Road of Stars

A fictional history

in which White Cloud seeks his father

and helps to build a railroad

Byron Grush

Published in the United States by Broadhorn Publishing, Delavan, Wisconsin.

ISBN-10:0692403205

ISBN-13:978-0-692-40320-4

Cover Image: *Indian viewing railroad from top of Palisades. 435 miles from Sacramento*. Hart, Alfred A., 1816-1908. Courtesy of Library of Congress Prints and Photographs Division Washington, D.C.

Back Cover Image: *Milky Way Arch*. Courtesy of European Southern Observatory, Chile

Photograph of Byron Grush by Vincent Federighi, © 2013

For Mary

The Song of Hau

On the stone ridge east I go.

On the white road I, Hau, crouching go.

I, Hau, whistle on the road of stars.

[In the Hau song above, the celestial Hau (red fox), is described as travelling along the Milky Way.]

—*Creation Myths of Primitive America*, by Jeremiah Curtin, [1898], at sacred-texts.com

1

The Old Man of the Mountain

Shasta Mountain, May, 1868

The boy had been searching the west side of the mountain all day. His people, the Wintu, did not venture above the sacred meadow as a rule. Today, however, White Cloud was following his father's footsteps, footsteps that had faded away over nine years ago.

The trail the boy followed was incised in memory: how often he had asked his mother to tell the story—now he knew it well. He had been only three years of age when his father had left the village. It was the year of the Pit River Massacre when 70 men, women and children of the Achomawi tribe, neighbors of the Wintu, had been viciously murdered by white Rangers. It was the year that many Indians who lived near the sacred mountain had been captured and herded like cattle in a forced march to the reservation at Mendocino.

His mother, Little Deer, and his younger sister, Little Wind, and he had been among those taken from their ancestral lands along Cottonwood Creek where steelhead trout were once abundant and game plentiful. Their fortunes had taken a turn for the worse. They had been taken to Nome Cult Farm, the West Place, a depressed and lonely location which would later be renamed the Round Valley Reservation by the white people. There the Wintu joined in a common struggle for survival with the Pit River peoples, the Yuki, Little Lake, Pomo and many other Native American peoples, all speaking different languages and holding different beliefs.

Hunting grounds, fishing waters, even foraging areas for acorns and grubs were inadequate to support the large numbers of Indians crowded together in that terrible place. Many starved. Many succumbed to disease. Some left the reservation only to be killed by white settlers who were paid bounties for Indian scalps and heads. The influx of whites, forty-niners seeking gold and free land, had drastically altered the native peoples' lives.

Little Deer kept Wintu culture alive for her children by telling them stories of her own life. Chief among these, as far as White Cloud was concerned, was the tale of James Grosh, the white man Little Deer had found half alive on the side of the mountain. This man she had brought to the village and nursed back to health. She had taken him for a husband.

James Grosh, his mother had told him, had climbed the sacred mountain to its very top where the Great Spirit Olelbis dwells. On his perilous climb he had been helped by the Little People who lived there. He had met and talked with a k'iyeh, an old man who lived in a cave just past the tree line where snow fields rose high above. On returning from the summit he had been attacked by a grizzly bear and barely survived. Little Deer found him bleeding in the brush near the foot of the mountain. Members of the Wintu village believed that this white man had been transformed by his journey to the top of the world. He was accepted as one of the people.

This man, White Cloud's and Little Wind's father, was no longer a white man, said Little Deer. He lived as one of the people, hunting and fishing and joining in dances and ceremonies. But one day news came that men from the village had been murdered by white settlers and their women had been taken. A raiding party was formed to avenge these deaths and James Grosh was expected to accompany them.

"We talked much of this," Little Deer told the children. "Poor James could not kill his own white brothers no matter how evil they had behaved. And yet he could not oppose his Wintu brothers in their fight against these whites. He needed guidance. He decided he must go again to the mountain. And he would go alone."

It was shortly after James had left the village that White Cloud and his family were taken to the reservation. Why had his father not come looking for them, White Cloud had wondered? Why was there no word of him? When he turned 12 years old and thus became a man, White Cloud resolved to find his father. He left Nome Cult Farm and made his way to the foothills of Shasta Mountain.

The boy had skirted across the timber line where cedar and ponderosa gave way to scraggly manzanita and thimble berry bush. The mountain, a series of volcanic cones, had created alluvial mud flats from which the steep slopes of several buttes angled upward toward cloud and mist. Outcroppings of tumbled rock, falls of talus and scree presented a formidable boundary between the forest below and the glaciers above.

White Cloud followed a dwindling flow of snowmelt toward its source near the edge of a snow field where he could see an abutment of red-colored rock rising wall-like against the alabaster glacier. This singular feature jogged a memory: hadn't his mother spoken of the red butte his father had followed in his ascent to the summit? Hadn't the old hermit of the mountain directed James toward this bizarre looking landmark? Hadn't his father talked of the presence of the Little People at this place?

As White Cloud stood looking up toward the red cliffs he heard a low whistling sound as if someone were playing a wooden flute. It could have been the wind winding its way across polished snow and jagged rock. But no...surely this was Waida Dikit and Tulchuherris, those two divine beings, performing in a musical contest. Certainly their flute playing had turned those cliffs to the deep crimson color they now exhibited. In any case, White Cloud now knew the direction in which he should search.

Great slabs of smooth rock formed terraces to the north of the cliffs. White Cloud climbed these hurriedly. His deerskin moccasins slid on the slippery surface and he plunged forward, catching himself with outstretched arms. The bag in which he carried all his worldly possessions fell from his shoulders nearly rolling off the edge of the terrace before he was able to check its headway. The quiver of arrows he carried clattered against the rock as he rose to his knees, then gained an upright stature. The mountain, he realized, demanded respect.

He continued, this time more slowly, glancing out across the vast terrain surrounding Mt. Shasta. The valley below stretched in an unbroken plain toward a horizon where peaks and crags of mountains one hundred and forty miles distant seemed pathetic challengers to Shasta's dominance of the landscape. It was no wonder that the People considered the sacred mountain a source of power. It was a place to visit but not to live. It was a place to offer prayers and seek guidance. The mountain could heal and sooth, give strength and balance, but there were dangers—dangerous spirits who guarded the interior realms of the mountain—spirits potentially harmful, especially to the young.

The flat slabs had now given way to smaller, rounder rocks and sheer walls of stone rose vertically along one side of the boy's path. At last he spotted a fissure in the wall, an opening barely the width of a man. He entered this and found himself in a long, narrow box canyon. At the far end of the canyon a shallow pool of water had collected in a hollowed-out depression. Melting snow dripped from the wall above this. An outcropping of rock next to the pool sheltered a cave in which White Cloud saw familiar objects: blankets, some pots and pans, several books.

Standing at the entrance to the cave was a man. He wore a long full beard and had shoulder-length hair which was parted into two long tresses tied by ribbons. His clothes were buckskin and well worn. Around his waist was a sash which supported a long sheathed knife.

Although White Cloud had been searching for this man, the "Old Man of the Mountain" of his mother's story, he was momentarily shocked and surprised. It was as if a mythical character from some child's folk tale had suddenly come to life to stand before him in undeniable realism. Mythical, perhaps, but he was not a spirit, White Cloud decided. He was a man—a 'elti-winthu'h—a white man.

"What have we here?" the man said after the initial moment of hesitation shared by man and boy. When the boy didn't say anything, the man tried asking him who he was in Wintu, which he spoke somewhat poorly. "Heket 'ibeym?"

"I know ya-paytu-qo'l, the white man's language. Speak in that if you will," replied White Cloud, amused at the man's attempt to use the Peoples' words. "I am called White Cloud, although net-t-a'm, my father, called me Ay-Zack."

"I'm sorry, I don't remember the words so well...it's been a long time since I was in the world. Why does your father call you that?"

"Net-t-a-np'eh 'iye 'be...I don't have a father now. He left us years ago. That is why I came here."

"Just how *did* you come here? This is not an easy place to find." The man gestured to the boy to enter the cave. "Here, come sit and talk to me."

There was a three-legged stool and a bedroll the color of dead grass. The bedding consisted of what looked to White Cloud like old army blankets, like the ones given to them at the reservation. The man pointed to the stool indicating that the boy should take it. He then sat cross-legged on the bedroll and studied the boy with eyes that seemed much younger than his outward appearance would suggest.

"I get few visitors," the man said, laughing. "Those who do come sometimes bring me food or tobacco or something to read."

"Sorry," said White Cloud. He reached into his bag and produced a piece of dried beef jerky. "This is all I have, but you're welcome to it. I wonder, the people that come here...if you ever saw my father."

"How is it that you speak English so well?"

"The Franciscan Brothers came to the reservation to start a school. The elders didn't attend because they believed the whites wished to steal our language from us the way they stole our lands. But my mother made me go."

"You said you came here because of your father. Why is that?"

"In the story my mother told me about him he once climbed the sacred mountain. He met and talked with a wise man living in a cave."

"A wise man? I doubt that!"

"This was many summers ago. He came to live at my village and marry my mother. Later he left us. He was not of the People, you see. He was 'elti-winthu'h, a white man—like you. When he left he climbed the mountain again. I think he came to see you."

"I think I understand. You want to find him. And you think I know where he is. I'm sorry to disappoint you, but I have a very bad memory. In fact, I don't even remember much about my *own* past, where I came from, even my own name! So you see, I wouldn't remember your father even if he did come here."

"Just before he came to live with my people he was attacked by a bear. That left him with three deep red scars across his chest. You would remember that if you had seen it."

The man was startled by this. His hand went automatically to his own chest. "A bear attack! How horrible. But he lived?"

"He did or I wouldn't be here now. I had hoped you'd remember talking to him the second time. That he may have told you where he was going."

"Do you know why he left your village?"

"Some said that he was afraid to go into battle. My mother said he wasn't afraid, he just couldn't kill his own people...the white settlers. He was living in two different worlds at the same time. So he left."

"Perhaps he returned home."

"I went to the spot where our village was. There was nothing there anymore."

"No, I mean his original home. He must have come here for gold, from the east. He might have gone back."

"My mother said he talked of a faraway land where his own father lived. I think it was called El-Ya-Noy. Do you know where that land lies?"

"Away across the mountains and further across the plains. It would take most of a year to get there. It is a long way…near the end of the road of stars!"

Water dripping from the cliff top echoed softly through the cave. A feeling of serenity might have come to White Cloud had he not begun to ponder his options. He could return to Nome Cult Farm where his mother and sister lived in poverty and hunger. He could roam around Northern California and Southern Oregon, hoping for some sign of his father and risk being taken or murdered by the Rangers or the soldiers. He could start on the long journey along the road of stars to El-Ya-Noy—where ever that might be. But with no horse to carry him, no food or money to sustain him, no idea of what dangers might lurk ahead on that mysterious road—this was perhaps the riskiest choice.

The boy's eyes fell upon the small pile of books. He picked one up. "I have seen this one before. The Brothers had one like it. I recognize this mark," he said, pointing to the cross on the cover of the bible.

"I've not had much use for it lately," admitted the man. "Perhaps you'd like to take it with you when you go."

"Thank you, but I've not mastered the reading of the marks as yet. Would do me no good to look at them. We Wintu never put down marks for our sounds as you white people do."

"And what of your mother? Is she well?"

White Cloud wondered why this white man, this scraggly old hermit would be interested in the welfare of his mother. Perhaps he asked this to draw White Cloud's attention away from his quest, to instill in him the guilt for leaving his family that a white man would have felt. Perhaps he did indeed possess wisdom—wisdom he was imparting to White Cloud in some subtle and mysterious manner. Perhaps White Cloud *should* return to the reservation.

"Do you not have some wisdom to give to me?" he said instead of answering the man's question.

"Zack...I like that name better than 'White Cloud.' May I call you Zack? I think it would be wise if you left California. There is too much danger here for you. Go east. Go to Illinois in search of your father's family. Tell them...tell them the story of your father."

"You don't think he is at that place, the El-Ya-Noy?"

"Perhaps he is. But if not, you would at least find a home where you would be safe."

"My mother and my sister?"

"Take them with you. This reservation where you live..."

"The West Place, it is called."

"That can't be a good place to remain. Leave while you are still young."

The man and the boy sat in silence looking at each other. White Cloud...Zack...felt a strange connection to this crazy hermit. His words had the ring of truth to them. Zack rummaged through his bag and pulled out a small stone carved in the shape of a fish that he had carried with him since he was a small child at the Wintu village. It was a magic charm, perhaps a century old, used to bring good luck when fishing or trapping game.

"I want to give you this," said Zack, "for your kindness to me and for your words."

"Thank you, Zack. I shall treasure it. It will bring me luck. And wait, I have something for you as well." The man reached under his bedroll and retrieved a round object. He handed it to the boy.

"It's a watch. It's not valuable...not gold or silver or anything, but I've had it for many years. I had it with me when I came here. Perhaps it too will be lucky. Oh, I'm sorry, I don't have the winding key anymore. It is lost. The watch will always tell the same time, I'm afraid."

"That's all right," said the boy. "Sometimes it's good that time stops. It's a wonderful gift." He gathered together his belongings and started for the opening at the other end of the canyon. He stopped and turned.

" 'Una hara-da. Goodbye."

"Goodbye, Zack. Olelbis be with you."

2

The Trickster of West Place

Nome Cult Farm was opened in 1856 in Round Valley, California, as an extension of the Nome Lackee Reservation, one of five California Indian reservations established by the United States Government in the 1850s to protect Native Americans, but also to segregate them from whites. The name Nome Cult came from a Wintu word for "Home" or "West Place." It might more properly have been called "Hell."

That Native Americans needed protection from whites wasn't a commonly held opinion. The gold rush of 1849 had swelled the population of nonnative settlers who hungered not only for gold, but for land. The native tribes possessed both. The "Redman" was hated, feared, and, to the settlers' way of thinking, needed to be eliminated at all costs.

In his Second Annual Message to the Legislature on January 7, 1851, California's first governor, Peter Hardeman Burnett, stated "that a war of extermination will continue to be waged between the two races until the Indian race becomes extinct...." The legislature budgeted over one million dollars to reimburse local militia and vigilante groups for expenses incurred killing Indians.

In 1850, the year California became a state, its legislature passed the "Act for the Government and Protection of the Indians," commonly known as the Indenture Law. Among other provisions, the act allowed Native Americans, including women and children, to be arrested by any citizen on a charge of vagrancy and held or sold, effectively making them slaves. An Indian caught loitering and without visible means of support would be brought before a judge who could "hire out such vagrant within 24 hours to the best bidder" for a period of four months. In 1860 this was amended to extend the period of indenture to age 25 for males and age 21 for females.

Now the reservation became a dumping ground for Indians driven off their lands. This allowed the vigilante groups, called "Volunteers" or "Rangers," to conserve bullets in their war of extinction: starvation and disease did the job for them. Rape and murder and abduction also took a toll.

Upwards of two thousand Indians from several different tribes lived at Nome Cult Farm. Clustered together they were easy prey for slave traders. California newspapers reported that parties in the Northern portion of the state stole young children and squaws and sold them to settlers who would "willingly pay $50 or $60 for a young Digger to cook or wait upon them, or $100 for a likely young girl."

There were, of course, treaties offered to the Indian tribes by the United States legislature: eighteen in the year 1853 alone. Indians traded millions of acres of their ancestral lands for the promise of protection under United States law and to receive new lands with abundant water and game—but the Senate refused to ratify the treaties.

Hostilities between the settlers and the tribes increased. The Yerka Herald said: "Extermination is no longer a question of time— the time has arrived, the work has commenced, and let the first man that says treaty or peace be regarded as a traitor." The city of Shasta offered five dollars for each severed Indian head brought to city hall.

Massacres at Indian villages became commonplace. To mention just a few there was the McCloud River Massacre, Bear Creek Massacre, Clear Lake Massacre, Blood Run Creek Massacre, Klamath River Massacres, Bridge Gulch Massacre, Yontoket Massacre, Achulet Massacre, Kaibai Creek Massacre, Silva Massacre, Camp Seco Massacre, Three Knolls Massacre, and the Massacre at Bloody Rock.

Some of these atrocities were orchestrated by the Copper City Volunteers, Cow Creek Volunteers, McCloud River Volunteers, Millville Volunteers, Pine Grove Rangers, Pit River Rangers, Red Bluff Rangers, Humboldt Volunteers, Hydesville Volunteer Company, Shasta Guards, Trinity Rangers, Yreka Volunteer Company, and others.

What usually happened was that some hungry Indians killed a rancher's cow or hog; on occasion, a settler was killed by an Indian in some dispute. Reprisals were harsh, visited upon whole villages by the militia groups where often hundreds of men, women and children were killed. Survivors of these encounters were marched to the reservation.

Estimates vary, but as many as 245,000 Native Americans lived in California in 1830. By 1890, their population was approximately 16,000. Not all of the decline was due to the actions of the militia groups, the army or from wars with other tribes. Some of the deaths could be attributed to diseases introduced first by the Spanish and later the Americans, and by starvation due to pollution of their rivers which killed the salmon, deforestation which limited the gathering of acorns, and isolation upon the reservation where food was scarce.

White Cloud had descended through thick groves of hemlock and cedar, crossed the meadow where Wintu ceremonies had been held in the days before the white man came. He struggled through matted scrub brush and emerged into the valley south and west of Shasta Mountain. His journey back to Nome Cult Farm followed an ancient trail past Castle Crags where the Modoc, armed only with bow and arrow, had battled the local white militia whose rifles had decimated their numbers.

To avoid the mining towns of Shasta, Whiskeytown and Weaverville, the boy traveled only by night. He stole past the hamlet of Hayfork and headed for the former site of a Wintu Rancheria. In 1852 this had been the scene of an atrocity called the Bridge Gulch Massacre: 150 Wintu had died and only three small children had survived. On he went.

Following ravines and creek beds through the mountains, he made his way to Eel Creek in the Yolla-Bolly wilderness. Here he hunted, watching for black-tail deer, wild turkey, grouse and quail. Notching his arrows with their blue-painted shafts and red obsidian arrowheads, he lay hidden in the brush. A young fawn wandered close by. With a silent prayer to thank the animal for its life White Cloud loosed the arrow and it found its mark in the deer's neck. Expertly, he gutted the deer and slung it onto his shoulders.

As he hiked through the wilderness he sang the Lightning's Song, Walokin tsawi:

Mínom tóror wéril chirchákum sáia
Dúne wérem winwar dún bohémum

I bear the sucker-torch to the western tree-ridge
Look at me: first born, greatest.

When he reached Nome Cult Farm he saw that the rail fence had been taken down again on the side where the white rangers' land touched the reservation. The rangers did this to allow their cattle to graze on the Indian farm land: this, of course, destroyed the crops. The government agents who ran the farm did nothing to stop the practice. In fact, they mismanaged the reservation so badly that the food allotment was now down to three ears of corn per person per day. White Cloud's deer carcass would barely put a dent in the inadequate food supply.

He found his mother busy making acorn soup. He let the deer carcass slide from his shoulders and greeted her. But the happy reunion he had expected turned into sullen consternation on both sides. White Cloud couldn't remember ever having seen such stormy indignation on his mother's face.

"Where have you been?" she demanded. "I imagined you to have been eaten by Old Sas!"

"I've been hunting, Mother," he answered. "But first I went to Bohĕm Puyuk to see..."

"And the spirits spoke to you? You had visions? You will be a healer now? I don't think so! You were not to go to the sacred mountain unless the elders told you to do so. Now they may think you to be a sorcerer. They may send you away."

"I may be going away on my own, Mother. Soon."

"What? What are you saying?"

"To Puidal Pom, the land far to the east. The Old Man told me..."

"What k'iyeh? What old man? Heket isuki? Who is he?"

"Don't you remember Mother? You told me the story of my father meeting a wise man on the western slopes."

"Ai! Now I'm sure you are enchanted! Don't mention this to anyone. And lose your desire to go east. I need you here."

"But Mother..."

"Had I known where you were going...oh, I would have needed to send Winishuyat with you. I would have tied him into your hair and he would have seen any danger that threatened you. He would have warned you and..."

"Mother, a little man the size of my thumb hidden in my hair is the last thing I would need."

White Cloud looked longingly at the acorn soup his mother was stirring. Noticing his hunger Little Deer said, "This is not for you. It is for your sister. She is bala kila'el. She has come into her time of first bleeding and must eat nothing but this soup."

"Where is my sister? Where is Wind-From-The-Wings-Of-The-Hummingbird?"

"Little Wind is still in seclusion in the young women's hut. You missed the five days singing. And that's another thing—while you were scrambling around places you shouldn't be, the other men were gathering acorns for soup and building huts. It is difficult to find the nuts and the bark to cover the huts these days. The white men have cut so many of the trees."

"Mother, you act as if everything were my fault."

"No my son, I'm just concerned about you. I lost one of my men to that mountain so many years ago. I don't want to lose another."

Tommy Wepa

In 1863 hostilities between whites and Indians in Butte County, California, had reached a climax. There had been several murders and then retaliations for the murders and then more retaliations for the retaliations which had left innocents dead on both sides of the conflict. In July over three hundred white people met at the Pense ranch and drafted a resolution which called for the removal of all Native Americans in the county. By *all* Indians they meant "those that are roaming in our mountains, as well as those upon the ranches in the valleys." Any that remained or who had returned after removal would "do so at the risk of their lives."

By August, at Camp Bidwell, the number of Hat Creek and Concow-Maidu Indians rounded up was between 500 and 600. The plan was to transport them to Round Valley to the Nome Cult Farm, 110 miles distant. The Pense resolution called for adequate supplies of food and water, good shelter and the use of horses, mules and wagons; however, funds ran drastically short. Captain Augustus W. Starr and 23 soldiers of Company F, 2nd Regiment of the California

Volunteer Cavalry led the forced march that lasted 20 hot September days and nights over the 6,000 foot crest of the North Coast Range.

Most had to walk. Some were too sick or too weak to travel and later reports stated that 150 Indians had been left along the side of that terrible route. They starved. They were attacked and killed by wild boar. This trail of tears for the Concow-Maidu would come to be known as the Death March and would be commemorated yearly even into the twenty-first century.

A young Concow-Maidu boy named Képetu was among the survivors of the Death March. He had been nicknamed Wepa, or "Coyote," because his mischievous antics as a small child reminded the tribe of that famous Trickster of Maidu legends about the First People. Wepa was only eight years of age when his family was herded along mountain roads by the soldiers.

He watched from a wagon as his father, sick and struggling to walk behind them, fell to his knees on the mountain pass. That was the last he would ever see of him. When the wagon broke down, Wepa and his mother, along with the other women and children who had been crammed into the rickety conveyance had to walk the remaining fifty miles to the valley. Temperatures reached 90 degrees.

Wepa and White Cloud had attended the English school together on the reservation. Although their native languages were dissimilar and their tribal customs differed, the two became fast friends. Ironically, it was learning the white man's language that had bridged the cultural gap between them.

Wepa, true to the puckish and rascally character of his namesake, loved to perpetrate the most outrageous pranks on the inhabitants of Nome Cult Farm. If it were at all possible he would embroil White Cloud in these shenanigans. The boy knew the story about Coyote (the mythical one) stealing fire to give to the First People. He thought it would be a great joke to steal the fire that the women used to boil water for washing. So one day he talked White Cloud into helping execute this hilarious gag.

Together they borrowed a wheelbarrow from a nearby white rancher's farm—without the rancher knowing about it, of course. When no one was looking they took a shovel and scooped up the burning wood and embers, deposited them into the wheelbarrow, then took off down the road as fast as they could travel. The wheelbarrow, being made of wood, started to burn.

Thinking to push it into a stream to extinguish the flames they gave the barrow a shove down a short hill next to a road which led back to the rancher's property. Instead of rolling down to the water, the wheelbarrow changed course and headed for the rancher's field of fresh clover where several cows were munching contentedly. The cows panicked at the sight of the burning barrow and ran, busting down a fence as they went.

The cows were lost into the valley beyond the ranch, the field also started to burn, and the reservation authorities were informed an attempt had been made by the obviously hostile Indians to destroy the ranch. Luckily for Wepa and White Cloud the identities of the imagined terrorists were never learned.

There were other pranks. They had sewn shut the flap of hide that served as a door to the sweat lodge. Luckily it had not been inhabited at the time. They had stolen the moccasins of a tribal elder and hung them high in a cottonwood near the stream. They had emptied a jar of cornmeal and substituted sand—this had perhaps been the most dangerous of all their pranks as it brought down the wrath of the women folk upon them. They might have been flailed alive had not the aforementioned elder taken pity on them and interceded. He apparently had a good sense of humor and gave the boys a lesser punishment: cleaning up animal dung from the entire reservation.

The day following White Cloud's return from the sacred mountain he sought out his friend Wepa. He told him the tale of his journey and his meeting with the Old Man of the Mountain.

"A spirit! Clearly this man is possessed of great power," commented Wepa.

"No, he is only a white man who lives away from his people," answered White Cloud. Then showing Wepa the watch the man had given him he continued:

"He advised me to go to this far-away land of my father's birth in order to search for him or at least to find his family. It is called El-Ya-Noy. Have you ever heard of it?"

"No, but it is in the white man's realm I would think. It means going among them. Very dangerous."

"We could go in disguise," said White Cloud, returning the watch to his bag.

"We?" Wepa was incredulous. Playing tricks even at high risk was great fun, but this? This venture could have dire consequences. "You want me to go with you?"

"Wepa, you have the cleverness that I lack. And you're fearless. Would you remain in this place of sorrow and pain...and boredom?"

"Ah, now you've touched on my weakness. Adventure! Better than stealing fire! Yes, I will go with you. But we must plan carefully how to go...and...in which direction does this land lie?"

"It is in the east. The miners come from there. So we go the way they came, only backwards."

"Some came by land, over the mountains in wagons. I know this is true. But we have no wagon or cattle to pull it."

"And some came over the ocean, Wepa. In great boats. This I think should be our path. We will go to the place of the big boats and find a way to ride on one."

"My friend, you amaze me. An almost impossible quest! I cannot wait to get started."

That evening they sat under the stars, away from anyone who might overhear them, and began to plan. There was no one they could ask for help; certainly not their mothers who would prevent them from leaving. They would have to gather the supplies they needed using the utmost stealth. It was decided that if they could not pass as white men they might be mistaken for Mexicans with the proper clothing. Wepa knew of a local rancher who had boys about their age and size and he knew when the rancher's wife hung clothes out to dry. It would be a simple matter to procure pants and shirts, but shoes or boots was another matter.

"If we are no longer to be of The People," said White Cloud, "then I will be known from here on as Zack Grosh, the name my father gave to me."

"And I will be Tommy. Tommy Wepa. Tommy after the name of my tribe's great chief, Tome-ya-ne, and Wepa because...because..."

"Because that's who you are. The Trickster Coyote of the West Place."

Two days later they were ready. White Cloud was disappointed that he would not be bringing his arrows and bow, but Wepa pointed out that Mexicans didn't use them. Wepa had finally located two pairs of boots. White Cloud complained that they hurt his feet and insisted on going barefoot, at least until they reached a city. The city of the big boats, San Francisco, was 180 miles to the south. It would be a long trek.

"I wish I could tell my mother goodbye," said Wepa.

"I do too. I don't want them to worry that we've been kidnapped or something. I have an idea—I'll tell my sister about our plans just before we leave. She can tell our mothers but not until we are many miles away. That way they won't be able to send anyone after us."

Night lacquered the land with opaque blackness. White Cloud moved by dead reckoning toward the hut where Little Wind was sequestered. He found it more by touch and smell than by sight although a weak crescent moon was making an effort to escape from the thick clouds above. A gray owl seemed to be encouraging the orb's progress with a slow staccato of hoots.

"Little Wind!" the boy called quietly, then entered the circular hut. The smell of still fresh bark covering the hut's exterior was supplanted by the stench of unwashed girl in the interior. He wrinkled up his nose.

"White Cloud, you should not be here. What if someone sees?" said the girl.

"No one can see anything this night. Don't worry. I came to tell you I am leaving. For a long time, I think. I want you to tell our mother...and Wepa's as well. But not for many days."

"I don't understand. Where are you *going*?"

"We are going to El-Ya-Noy. To find father. It's a long way from here. We have to go by the big boat with the great white wings."

"I am afraid for you. I wish you would not go. I know our mother would not let you."

"I would take you both with me if she would come, but she would not. All I can do is find father and then try to bring the two of you to El-Ya-Noy somehow."

"Oh, White Cloud, I don't think you have thought this out very well."

"Maybe not. But it is my task and my future. I've been to the sacred mountain and learned that much."

After White Cloud had left, Little Wind settled back onto the animal hides which served her for a bed. Although it had broken a strict taboo she was happy about her brother's visit. Why she had to be cooped up in this smelly dark hut just to come of age was a complete mystery—an irritating one, at that! Only a few more days now. Then what? Would she be married off to some broken-toothed old coot? All the young men of the tribe had either died in battle or run off. Run off like White Cloud was doing! Another thing to worry about.

She heard scratching at the hut's doorway. "White Cloud? Is that you?" she called. No answer. Suddenly two large figures pulled back the door flap and burst into the hut.

"Here's another one," said one of the men. Little Wind knew by the fact that he spoke in the white man's language and further by his smell that he was not one of the People. She began to scream but the man placed his large, dirty palm over her mouth.

"Take her. Tie her to the mule with the others and let's get out of here," said the other man. They dragged Little Wind from the hut. Although she struggled and fought she was soon secured to the back of a mule that smelled only slightly better than the white men.

Zack and Tommy Wepa had left Nome Cult Farm that night unafraid of discovery in the nearly absolute darkness. The bags slung over their shoulders were filled with dried jerky and they had brought with them the few possessions they treasured too much to leave behind. They had dressed in the stolen clothes, certain that if anyone saw them they would not be recognized as Indians.

"What if we meet some Mexicans?" Zack asked. "Do you speak Mexican?"

"No. Do you? Well, if we meet any we'll just tell them we're Indians."

"Brilliant!"

They ambled along the dirt road leading away from Nome Cult Farm. It wasn't long, however, that two men on horseback leading a third animal came galloping down the road forcing them to jump into the nearby brush to hide. They couldn't see the men well but thought they were white men because of the sloppy way they rode their animals. Then they thought they heard muffled cries as the men rode by—cries like lambs being driven to the slaughter. Alarming cries, with a desperate human quality to them. But before they could investigate, the men had disappeared into the darkness.

3

Into the Wilderness

Following the Eel River back into the mountains, Tommy Wepa was unable to shake the eerie feeling that he was retracing the path of the Death March. Were they to go through the Mendocino Pass and up over the Coastal Range they would indeed be heading directly for the Bidwell Ranch near Chico, a place where they would have been most unwelcome. They would be doing so at the risk of their lives.

They trudged more southerly, toward the ancient lands of the Yuki, where there were no roads or trails, and therefore, no white men. Long, flat ridges bristling with chaparral of saltbush and rabbitbush and spotted with scraggy cedar provided access up to the higher realms of wilderness they would need to cross. There ponderosa pine and Douglas fir dominated giving home to spotted owl, groshawk and prairie falcon. Occasionally a meadow of short grass and wildflowers of varied and brilliant hues broke out of the shaggy forest like a peaceful oasis. Clear streams sparkling like a rush of diamonds provided sparse watering holes for marten and fox. Where the larger river and its spring-fed tributaries flowed through deep valleys below the ridges, beaver built their dams and river otter frolicked in the muddy shallows.

Again Zack complained about having left his bow and arrows behind. What glorious hunting he was missing! Near the foot of the mountain peak to their north roamed herds of tule elk. Black bear and badger were abundant as well. When they stopped to camp for the night they set traps and snares hoping to catch smaller game: rabbits, squirrels or kangaroo rats.

Before they left the banks of the Eel they fished. Zack had borrowed a dip net from the reservation's fishing equipment. It was a small one, a net woven of hemp attached to a bent hoop of willow. He searched for a long straight tree branch to use as a handle. The river was lush with salmon, trout, and suckers. They were too far from the mouth where the river emptied into the ocean to see any of the Pacific lamprey that were considered a delicacy among the Wiyot people who lived further north. Legend had it that early explorers, fascinated by the strange eel-like parasite that attacked itself to other fish, had traded a broken frying pan to the Indians for a basket full of lamprey. These Europeans named the river the Eel, mistaking the lamprey for that more familiar animal.

Sediment from landslides of the loosely packed soil along the river made it difficult to see the fish. After several attempts, however, Zack netted a good-sized salmon and the boys settled down to feast upon it. Zack sang Olelben tsawi, the Song of Olelbis:

> *Olél bohéma ni tsulúli káhum síka ni*
> *I am great above. I tan the black cloud.*

"What's that about?" asked Tommy, not following the words in Wintu.

"Olelbis is all-seeing and all-knowing. He transformed everything that is from everything that was. Once he drew his finger down from the sacred mountain and made the great river. Then he made the animals and fish and all kinds of food for the People to eat," answered Zack, beginning the Wintu creation story.

"Oh no...that is not how it happened," interrupted Tommy. "Coyote was out walking. Along the north side of the great water he found Turtle. He tied a rope to Turtle's leg and sent him down to dive for mud. It took five tries, each time he had to add more rope. Finally Turtle brought up a clod of mud. Yâhâsin-yepâni made it into a flat cake and floated it on the water. It spread out in all directions and made the earth we now live on."

Zack and Tommy relished sparring with stories learned from elders—different in detail but strikingly similar in substance. To both of them everything in the world was related. Everything was descended from the world of the First People, who, in turn, were created by a supreme being. To Tommy, the personification of various animals, Coyote, Fox, Bear, Turtle, signified the interdependence and oneness of man and nature. Zack's stories, though peopled with human-like spirit beings, echoed the same philosophy.

"Wokwok was the son of Olelbis and Mem Loimis," Zack began again. "Bits of him fell to earth and became the elk and the brown bear and the raccoon. The end of his little finger became the earthly Wokwok who walked about as a man. He is the greatest source of power."

Tommy took his turn: "Hiki was the great serpent who created all the valleys as he slithered across the land. Kuksu was first man."

"We know of Kuksu," said Zack. "Our brothers to the south have dances and ceremonies for the dreaming times. Kuksu is the guide for this."

"We Maidu and you Wintu have much in common."

"We are brothers, are we not?"

"We are brothers, my friend."

Embers once glowing golden-red had passed into cold grayness. The smallest creatures had emerged to claim their nocturnal hunting grounds: a mountain shrew foraged for snails and grubs; a pocket gopher peeked from its burrow near an incense cedar; a bat gamboled and fluttered scooping tiny insects from the night air. Up slope a pasty pink-faced opossum scrambled to the tree tops to await the rising of the sun.

Dawn light filtering through pine needles woke the sleepers. A bit of fish served as a breakfast. Zack retrieved his moccasins from his bag and slipped them on. "As we climb higher the stones will become sharp," he told his companion.

"Don't you want to try out the boots I went to the trouble to steal?"

"I can't feel the earth with my toes through those things," Zack explained. "And these heavy clothes itch my skin."

"Better get used to it. I'll check the traps," said Tommy and took off into the forest. He had rigged a clever trap by balancing one flat rock above another using a short stick and had baited it with crushed acorns. It looked a bit like an open clam shell. The stick had been knocked over by a vole which now lay wedged between the two rocks, conveniently flattened and dead. They had also caught a rabbit in a snare and would now have fresh meat to add variety to their diet.

It was not a difficult climb: they gained several thousand feet of altitude in only a few hours. Twisted cypress hung from crags of rock. Steep canyon walls showed evidence of ancient petroglyphs, scratched and painted images unreadable now even to the ancestors of their makers. Soil like dust, like gravel, like the ground-up bones of Wokwok made Tommy's boots slip and slide; not so Zack's moccasins. The wooded areas were filled with kákeni, spiritual beings who might be persuaded to bestow supernatural powers on them, or so the boys imagined. Less benevolent monsters lurked there as well. It was usually best to avoid them. The higher they climbed the more fantastic were the vistas presented to them. Distant snow-capped peaks stood stark against the turquoise sky. The rocky terrain became dry and green-blue with serpentine soil. Scrub manzanita clung begrudgingly to slopes where even not even stubborn cypress took root. Wild flowers no longed ornamented the mountain.

They had crossed over the high point and now they were descending. Ecosystem gave way to ecosystem. Plants and trees appeared in diverse abundance. Bald eagles circled. Woodpeckers sounded a welcoming tattoo. Ahead lay the vast flood plain of the Sacramento River Valley.

The valley was once a great inland sea, isolated by the tectonic rise of mountain ranges, then drained, leaving a thin ribbon of river to meander through fertile fields and forests. It is 6,500 miles square, 200 miles long and from 10 to 50 miles wide. It is bordered by the California Coastal Range on the west and the Sierra Nevada Mountains on the east. Its principle rivers are the Feather and the Sacramento.

The Sacramento River originates in the Klamath Mountains and winds its way 400 miles south to Suisun Bay, part of San Francisco Bay, and then into the Pacific Ocean. Whales and sea lions have been known to travel up the river in search of food. It became a major waterway in the nineteen century, connecting all the northern mining communities in Trinity County with the hub city of Sacramento and the port of San Francisco.

The valley was a good place to grow things and the early European settlers set about cutting trees and planting crops and raising cattle. But the river tended to flood, not having the ability to drain away the spring thaw. The settlers built levees and tried to straighten out the river that twisted and undulated like an unruly snake. That worked for a while.

In December of 1861 the town of Nevada City, California, recorded six inches of rain falling within a 24 hour period. San

Francisco had nearly nine inches. Strong gales began to blow. Ten to fifteen feet of snow piled up in the Sierra Nevada. In January the temperature dipped to 23 degrees. And then the flooding started. It lasted 43 days.

By January 9, 1862, water broke levees on the American River and rushed down the Sacramento at a startling pace. By noon Sacramento streets were under water. The water level rose at the rate of one foot per hour. There seemed to be no dry land in the valley from Red Bluff down to the city. The Feather, the Yuba and the American Rivers were also claiming drowning victims. By January 10 the high water level in Sacramento was at 24 feet above normal.

It got worse. More rain fell. More and more California cities were affected. Politicians in Sacramento voted to move the capital to San Francisco. Native Americans living near Marysville moved to the foothills of the mountains and warned the settlers that more water was coming. By the end of January there was a coating of ice three-quarters of an inch thick on everything in the city of San Francisco and six inches of snow had fallen in Napa. In the town of Folsom they measured the water at 183 feet above sea level.

Six years later, Tommy Wepa and Zack Grosh stepped out onto the tule marshes of the Sacramento Valley. There was little evidence of the old flood or of the grief of the people who had lost loved ones and property to it. There were new levees and a belief that it would never happen again. But of course, it would.

"These boots will keep your feet drier than those moccasins," Tommy told Zack.

The river was twenty miles east of their location now, sitting on a ridge that bisected the valley and left a wide shallow trough on either of its sides. They would move through rugged foothills and across streams, wade through marshes where frog and waterfowl complained of their passage with croaks and quacks, trudge through stands of tough and tall wild grasses and enter thickets of young trees where squirrel chatter would seem to urge them onward. There were patches of dead ground where alkali stunted all but the most obstinate of weeds. There were vibrant carpets of California poppy, swinging red-headed in warm breezes. Elk, deer and antelope which had roamed freely through the valley in the days before the white man came were now no longer to be seen, having been hunted nearly to extinction. They would see a few raccoons and an occasional skunk but none of the larger animals.

They traveled across the valley toward the small mining town of Butte City. Once one of a handful of mining camps like Shirttail, Bedbug (later called Freezeout, then Ione), Muletown, Hogtown, Suckerville and Helltown, the town of Butte City prospered from its location on the banks of the Sacramento River. A wall of timber land a mile wide bordered the river on its western bank; the town grew up one hundred buildings strong along the eastern shores.

The timber from Butte City was harvested and sent downriver to become the principle fuel for steam-powered boats that cruised up and down the Sacramento carrying goods and passengers. There was such an abundance of oak, willow and sycamore that it seemed the supply would last forever. Of course, it would not.

In some parts of the thick woods wild grape vines intertwined making passage nearly impossible. Near the river mosquitoes swarmed and attacked in swirling clouds. Tommy and Zack had smeared mud on the exposed parts of their skin to ward off the insidious biting bugs. Where a white man might have become lost in the jungle-like approach to the river the boys relied on their innate sense of direction. Yet it was slow going: there were no paths, not even animal trails to follow. Zack had reluctantly donned his white man boots and now began to appreciate the protection against brambles they provided.

At last a fresh and moist breeze wafted through the forest signaling the proximity of the river. The timber thinned and sounds of water fowl reached their ears. Now they sat on the river's soft shoulder contemplating the ebb and flow of the mighty waterway.

"Now what?" asked Zack. "Do we cross it? And if so, how?"

"This runs down to the big water where we go to find the boats with wings to take us to El-Ya-Noy," said Tommy. "We follow it."

For a while they simply sat and watched. The current was swift and broken branches of trees were carried in its rush. Then a single log came around a twist of the river's coarse. Followed by another. And another. Then...

"Do you see what I see?"

"What is that?"

"A raft. I think...I know what it is. The white men cut down the trees to build dwellings and to feed to their boats. They lash them together to float down river."

As Tommy spoke, another man-made raft came around the bend. These were crudely made flotilla, to be sure. Not meant to transport living beings, only to hold themselves together for the trip down stream. But to Tommy and Zack they seemed like the most luxurious ocean liners imaginable.

"There's our ride," Tommy said.

They ran to the bend where a low promontory of crumbling rock rose above the bank. Looking up stream they could see more of the lashed-timber conglomerations careening down toward them. Tommy scrambled down to the bank and broke off a young sapling near its roots. He began to strip its limbs with his knife. "Get ready," he told Zack.

The leap they made could hardly have been called elegant. The raft tipped and tumbled and the boys clung and counterpoised and the river lapped and would have swallowed them whole had they not found their balance. Tommy demonstrated the purpose of the pole he had manufactured and maneuvered the raft closer to shore yet shy of eddies and snags. They were off, afloat, bobbing and wobbling, but en route to the big water and traveling in style.

Just how faraway the big water actually was, they didn't know. It was, perhaps, 118 wet, water-logged miles to Sacramento and another 125 to the bay of San Francisco. Or less. Or more. The river looped around so much that its precise measurement was sometimes mostly speculative. All they knew for sure was that they were no longer walking—in boots or out of them. Once they had gotten used to the navigation of their craft, which primarily entailed pushing off from snags using the pole, they began to relax.

Drifting past the drooping willows, past the bleached skeletons of fallen sycamores poking from the shallows, past long-legged herons standing idle in the reeds, past swirling eddies and dead-ended channels and the adjacent fringes of wildflowers that met the banks once the forest receded—this gentle, dream-like cavalcade lulled. Laughter came easily now: you are soaking wet; you are covered with mud; your clothes don't fit; your boots are filled with water—you don't look anything like a Mexican.

The river, serene and polished, flowing like melted wax, suddenly became reluctant, agitated, irascible. Behind them the very air seemed to thicken. A presence, way up river but impending, instigated the scattering of water fowl, the sudden silencing of fauna, the deepening of a hollow, encompassing, dark mood: evacuated tranquility. The river buckled, surged. The silence left behind by the escaping wildlife was replaced by calamitous commotion: the clinking, the clanking, and the clattering of mechanisms so foreign to the placidity of the river environs that Olelbis himself felt shock and awe.

Came a beast, a behemoth that blasted and belched and snorted and groaned as it pushed arrogantly through the great river, oblivious to its subtleties. Twin stacks like horns adorned it, spewing acrid fumes and sparks into the once pristine sky. It gobbled down the river churning and spraying and generally making a mess of things; creating a wake that sucked and sent spinning everything contingent to its path.

A riverboat. A steam-driven paddle-wheeler, intent on chugging and splashing its way along the tangled waterway with aplomb, with eminent domain. It pushed aside the rafts of logs as if they were toys in a child's game of jacks. Tommy and Zack, vulnerable on the flimsy raft, paddled and poled frantically toward shore. A wall of water from the wake of the boat sent them flying against the muddy bank with an impact that nearly broke the log construction apart. They rolled in mud—but at least they were safe.

They looked back at the thing, garish with gilded ornament and large lettering (which the boys couldn't read) announcing to the passing world its name: the Shasta Belle. On the deck of the riverboat stood a man. He looked out over the river and saw the two boys, near victims, staring back wet and weary and wondering at the sight of the strange beast upon which he rode. He acknowledged them with a slight nod.

4

Little Wind

Along the Russian River in Mendocino County, California, a generous Mexican land grant of 17,754 acres was given to Fernando Feliz by Governor Manuel Micheltorena. Feliz named his new property Rancho Sanel. The date was 1844. In 1848, when California was ceded to the United States by Mexico, the Treaty of Guadalupe Hidalgo provided that all land grants would be honored. By 1858, tracts of land divided up from the original grant in a section called Knight's Valley were beginning to be sold. A parcel of 316 acres was purchased in 1859 by Benjamin Wood, a man who had come to California from Barnwell County in South Carolina with one of the first waves of gold rush prospectors.

Wood had had his fill of the gold fields. He hadn't gotten rich, but he had saved enough from his diggings to purchase the ranch and a small held of cattle. He sent for his wife, Eudora, and his two sons, Jerrod and Clayton, to join him. The younger of the two sons, Clayton, was 13 years of age and accompanied his mother on a ship to Panama, crossed that country by train, and sailed on up to San Francisco the following year.

Jerrod Wood, however, was 17 years of age and restless. He remained in South Carolina, captivated by the political fervor in his home state. That spring the Democratic Party held its convention in Charleston and split angrily on the issues of slavery and secession. The Republican Party held their convention in a small town in Illinois called Decatur, and nominated a native son who, although he had moderate views on slavery, none the less was a potential threat to the pro-slavery powers of the American South: Abraham Lincoln.

In November, Lincoln was elected President of the United States of America. In December, South Carolina became the first state to secede from the Union. By February of 1861 six states had seceded and formed the Confederate States of America. More would follow.

Feeling ran deep: there was an assassination attempt on the president-elect before he was even sworn into office.

In April, Confederate troops bombarded Fort Sumter in South Carolina, successfully capturing the fort and initiating a war with many names: the War of Succession, the War of Rebellion, the War Between the States, the American Civil War, Hell on Earth. In May young Jerrod Wood enlisted in the Army of the Confederate States of America.

Assigned to Hagood's 1st Regiment Volunteers under Colonels Duncan and Hagood, Jerrod found himself shoring up the earthworks near the fort at Secessionville. It was June of 1862. The fort, built on a peninsula formed by creeks in a marshy area of James Island, South Carolina, was about to come under attack by Federal forces.

Colonel Hagood deployed his troops along the right flank while Colonel Lamar commanded those at the fort. The Union Army had war ships at the mouth of the river and some 3,317 men at the ready with 1500 more in reserve. The Confederates numbered around 750.

What should have been an easy victory for the Union was mired in mud and bogged down by inexperience. Besides the muck and vegetation through which they crawled, the Federals faced big guns trained on them from the fort: an 8-inch Columbiad, a 24-pound rifled gun, a 24-pound smoothbore, and an 18-pounder. These were filled with grape shot, nails and glass and sometimes pieces of rusted iron chain.

On the road flanking the fort Colonel Hagood commanded what was known as the Advanced Guard, although most of the men were as green as the soggy cotton fields they defended. He had two of the 24-pound guns but no one who knew how to operate them. He selected four of his own 1st Regiment Volunteers and ordered them to load the artillery piece. One of these soldiers was Jerrod Wood, about to see combat for the very first time.

The gun Jerrod and the makeshift crew were manning wasn't a light field piece, the type that could be pulled along by a team of horses. This was a massive piece of metal, 10 feet long with a bore nearly 6 inches in diameter. It weighed 5,800 pounds and was adjusted for the firing angle by using long wooden handspikes to tilt and rotate the barrel which sat on chassis of thick wooden beams.

Two of the men forced the sponge on its long wooden handle down the throat of the monster, twisting and cleaning the bore. A 5-inch wide powder cartridge was pushed into the muzzle using a rammer, followed by grapeshot and a packing wad. Jerrod and another man aimed the big gun with the handspikes and then adjusted the elevation using a hand crank on the chassis. The first firing would be observed for accuracy of range and trajectory so that adjustments could be made.

The powder cartridge, placed at the back of the bore, was pierced by inserting a punch into the vent hole just above it. Then Jerrod, clinging to the top of the gun's framework, pushed a friction tube down the vent, yelled, "Ready!" and jumped. One of the men stood to the rear of the gun holding a long piece of lanyard, waiting for the command to fire. When it came he pulled the lanyard, setting off the friction tube which in turn ignited the cartridge and...boom.

No, not just a boom: a thunderous, ear-shattering, nose-bleeding, shock wave of sound that shook the earth and reverberated in the men's minds and souls for days afterward. Nothing could have been as terrible as that hellish noise—nothing, except perhaps the hole it blew in the Union lines where fragments of uniforms, weaponry, and body parts splattered into a glitteringly bloody, expanding haze as if a red sun had gone supernova.

Of the officers it was said that there was an incompetent on one side and a drunkard on the other. Mistakes were made, soldiers fired willy-nilly hitting nothing. The enemy marched right past one commander's position unscathed. There were reserve troops stationed nearby that weren't brought up. But on the Union side, there were 689 casualties, of which 107 died. The Confederates had 207 casualties with 52 killed. All in all it was a splendid beginning for the War Between the Blue and the Gray, the War Between Brothers.

The Union failed to take the fort, which put a "win" on the Southern States score card. Jerrod Wood, standing numb beside the still smoking canon, suffered a severe head wound from returning musket fire and spent his remainder of the war—and his life, in a hospital room in Charleston. When news of his son's death reached him in California, Benjamin Wood wept.

Little Wind had arrived at the Wood ranch tied to the back of a mule. Her dignity hurt almost as much as her bruised and battered body. Her captors had argued with Benjamin Wood over price and settled finally on $40 for the Indian girl child—further insult added to her already injured pride. This was slavery! But to Benjamin Wood, grieving as much for the loss of the way of life of the American South, his former home, as for the loss of his son who had fought so gallantly to preserve it (he believed), it was merely business as usual.

Eudora would take the child into the household to help with chores. It was a bit of a luxury to be adding to staff again, but it had been a good year for the cattle ranch. And Indian labor was cheap in the long run. Besides, Eudora had to cook and clean and keep house for the men folk (Benjamin and son Clayton) and keep track of Minnie, the Indian woman who helped cook and who in turn had to cook and clean and keep track of the ranch hands, Randal Gallagher and Peter Obermeyer, who in turn were responsible for the whereabouts of the four Mission Indians that worked for them as cowboys...which...well, it was complicated.

"Get a move on, Missy," Eudora Wood yelled at Little Wind. "Into the house with you. And no sass! If there's anything I can't abide it's a sassy Injun." Little Wind just stared at the woman. Deciding erroneously that the girl understood no English, she grabbed her roughly by the arm and herded her toward the house. Then she called for Minnie.

Mrs. Wood fretted about road dust, grit and grime, and what she called "Injun cooties" which she was sure were crawling all over Little Wind. She pushed Little Wind at the Indian woman, Minnie, saying, "Into the tub with her. Lordy! I can't even tell if she is a girl child or a boy child." And Little Wind soon found herself immersed in a tub of luke-warm soapy water being attacked by a scrub brush.

Minnie tried several dialects on the girl, getting no response. Little Wind recognized in the woman's tone a certain positive regard, and so, using a term of respect for the woman's age she said, "I speak English, Grandmother."

"Ah ha! You do huh? Maybe you shouldn't let on about that. Give you an advantage here at the ranch."

"I'm not planning to stay here at this place."

"Oh you will. Try to run away, they catch you. Then you get punished. You stick close to me. It can be good here. You see."

Minnie had a wrinkled prune of a face and a colossal girth that gave her the silhouette of a ripe pear. She lifted Little Wind from the tub effortlessly and wrapped her in a blanket, rubbing her dry. "We find you something to wear. Burn old clothes," said Minnie.

Later that evening, Little Wind sat at a long, rough-hewed wooden table at the back of the kitchen. She wore a large man's flannel shirt which functioned as a dress of sorts, reaching, when she stood, below her knees. It would have to do, Minnie had told her, until they could get some decent Christian clothing for her. What Christian clothing might be like, Little Wind had no idea.

Around that same table sat the four Indian men and the two white ranch hands. Minnie presided at the head of the table and mumbled some words in a rapid drone which Little Wind later learned was called "grace." It seemed strange to the girl that men of the People could be sharing a meal with men of the enemy white race. Very strange.

Minnie and the four men had grown up at the Mission San Miguel Arcánge at San Luis Obispo. During the Spanish rule of Las Californias in the late eighteenth and early nineteen centuries the Franciscan Order had established this and other missions. Native Americans from the surrounding area were forced to live and work at the mission, and were subsequently Christianized; the Spaniards believing that the Indians' salvation could only be brought about by exterminating their heathen beliefs and cultural practices.

But the mission had its own ups and downs. The Mexican government had secularized all mission lands and in 1846, the mission was sold and turned into a private residence. Fleeing, the Mission Indians, as they came to be called (having little tribal identity left to them), found work at the farms and ranches of Californios, the Spanish settlers. Some, like Minnie and the four Indian cowboys now seated around the table, had ventured further north, finding work on Fernando Feliz's Rancho Sanel. When Benjamin Wood purchased his ranch from Feliz they came to work for him. Men like Benjamin Wood saw the potential of Indian labor: Mission Indians worked for food, shelter and clothing and received no pay. That was good for business.

The men were now talking in low voices in a strange language that Little Wind could not understand. She learned later it was called Spanish, although it seemed to be a mixture of that, English and some Native American dialect. They were a scruffy bunch, sun-burned (the white men) and covered with a fine patina of yellow dust of the kind kicked up by cattle hooves from desert waste lands (although Mendocino Valley was far from being a waste land). Minnie pointed to them, one by one, by way of introduction for the girl:

"Pete…Randy…" she said, indicating the two white men. "And," (the Indians), "Mathew…Mark…Luke…and John."

This must be a dream, thought Little Wind. A bad dream. Soon she would wake up and run to tell the dream to the shaman who would interpret it for her. He would tell her it meant that she should respect her elders or something equally irrelevant. But no, it was not a dream.

The one called Randy gave her a broken-toothed grin and said, "Girlie…go get me some more coffee." Little Wind glanced at Minnie whose subtle expression, the slight tightening of prune wrinkles and the squinting of slit-like eyes told her she need not obey. She looked at Randy blankly and shook her head.

"Get it yourself," bellowed Minnie and Randal Gallagher, much to the surprise of Little Wind, seem to shrink back into his chair and nod obediently. "This girl," explained Minnie, "works in the house *for me*. Get it?"

At least she had a friend, thought Little Wind. And she had to admit that the food, a mixture of meat and beans flavored with chiles and wrapped in freshly baked tortillas, was considerably better than the fare she had endured on the reservation. Perhaps it wouldn't be so bad here after all.

The kitchen and Minnie's quarters, which Little Wind would be sharing, were positioned far at the back of the rambling ranch house. The family took their meals in a separate dinning room connected by a walk-in pantry to the kitchen. The house had evolved, addition by addition, from the original, single room log cabin Wood had built with his own hands when he had acquired the land. It still smelled of fresh pine sap. The ranch hands stayed in a bunk house a sufficient distance from the main house to mute the songs, swearing and general rowdiness which filled their evenings and occasional idle times.

Little Wind was initiated into the daily routine. Dust seemed to leak in through every crack and constantly required the application of rags and brooms to clear it away. Breakfast was always elaborate, eggs or griddlecakes, ham or bacon, and lots of coffee. The work was not hard, but it was exhausting. In the next few days the girl had little opportunity to talk to Minnie: when they retired after the workday was over she fell into bed and was soon sleeping soundlessly (unlike Minnie who snored).

She tried to make sense of it all. Rarely did she come into contact with the Wood family. That was just as well as Mrs. Wood was curmudgeonly inhospitable and the Mister was distant and often absent. The son, Clayton, was always off working the ranch with the hands and had hardly given her any notice when he was around. The Mission Indians and the two white ranch hands were present for breakfast and an evening meal—but this was not always a very pleasant experience.

The one called Randy had a habit of leering at Little Wind and he chewed with his mouth open. Which was worse, she hadn't decided. None of the men talked to her nor did they seem intent on ever acknowledging her presence. One day, however, as she was carrying water from the well which was some distance from the house she felt she was being followed. Turning, she caught a glimpse of a dark figure ducking behind an old oak. Cautiously, she ambled toward the house at a reduced pace, then slammed the bucket onto the ground and whirled. There behind her stood Randall Gallagher, lips knotted into an ugly smirk, his hands rubbing against the coarse cloth of his trousers, as if he were wiping away something that clung to his palms—something uncomfortably sticky.

Perhaps that was the moment when Little Wind made her decision to leave the Wood ranch. She wanted to see her mother once more and to relate that her brother, White Cloud, had gone voluntarily from the reservation, that he had not been kidnapped as she had been. The scheme needed a good solid plan in order to be successful.

She began to collect some of the table scraps that wouldn't rot and start to smell: bits of dried meat, vegetables, bread. She hid these wrapped in a napkin under her mattress. She now had a simple dress that Mrs. Wood had bought for her on a shopping trip to Ukiah, the nearest town. For her journey cross country, she needed something more substantial. She managed to steal a pair of men's trousers from the wash line and cut them down to fit. A paring knife borrowed from the kitchen and a short length of rope completed her traveling kit. She was ready.

Minnie was snoring. A breeze fluffed up the gingham curtains. Little Wind retrieved the bits and pieces of her salvation, the food, the clothing, the knife, from under her mattress. Silently she slipped on the trousers, tied them tight with the rope around her waist. Cat-like she moved through the house. Cautiously she opened the door. And ran. Past the bunk house where a soft glow showed behind a dirty window: an evening's pipe nearly spent? Past the old oak tree and the well. Across a rail fence and into the night ran the Native American girl, plucky and determined and frightened beyond all belief.

The only flaw in her plan was that she had no idea exactly where the ranch was located nor did she know in which direction the reservation might lie. No matter. She was escaping.

Slow going through brush and thicket. Loose rock on ridges, sloppy mud near creek beds, the sweet sad song of coyotes from here and there and everywhere. Tired. Uncomfortable in baggy, cut-off denims. Feet torn by brambles. Moon behind clouds. Finally, exhausted, she rested.

She had climbed a steep hill where rows of grape vines hung, their twisted tendrils and broad leaves affording some shelter from searchers—if searchers were in fact coming. She sank—onto the soft earth, into a blessed deep sleep. She hadn't planned on dozing off, but her tired body overrode her desire to remain vigilant. She was safe for the time being. Only a timid field mouse was aware of her, explored her kit bag, borrowed a few morsels of bread.

It wasn't the sun that woke her. It was the footfalls of the horses. Near—too near! She ran through the vineyard, straight rows of plantings kept between her and the approaching clump-a-clump of her pursuers. They moved along the base of the hill, parallel to her flight. Was it a coincidence or had they seen her? If only she could angle off in a different direction! But the grape vines made too thick of a barrier. On an impulse she reversed direction. Now the hoof beats came softer, receded. She slowed her pace and searched for a way through the vines.

By ducking low, sometimes crawling, she moved up the hill through the vine rows, away from the road that the horses must be following. She came finally to the apex of the hill. Now the vineyard rows descended the slope, reached another road and another hill with yet another section of vines. And up the road came two men on horseback: Peter Obermeyer and Randal Gallagher. The road had wound around the hill to come out on its other side.

They had spotted her. Panicked and breathing hard she ran down the row of grapevines in the opposite of the direction they had come. But the men split up, one riding up the road, the other down it. Either direction she ran, one of them would be waiting for her. She dropped to her knees and began to crawl, back down the hill cutting through the vine rows. Maybe she could still elude them.

One more row and she would be at the road at the base of the hill. She froze and listened. There was only the wind rustling the leaves. She risked a peek, poking her head under the last row. Nothing. She crawled through, stood, waited for any sound, any sign of the enemy. Feeling uncomfortable she backed up into the protection of the vines, but as she moved, she brushed against something much more massive than a grape vine. Slowly she turned. A man had materialized right behind her.

"Found you little missy," he said.

She looked up into the very blue eyes of Clayton Wood.

"Lucky I found you before those other two!" He took her by the arm and led her to his horse which was hobbled just down the road out of sight. "Yep. Real lucky!"

5

City of the Holy Sacrament

Rivers are providers. The life blood of a land pulses through its rivers. River water thicker than blood. River water that nourishes growing things. River water that turns deserts into gardens. But as rivers giveth, rivers also taketh away. Hopes and dreams of hard-working people are often drowned in the floods of raging rivers.

Rivers connect. Avenues of commerce are spawned, cultivated and nurtured by rivers. Towns arise along the banks of rivers. Industries thrive from trade upon the rivers. And then the rivers cleave. As rivers cut new channels, communities are isolated, left high and left dry. Giveth. Taketh away. The river is ambivalent.

Rivers sustain life. Swimming things, flying things, things that scoop up their food with claws and paws, things that lash out with sticky tongues, even human things that pluck out of the living liquid those other live things—or grab for shiny golden objects that never lived—all these things are fed by rivers. Just as surely, rivers also deprive. As the river loses its balance, life diminishes then disappears all together. Rivers may kill. Rivers can also die.

River, creek, channel, brook, branch, stream, estuary, rivulet, runnel, rindle, rill—whether ripple or swell, cascade or trickle, in the river there is always movement. And movement is the fabric into which time is woven and the cloth by which eternity is measured. The river *is* eternity.

But for two youths, born of indigenous peoples for whom the river's embodiment of all things eternal is self-evident, the river was also a great way to get from one place to another. The current carried them swiftly down river toward the new state's largest city: Sacramento.

Their raft of fresh cut timber dipped and swung as the river manifested its endless repertoire of movement: surging, boiling, rolling, or slipping silently, smooth as polished silver, or suddenly

37

stagnant, brought up abruptly against solid, unyielding shore, tossed back in eddies, swirled in whirlpools, plummeted across boulders older than the river.

Avoiding shoreline snags meant keeping to center stream where there was imminent danger from a constant parade of steamboats. How different this river was from the time when their people traveled it in boats made of tule reed, fished it by stretching nets from bank to bank, drank from its pure flowing waters. Now unnatural things floated there: the jetsam from the white invaders' abominable, fire-breathing behemoths: the steamboats.

As they neared the city the sky seemed to lose its color. Trees seemed stunted. River banks were heaped up into levees of dirt that constricted the river, made it angry and turbulent. At a narrowed channel workers stood armed with long pikes. They reached out to the floating log rafts, hooked them, brought them toward their collection point where they hauled them out of the river and stacked them in neat piles. Tommy and Zack were headed directly for the loggers. The boys would have to get off of the log raft quickly.

They jumped, ran, were chased, were yelled at with angry and incomprehensible curses. Darting along the levees they barely evaded capture. Rows of boats lined the banks; they ducked between them. A city rose up behind the boats, made of brick and painted wood and glass.

"Is this the city of the big boats?" Zack asked Tommy.

"I don't think so. There are no boats with wings here. The big waters are not here."

"What do we do now?"

"Why don't we explore?"

A broad avenue ran the length of the waterfront between the buildings and the levee where stevedores and roustabouts worked unloading and loading steamboats and barges. The city sprawled back from this in a geometric grid of block after block of masonry structures, many having three stories and colonnaded porticos.

Because of the floods in the early 1850s and especially because of the devastating monster of a flood in 1862, Sacramento needed a plan to guard against rising waters. Being located on the Sacramento River was the basis of the city's economic growth. So instead of moving the city to higher ground, they simply raised its streets. Stone walls were built, ten feet high, on either side of the avenues and then the space between them was filled in with dirt.

The city officials gave the building owners the task of raising their individual sidewalks to the level of the new, higher street. Since their first floors now looked out at brick walls, many of the merchants raised their entire buildings the necessary ten feet using jackscrews. Others built up an additional story or two, making the original first floor a basement. The old sidewalks were now beneath the new ones, creating a labyrinth of tunnels. The project would take 13 years to complete and was still underway when Zack and Tommy reached the city.

In some places the streets had been raised but the sidewalks remained gapping holes, dangerous precipices where an unwary person could tumble to certain injury. In other places the sidewalks and storefronts had risen to the prescribed height, only to be adjacent to a cavernous, unfinished street. Wagons of dirt fill were dragged up ramps by weary horses. Wheels stuck in mud. Workers cursed. But life in the City of the Holy Sacrament continued with its usual fervor.

Zack and Tommy wandered along the elevated sidewalks fascinated by the variety of goods displayed behind the dust-covered windows. Bolts of bright-colored material, sacks of coffee beans or wheat open at the top to reveal their contents, curious machines (sewing, apple-peeling, typewriting) whose purposes the boys were unable to fathom, long barreled rifles, pocket-sized pistols, serrated knives, red, yellow, and green painted cans and boxes with pictures of corn or carrots or lima beans or the smiling face of a beautiful woman, shovels, picks, hoes, rakes, coils of thickly braided rope, water-filled glass bowls swarming with tiny fish sparkly with metallic blue or golden scales, watches...

Zack stopped suddenly in front of Floberg and Conrad, Watchmakers & Jewelers. The window provided a view of dozens of pocket watches, silver, gold, and pewter, with chains and fobs and dangling little winding keys. More astounding was the store's sign, a giant pocket watch which hung above the sidewalk to advertise the shop: on its face was painted a pair of unblinking eyes and a mouth grinning with perfect teeth. Zack's attention, however, was focused on the winding key on one of the watches. The missing element of the watch he carried as a talisman was its winding key. What if...

The boy entered the shop. The proprietor was occupied with a customer, a woman whose bustle and flamboyantly feathered hat nearly filled the shop. Zack went to the window, reached and retrieved one of the winding keys. He turned, meaning to ask the proprietor if he could try the key on his own watch, but the man, seeing a dirty and disheveled street urchin clutching something that obviously belonged to the store, leaped from behind the counter and rushed toward him yelling, "Hey you! Give that here."

Zack ran from the shop grabbing Tommy's arm as he fled. They plunged recklessly up the sidewalk, nearly failing to notice that it ended abruptly in a deep pit. The shopkeeper, furious and determined to recover whatever it was the boy had stolen, was storming after them. They jumped, landed hard on the wooden planks of the old sidewalk, gained their footing and took off running through the underground city.

There were buttressed walls of brick on one side, boarded up storefronts on the other. Here might be a spacious area, the footprint of a building which had been jackscrewed up above it. There might be a mountain of crates and barrels, storage for some establishment that once fronted on that subterranean spot. Cisterns of stone, pipes and wires, red-eyed rodents that scampered into cracks in the walls at their approach, hanging webs of dust—all were barely discernable in the gloom of the underground tunnel. Corridors branched this way and that. Water tricked in lazy streams. The air was moist and smelled of mold and decay.

The tunnel dead-ended at a brick wall. Catching their breath and listening for the footfalls of their pursuer, they stood in the darkness, marveling at the extent of the underground city. Hearing nothing but their own breathing and the dripping of water, they sank to the ground in exhaustion.

"What was that all about?" Tommy asked of Zack.

"Only this," he answered, showing the winding key to his companion. "It's to wind the watch. I didn't mean to steal it. But the man came at me so fast..."

There were spots of light back down the tunnel at junctures where the ceiling, the bottom of the raised sidewalk, had a grate to allow water to drain below into the tunnel. There were also some places where glass bricks had been placed into the new sidewalk to give sparse illumination to the space below when it was used for storage—or other things. The boys rose and set off in the direction they had come. At the first intersection they turned a corner.

They searched for a way out of the tunnels, turning here, forging ahead there, and began to despair of being lost. They were encountering nothing like the opening into which they had jumped.

"Maybe if we go through one of these store fronts," suggested Zack. They tried a door, then another and another, but found them locked and boarded up. There was nothing to do but to keep moving.

There was light and sound and the sticky, sweet smell of something burning just up at the next turning. They ventured a quick look around the corner and saw an abandoned storefront from which issued the light and the sound and the smell. They approached, wiped a circle of damp dust from a window and peered through it. The interior was lit by candles in whose flickering shadows they could just make out the reclining forms of men with long stemmed pipes protruding from their mouths. The air was filled with smoke.

"What is it?" Zack asked. "Are they demons?"

"I don't think we should try to find out," said Tommy.

They continued searching for an exit, trying doors and windows. The pools of light from the openings in the sidewalks above them were beginning to dim: the afternoon was waning. They turned off into another series of tunnels where faint illumination suggested they would encounter another occupied storefront. As they approached this one they heard music, or something like music, and laughter.

"More demons?"

"Perhaps not. It sounds like somebody's celebrating."

Twelve and thirteen year old boys are not supposed to know about brothels, certainly not Native American twelve and thirteen year old boys. But Zack and Tommy were about to be introduced to one. The door was not locked or barred so in they went. Girls, Asian girls not much older than Zack or Tommy, sat on velvet-covered wing-back chairs. Some wore European clothing complete with hoop skirts that bulged and ballooned, revealing the inexperience of the wearer. Some wore—Zack and Tommy had never seen costumes quite like these—corsets and stockings and lacy underthings. It seemed everything in the room, clothing, rugs, furniture, wallpaper, was a deep crimson, as vivid as the glistening red cosmetic paint on the girls' lips.

"Oh-oh," exclaimed Tommy.

The source of the music was a Chinese man in traditional dress seated cross-legged on the floor and playing a strange-looking stringed instrument. A Chinese woman who looked to be about one hundred years of age came over to them, scowled and said, "You too young. You go way now."

"We're just trying to get back up to the street," explained Tommy.

"No street here. You go. I get headman. He fix you good." The woman disappeared through a doorway to summon help.

Zack looked at Tommy. "We'd better get out of here," he said.

One of the girls rose from her chair, brushing her hoop skirt out of the way of a small table set with glasses filled with some liquid— red, of course—and came up to the boys, taking each by the arm. "Come this way," she said.

She ushered them through another door and out into a part of the tunnel leading in a different direction from which they had come.

"You want leave? You take Mei Lim too? I show you way to go."

And without waiting for an answer the girl moved quickly down the tunnel. The boys followed, not wishing to meet the "headman" who was going to fix them good. How she found her way through the darkened corridors they could only wonder at as they followed obediently. The circuitous route they took led slowly upward. Finally they reached a rickety old stairway which seemed to lead to nowhere. They climbed, found themselves in an alley at the level of the raised street.

"Must leave here quickly too," said the girl. "Must have other clothes." She then slipped the straps of her costume off of her shoulders and the hoop skirt fell to the ground. She stood in the dark alley dressed in a chemise bodice and long white split drawers.

"Which way is the river?" asked Tommy.

"Come. I show. Where we go on river?"

"We? Ah…well…*we* are going to the big water to find a boat with wings to take us to El-Ya-Noy. You know where that is?"

"I not know this place. Big water you speak of is ocean? We go Dai Fow. Leave Yee Fow right away. You Indian boys?"

"No, we're Mexicans."

"No, you not Mexicans. You Indians. I know. We go now before bad people come."

The Shasta Belle rolled gently in the wake of a large steamer passing down the river. She was moored on the levee near the section of town called Yee Fow, Sacramento's "Second City," its Chinatown. Mei Lim had led Zack and Tommy through the muddied streets and alleyways and across Front Street, the broad avenue bordering the levees where the bustle of maritime industry continued day and night.

"We hide on that one. It leave soon for Dai Fow. Ocean there," she said, pointing to the Shasta Belle.

Mei Lim, still clothed only in her undergarments, was hiding behind a row of barrels which reeked of strong ale. She hadn't explained as yet just how they were going to get onto the boat. Tommy watched as dockhands hefted heavy crates and carried them onto the riverboat.

"I have it! Wait here a minute," Tommy told his companions.

There were a number of wooden crates stacked along the levee waiting to be loaded. Tommy studied these and selected a small one. He pried the lid off of it with his knife and tipped it over to empty its contents. Dishes packed in excelsior clattered out of the crate and crashed into pieces. The noise was unnoticed in the clamor and confusion of the busy waterfront.

A few minutes later, two young stevedores carried a wooden box up the ramp to the deck of the Shasta Belle. If they caught anyone's eye they were assumed to be two Mexican boys working on the docks, or at least, that is what Zack and Tommy hoped. They set the crate down behind a row of others. A voice came from inside: "Hey, careful!" Mei Lim popped out of the crate like a playful jack-in-the-box.

Pitch-dark night came early, flowed over the levees as if someone had tipped over a bottle of ink; clouds obscured the starlight and the moon had not yet risen. Tommy waited for the sounds of snorting and snoring to come from the crew's quarters, then did what he did best: he stole some trousers and a shirt for Mei Lim.

"Now we are *three* Mexicans," Tommy proclaimed as he presented the Chinese girl with the clothing. Mei Lim just shook her head.

Zack settled down for the night. Things had happened so rapidly and in such a convoluted manner that he hadn't had time to sort them out in his mind. They were on their way! It seemed incredible. He thought about Tommy. A year older but possessed with spirit and bravery and yes, cleverness that Zack could only aspire to. Was it bravery or was it foolhardiness? It didn't matter because without Tommy's dauntless energy, his intrepid (but often reckless) pluck, Zack might still be sitting back at the reservation.

And then there was the girl. How had that happened? It was true that without her help they might have been lost in the underground city forever. It was also possible that they had become paladins, delivering an imperiled damsel from a degrading and wretched existence. The pitiful helping the pitiful. But now what? They couldn't bring her with them to El-Ya-Noy...could they?

"Girl," Zack said, "what is your name again?"

"Mei Lim. Chen Mei Lim is full name but don't use family name. Sold me to headman. Hate them now."

"Mei Lim, do you intend to go with us to El-Ya-Noy?"

"I go Dai Fow. It mean Big City. Lots of Chinese there. Same place you get boat."

"Why did you help us?"

"I want to leave evil place for long time. Can't go with white men who visit. They even more evil. I see you boys. Know you kind. Know you help me. So I help you."

They slept on the deck behind the crates. They slept the sound sleep of total exhaustion and were not awakened when the Shasta Belle's great wooden wheel began to churn the silty Sacramento River.

Christian Kopp had been a mate on the Shasta Belle since two years ago that April. He was proud of his ship, and thought it the best stern-wheeler on any river in the state of California. She had been built in Greenmanville, Connecticut, along the Mystic River, taken apart, placed on a bark that sailed around the horn to arrive at San Francisco, reassembled and sent to ply her trade on the upper Sacramento River. Her draught, when she was not loaded, was only eighteen inches: sufficient to navigate all the way to the mouth of Clear Creek some forty miles above Red Bluffs where low water repulsed most steamers.

The Shasta Belle was not the largest of steamers: only 160 feet long and 28 feet wide of beam. She had two engines and three boilers. Her accommodations for passengers included 14 double staterooms and 12 open berths. Her salon ran the length of the Texas deck, complete with hanging crystal chandeliers and an ornate carpet decorated with the squiggles and curlicues of some fantastic plant life.

Christian Kopp was no newcomer to paddle-wheelers. He had shipped on several riverboats and had been part of the crew of another boat named Belle, whose boiler had exploded at Russian Ford, 11 miles above Sacramento in February of 1856. The incident was imprinted in his memory and had instilled in him a certain cautious nature, an obsessive tendency to check and double check the well-being of any vessel on which he shipped.

That Belle (not this one) had been waiting out a fog, a thick gray-white blanket of rarefied moisture that obscured river and river bank so thoroughly that Captain Charles Houston lay to and ordered the boilers shut down. When finally the fog began to lift the Captain sent a young Christian Kopp, then the ship's cabin boy, in search of the first engineer, a man called Elrick.

"Tell him to get up some steam," said the Captain. "But no more than eighty pounds. No need to rush down river when a blind bat can see better than us."

Kopp did as he was told and assumed that Elrick had relayed the orders to the fireman. Indeed, the sounds of rumbling water in the big boilers and hissing steam from the escape cocks could be heard clearly throughout the boat. Kopp went to get some breakfast.

Perhaps there had been much more pressure than the requested eighty pounds. Perhaps there had not been adequate water in the boilers or perhaps the iron was faulty. Whatever the reason, the explosion ripped the Belle apart, broke her in two. Everything but the aft section immediately sank.

Kopp watched in horror as a piece of exploding boiler struck a man squarely on the head and splattered his brains and his blood onto the man standing next to him. Another man was blown through the washroom door, his trousers still pulled below his knees.

There were some miraculous escapes. One man had been sitting in front of an iron stove, his legs straddling it on either side. The explosion propelled the stove through the hurricane deck but left the man unscathed. Another man lost his hat to a flying fragment of metal which parted his hair but left his head still connected to his body. Others were not so lucky.

The fireman, William Green, was fished from the river by rescuers. The upper part of his body was missing. People hung from the edge of the deck as the boat slid beneath the surface. The dead numbered somewhere between ten and twelve; there had been about sixty passengers and crew aboard. Not the worst disaster on record, but Christian Kopp never forgot the incident; in fact he spent the next six years as a landlubber, working on the docks or in the warehouses, afraid to return to the river.

But she beckoned. Her sparkling smile of sun-flecked swells seduced him as surely as if she had been a spurned lover, begging for reconciliation. After that he worked on series of steamboats and advanced in his profession. When the position of mate on the Shasta Belle became available Christian jumped at the chance. Something about the name though, the Shasta *Belle*, made him apprehensive. Perhaps it was just superstition.

The Shasta Belle was pulling away from the harbor of Sacramento, winding through the maze of small and large boats that clogged the river. Christian Kopp left the pilothouse, a glass-enclosed box perched atop the paddle-wheeler's upper deck, and began his tour of inspection. He spent extra time in the room where the boilers were being stoked, examining gauges and water lines, and making sure the firemen were well aware of his presence.

"Keep an eye on those gauges," he cautioned. The men cast angry glares at his back as he exited the boiler room.

They were well past Sutterville and Riverside and approaching Freeport when Kopp's tour took him to the main deck. He leaned against the hog mast, felt the tension on the hog chain that kept the hull from sagging, and looked out over the river. Hydraulic mining was filling the rivers with silt and debris. Some of the sloughs in the lower river delta were becoming impossible to navigate for ships with a greater draught than the Shasta Belle. The gold miners, obsessed with extracting the minutest specks of gold were laying waste to entire hillsides, washing them away with high-pressure hoses, killing the rivers. It would be years before the practice would be outlawed.

Kopp moved toward the bow of the boat where crates were stacked and the crew sometimes idled to smoke or tell stories or otherwise shirk their duties. Seeing no one, he was about to return to the pilothouse when he heard the sound of voices coming from behind the crates. Then he saw them: three young boys—stowaways!

"You there!" Kopp called. "Come out from behind those crates. What are you doing here?"

With a start he realized that one of the "boys" was in fact, a girl. This complicated things in Kopp's mind. He might have been tempted to simply throw the youths overboard. But a girl might drown.

"Who are you? Are you a bunch of Indians?" Kopp asked.

"No, Sir. We are Mexicans," replied Tommy.

"No, you aren't. You're Indians. Well, what have you to say for yourselves?"

"Please don't put us off. We'll work for our passage. We just need to get to El-Ya-Noy."

"Dai Fow," said Mei Lim.

"Oh swell," said Kopp. "A Chinese girl and two Indians. What ever will I do with you?"

6

San Francisco Bay Blues

Zack had woken to the bobbing of the boat and the acrid stench of burned wood, coal tar and over-heated iron. Sea birds swirled overhead, calling for handouts. Boards creaked and taut ropes sang in the wind. He roused the others, eager to share a dream that had come with him as he woke.

"I was riding a fast horse along the road of stars," he related. "It was snow white with a long mane and galloping like thunder. We came to a cliff and the horse jumped out into the empty space but we did not fall. We flew like a great bird and sailed through the clouds. But a huge eagle came after us, clutched the horse in its talons and I fell…"

"What happened?" asked Mei Lim. From her own culture she had acquired a respect for the power of dreams, their tendency to be prophetic. A flying horse was an omen—but of what?

"I woke up."

They sat in silence for some moments. The boys fished through their bags to find what little food stuffs were left.

"What will you do in Big City," Zack asked Mei Lim. "Aren't you afraid you'll be put back to work in another…another evil place?"

"Where I was came only Fah Kay Yen, Flower Flag People…you call white men. Not high rank to work for white men. Lowly persons treated badly, whipped and told we no good. Bad, bad life. I go Big City and find place where only high Chinese come. Then I treated like princess. Many fine clothes. Good food. Better life there. You see."

"But…oh, I don't know. Wouldn't you rather take a husband? Raise a family? Not have to…you know…do those things?"

"How I can be married? No way. I am already marked. See?" Mei Lim pulled back her sleeve to reveal a tattoo on her arm. It was a Chinese character in red ink.

Zack was about to ask the meaning of the character when the first mate, Christian Kopp, discovered them.

"Oh swell," Kopp was saying, "a Chinese girl and two Indians. What ever will I do with you?"

Zack looked up into a pair of gray-green eyes sunk into a prematurely aged face. The man was big in the way that a brown bear is big when standing on hind legs to devour a salmon. He wore a uniform with stripes on its sleeves, which gave Zack to think that this was the captain. What indeed *would* he do with them? Zack imagined the bear hug and the hurtling out, over and into the cold water that was certainly in store for them.

Yet if he read the man's expression correctly—the eyes that sparkled ever so slightly, the lips drawn tight into a straight line but creeping up at the edges, the sudden twitching of the nose like a chipmunk examining a walnut—perhaps all was not lost. There was kindness hiding behind that forced solemnity, wasn't there?

"Please, Captain," Zack began, "we aren't hurting anything. We can pay for our passage. See? I have this…" and Zack produced the watch from a pocket, offered it to the man.

"Hmm…" Kopp looked at the watch, shook it, listened to it, gave it back to the child. "It don't work, son. Ain't worth the price of passage I'm afraid."

"Oh well, it needs to be wound." Zack searched through his pockets to find the winding key he had stolen. "See…"

But trying to insert the key into the slot on the watch proved to be a dismal failure. It didn't fit. Crestfallen, Zack looked up at the man with the most sheepish look he could muster.

"And I'm not the captain," said Kopp. "I am, however, the person in charge here and now and *I* will determine your fate. Now, have you any skills?"

Zack kicked at Mei Lim as she started to answer. Her skills, although they would probably be appreciated by some of the crew, were not, so far as Zack was concerned, a bargaining point at this juncture. "We will work hard," Zack said. "Anything you need done. We're strong. We can help unload the cargo."

"I tell you what. Do you know what a snag is?"

"Something in the water, like a tree or a rock that the ship might hit?"

"Very good. You three go up to the bow and look for snags. If you see one you pull that rope over there. You see it? It rings a bell in the pilothouse. If we get to San Francisco without hitting any snags you will have earned your passages."

Christian Kopp wasn't worried that the three children might be too inexperienced for the job or that they might shirk their duty. There was already a man stationed on the hurricane deck watching the river. But giving these urchins some responsibility made him feel that he was handling the situation in a positive manner. Of course, he could always just throw them overboard.

Zack, Tommy and Mei Lim positioned themselves along the flat bow of the Shasta Belle. The water rushed under the boat at a dizzying speed. Bits of flotsam, leaves, small twigs, a dead bird, an old boot, flashed past. Along the river were small settlements with landings where farmers could load their produce onto steamboats. The Shasta Belle passed them by. She entered the middle fork of the river delta, a route called Steamboat Slough, favored by the larger and faster boats.

Steamboat Slough was slowly filling with silt from the slickens, the waste and debris from hydraulic mining that washed down the river. It was now half as deep as it had been only ten or fifteen years before. Still, with its shallow draught, the Shasta Belle slipped easily along.

There were places where the wrecks of boats poked ugly skeletal remains above the surface: the sloop Wasp, the schooner Bianca, the steam barge Star of the West, the Eliza, the Fanny Ann, the F. W. Crawford, the General Reddington, the Monitor, the Nevada, the Sophie McClean, the Yosemite, and many others littered the river from Sacramento to Rio Vista. Some lay deep; others were hazards to navigation.

Their tenure at the bow of the Shasta Belle had been boring at best. Zack had expected a more challenging assignment, one entailing brute force labor or perhaps a sophisticated appointment like cabin boy or waiter in the salon. But snag spotter! He was beginning to believe they had been simply put aside where they wouldn't cause trouble or be noticed by the rest of the crew. Then he saw the wreck.

It was almost invisible; a swirling mat of leaves and brush had clung to it, obscuring its sharp contours. The burned-out hulk of a steamer sat directly ahead, mostly submerged but lethal as a killer whale should they strike it at their present clip. Zack ran to the bell rope and pulled it repeatedly. Up in the pilothouse the pilot, hearing the bell ringing, immediately threw the paddle-wheel into reverse and swung the Shasta Belle toward the middle of the river. There was a loud crunch as the Shasta Belle grazed the submerged wreck.

The impact nearly threw Tommy and Mei Lim overboard, perched as they were on the bow. The boat was turning sideways in the middle of Steamboat Slough and coming to a halt. Men ran to the lee side to look at the damage. Luckily, the hull had not been breeched; they were not sinking. Christian Kopp was on the hurricane deck, fuming and taking the lookout to task for not having noticed the wreck. Zack was still gripping the bell rope, his knuckles turning white, his breath coming hard and fast.

After the steamboat got back underway Kopp came to the three stowaways. "You probably saved us from a very bad wreck," he told them. "Are you hungry? Would you like some food?"

Kopp couldn't allow the stowaways to mingle with the crew nor to enter the salon on the Texas deck where the first class passengers were clustered around a long table heaped with plates of fish and various meats. He could, however, scrape together some left-overs, and this he had done, bringing them a bag filled with bits of smoked fish, fresh cod, herring, shrimp, venison, roast beef, apples, grapes, figs, nectarines and other delicacies. Zack marveled, not only at the food, but at the fact that here was a white man being kind to them. It was a new experience for the boy.

The Shasta Belle glided past corn fields and swampy stands of tule reed. Steamboat Slough widened and emptied into a broad bay, eight miles wide and fifty miles long, whose exit into the Pacific Ocean squeezed through a channel a mere mile across. On a peninsula, protruding into the bay like a sore thumb, sat the elegant, decadent, and awe-inspiring citadel of San Francisco.

In the early years of the 1849 California gold rush, San Francisco was the terminus for gold-seekers who sailed from New York, London, Australia, Chile, Argentina, and China on barks and clipper ships that rounded Cape Horn or came up from Panama or from across the Pacific ocean to dock at the wharves along the bay front. Many crews deserted their vessels to prospect for gold and the bay became clustered with the masts and empty hulls of ghost ships.

The city had been laid out in straight lines following the typical method of city planners of the day. A grid of squared blocks extended from the piers on the waterfront back and up sand hills that had been heaped up by the sea eons ago. This resulted in steep avenues difficult to climb. An effort to correct their grades was undertaken, gouging and scraping away at the hills and providing employment for many San Franciscans.

As more ships arrived bringing travelers and commercial goods, more docking areas were needed. The waterfront was filled in with dirt excavated from the steep streets. New wharves were built out onto the filled-in areas, sometimes over the corpses of abandoned sailing ships.

Perched on the hills, houses of the wealthy and the not so wealthy sprang up surrounded by glorious gardens of nasturtium and fuchsia, with climbing rose vines and towering pine trees, lilacs, urns of chrysanthemums and pots of geraniums. The houses hung on the impossibly sharp inclines like jeweled boxes suspended in mid-tumble.

The Shasta Belle couldn't dock at the huge Central Wharf where the volume of traffic exceeded even its impressive 500 foot length. They passed on to the Pacific Street Wharf, newly built to compete with the Central and the many other private wharves that splayed out into the bay like quills on a porcupine.

As the name implied, the wharf fronted on Pacific Street, one of the first to be cut through the hills and a destination for some, for if one ambled up the street one found oneself in the notorious district called the Barbary Coast. Then if one followed the street as far as Portsmouth Square, one found oneself in Chinatown.

San Francisco was a city of opposites, mixed together into a rich stew of contradictions. The refined culture of the newly rich co-existed with a disreputable underworld of gambling, prostitution and drugs. The opera house rubbed shoulders with the saloon. Expensive hotels were within walking distance of dives where errant sailors, drunks, rowdies, petty thieves, and other despicable characters imbibed large quantities of alcohol and, in various unsavory ways made merry. Miners came to "Friscoe" who had gold dust to spend and there were gamblers and pretty (and not so pretty) ladies waiting there who were ready and willing to take it from them.

Zack and Tommy had tagged along with Mei Lim who seemed to have the directional sense of a homing pigeon and headed up Pacific Street toward Chinatown. Perhaps their own sense of chivalry would not let the young girl wander through the now darkening streets alone, or perhaps they simply had no where else to go. They followed a few paces behind her as she stopped occasionally to talk to anyone who was Asian who might supply her with directions.

She narrated their progress as they passed Fay Chie Hong (Fat Boy Alley) and Fo Sue Hong (Fire Alley). The Chinese place names bore little resemblance to the labels assigned to them by the City of San Francisco, but they functioned much better for the residents of the district who were familiar with the street where a 240 pound child had lived or an alley where a fierce fire had destroyed many houses.

Bartlett Alley, which they had turned down to cross to Jackson Street, was known as Buck Wa John Guy, which meant "the grocery man who speaks Chinese." From Jackson they entered an alley called Cum Cook Yen after a restaurant that was located on it and stopped to gaze through its window. Looking past pale pink silk banners and hanging tassels of gold and red they could see a large round table around which were seated several Chinese men dressed in splendidly elaborate traditional costumes as well as six Flower Flag People (or white men as Zack and Tommy thought of them).

One of the white men stood speaking to the group. He used wide, extravagant gestures and elicited laughs and guffaws from the other white men. The Chinese were unmoved. The man had dark, curly hair and a broad, walrus-style moustache. He wore a suit coat with velvet lapels and a small, neatly done string tie. Something about him struck Zack; perhaps it was the enthusiasm he was garnering. He certainly had a presence that even a young Wintu boy could appreciate.

Mei Lim asked a passerby what occasion was being celebrated inside the restaurant that included the Fah Kay Yen. There followed a fairly lengthy conversation in which Mei Lim sometimes resorted to sign language to compensate for the differing dialects. She then explained to her companions that a banquet was being held in honor of some distinguished white men.

"You know of the Six Companies?" she asked. Seeing the doubtful expressions on the faces of the two Indian boys, she continued. "These are leaders of our people who help those who come from China to here. All not speak same or come from same province. When arrive are directed to which company that help them. Companies help with jobs, with sickness, with death. Send bones back to home. They give dinner for important Fah Kay Yen."

They watched as dozens of bowls of exotic food were placed in front of the diners: fried shark's fin, stewed pigeon in bamboo soup, chicken with water-cress, bird's nest soup, roast duck, pickled cucumbers, and steaming rice. Mei Lim giggled at the white guests' attempts to eat with chop sticks. Zack was delighted to finally see the young Chinese girl laughing.

"Could the Six Companies get you a job?" Zack asked Mei Lim. "A different kind of job, I mean."

"They not interested in help woman. Woman not worthy. I look for help from Madam Ah Toy. She help joy-daughter like me."

"Who is this Ah Toy person?"

"She come Hong Kong to Big City many years ago. She then slave but her feet unbound. Too big I guess. Owner die on ship. She start business on her own. Very beautiful. Miners like look at her. She charge for 'lookee lookee but no touchee.' Get very rich. Bring girls from China. Expand business."

"Mei Lim, I don't think you should..."

"You come with me far as place of Ah Toy? Maybe she also help you get to El-Ya-Noy. Very important woman. Know everyone."

They had been waiting in the foyer for sometime. Entrance to Ah Toy's salon had only been allowed after Mei Lim had showed the tattoo on her arm to the fat, sweating mountain of a man who had answered the door. Mei Lim thought the appointments of the room in which they waited were less impressive than she had anticipated; the furnishings were old and tattered and the wallpaper was drab. A moth-eaten curtain functioned as a door at the back of the room. As she mentally compared the space to the one in the underground city in Sacramento the curtain parted and a tall, broad-shouldered woman entered.

She was dressed in a cream-colored silk jacket decorated with dragons and wore pale blue pantaloons. High-heeled wooden sandals increased her already considerable height by two more inches. The ebony black hair piled high on her head was held in place by ivory combs from which dangled golden tassels. Her eyebrows had been shaved and penciled back in as thin black lines that accented her ebony eyes. Her face was still beautiful but time-worn. White rice powder barely covered her worry lines.

Zack and Tommy waited as Mei Lim and Madame Ah Toy conversed in Cantonese. Now flanking the woman were two very large men: bodyguards, Zack concluded. As mean and ruthless as the two men appeared, Zack was more frightened by Madame Toy. Her expression was frozen in the kind of snarl you might see on the face of a hungry predator seconds before it swallowed your head.

Finally Madame Toy nodded to one of the men who took Mei Lim by the arm and escorted her through the curtained doorway. It happened too quickly for Zack or Tommy to react. Tommy stepped forward but the remaining bodyguard blocked his way. Ah Toy looked at the boys sternly, then her face broke into a smile exposing yellowed teeth.

"Do not worry about the girl," Ah Toy said. "She will be treated well. She thinks she knows everything, but she knows nothing. I will teach her. As for you, her companions and protectors, I have assured her I will help you also. You wish to go to the east, do you not?"

"Yes we do. To El-Ya-Noy," replied Zack.

"You go tomorrow morning early to the docks. Look there for a man name of Bathhouse Jake. You'll recognize him by his two front teeth. They are sold gold. He is taking a group of men toward where you wish to go, though perhaps not all the way. You don't have anything against working your way there, do you?"

"We're good workers. Thank you ma'am. Please be kind to Mei Lim. She's a good girl."

"Off with you now. And don't come back!"

Ah Toy turned and swished through the curtained doorway as smoothly as if she had wheels instead of feet. The bodyguard took a step toward the boys. Within seconds they were back outside and running up the alley.

The darkness in the alleys was offset by paper lanterns hanging at intervals which swarmed with moths and other flying insects and cast pale pools of light onto the paving stones. Windows, barred by bamboo spilled stripes of light from houses where people were gathered for the evening meal. The smells of cooking leaked into the alley mingling with wood smoke from the chimneys. Zack and

Tommy slowed their pace, trying to retrace the steps that had taken them to Ah Toy's bordello. They expressed sadness and worry at the plight of Mei Lim as they crept through Chinatown.

Ahead of them was the alley where the boys had peeked into the restaurant. Two white men came out of a door and strolled up the alleyway just ahead of them. Zack recognized one of them as the curly-headed man who had entertained his cronies at the banquet earlier. It was impossible not to eavesdrop on their conversation.

"Ah, Bret," the curly-headed one was saying, "I don't think our Oriental friends appreciated my humor."

"You can be a bit abstruse at times, Sam."

"Enigmatic, you mean? Esoteric? Perspicacious?"

"Perplexing but definitely insightful, even profound..."

"I do appreciate your comments about my book, Bret. I'm going to make most of the cuts you suggested."

"Good. And I think the newspaper articles from the Alta can stand pretty much as is. They were brilliant pieces."

"Yes, those bastards gave me hard time about those. Didn't want to give me back the rights."

"Sam, why don't you let me publish a few chapters of your book in the Overland Monthly."

"That rag you edit? Well, of course you can. But Bret, you should write more fiction yourself. You remember that story we talked about? The one about the gold miners and the big flood of '62?"

"Yes, maybe I should. You seem to be getting a lot of attention with *your* prose. By the way, what are you calling this book?"

"Well I don't know. Maybe something like 'My Great Pleasure Excursion and Travels Abroad with Idiots like Myself.' I want to go back to New York tomorrow and edit the book on the boat. Some fools want me to lecture next week, though. Of course, I can use the money."

"An ocean voyage where you work...that should be relaxing! Will you go or stay and do the lecture? Well, here's where I turn off. Good luck with your book."

"By, Bret. Take care."

Soon Zack and Tommy were trailing several yards behind the man called Sam. Suddenly, as happens in the alleys of Chinatown, two dark figures exploded from a shadowy doorway and leaped upon the man, knocking him down. Tommy was the first to enter the fray followed closely by Zack, swinging his bag.

Tommy had pulled one of attackers off of the man named Sam and was tussling with him. Sam was giving a good account of himself, helped along by Zack whose well-aimed bag of dried meat and fruit connected repeatedly. Tommy's opponent wriggled from his grip and took off up the alley, his footsteps echoing on the cobbles. The other attacker rose and aimed a kick at Zack. Zack managed to grab the man's foot in mid-kick and twist it, tumbling his attacker to the ground. This man then scrambled to his feet and ran away.

Dusting himself off, the man called Sam felt for his wallet and finding it intact gave a grunt of relief. He looked at Zack and Tommy, trying to decide if he was still at risk of being robbed. As the boys were standing motionless, their body language not being aggressive, Sam decided to be optimistic.

"I can't thank you boys enough," said Sam. "I'm Samuel Clemens. You've heard of me? No? Just as well. You're Indians, aren't you?"

"No," said Tommy, "we're Mexicans."

"Hmpf. I don't think so. I think you are certainly Indians. No matter. I would like to do something for you for helping me out of that jam. Are you hungry?"

Sam Clemens had hired a horse-drawn carriage and soon they arrived at the corner of Montgomery Street and Sutter where an imposing edifice, four stories high and an entire city block long, stood as a monument to San Francisco's place in the nineteenth century world of culture, wealth and elitism: the Occidental Hotel. Sam ushered the boys (against the doorman's objections) into the hotel's restaurant.

"Tell Bill Hooper that Sam Clemens is in the restaurant with some friends," Sam said to the maitre d' hotel who looked askance at the rough-and-tumble clothing and dark skin of the two boys. Hooper was the proprietor of the Occidental and a good friend of Clemens who always stayed in his hotel when he visited San Francisco. "And tell the Professor to make me a good strong Martinez and rustle up a dozen Olys on the half shell for starters."

They were seated at a table next to the bar where they watched as the bartender, Professor Jerry Thomas, was putting the finishing touches on one of his signature cocktails, the Blue Blazer. Thomas set whiskey on fire and poured it artfully from glass to glass. Sam pushed the menu toward the boys. Sensing their inability to decipher the hand-lettered writing on the yellowed parchment he began to read:

"The Golden Gate Restaurant of the Occidental Hotel, Menu for June 28, 1868: Bouillon, Chicken A la Creole, Boiled Yaquina Bay Salmon with Sauce Crevettes, Santa Cruz Mackerel Grille Maitre d'Hotel, Saucisson de Lyon with California Ripe Olives, Boiled leg of Mutton in Caper Sauce, Roast Ribs of Beef, Corned Beef Tongue Chilienne, Navel Orange Beignet au Curacoa, Garden Peas Mashed, White Turnips, Fried Parsnips—anything here strike your fancy? No? Ah, desserts! How about Citron Cake Lemon Wafers, Cocoanut Jumbles Sugar Kisses...oh, here you go...Indian Pudding, Wine Sauce."

The waiter arrived with a plate heaped with oysters. Clemens ordered the roast ribs of beef all around, the garden peas, another glass of the new cocktail which the Professor called the Martinez for himself and a sarsaparilla for each of the boys. Zack and Tom, mesmerized by the shards of light bouncing off the crystal pendants on the room's chandeliers were the perfect captive audience for Clemens who embarked upon an elaborate commentary on everything in general.

"My friend and colleague, Bret Harte, has just finished reading the manuscript of my new book, a sort of travel narrative of my recent trip to the Holy Land. Of course, the Americans that I traveled with affected foreign airs in order to hobnob with the local dilettantes and supplied me with never-ending entertainment, often more intriguing than the sights. Now I've received an invitation to speak next week at the Mercantile Library Hall—of course there is generally a wide spread opposition to my lecturing, sometimes to the point that the audience takes up a collection in order to dissuade me from talking—that's a joke, boys—and besides, I did so wish to be on a steamer headed back to the east tomorrow..."

"Mr. Clemens, Sir, do you say you were going to the east? Is that near El-Ya-Noy?" asked Zack.

"El... you mean Illinois? Well, no. I'm going to New York. Illinois is more or less out in the prairies, what we used to call the Wild West. Little did we know! You have an interest in Illinois?"

"We're going there. Only, we aren't sure exactly how to get there."

"Well, you could go by coach. I think you had better tell me your story. Wait 'til I get my notebook out."

The meal progressed with Zack telling Clemens the tale of their adventures and Tommy filling in points here and there. Clemens was particularly interested in the part of the story where the boys had floated down river on a raft.

"You boys sound to me like two innocents abroad. I wonder if you know what you're in for."

"Maybe you could take us with you to this Nu-Yor. Then we could take a coach to El-Ya-Noy."

"Take you…I suppose I might do that if you could be of some service to me. Can you read and write? No? Well, come see me after my lecture next week. Maybe we can work something out. My heart goes out to you boys."

A giant of a man with a round head and puffy face with the complexion of an old shoe sauntered over to the table and slapped Clemens on the back. "Sam," he said, "I've missed you at Stahle's Turkish baths. When you're done here come over to the bar and I'll give you a few on the house."

"Boys, I want you to meet an old buddy of mine, Thomas Sawyer. Tom and I go back to my days looking for gold out in Nevada. He's as rough as they come, a fireman and saloon owner and hero of a steamboat disaster where he saved 92 lives."

"It was 26, but I wasn't exactly counting."

"Tom, these two boys saved my skin—and my wallet—earlier tonight. Say hello to Zack and Tom."

"Hello boys. You're Indians, aren't you?" said Sawyer.

7

If Horses Could Fly

"Hurry up now, child," said Minnie, taking the iron pot of chile-flavored beans from Little Wind and directing the young Wintu girl to climb onto the back of the buckboard. Benjamin and Eudora Wood and their son, Clayton, already had squeezed onto the front seat and were anxious to begin the ten-mile journey to their neighbor's ranch where a cook-out was being held in honor of an esteemed visitor to the valley. Leland Stanford, the former governor of the state of California, had come to inspect, and possibly acquire, a prize colt that the neighbor had raised. Everyone in the valley had been invited and was headed for the festivities.

Minnie handed up the beans and climbed up, hefting her considerable weight with the unlikely agility of a pirouetting hippopotamus. Benjamin Wood snapped the reins and the buckboard lunged up the drive followed by the two ranch hands, Randal Gallagher and Peter Obermeyer, riding on horseback.

The air was still damp from a brief sprinkling of early morning moisture, hardly substantial enough to be called a rain, but adequate to paste down the trail dust. The sun was burning off a thick haze and appeared red-gold against the dull gray sky. Off to the side of the trail in a flowering shrub, a swarm of hummingbirds sampled sweet nectar.

Leland Stanford had come to California in 1852, like so many others, drawn by the prospects of easy and immediate wealth in the gold fields. He operated a general store with his brothers for a time, gravitating, because of his former background as a lawyer in New York, toward politics and became a Justice of the Peace in Placer County. By 1856 Stanford had moved to San Francisco and become one of the "Big Four," the most powerful businessmen in California, gaining him the apt designation of "robber baron."

The Big Four, Stanford and Charles Crocker, Mark Hopkins, and Collis P. Huntington, were the controlling interests of the Central Pacific Railroad and the Southern Pacific which had became a holding company for the Central; Stanford was its president and used his influence to win the coveted contract to build the western leg of the First Transcontinental Railroad.

On his second attempt for the office Stanford was elected to be the eighth Governor of California. In his inaugural address of 1862 he stressed California's continuing support of the Union in the War Between the States, but exhibited a bent toward racism in his diatribe against what he called the dregs of Asia. He said, "It will afford me great pleasure to concur with the Legislature in any constitutional action, having for its object the repression of the immigration of the Asiatic races."

A curious position for him to adopt since the Central Pacific Railroad not only hired large numbers of resident Chinese laborers but took an active role in their importation in order to swell its workers' numbers. The Chinese, after all was said and done, were much more efficient than white workers, worked for about half the wages, and supplied their own food. Besides, the white laborers were mostly Irish and considered by the Big Four to be drunkards and low-lifes.

Stanford owned two wineries and considerable tracts of land in various counties. He had begun to breed race horses and this was the reason he was abroad in Mendocino County today. Stanford was of the opinion that thoroughbred stock was the key to siring good trotters. Most breeders of the nineteenth century discounted this notion and felt that training was the only essential ingredient to achieve speed in a race horse. But they ran their racing stock to the point of exhaustion, a situation Stanford deemed both inefficient and intolerable.

Paco Melendez, Stanford had been informed, raised his colts with a gentle hand. Melendez had a yearling named Bucephalus, a bay with a long body and well muscled shoulders and withers. The colt was young and spirited and showed great potential for harness racing. When Stanford's master trainer, Charles Marvin, spotted the horse during a tour of breeding ranches, he knew Stanford would be interested. Now the former governor was at the Melendez Ranchero to evaluate Bucephalus.

The Woods' buckboard had rumbled up the road to the Melendez Ranchero. Ben Wood parked at the end of a long line of carriages and wagons. The Woods and their group ambled up the road toward a rambling, dust-colored adobe where long tables had been arrayed on the front lawn and the huge carcass of a hog turned and sputtered on a spit over an open fire.

Little Wind, carrying the bean pot, couldn't help staring at the profusion and variety of horse-drawn vehicles: some fancy with painted designs and brass lanterns, others more utilitarian, decrepit and mud-splattered. One wagon in particular caught her eye. It looked like a little house on wheels, painted with shiny black lacquer and emblazoned with scrolling gold lettering. Had she been able to read the lettering, Little Wind would have been informed that this was the property of one E. J. Muybridge. It was also labeled as the "Helios Flying Studio."

A small crowd of people was watching a man lead a brown horse around by a rope in a fenced pasture across the yard. Two men and a woman who Little Wind deduced were Mission Indians were setting plates and trays of food on the tables. She hurried to add her pot of beans to these offerings. A man with dark bushy hair and a long pointed beard was opening a tripod and positioning in at the foot of one of the tables. He attached a box to the top of the tripod and mounted two brass cylinders to the front of that.

Mystified as to what the contraption that the man had assembled might be, Little Wind approached for a better look.

"Hello, little girl. A fine day, isn't it?" said the man. "You're wondering what this is all about, I would wager."

He seemed so polite and soft-spoken to Little Wind: something she rarely experienced when being around white people. She smiled at the man.

"This is a stereopticon camera," he said. "You see these two lenses? They focus on the same image but at slightly different angles. I develop the pictures and mount them side by side. If you look at them through a special viewer they appear to have depth. Just like in real life. Would you like to see some slides?"

Little Wind nodded, but then looked around to see if Minnie was watching her. Believing she was unobserved, she followed the man to the wagon she had seen earlier, the one with the gold lettering. The man rummaged around in the back of the wagon and produced a stereopticon viewer, a very strange looking device, something that Little Wind had never seen before. He inserted a piece of cardboard with pictures on it into a holder on the viewer and held the other end of it up to Little Wind's eyes.

She almost staggered in astonishment. Before her eyes stretched a deep vista. The silver ribbon of a river cut through a mountain valley along which giant redwoods rose. She pulled her head away from the viewer and saw only the side of the wagon. She blinked.

"See? I told you so. Here's another," said the man, putting a different slide in the viewer.

Now she saw a stately building lined with pillars sitting at the end of a broad avenue which was filled with people and carriages. She reached out, trying to touch the scene in front of her. Again she had to pull away from the viewer. She was reeling, beset with vertigo and unreality. The man handed her a stereo slide so she could see that the images were actually flat, just photographs.

He brought out a whole box of the slides, handed her the viewer and told her to experiment with looking at the pictures. She looked at city scenes, mountain scenes, children and animals, buildings and houses. She was beginning to get the hang of it and thoroughly enjoying this new adventure when a loud voice startled her:

"Whadya think yer doing?" It was all too familiar a voice—the rasping, venomous rumble of the voice of Randall Gallagher, the vindictive ranch hand who seemed to hate her and who tormented her at every opportunity.

She dropped the stereopticon viewer and wheeled to stare into Gallagher's scowling face.

"Now, now," Muybridge said, "I was just entertaining the little lady with some views. No harm in that. Perhaps you'd like to see some?"

Gallagher just sneered. "She don't need no entertainin'," he replied. "She's just a dumb injun. She better git back to work or there'll be trouble!"

"Better go, dear. You come back later when you have some free time," Muybridge told Little Wind.

"She ain't never got no free time," said Gallagher. "She ain't exactly free."

Little Wind and the Mission Indians, being servants, weren't allowed at the two long tables during the cookout. They stood respectfully, awaiting orders. The photographer had taken a picture of the festivities, angling his camera so that the perspective added to the depth that would be seen on the stereopticon slide. He then took a seat across the table from Leland Stanford who was gnawing on a chunk of roast pork.

"Nice to see you again, Eddy," Leland told Muybridge. "Have to have you up to Palo Alto one of these days. Marvin's been doing a great job training the horses. Like to have you take some pictures of them."

"I'd like that, Lee. Really would. But I'm headed back out to Yosemite Valley. I want to make more photographs of the wilderness there. It's spectacular."

"You know, another thought occurs to me. We're making great progress crossing the Sierra Nevada with the railroad. Some of the scenes of the Celestials cutting through the mountains would make spectacular pictures too!"

"Celestials? The Chinese you mean? Ah…building bridges, digging tunnels…I don't know, Lee, I'm more interested in the purity of nature, not in its destruction."

"Destruction? Why we're creating the most important monument to progress in the history of this country. Why, think of it! Linking the east and west coasts, opening up vast territories for exploitation…. The journey that took the pioneers months and months to make will only be a matter of days!"

"But at what cost? Indigenous people will suffer from the loss of their lands. Wildlife will be disrupted. The natural beauty of the mountains and valleys will be smudged by the acrid black smoke of your 'progress'. No, I have no desire to immortalize acts of violence against the environment by photographing them."

"I'm sorry you feel that way. But I still want you to come to Palo Alto. I want you to photograph a flying horse."

"Now you *are* intriguing me. A flying horse, you say? What is this all about?"

Leland Stanford told Muybridge about the ongoing debate among the elite land and horse owners of California (of which he was a charter member). Some claimed that a galloping horse needed to have at least one of its feet touching the ground at all times. Others,

Stanford included, thought there was a point at which the horse "flew" above the ground with all four feet elevated. Although it was impossible to prove this either way, the debate continued and there was even a standing wager against the time such proof could be offered. Leland now had a brilliant idea: why not photograph the horse in motion? Could it be done?

"Of course it can," answered Muybridge. When I get back from Yosemite I'll get in touch with you. We'll set something up."

The relationship between the Anglo and Hispanic land owners was civil, each sharing a common sense of belonging to the land— although the American citizenship of those of Spanish and Mexican heritage had never been fully acknowledged by the white settlers. The ranch hands, however, who had no vested interest in the land other than that it provided them a livelihood, were not constrained by the same social conventions as their employers.

Friction between the lower class whites, like Randall Gallagher and Peter Obermeyer, and their counterparts on the Melendez Hacienda erupted shortly after the cookout ended. Verbal taunts soon gave way to serious stare-downs and the orchestrated bumping of shoulders. Push, shove and fisticuffs were boding and it seemed some kind of friendly competition was needed to forestall an actual fight.

A rodeo of sorts was organized with a roping contest between the cowboys and the vaqueros. A calf was turned out in a small corral. The object was for a man on horseback to chase down the calf and throw a lasso over its neck, tie off the rope to the horse's saddle, jump off and while the horse kept the rope taut, throw the calf to the ground and tie three of its legs together. The man doing this in the least amount of time won the event.

Little Wind saw that Paco Melendez was perched on the rail fence with a gold watch in his hand. He flipped the watch open and raised his other arm in the air, ready to signal for the first event to start. Little Wind thought of the watch that White Cloud had shown her and wondered if it opened up like this one did. She wasn't sure what made her think about this—perhaps it was that this was only the second pocket watch she had seen in her entire life.

The air was thick with dust and the smells of leather, horse and man sweat, and the pungent scent of the frightened calf. Now the rail fence was crowded with onlookers, cheering for their fellows and booing their rivals. High-heeled boots clicked against the fence. Horsemen galloped after the calf, rope lassoes sang through the air and encircled the poor animal's neck and shoulders. Someone kept score on a slate. The vaqueros had the best times so far.

Mexican-American ranch hands considered themselves accomplished charros in the tradition of the charreada of old Mexico, a more elaborate and organized rodeo-like event brought from Spain two centuries earlier. Their skill at roping was soon evident and the anglos like Gallagher and Obermeyer were hard pressed to beat their times.

Randall Gallagher mounted his horse and gave the ready signal. Señor Melendez gave his own signal to release the calf into the corral. Randall had roped many a calf and steer at branding time so the bravado that he showed was not unwarranted. His first throw of the lasso was successful.

His horse knew exactly what to do and soon Randall was leaping from the saddle to hog-tie the calf—only something went wrong. The lanat was lose around the calf's neck, the horse allowed too much slack, the man's boots slipped in the dust, or he tripped over the rope—whatever the reason or combination of reasons, Randall Gallagher suddenly found himself tangled up with rope in a squirming pile of man and calf.

Hoots and hollers went up from the spectators. Randall extricated himself from under the animal, retrieved his rope and led his horse out of the corral, much chagrinned and ready to turn his anger against the first available person—preferably one of an inferior race—that he met. The Mission Indians backed away from him. The Hispanic ranch hands gave him a wide berth. Even Peter Obermeyer avoided him. He smoldered.

Randall hobbled his horse next to the buckboard. When he looked up he saw Little Wind returning to the Woods' buckboard with the now empty bean pot. Under his breath he was snarling but he forced a smile to appear on his face and hailed the girl:

"Hey there, little princess. Want the big man to give you a hand with that heavy pot?"

Little Wind was still pretending not to understand English, a charade that was not altogether successful. Randall had suspected for some time that the "dumb Indian" was not as dumb as she appeared.

As she approached he wrenched the pot from her hands and tossed it into the buckboard.

"There. Now, don't you want to thank me?"

Gallagher reached toward Little Wind with both arms but the girl backed away, anger showing plainly on her face. He tried again to grab her and this time managed to encircle her in a bear hug. Little Wind squirmed, then stomped down as hard as she could onto one of Gallagher's booted feet. He merely tightened his grip and laughed.

Little Wind twisted back and forth and then slipped down and out of the big man's embrace. Randall, surprised and not at all amused, stood gaping at her as she landed a hard kick to his groin. He doubled up in pain. *Now* he was getting angry.

She took off running as fast as she could. It wasn't long before Randall Gallagher had recovered enough to pursue her. She ducked in between carriages but still he came, gaining little by little. As Gallagher rounded the corner of a particularly large carriage he saw Clayton Wood walking up the path toward them. He stopped in his tracks and smiled at the boss's son. Little Wind was still running and hurried past Clayton who looked at her with curiosity, then looked at Gallagher. Clayton seemed to understand the situation and went to confront his ranch hand.

Without turning to see that the two men were arguing, Little Wind hurtled ahead. She had no real destination in mind and definitely had no plan. She would have to return to the ranch, she knew, and once there, Clayton Wood would not always be around to save her from the clutches of that miscreant, Gallagher. As she thought about this she saw ahead of her the ebony and gold wagon that belonged to E. J. Muybridge. The photographer was just climbing onto the seat and picking up the reins of his horse. Without considering the consequences of her next action, except that she was certain that this was the lesser of two evils, Little Wind pulled open the door at the rear of the wagon and climbed inside.

8

The Best Laid Plans of Mice and Men

It may seem ironic that the two Native American youths were now to be reintroduced to the cultural mores of the white race (their previous indoctrination having been conducted by Franciscan Brothers intent on erasing their "savage" and therefore heathen identities) by two drunken, free-thinking men of the world like Samuel Clemens and Thomas Sawyer, but then, the fates, be they Greek, Anglo-Saxon, or Wintu, are often fickle when it comes to intervening in the affairs of mortals—even those who are on a mission. Zack and Tommy had no where to go after the meal at the Occidental so they accompanied Clemens and Sawyer to Sawyer's saloon on Mission Street which was called the Gotham.

On a wall inside the saloon were hung firemen's helmets, a fire axe, bugles, nozzles, hooks and other paraphernalia from Sawyer's part-time job as a volunteer firefighter. A long fire hose was unraveled and snaked across the top of the mirror behind the bar in an artful though rustic display. Sawyer escorted Clemens and the boys to a table near the back of the establishment and ordered up a whiskey and soda for himself, a double Scotch for Clemens and seltzers for Zack and Tommy.

"I don't have any sarsaparilla on hand," he explained. We usually don't get children in here."

"Children!" complained Tommy. "We are considered to be grown men by our people. But thank you for protecting us from the evil drink you are having for yourselves. We have seen its effects on *your* people"

"Yes, I suppose you have. My apologies, Chief. Well Sam, what have you to say for yourself? Back in our Virginia City days you always had a good tale to tell," said Sawyer.

"Tom, I think you should spin your own yarn for the boys. Tell them about the wreck of the Independence."

"They don't want to hear about that."

"Sure we do," said Tommy, hoping that if he were cordial the friction between him and the saloon keeper might dissipate.

"Well," began Sawyer, "we was out of Acapulco headed to Friscoe with a full load of passengers—oh, 350 maybe. I was shipping as fire engineer. Just off Baja we struck a reef. We was taking water. Cap'n Sampson tried to beach the steamer so's to get the passengers off safely but she swung in the surf and hit the reef broadside, making things worse.

"I ran down to the boilers but the sea water was cooling them too much to get up enough steam to get us to the shore. The coal was wet and we started busting up anything we could find that would burn and throwing it on the fire. Trouble was, the furnace then got out of control and set the boiler room on fire. Flames shot up through the smoke stack and reached the upper deck. That's when the panic started.

"People was screamin' and running helter-skelter and some was jumpin' off the ship. I saw the chief engineer and his stoker jump into the water and flail around like they was drownin'. Couldn't swim, I guess. So I jumped in and grabbed the both of them around the waist and swam for shore."

"That's not even the half of it, Tom. You swam back and rescued another. And returned again, and again—over twenty times," Clemens said.

"Well somebody had to do it. It weren't nothing anybody couldn't of done."

"Anybody with the constitution of a sperm whale."

"Well, Sam, you was a pilot on the Mississippi. You must have a story or two to tell."

And so it went. Sam Clemens related a few yarns, especially of ship wrecks on the Mississippi, but failed to allude to the death of his own brother on a riverboat whose boilers had exploded. Sam blamed himself for having gotten his brother the job and was reluctant to talk about the tragedy. The stories bounced back and forth between the two men like tennis balls. And the drinks kept coming.

"One of these days, Thomas, I'll write a story about you. About your wild days as a young boy. These two boys here remind me of my own youth. They're out having adventures right now. You should

70

hear some of their story," said Sam. But of course, neither boy could get a word in edgewise.

In fact, sometime well after midnight the boys crept away from the table and found a quiet dark corner in the back of the saloon where they could curl up, use their rucksacks as pillows, and fall into a well deserved and very sound sleep. When they woke it was early morning. The air in the room smelled of booze and tobacco and mold. Light filtered in through the front window, its stained glass casting fantastic shapes on the dirty floor. No one was present but the two boys.

The front door was locked but they found a rear entry where the latch could be worked from inside and quickly exited into the alley. The sun had risen over the bay and white gulls gyred against its pale pinkness celebrating the new day with screeches and squawks in the typical manner of gulls. It was not difficult to determine in which direction the waterfront lay: its breezes beckoned with a freshness and exhilaration which the streets of the city did not possess. Moreover, every person awake and abroad at that hour seemed headed toward the bay.

They were presented with a formidable problem: there were a great many wharves and piers and landings and they had no idea on which to look for the person whom they sought. They sought, with a dubious resolve, the gold-toothed Bathhouse Jake—he who could whisk them eastwardly toward their goal, or so Madame Ah Toy had said. He would take them there, but maybe not all the way, she had said. They wouldn't mind working their way there, she had asked? They would not need to worry about Mei Lim, she had said.

"I don't know about this," Zack told Tommy.

"What choice do we have? We have no money. We could wait and see if that Sam fellow would take us along with him, but he isn't going to El-Ya-Noy. And he didn't say he would take us...only maybe." They began the search for Bathhouse Jake.

Bathhouse Jake MacConnell was an Irishman from West Claire who had immigrated to the United States during the Great Potato Famine in 1847. He was a rough, uneducated man with a flat face, deep emerald eyes and shaggy, sand-colored hair and stood nearly six feet tall. Determined to shed the fetters of poverty that had followed him from Ireland, MacConnell sought out the power brokers of the blossoming city of San Francisco and soon became an indispensable enforcer for the seamier side of the Golden Gate City's political spectrum.

Established and now flush, MacConnell then branched off on his own into the lucrative field of procurement. Having contacts on both sides of the law enabled him to operate with relative impunity. His familiarity with the daily operations of the waterfront convinced him that the highest profit was to be made not in quality, but in quantity. Indeed, he moved massive quantities of goods, mostly imported from China: opium and contraband, new recruits for Madam Ah Toy, and Chinese workman for the Central Pacific Railroad.

Today, however, Bathhouse Jake was supervising the transfer of iron rails from a steamer recently up from Panama to a barge that would take the materials up river to Sacramento. It was a legitimate undertaking with no risk although as with all his activities, the authorities were paid to look the other way. Occasionally it was healthier to engage in a legal enterprise such as this contract work for the railroad. Occasionally a little contraband slipped through as well.

Only last week, for instance, the police, at the prompting of the Six Companies, had seized 43 Chinese girls as they were brought off a China clipper. The newspaper, the Sacramento Daily Union, reported that the girls were between the ages of 8 and 18 and destined for lives of prostitution. They were promptly sent to the Magdalene Asylum until they could be placed with "good American families" where they would be taught skills enabling them to work and earn an honest living (like cleaning and washing). Madame Ah Toy was furious. Bathhouse Jake had been lucky to have escaped prosecution that time, but as reformers were always putting pressure on the police to clean up San Francisco, there was no sense taking chances. At any rate, the railroad provided equal opportunities for graft.

Two independent rail companies had been commissioned to build the First Transcontinental Railroad: one starting from the Mississippi River and the other from California. The Central Pacific Railroad, owned by the Big Four, was in competition with the Union Pacific Railroad to lay the most track before the west-bound and east-bound routes came together—and there were now only about 1000 miles left to complete. The more track they laid the more

Government bonds they could collect and the more of the right of way they would eventually own, hence it was a race to the finish.

The Central Pacific was the more efficient of the two rail companies having hired experienced surveyors and engineers and having made the good decision to use the Celestial workforce, their imported Chinese laborers. However, the CPRR was at a disadvantage in two ways: they had to cross the Sierra Nevada and they lacked the ability to produce the needed materials and equipment.

Whereas California redwood and quarried stone were readily available for building materials, the iron rails, spikes and even the locomotives and railcars had to be brought from the East by ship. This was expensive and time consuming and allowed for many extras hands to dip into the pot of gold that was railroad construction. MacConnell had his in up to his elbows.

By the time Zack and Tommy had finally located Bathhouse Jake, most of the rails had been loaded. Each one weighted over 500 pounds and required five strong men to lift and carry it. Bathhouse Jake was standing alongside the barge which was filling up with rails and which would be pushed across the bay and up the Sacramento River by a stern-wheeled steamboat in a matter of a few hours. The boys approached him and were greeted by a smile that exposed MacConnell's solid gold two front teeth.

"Hey there me lads, where you be goin' now?" he said, amused by the sight of two grimy street urchins who looked as if they had stepped out of a story by Charles Dickens.

"Sir," said Tommy, "are you Bathhouse Jake?"

"That be me, laddie. And who might you be? And what business have ya here?"

"Madame Ah Toy said to find you. That you might help us go east—we'd work for it, you see. I am Tommy Wepa and this is Zack Grosh. We're…"

"You're Chinese, I reckon."

"No, I'm Maidu and Zack is Wintu. You would call us Indians, although we're not from India, you know."

Bathhouse Jake laughed. "So the Dragon Lady sent you, huh? She usually deals in females of the species. Well, you want to work, aye?"

"Yes Sir."

"Think you could lift one of those rails?"

Zack and Tommy looked at each other, aghast. "Well, we…"

"Oh, I 'spect I could find sometin' fer ya ta do," said Bathhouse Jake. Most men in his position would have chased the boys away or worse, sent them to the court system to be sold off into indentured servitude as the law provided. But MacConnell remembered Ireland during the Gorta Mór, the Great famine. He remembered how the British government had not helped the starving farmers except to filter them through the workhouses, creating a nation of paupers. How the Poor Law withheld aid from anyone owning more than a quarter acre of land. How the only charity had come from unexpected sources: the Quakers, the East India Company, Queen Victoria herself, the Ottoman Empire and remarkably, a Native American tribe in the New World called the Choctaw.

The Choctaw had experienced starvation and despair during their removal from their ancestral lands, and their forced march along the Trail of Tears. Sixteen years later, hearing of the plight of the Irish, they had collected $710 and sent it to Ireland. That was in 1847, the same year MacConnell left for the United States. Now MacConnell felt a special affinity toward Native Americans. He would help these two Indian boys who, if they were observed to be unemployed could be taken by any citizen and enslaved.

"There's a new group of coolies waitin' on shipboard. I'll put you in with them. Come along, I'll introduce you to the overseer."

"Sir? Will we be going to the East?"

"Oh yes. Just blend in. Do what they tell you to do. You'll be fine."

As Bathhouse Jake led them toward a paddle-wheeler moored just down the wharf Zack said, "Tommy? What's a coolie?"

"I don't know, Zack."

"Tommy? Why doesn't that boat have wings?"

"I don't know, Zack."

"Tommy…"

"Quiet now. We're going to El-Ya-Noy!"

It wasn't until the paddle-wheeler, pushing the loaded barge ahead of it, had swung out into the bay, crossed over and headed up Steamboat Slough that the boys sensed that something was wrong.

"We aren't headed to the ocean," said Tommy. "This looks like the very same river we came down before."

They had discovered what the term, "coolie," meant and were now huddled with perhaps one hundred Chinese men on the main deck of the steamboat. They had been unable to find any that spoke English, much less Wintu or Maidu. The man that Bathhouse Jake had called the overseer was nowhere to be seen.

The day was hot for the end of June, not exactly a swelter, but a kind of smothering, baking, breezeless heat augmented by the closeness of one hundred unwashed Celestials recently arrived from a long ocean voyage, having been sequestered in steerage, and now reeking of the odors of damp clothing, rotting food, and ages-old bilge water. As if to cover up this desolate landscape of soiled humanity, sparks and soot from the stacks dropped like dirty snow onto their heads. Zack and Tommy eased their way toward the edge of the deck, desperate for fresh air.

"We could swim for it," suggested Tommy.

"I'm not a strong swimmer. Better than you are though. We'll have to wait until the boat docks somewhere. It's the only sensible thing."

"Why do you suppose Bathhouse Jake put us with all these Chinese? We said we wanted to go to El-Ya-Noy."

"Did we? I think we just said 'to the East.' And look, we *are* traveling in roughly that direction. Do you think there is a river that goes all the way to El-Ya-Noy?"

"I wish I'd paid more attention in school. Maybe I'd know about geography."

"All I remember was that they told us some Italian fellow discovered our land. Like we weren't here before that! I don't know if their information was all that reliable."

"Well, we may as well enjoy the ride for now. I wish some of these fellows could talk English."

They stood at the rail watching the brown rolling sludge of Steamboat Slough slip past the ship. The great wheel at the stern slapped and churned the river with a rhythm like the beating of a drum. Zack sighed, thinking of his days as a young child in the village when drum sound meant dancing and chanting and talking to the spirits—spirits who now seemed to have abandoned him and his people.

What did he really remember about his father? Had he been kind? Strict? Distant? He was tall, pale-skinned, protective of his wife and children—of that Zack was sure. Why then had he left? Why no word? Why was he, Zack, devoting this crucial time of his young life to searching for him? Why was he following this road of stars toward the unknown?

"What...have you returned so soon?" said a voice behind the boys. They turned and saw a man in a uniform, his arms folded across his chest. "Well?" he bellowed.

At first Zack and Tommy didn't recognize the First Mate of the Shasta Belle, Christian Kopp. Was it possible they were on the same boat that had brought them down river to San Francisco? Yes, it was true: there did stand Christian Kopp. His eyes danced with humor, betraying the serious frown he was affecting for the boys' benefit.

"Captain! We..."

"I'm not the Captain, lad. Only the First Mate. I thought you two bogus Mexicans were shipping out to sea. What happened? Are you now pretending to be Chinamen?"

Zack explained, relating the tale from their encounter with Madame Ah Toy to their conversation with Bathhouse Jake. "Unless this river goes all the way to El-Ya-Noy I think we've made a mistake," he said at the end.

"I'm very much grieved to hear that the young Asian girl wasn't able to escape from her profession," Kopp commented. "And as for Bathhouse Jake, of course we know that hooligan. We wouldn't have this cargo except for his finagling. The captain trusts him, but as for me...well...I think he saw a way to pad the numbers of these coolies. Gets so much a head, you see. But he didn't entirely lead you astray."

"What do you mean?"

"If you stick with the railroad you'll be headed more or less straight toward your desired destination. I hear the line is almost finished. Work your way east with this lot and then hitch up with the Union Pacific. Take that to Illinois."

"I don't exactly understand. What's the Union Pacific?"

"The other railroad. They are building west while we are building eastward. We'll meet in the middle. You can then take a train all the way from one coast to the other. It will probably kill the shipping business, but that's progress. It's an amazing time we live in."

Yes, thought Zack, an amazing time for white people. A demoralizing time for the Wintu and their brothers. Land stolen. People slaughtered. People enslaved. The Great White Father in Washington had made treaties. The people had kept the treaties. The whites had broken them. An amazing time if you're a white man.

"You think we can get to El-Ya-Noy if we go with these Chinese and work finishing the railroad?" Zack asked Kopp.

"I think so. You'll have food and clothing and you'll even get paid. You'll have enough money to ride the rest of the way in style, I should think."

"Tommy?" said Zack. "What do you think? Should we give it a try?"

"I don't think we've much of a choice, Zack. And as you pointed out, we aren't very good swimmers."

Tommy, thought Zack, is always so ready to jump toward adventure. Me, I'm more apt to jump overboard. I guess I need his enthusiasm to spurn me onward—although sometimes I wonder if we're headed for disaster! This white man, is he telling us the truth? Do they ever tell the truth? Did the Old Man of the Mountain give me good advice? Or did he only give me a watch that doesn't work?

Zack's hand went to the watch in his pocket. He looked up into Christian Kopp's eyes, trying to read in them honesty, concern, wisdom. Perhaps he saw empathy in the first mate's countenance; maybe it was only pity that wrinkled the man's brow, drooped the corners of his eyes. I am half white, thought Zack. I'm half my mother and half my father. I understand the half that comes from my mother—I am struggling to understand the other half. I must know who I am.

9

The Photographer

Little Wind, hiding in the photographer's traveling darkroom, a modified carriage, had been buffeted and bounced and battered as the Helio Flying Studio rumbled over mountain roads. Chemical smells accosted her senses sending her to the verge of delirium. It wasn't just dark; there was a total absence of light, a blank and black world where even the little flashes her retinas produced were lost in the void. For a while, Little Wind believed she had died and been dragged down to the underworld where demons would soon come to devour her. Then she began to wish for death to put a final ending to the misery of being trapped in this insufferable conveyance.

It stopped. The creaking, the bouncing, and the darkness. A crack of light worked its way down the edge of the door then widened and a flood of excruciatingly painful brightness assaulted her—a wall of white agony against which she threw up her hands to shield her eyes. Slowly she opened her fingers enough to peer at the outside world. A great hulking shadow was centered in the light. A mountain with a halo of sunshine? No, a man. A Man who laughed. A man who pulled her from the carriage and stood her upright on the ground.

"Well, well," said the man. "What have we here?"

It was several minutes before Little Wind's eyes adjusted to the light which she now saw was not the brightness of morning sun but the weak and fading illumination of dusk. The crisp freshness of the air revived her to the extent that she could focus and remember who she was, where she was and who the man who stood softly laughing before her was: the photographer, Edward Muybridge.

He was holding her by both arms. She realized suddenly that he was holding her upright and that her legs hadn't the strength to allow her to stand on her own. She gulped in a mouthful of mountain air.

"You'll be all right in a few minutes," Muybridge told her. "Maybe you should sit down."

Muybridge set about making camp, lighting a fire and bringing things from the carriage. Soon there was coffee brewing and a pot with vegetables and meat bubbling over the fire. The aroma of food cooking chased away the evil smells of the traveling studio which still clung to Little Wind's clothing.

"We'll be staying here for the night. I'll see if I can find some blankets for you to wrap up in against the cold. You don't have to tell me why you were hiding in my wagon. I can guess. But, my dear girl, what am I to do with you? I'm headed for the wilderness to climb mountains and photograph the great valley vistas and the waterfalls and the storm clouds forming above peaks and the trees tall as the mountains themselves. I can't leave you here. I can't bring you along. Where shall I take you?"

"Please don't take me back to that ranch. Or to the reservation. Anywhere but those awful places. Take me with you. I could help out. I could cook, wash your clothes, feed your horse."

"I'm sorry but I really can't think of any use you could be to me. Although…. Maybe I'll photgraph you. I've made some plates of Indians. But your clothes…they're not native."

"No. The Missy dressed me up in white people's clothes to work on the ranch. They burned my old clothes."

"Of course they did. Well, maybe we can stop at an Indian village somewhere along the line. You know, when I went back to England in the early 60s…I was born there, you see…that was when I learned photography…I met many interesting people in that profession: Roger Fenton, Julia Margaret Cameron, and this fellow who called himself Lewis Carroll. Carroll photographed a lot of young girls about your age. Very evocative and most charming photographs they were. If I make one of you I'll send it to him. I know he'd love it."

"I don't understand how you make those things," said Little Wind. "They look so real. But if they are so real, then why don't they move?"

Muybridge was stumped by the girl's question. "Move? Why the whole idea is to freeze time…to stop movement. Otherwise it would be just a blur. You see…" Now he had to stop and consider just how much this girl, an Indian, a fragile being that most people would consider to be an ignorant savage, could comprehend about the science of photography.

"Well, you see…" he began again, "there is a liquid we can paint on glass that turns black when light hits it. Are you following me so far?"

"Like a fire burns wood and it turns black?"

"Yes, something like that. So we take a lens and it can focus an image of the world onto the glass such that the liquid darkens where there is the most light and stays lighter where there are shadows. You see, light turns it black and black leaves it white. We call this a 'negative.' "

"Black is white and white is black. Of course, that's perfectly clear," said the girl, giving little effort to disguising the sarcasm in her voice.

"Exactly. We clear away the white so we now have a piece of glass with dark areas where the light was brightest and clear areas to whatever extent there were shadows. If we then paint this same liquid on paper and place the negative against the paper and expose it to light we can reverse the image and so that then it looks real. Here, I'll show you what I mean."

Little Wind tried to appear interested as the photographer extracted a glass plate and a print from the wagon. She was fascinated by the photographs but still quite confused by the complicated process. Muybridge babbled on and on about it, perhaps excited to have an audience, albeit one that was an "ignorant savage."

"It was Doctor Gull who enticed me to pursue photography…well, not directly. You see, I was intent upon traveling back overseas. It was 1860. I took the overland stage from San Francisco in order to eventually get to the east coast and board an ocean vessel. It was a comfortable trip until we reached the wide plains and steep hills of Texas. The fool driver cracked his whip and the horses took off at a gallop. We began descending a steep slope when it became apparent that the brakes were not working. We went off the road and hit a tree.

"I was one of the lucky ones, with only a head wound. Two men died! Everyone had some form of injury. I later sued the bastards, that is, the stage company. But I spent many days in bed with double vision, no sense of smell or taste. I had confused ideas for months. However, I got to New York and hence to London where I was treated by this very eminent doctor, Sir William Gull who prescribed rest, spending time outdoors and breathing the fresh sea air. I began to be aware of the beauties of nature and wished there were someway of capturing the experience I was having. Also, this regiment of relaxation made me feel idle and useless, so I took up photography."

They had finished the makeshift stew that Muybridge had prepared and as night had fallen with the usual concert of crickets chirping and owls hooting, Little Wind stretched and yawned. Muybridge threw more sticks on the fire and unrolled a woolen blanket nearby for the girl.

"I must say, you are very light-skinned for an Indian girl," he said as she curled up under the blanket.

"My mother is Wintu and my father is 'elti-winhu'h—a white man. I get some lightness from my father."

"And where are your mother and father now?"

"Mother is still on the reservation, I suppose. We don't know where my father is…or if he is even alive. My brother, White Cloud, has gone in search of him. A foolish thing to do, I think, but that is the way he is. And I hope he is well."

"Where did he go? Looking for your father."

"A place called El-Ya-Noy."

"Well, sleep now. Tomorrow we'll be back in San Francisco at my gallery. We'll sort things out then. Goodnight."

"Thank you Mister Muy…Muybridge. You too—sleep well."

Selleck's Cosmopolitan Gallery of Photographic Art was located at 415 Montgomery Street near the Merchant's Exchange Building, three blocks from the Occidental Hotel where Samuel Clemens stayed, and a stone's throw from Chinatown and the wharves of the Embarcadero. In the window sat a card announcing for sale by Edw. J. Muybridge, the photographs of the Scenery of the Yosemite Valley by Helios, comprising "260 views of the various falls, precipices and the most picturesque and interesting points of sight in the valley." One could purchase up to 100 different half-plate prints of 6 by 8 inches, or full-plate prints of 14 by 18 inches for $1.25 each, and 160 different stereo views for $4.50 per dozen.

Muybridge's long time friend and partner in the gallery, Silas T. Selleck, met him and Little Wind at the door. Selleck was also a photographer. Although the daguerreotype process had become obsolete due to the advent of wet-plate colloidal photography, Selleck still operated a studio for producing the small silver images next door at number 413 ½. He also used wet plates for less expensive portraits.

While Selleck photographed families and made portraits of people sitting in front of elaborate backgrounds, Muybridge preferred to venture out of doors and pursue subject matter less human, such as buildings and landscapes. He had somewhat of an aversion toward working with people. Still, Muybridge had learned much of his craft from Selleck when the two had first met in New York City and now they seemed to compliment each other, their individual specialties covering the gamut of marketable picture making.

"Edward," said Selleck, ushering Muybridge and Little Wind into the gallery, "I'm glad you're back. We're having quite a run on your Yosemite pictures."

"That's good to hear. What about my photographs of San Francisco?"

"Not so much. But we have orders from back east for as many stereo slide sets as we can produce of the landscapes." Silas Selleck had embraced Muybridge and now focused his attention on Little Wind. "And who is this, if I may ask?"

"Silas Selleck, meet Little Wind, also known as The Wind From The Hummingbird's Wings...did I get that right? Yes. She sort of latched on to me up in the Mendocino Valley. I couldn't actually leave her out in the wilderness, so I brought her along."

"Very civilized of you. What are you going to do with her?"

"I was wondering if perhaps you and Sarah might take her in. She has nowhere to go and the authorities would just send her to a reservation where she'd starve."

"Oh I don't think my wife would like that. We already have three children."

Little Wind, who had been strolling through the gallery looking at the photographs on display, had been listening, her anger mounting by the minute. "Why do you talk about me like I'm not here?" she demanded. "And why don't you ask me what *I* want to do?"

"All right then, what *do* you want to do?" asked Selleck.

"I want to go with Mr. Muybridge. To photograph mountains and rivers and trees. I can cook and wash and..."

"Oh, no, Little Wind," said Muybridge. It would be too dangerous. I climb up on cliffs and hang over precipices with the heavy camera and sleep in the snow and get chased by bears and mountain lions and…"

"And, Edward, if I may interject something at this point, you may have a new commission coming up."

"Really? And what is that?"

Silas Selleck then explained that the United States Government was attempting to turn public opinion around concerning the recent purchase of the Alaskan Territory. When Secretary of State William Seward had given Russia over seven million dollars for a frozen waste land on the very edge of the known world he had come under severe ridicule. It became know as "Icebergia," "Seward's Folly," and "Walrussia." It was felt that a series of photographs by a famous photographer known for his artistic work in wilderness areas might heighten public acceptance for this, the largest real-estate deal since the Louisiana Purchase.

"They want you to go with General Halleck to Sitka where the military has its headquarters and from there venture out photographing everything and anything that might illustrate the commercial value of the region."

"Commercial value? Silas, you know I oppose the exploitation of nature."

"But Edward, if you don't do it, someone else will. Maybe Watkins or Weed. They can't show the beauty of the place like you can. That's how you'll save it. There's nothing up there anyway that anybody'd want."

Little Wind had resumed her browsing during this somewhat boring interchange between the two men. She stopped at a picture of a crowd of people surrounding a giant of a man dressed in a Chinese costume. "Oh my!" she said. "Who is that giant?"

Muybridge looked at the photograph. "That is Chang Woo Gow," he explained. He is the tallest man in the world: eight feet and three inches tall. I photographed him at Woodward's Gardens. He's one of the main attractions there. Say, you might like to see that place. It's just down on Mission Street."

"What do you mean, 'attraction' ?"

"People pay to see him. Well, at least in the sense that they pay to see the gardens. Costs 25 cents…10 cents for children…and well worth the price of admission! The place is two city blocks long. There is also a man only 25 inches tall. Woodward has animals from all over the world: ostriches, flamingos, lions, monkeys, bears, camels, and he even has a five-legged dog and a calf with two heads!"

"Why would I want to see that?"

"Well, people do."

"I'd rather go to Alaska with you."

"Little Wind, I told you..."

"Edward," interrupted Selleck, "I hope you'll come to dinner tonight. Bring your companion. She can meet my wife and my children. You never know, they might hit it off. And think about this Alaskan thing. It could be very good for you."

The Sellecks lived at 1429 Taylor Street near an intersection with Jackson Street where a cable car would one day descend the steep hill. The children, Edwin, seventeen, Nellie, ten, and Catherine, eight, stood at attention in order of height as Silas greeted his dinner guests in the foyer. Then, at a nod from their father, as if released from a mesmerist trance, the three sprang to life and scurried away.

"Ah, the children," said Silas Selleck. "The blessed children give me no end of delight...and worry."

"Worry, Silas?" asked Muybridge.

"They are growing so fast. Young Edwin will soon be done with school and talks of the merchant marine."

"Indeed. Does that worry you more than if he had a desire for military service or...?"

"Did you see his attempt at the growth of side whiskers and mustache? The young are always so ready to abandon the sweetness of youth for a taste of the bitterness of age! Well, come in, come in! Sarah is waiting for us in the parlor."

Little Wind stayed close to Edward Muybridge, not cowering exactly, but needful of the intimacy of his familiar bulk and solidity as she drifted into a strange, unimaginable environment of plush chairs and patterned carpets, gaslights and oil portraits, and into the presence of Sarah Selleck, smiling, appareled in a polonaise gown with soft bustles dyed brilliantly purple, her hair tumbling lightly down the back of her neck in a cascade of light brown curls—Little Wind was appalled at her own appearance even though the kind Mr. Muybridge had shopped for and bought for her the party dress she now wore. It was an unfamiliar feeling to be in awe of such an alien presence, this beautiful white woman for whom she could muster no animosity, no fear, no repulsion. She was spellbound.

But this spell was shattered by the inflection, or lack of inflection, in Sarah Selleck's voice when she greeted the Wintu girl. Pleasant, but without warmth or sincerity, Sarah Selleck's bland intonation unsettled Little Wind in the same way Eudora Wood's had when the ranch mistress had addressed Little Wind, masking her hatred with syrupy, sing-song condescension.

"Come along, dear," said Mrs. Selleck, "our dinner is waiting." The woman took Little Wind by the hand and led her into the dining room. Another exotic interior! A huge table of polished wood over which hung an elaborate iron chandelier supporting clear glass globes in which gaslight danced. Plates of bone-white china adorned with painted flowers, twisting vines. Rows of silver knives and forks and spoons whose bright surfaces reflected the undulating wisps of flame above. Starched white napkins folded—and this intrigued Little Wind the most—into the shapes of birds. And glassware! Goblets and tumblers and slender stemmed wine glasses and little cut-glass dishes filed with salt. However, more unbelievable than these was the food.

There was soup. Not the thin broth of pounded acorns that Little Wind was used to, but a thick, rich, *green* and flavorful pea soup substantial enough to have satisfied the girl's hunger by itself. She mimicked the other children who raised spoons deftly to lips and sipped silently and without spillage. She saw the matron of the family smiling slightly at her and was glad of the instruction in etiquette given her earlier by Muybridge.

A salad of greens followed and then a golden-brown turkey the size (Little Wind thought) of a dog was carved by Mr. Selleck. The two Selleck girls received drumsticks, one of which would have fed an entire family on the reservation. A toast with wine glasses (the children's wine was watered down considerably) and the meal and conversation among the adults began in earnest.

After the detailing of the domestic and commercial affairs of the San Franciscans and the somewhat exaggerated narrative of the photographer's recent travels, the issue of the errant girl, which could no longer be avoided, was broached.

"I understand, dear Edward," began Sarah Selleck, "that you are looking for a situation for your ward."

"A situation...yes, indeed. The poor girl cannot be left on her own in this modern world that is so hostile toward her race. If you could see your way toward taking her in..."

"Mother!" interjected the boy-man, Edwin. "You mean you'd take in that..."

Little Wind, whose anger once again was getting the better of her blurted out: "Filthy Redskin? Dirty Injun? Ugly savage?"

"Little Wind!" cautioned Muybridge. "Remember yourself."

"I'm sorry. It's just that...we're people too. We have families and homes and beliefs just like all of you. Only a little different."

"Of course you do, my dear," said Sarah.

"Only *we* live in harmony with the land, not taking from it all of its soul. You come and dig for yellow metal that has no meaning and then kill the fish and cut down the trees without regard for animals or the people who were here before you. You steal the land from us and if we won't move off of it, you kill us!"

"That's enough," shouted Muybridge. He had an irritable and irrational streak stemming from his head injury which sometimes surfaced. "I'll take you back to the reservation tomorrow."

"No, Edward," said Silas Selleck. She can stay here...for a time."

"Silas? Do you really think...?" Sarah said to her husband.

"We took in the Humbolt boy, when his parents died from smallpox."

"Yes, but that was just until his relatives back east sent for him."

Then Muybridge said: "If you could see your way toward boarding the girl...and she could cook and clean for you, and I would help with her expenses...just until I get back from Alaska..."

"Alaska? You're going to Alaska?" asked Edwin Selleck, his eyes lighting up, his dander at the prospect of the Indian girl coming to live with them ebbing.

"Yes, I am thinking of accepting a commission to photograph in the new territory."

"May I come with you? You'll need a crew to help you with your equipment."

"Well, Edwin, I don't know," answered Muybridge, looking at Silas for a response. Silas shrugged.

Then came the orange sherbet. Little Wind eagerly gulped hers and was rewarded with a sharp pain at the bridge of her nose. After dessert Nellie and Catherine took Little Wind to see their playroom.

The girls were only slightly younger than she was and possibly were the only family members who were not jaded or prejudiced.

As they left the dining room Little Wind heard snippets of conversation from the adults: "...she's certainly got an attitude, but maybe I can teach..." and "...his wanderlust might be sated if you let him come..." and "Mother, I *really* want to go to Alaska."

The playroom was a wonderland of bright colors and whimsical shapes: a hobby horse painted scarlet and turquoise and green, porcelain-headed dolls richly clothed and posed against a doll-sized table with a china tea set, a miniature carousel that chimed as it rotated, a pile of dress-up clothes including an Indian headdress—the latter item derailed Little Wind's delight in seeing the toys and dolls.

She had just begun to relax, to feel sorry about her outburst, to envision herself living with this family in their fancy house. But now she realized a harsh truth: that she could never be comfortable here; she didn't belong. Now she was more determined than ever to accompany Mr. Muybridge on his trip to Alaska—where ever that was.

10

Crossing the Sierra Nevada

The United States of America and the Emperor of China cordially recognize the inherent and inalienable right of man to change his home and allegiance, and also the mutual advantage of the free migration and emigration of their citizens and subjects respectively, from one country to the other, for the purposes of curiosity, of trade, or as permanent residents.
—Treaty with China, proclaimed July 28, 1868

Whereas in the opinion of the Government of the United States the coming of Chinese laborers to this country endangers the good order of certain localities within the territory thereof: Therefore,

Be it enacted by the Senate and House of Representatives of the United States of America in Congress assembled, That from and after the expiration of ninety days next after the passage of this act, and until the expiration of ten years next after the passage of this act, the coming of Chinese laborers to the United States be, and the same is hereby, suspended; and during such suspension it shall not be lawful for any Chinese laborer to come, or having so come after the expiration of said ninety days to remain within the United States.
—The Chinese Exclusion Act of 1882

Sacramento, California, late July, 1868

The levee protecting the City of Sacramento from the floodwaters of the American River provided a wide embankment where the thousands and thousands of pounds of iron rails could be transferred from the barge to a waiting railroad flatcar. Toting the rails was the first work these Chinese men who now poured from the deck of the Shasta Belle were doing for the Central Pacific Railroad.

They were joining an army of their countrymen who numbered somewhere between ten and twelve thousand, comprising perhaps eighty percent of the CPRR's workforce.

There were also Native Americans, Piutes and Shoshones, who had been hired by the railroad as part of a treaty when it gouged a pathway through their lands. They called the Chinese "The Yellow Ant People" because they worked so hard and seemed to swarm all over the building sites. And there were also Irish, Welsh and Cornish railroad workers who had now become a minority. They thought the Chinese were weak and effeminate, incapable of hard labor. But the Chinese outworked them and gained the respect of railroad officials and their white foremen. They had, after all, built the Great Wall of China.

Now the train, loaded with supplies and more workers, pulled away from Sacramento, crossed the high, 700 foot-long trestle over the America River and started a trek along the finished sections of the Transcontinental Railway. Steamboats blew their whistles and people standing along the route waved, aware that something miraculous was happening—something that had started in their own city when the first rail was laid, the first spike was driven at Sacramento on October 26, 1863.

The train rumbled easily over the flat, gently rising Sacramento Valley floor to the small town of Junction eighteen miles away which the builders had first reached on February 29, 1864. From here the approach to the Sierra Nevada was gradual and followed the path the river had cut through the foothills many millennia ago. Thirty-one miles from Sacramento lay Newcastle.

The railroad builders had laid tracks to Newcastle by June 6, 1865 and here the construction was delayed for lack of materials and manpower. From this point to Truckee ninety miles of deep cuts and fills to maintain the grading would be required. It was here that the idea of using Chinese labor was implemented in spite of the prejudice of railroad management and the jealously of Caucasian labor.

Now, three years later, Zack and Tommy watched from the open door of a freight car filled with the sweating bodies of the Celestial workforce as the train wound its circuitous way up the mountain. Just west of Auburn they entered Boomer Cut, 800 feet of excavation where a depth of 65 feet of cemented gravel, shale and sandstone had been blasted away. Then beyond Emigrant Gap the tracks clung to the sides of the hills where solid granite had been carved into flattened roadways by pick and shovel and black powder. Trestles bridged ravines and ahead lay several short tunnels.

Fifty miles out from Sacramento the engine began to slow. Just ahead, Zack, leaning out the door into the wind, could see the engine approaching the Dry Creek Bridge. It was a tall, spindly-looking conglomeration of impossibly thin sticks of wood that seemed to be the imaginative invention of some giant child. Here were four long spans of forty-five feet each. Zack was sure the weight of the train would tip the rickety thing over into the valley below.

"I wish," Zack told Tommy Wepa, "that these Chinese gentlemen could speak English, or that we could speak Chinese. It's going to be rather lonely for the two of us having only each other to talk to."

"Excuse please. I speak English," said someone standing behind the boys. "I am Lee Shao," said a tall Asian man, "and this is my companion, Fong Dun Shung, who also speaks your language."

"Well, it isn't exactly *our* language," replied Zack. "I am Zack Grosh, a Wintu...that's an Indian tribe...and this is Tommy Wepa, a Maidu."

"Indians. We have heard of the Indians back in homeland of China. In fact is well-known that the beggar-monk Hoei-shin discovered Tahan—I think you call Alaska—and visited Fusang— what you call, I believe, Mexico, in reign of Emperor Xiao Wen Di, in Wei Dynasty."

"Ah...we're not Mexicans, you know."

"Of course. I know that."

"This Hoo person, he wasn't from Italy, then? They told us an Italian discovered America."

Lee Shao laughed. "No. In fact, Chinese discovered Italy too. This was done by Zheng He in Yuan Dynasty. He sail all over world."

"You know a lot of things. How come?"

"I am scholar. Read many things: memoirs of Hoei-seng and Song-yun and writings of Fa-hien."

"I can't read. Neither of us learned."

"Unfortunate. My friend Fong Dun Shung is also very learned man. He knows all the herbs. Will be of great value to workers of railroad."

"Why did you come from China to work on the railroad? It sounds like you both should be teachers or doctors or something important."

"Ah, you know little of China. At home in Dimitao we might earn what in American money would be three dollars…maybe four a month. Here we are paid thirty dollars a month. We came here to work at Gam Saan, the Golden Mountain, but the railroad gives us more gold for less work."

The train's whistle wailed and wind whipped acrid black smoke into the freight car as it clattered around a sharp curve high on the mountainside. Below was the town of Colfax. Just ahead was a vertical slope of hardened granite which had presented the builders with a nearly impossible task. They had named it "Cape Horn" for it resembled that perpendicular promontory in the angry and forbidding seas of the Drake's Passage. It rose 2500 feet above the American River and afforded no footholds for man or beast, no avenue for the graders to follow.

The Celestials had woven large baskets from reeds and vines. Each basket could hold two or three men, its sides coming up to their waists. They had placed loops at each of the four corners of the basket, symbolic of the Four Directions, and attached long ropes to these. Prayers were inscribed on bits of paper which were pasted inside the baskets.

From the top of Cape Horn the men were lowered down the steep rock face. The wind caught and swung the baskets as they descended. At the prescribed height to match the road bed where the rail line had previously ended the Chinese workers chipped away at the rock. They drilled holes which they filled with gunpowder. They inserted long fuses into the holes. They would light the fuses and other workers would haul the baskets swiftly back to the top before the explosion carried away chunks of the granite wall—and chunks of the basket men. They were usually successful in escaping the blast, but some were unlucky: perhaps the fuses were too short or perhaps their prayers had not been worded correctly.

Now the train on which Zack and Tommy rode crawled across the face of Cape Horn like a column of confused spiders. Below them lay the vast panorama of the river valley where the mining towns of Gold Run, Little York, Red Dog, and You Bet were clustered along river bars of gravel and where gold miners still dug and shifted and panned—and hoped. Now they traversed a trestle, 1100 feet long, attached to the rock wall like the spiders' web.

Ahead was Dutch Flat. Then, at mile ninety-four from Sacramento the train would reach Cisco near where eleven of the fifteen tunnels the CPRR had had to carve into the ancient mountain stone were located—and where its crews had encountered the worst winter in memory. Drifts of heavy snow twenty feet deep had covered the mountain slopes and often cascaded down onto the workers. In spring frozen corpses were found with shovels still in their hands, standing upright like marble statues.

This was Donner Pass, over 7000 feet above sea level and infamous for the tragedy of a group of early pioneers, the Donner Party, three families from Springfield, Illinois, who, in 1846 became trapped by heavy snowfall high in the mountains above Truckee Lake. The story of their deaths from exposure, murder and cannibalism was sensationalized in newspapers across the nation.

But in 1866, the railroad was still shy of the summit. The railroad owners ordered the work on the tunnels to continue in spite of the harsh winter snows. Locomotives would have to be pulled by hand over the mountain if necessary, said the owners. The Celestials never faltered. They cut a road through the dense forests and placed locomotives and wagons loaded with black powder and nitroglycerin on sleds made of logs. Teams of mules and hundreds of Chinese men tugged and pushed and finally got the supplies up the mountain.

Work on the Donner Summit Tunnel proceeded through the winter of 1866. The tents and shacks the Chinese lived in were totally covered with snow; they dug air shafts and chimneys and tunneled through the drifts to get to the work site. Some of the tunnels under the snow were wide enough for the passage of horse-drawn sleds. Finally, however, the snow stopped work on the tunnel until the spring thaw.

When it was finished the tunnel was 1,659 feet long. It was 124 feet below the surface and had consumed many kegs of blasting powder every day. The crews had also used a new invention, nitroglycerine, which was so unstable it was banned from transport and had to be manufactured on the spot. It often blew up prematurely, killing its handlers.

Because of the dangers and the terrible working conditions the Chinese asked for a raise in salary from thirty dollars to forty dollars each month and for a shortened workday of ten hours, eight when drilling in the tunnels. They also objected to being whipped by their white supervisors. The owners refused these demands and so in June of 1867 the Celestial workforce went on strike. The owners withheld food and pay and threatened to replace them with Blacks imported from the eastern states. After only one week the strike was over.

Zack had been leaning out of the door again watching the engine spewing clouds of black smoke from its funnel-shaped smokestack as it rolled along the tracks. All of a sudden the front of the engine disappeared into the wall of the mountain! The train was entering tunnel number 6, the Donner Summit Tunnel, the longest, darkest and, for the young Wintu boy, the most terrifying entrance to the underworld he could imagine. If the mountain could swallow this great snake of a train what chance did a small boy have to survive the dangers and demons lurking within it?

His experience and knowledge of mountains was based on Shasta, the sacred mountain: a dangerous place where one could get lost or go crazy just as easily as being healed by the good mountain spirits that dwelt there. There was also a hidden realm inside Shasta Mountain where evil spirits lived. One might encounter doorways that opened and led into the home of the Little People, who were neither good nor evil but exhibited both qualities simultaneously, making them especially dangerous.

How much more power must this mountain have to swallow a mechanical monster that roared and breathed fire and belched soot and sparks?

Once inside the tunnel, the absolute darkness, the heat and the smoke and the collective unrest of the Chinese riding with them caused Zack to reel and smack up against Fong Dun Shung, the Chinese herbalist. The herbalist felt rather than saw that the boy was about to faint and was in danger of falling out of the open doorway and into the tunnel. He grabbed Zack by the arms and steadied him.

The train emerged from the tunnel and a blast of cold mountain air cleared the freight car of smoke. Blinding daylight entered the car, flashing through a stand of tall pines that broke the light into alternating beams; the stroboscopic sunlight and the train's joggle and clatter only aggravated the boy's giddiness.

"Easy now, boy. Let Qi settle. Breath deep," Fong said.

"Is boy all right?" asked Lee Shao.

"He will be. Get herb box from traveling bag please."

Lee Shao rummaged through the bag of processions that lay at Fong's feet and retrieved an ebony-colored wooden box with brass hinges. He opened it.

"Find container marked 'huang lian.' Is any water to be had? No? Rub some huang lian powder between palms. Good. Now blow at face of boy. This medicine, called goldthread by some, is bitter but has the nature of coldness. Will take away heatstroke of boy...I hope."

Zack had breathed in the powered goldthread and the combination of the herb and the fresh air revived him. Tommy had watched as one Chinese man had grabbed his friend and another had spat a white powder at his face. Was this some kind of attack or was it merely a greeting ritual of the Yellow Ant People or...? Before Tommy could determine what his companion's immediate fate might be, Zack was smiling and thanking the man called Fong Dun Shung.

The train began a long descent, winding through a series of serpentine switchbacks around Donner Lake. Ahead between Blue Cañon and Truckee the train would pass through thirty-seven miles of wooden snow sheds the work crews had built over the rails to protect the railroad from avalanches during the winter months. The tracks then followed the Truckee River Canyon through the Carson range east of the Sierra Nevada. Construction had reached Truckee by April and extended to Reno, Nevada, by May. When they arrived at Reno Zack and Tommy would have traveled 154 miles across the Sierra Nevada from their starting point at Sacramento. They reached Reno by nightfall.

There hadn't been a Reno before the Central Pacific emerged from the Truckee Meadows in May of 1868. There had been a Fuller's Crossing where Charles Fuller had bridged the Truckee in 1859 and built a hotel which he later sold to Myron Lake who then renamed the place Lake's Crossing. There was now a toll to cross the bridge and Lake had added a restaurant, a gristmill and a livery stable.

Lake's Crossing was a major stop-over for people coming from California to work at the silver mines in Virginia City and the Comstock Lode but it wasn't exactly what you'd call a town.

The CPRR changed all that. At the construction "front" where the railroad crews pitched their tents, entrepreneurs arrived and streets were laid out and buildings sprouted almost overnight. The new town was named Reno after a Union general who had fought in the Civil War, Jesse Lee Reno. General Reno had caught a musket ball in the chest during an enemy engagement at Fox's Gap, Maryland. He was said to have told another general, "Hallo, Sam, I am dead." He did die shortly thereafter and the men of his brigade shouted his name at future battles—"Remember Reno!"

There were thousands of laborers camped at Reno. When Zack and Tommy and another hundred or so Chinese descended from the train the resident workers had finished their twelve-hour workday and had returned to camp for dinner.

The Irish and Welsh and Cornish workers dived into a meal of meat and potatoes, bread and butter, and strong drink. The Chinese took time-out to fill tubs made from old powder kegs with hot water from a communal boiler to wash and change their clothing. They drank tea and ate traditional Chinese meals of rice, vegetables and bits of pork or chicken. Often they would have bamboo sprouts, mushrooms, seaweed, and different kinds of dried fruits, much of which had to be imported from China. The Chinese were much healthier than their Caucasian counterparts.

Zack and Tommy stayed close to Lee Shao and Fong Dun Shung, the Chinese men they had met who spoke English. The new arrivals were being divided into smaller groups according, apparently, to which province in China they had come from or which of the Chinese Six Companies had sponsored them. A great deal of conversation in Chinese occurred while Zack and Tommy waited and hoped they would not be separated from Fong and Lee.

There was a meal to be prepared by the cook assigned to their work gang. Lee Shao explained to Zack and Tommy that he had argued for the boys to be included in his gang and that the white foreman had relented only if they were to work as the cook's helpers, helping with meals and carrying the kegs of warm tea up the line for the workers, and thus being kept from harm's way—and from causing trouble.

"I'll be giving you some Chinese language lessons so you can at least understand what you're being told to do," he told them. "Come along now and I'll introduce you to our cook, Hu Qiang."

The cook, Hu Qiang, whose name translated into something like "having the strength of the tiger," was a large man, perhaps in his forties, wearing the blue quilted suit that the Irish workers thought looked like pajamas and made fun of, and a long braided queue which hung down his back nearly to his knees. In spite of his age he did appear to possess the strength and ferocity his name implied. When he spoke he seemed to growl.

There was some discussion between Lee Shao and Hu Qiang and much waving of hands and at last Lee turned to Zack and Tommy and told them that the cook would accept them as servants but would not teach them the art of cooking. They could carry things and make tea but for now they were to stand well back and just watch. They nodded in agreement.

It turned out to be a simple meal of rice, vegetables and smallish pieces of chopped pork, seasoned with spices and flavors Zack and Tommy had never before tasted and which, they had to acknowledge, was exceptionally delicious. Their tasks were to hand out bowls of food to the members of their work gang, some two dozen in all, retrieve the wooden bowls once the men had finished eating, and scrub them clean in hot water.

After dinner most of the men sat around a campfire and played fan-tan, a gambling game in which the players made bets as stones were removed four at a time from a heap of an unknown number. Whoever predicted how many were left—one, two, three or zero—was the winner. Zack noticed that Fong Dun Shung was quite an enthusiastic player but seemed to be losing most of the time.

A little over five-hundred miles of track remained to be laid between the front, now at the town of Wadsworth, and the terminus where the Central Pacific would meet the Union Pacific—a place yet to be determined. The terrain ahead of them was perhaps the easiest of all that they had as yet encountered but now there was an enormous pressure to lay more track than their competitor did. It was a matter of pride and of money and the race was on.

11

An Alaskan Odyssey

San Francisco, July 29, 1868

Edwin Selleck was having a row with his mother. The muffled words were not discernable but Little Wind could tell something was amiss—and imminent. She pushed the door to her room partway open and strained to listen. By now, however, the argument was over and Edwin was stomping upstairs and down the hallway. She eased her door shut. Edwin was banging something around in his own room and muttering to himself. Little Wind waited.

There were bumping sounds as Edwin dragged something down the stairs of the Selleck home. The argument began anew, and this time Little Wind stood at the top of the stairs and heard, and understood, and reveled in the knowledge: Edwin Selleck was leaving home (which in itself was a great relief to Little Wind as the two did not get along) and was leaving San Francisco *with the photographer Muybridge* to go to Alaska!

The Sellecks had been kind to have taken in the Wintu girl and had treated her well, given her fine clothes to wear and sumptuous meals to eat and had begun to instruct her in the etiquette and manners of the non-Indian world. She was grateful for their efforts and had even endured the taunting of their eldest son, Edwin, but this life seemed like just another prison to her, albeit one of silk and crystal and polished oak.

She had been waiting for an opportunity like this one. Quickly she put together a few articles of clothing and tied them in a bundle she could carry easily. She slipped down the backstairs and exited the house through a side door. She was in luck: she could see Edwin disappearing around a street corner. She followed, hanging back so the boy wouldn't notice her. He walked swiftly toward the harbor.

At the Jackson Street wharf Edwin stopped and looked around. He spied what he was searching for and began to walk up the long pier toward several steamboats that had been moored there. Little

Wind followed more closely now, not wishing to lose sight of the boy should he climb aboard one of the vessels and disappear. She ducked behind a piling as Edwin turned to look back in her direction. Then she saw him climbing the gangplank of a large ship. Now she waited until he had passed out of sight onto the deck of the ship.

The SS Pacific was a steam-driven side-wheeler with a length of 223 feet, a 33-foot beam and a tonnage of 876 tons. She had a wooden hull and three masts which towered above her single smokestack. She had been built in 1851 and during her early years had run between Panama and San Francisco shuttling passengers and freight. She had been wrecked once, sold twice and had seen service during the Fraser Canyon gold rush in British Columbia ten years ago. Her current owners were Holladay and Brenham and she made frequent trips up the coast to Vancouver and beyond. Rumor had it that her playboy owner, Ben Holladay, used the ship for drunken private parties lasting from San Francisco to Alaska and back.

The Pacific had been chartered by General Henry Wager Halleck. General Halleck was on an inspection tour of military forts in the Territory of Alaska. Halleck had been a lawyer and a scholar and was an expert in military art and science earning him the unfortunate appellation of "Old Brains." During the American Civil War, Halleck rose to the position of Senior Army Commander in the Western Theater and then to general-in-chief of all U. S. armies. But his subordinate, a Lt. General Ulysses S. Grant, was promoted over him and Halleck was demoted to become Grant's chief of staff.

After the war Halleck had quarreled bitterly with another general, General William Tecumseh Sherman, and as punishment was transferred to California to command the Military Division of the Pacific. This included the states of Oregon, California and Nevada, and the Territories of Alaska, Washington, Idaho and Arizona. The military force of the Division of the Pacific consisted of only two regiments of cavalry, one of artillery and four of infantry. It was a bit of a comedown for the former general-in-chief of the United States Army.

General Halleck had placed Major General Jeff C. Davis in command of the Department of Alaska. Halleck and Davis submitted reports to congress characterizing the indigenous peoples of Alaska as hostile and apt to murder whites at every opportunity. They referred to them as "Indians" although most were Eskimo, Aleut, Inuit and other native tribal entities having little or no relationship to native peoples of the American West. They did this to establish the need for increased military presence, a feathering, as it were, of their frozen nest.

Earlier in the month The New York Times correspondent in San Francisco reported that "Dispatches received at the military headquarters from Alaska state that the troops are in excellent health. The Indians now regard the occupation of Sitka and other places with a not friendly interest." And the general attitude toward the purchase of Russian America remained that it had been a serious and expensive mistake. New York Tribune reporter Horace Greely called Alaska "an ice-hard nothing, not worth taking as a gift."

Major General J. C. Davis, commander of the military presence in Alaska estimated that the new territory was about 578,000 square miles with a population of less than 2000 whites and about "60,000 half-breeds and Indians." From his headquarters in Sitka he was in charge of six military posts each garrisoned by a company of artillery or infantry. Some of the forts were better secured than others and were generally located adjacent to large centers of native population—located with their gun batteries aimed at the settlements in case of hostilities.

The voyagers to Alaska included Halleck's aides and an entourage of civilian dignitaries whose presence was intended to double-check the general's findings. Among these upright citizens, besides Edward Muybridge and his new assistant, Edwin Selleck, was the Reverend Anthony Kulver, an amateur painter specializing in landscapes of the American West.

Rev. Kulver was a philanthropist and a humanitarian who had worked closely with religious groups to help slaves who had been freed by the Emancipation Proclamation. He also advocated for the rights of Native Americans and had tried to improve living conditions on the reservations in New Mexico and Arizona. It was unlikely that Kulver and Halleck would find any common ground during the trip.

Black clouds billowed from the ship's smokestack and the shriek of its whistle sent a flock of seagulls spiraling into the sky. Just behind the smokestack stood the tall triangular support upon which tilted the ship's walking beam, a long diamond-shaped structure of iron struts which turned the paddles when it was set to rocking by a steam-driven piston. The whole affair was an unfamiliar and bizarre-looking machine which confused and frightened the young Wintu girl who had hidden behind its wooden supports. As the walking beam began to move, Little Wind scampered from her hiding place and ducked behind a lifeboat.

The SS Pacific backed away from the Jackson Street wharf, her whistle screaming, white steam mingling with black smoke, and headed for the Golden Gate, the strait that connected San Francisco Bay to the Pacific Ocean. Once out into the ocean and past the Point Reyes peninsula, the boilers were brought to a roaring full boil and the Pacific plunged ahead through a cold and choppy coastal current.

The prevailing winds blowing south along the California coast produced an upwelling of the surface that tended to push the ship out to sea. Until they reached British Columbia and escaped from the North Pacific Gyre into the Alaskan Current they would be fighting wind and water with a will of its own, but the SS Pacific was a capable and sea-worthy ship with a hardened crew and an experienced captain; it was up to the task.

Captain William C. Sprague stood at the wheel in the pilothouse. Sprague looked more like a dime novel cowpoke than a sea captain with his long and unkempt handlebar mustaches and his battered, wide-brimmed Stetson hat. He was slim, clothed in a dark suit and vest with a gold watch chain dangling from a pocket. His first mate, Daniel Bucket stood next to him. Bucket was surveying the deck of the ship from his vantage point in the pilothouse, checking that no cargo was shifting and that no cables were loose. He saw something unusual.

"Cap'n, Sir," said Bucket, "were there any children along with the passengers?"

"Hmm...I don't believe I noted any on the manifest. Why do you ask?"

"Because there's one down there behind the long boat. That's not a proper place for a child."

"No it is not, Mr. Bucket. Please see to it that the child is sent back to its cabin. I don't want any incidents on this voyage!"

Daniel Bucket took the steps to the main deck two at a time. He nearly collided with Edwin Selleck who was strolling along the deck, watching with fascination as the shore receded into the distance.

"Did you see her?" asked Bucket.

"See who?"

"The child. She was behind that boat but she's gone now."

"Sorry. I haven't seen any child. Is it important?"

"There aren't supposed to be any children on this trip. I think she may be a stowaway. We can't have that kind of responsibility so if you see her, please let me or the captain know."

"Of course," said Selleck. He watched as the first mate climbed the steps back to the upper deck. "I bet I know who it is," he thought to himself.

Edwin Selleck approached the lifeboat and lifted the canvas cover a few inches. "I know you're in there," he said. A few minutes later a small head emerged and Selleck helped Little Wind down from the lifeboat.

"And just what do you think you're doing? The mate said there weren't to be any children on the boat."

"Oh?" answered Little Wind. "Then what are *you* doing here?"

"You better come with me. We'll go see Mr. Muybridge. I'd just as soon see you get put off the boat right now, only...can you swim?"

The Pacific had a small salon; nothing like the grand spaces of the Mississippi riverboats, but large enough for some chairs and tables and a wet bar. Edward Muybridge was seated at a table talking to Reverend Anthony Kulver. Muybridge was telling the reverend about his photographs of Yosemite. Kulver was showing the photographer a sketch book he had brought with drawings of mountains and the Columbia River. When Edwin approached with Little Wind in tow Muybridge was furious.

"She snuck on board, Mr. Muybridge," Selleck told him.

"I see that. Little Wind, what the devil do you think you're doing on this ship?"

The girl hung back. Whatever confidence in herself she might have had, whatever belief she had held that the photographer would welcome her was now shattered. She said nothing but dropped her eyes.

"This is no place for a child. Do the Sellecks know you're here? Of course not. I could get in trouble for allowing you to be here...I...I will see that you are put off at the first port."

Little Wind had never seen Muybridge so angry, so red in the face and shaking. She then looked at Edwin and saw that the boy was grinning. Grinning! Now *she* was mad. She yelled back at Muybridge:

"No you won't! I'm staying...and that's that!"

Now it was Rev. Kulver's turn to enter the confrontation. "My dear," he said to Little Wind, "you are one of the People, aren't you? What tribe are you from? My name is Reverend Kulver."

Little Wind looked at the man who had just addressed her in soft, kind tones. He was about 35 years of age and was slightly balding. He had bushy sideburns but was otherwise clean-shaven. He didn't wear the backwards collar she had seen other white preachers wear and he definitely did not remind her of the Franciscan brothers. But at least he didn't have the aggressive mannerisms of most of the non-Indians she had met.

"I am of the Wintu," she replied.

"Edward," said the reverend to Muybridge, "I think you should calm down a bit. You obviously know this girl. Who is she?"

Muybridge told Kulver the story of his first meeting with Little Wind, of their traveling together and of his placing her with the Sellecks. Kulver smiled and nodded then turned back toward Little Wind. "I'll be happy to take care of you during the voyage, my dear," he said. "Unless, of course, Mr. Muybridge..."

"Oh for Chr...for Pete's sake, Anthony. The girl can stay with Edwin and me. But we have to send word back to Edwin's parents. Tell them where the girl is. Actually, they may be happy to be rid of her."

"Actually," said Edwin. "I'd be happy to be rid of her as well."

Two days later the Pacific passed opposite the mouth of the Columbia River where in 1811 Fort Astoria, the first permanent American settlement on the Pacific coast had been established. It was home to the Pacific Fur Company, owned by millionaire John Jacob Astor who had helped to open up the Oregon territory for the early pioneers. If one were to travel up the Columbia to its confluence with the Willamette about 100 miles distance one would reach the bustling city of Portland.

Near the end of the Oregon trail, Portland was once known as "Stumptown" because during its early period, around 1845 or so, the town grew so fast that the stumps of trees cut to make roads were left standing. They were white-washed to make them more visible and people hopped from stump to stump to cross the muddy streets. The town was fast becoming a major trading port with its access to the ocean, the two great rivers, and the fertile agricultural areas that surrounded it.

The following day the steamer had rounded the tip of the Olympic Peninsula and entered the Strait of Juan de Fuca. To the southeast was the entrance to Puget Sound and another boomtown, Seattle. Its chief commodity was lumber and its major avenue, Yester Way which descended a muddy hill, gained the nickname "Skid Road" as loggers sent cut timber skidding down it to Henry Yester's sawmill. To the northeast were a series of islands rising from the misty seas, great lumps bristling with Douglas fir and red cedar, home to trumpeter swans and bald eagles, black-tailed deer and elk, sea lions and Orca whales.

As the Pacific passed these islands, called collectively the San Juans, Little Wind stood at the rail fascinated and thinking she must have reached the very end of the world. A cold, damp vapor, windless but penetrating, came upon them as mist enveloped the boat. The islands appeared and disappeared in the fog like images from a dream. The light gray blanket of mist touched the gray-green waters of the sound and merged into a continuous wall of blankness.

The ship steamed into the broad Straits of Georgia that separated Vancouver Island from the mainland of British Columbia. They passed to the west of a small settlement called Gastown after the residents' favorite tavern owner, "Gassy" Jack Deighton. Some years later it would be incorporated under the name of the City of Vancouver. Little Wind, still standing at the rail felt a heavy hand on her shoulder. She turned to see that Edwin Selleck had come up behind her.

"Well, Windy," he said, "we're almost to port where I'll be rid of you forever."

"Why are you so mean to me?" Little Wind asked.

"Why did you have to come along and ruin everything for me?"

"I haven't done that. Why do you say those things? I've never done anything to you."

"You don't get it, do you? I have this good relationship going with Mr. Muybridge. I can make something of myself with his help. But you...you first came into my family and I had to deal with Mother and Father telling me to be kind to you, to help you and teach you things. Like I didn't have my own life. Now you show up on this boat!"

"Please, Edwin, let's be friends. I won't get in your way. Just be kind to me. You...you could be a big brother to me. If you only..."

"Big brother? Say, where is your *real* brother anyway? Why don't you go find him?"

Later Little Wind sat on her cot in the stateroom she shared with Muybridge and the Selleck boy. She couldn't help the tears rolling down her cheeks. Angry and hurt and feeling very much alone, the girl refused to break into a sob. She sniffed back the tears, wiped her eyes and lay back thinking about her mother, her brother and the life they had had in their village, before moving to the reservation. She thought about her stay at the ranch, how there she had been in reality only a slave with no human rights, how she had been treated as subhuman. She thought about her short stay with the Sellecks, all the wonderful things they owned, things that had little meaning for a young Wintu girl out of her element, a girl who could never appreciate wonderful things. She fell asleep and did not dream.

Excerpt from the journal of Reverend Anthony Kulver:

August 4, 1868. We have made landfall at Nanaimo, a trading post about midway up the coast of Vancouver Island. The Hudson's Bay Company has built a bastion here and has its long tentacles wrapped conveniently around the local industry, coal. The photographer, Muybrdige, embarked with his assistant and a wheelbarrow loaded with equipment—I assume a sort of portable darkroom. Indeed the native tribes here are very colorful, building tall sculptures carved from a single tree trunk which have many representations of faces, animal, human and mythical. Muybridge seems more interested in the buildings and sculptures than the people and will only photograph them at a distance, standing in groups— perhaps to add scale to the photograph. Had I the time I should like to make a portrait of the chief here.

Early in the morning the Pacific pulled away from the small pier at Nanaimo having taken on fuel and supplies. Edward Muybridge struggled with his heavy tripod and view camera attempting to photograph the passing Vancouver Island from the deck of the moving ship. Edwin Selleck steadied the tripod as Muybridge pulled the slide from the glass plate holder and prepared to make an exposure. He waited, feeling the rise and fall of the ship as it ventured up the strait. There was a moment when the ship either reached the crest of a wave or settled in its trough when the rocking and bobbing of the boat was lessened. He chose his moment and removed the lens cap from the lens and then quickly replaced it.

"Damn," said the photographer. "What I need is a fast shutter. Something spring-loaded might do."

He was beginning, although he didn't realize it at this particular time, a lifelong obsession with the capturing and fragmenting of motion. This obsession would evolve and he would invent or adapt methods of capturing *sequences* of motion—and his work would become a significant harbinger of the development of cinema. For the time being, he was just another photographer of landscapes and maker of stereopticon slides.

The route along the north-eastern shore of Vancouver Island was through a narrow channel which might almost have been mistaken for a broad river. Here, cutting through the bluffs were the Seymour Narrows, three miles of turbulent current which had caused mayhem for more than a few ships. The tides ebbed at 10 to 15 knots and in the center of the channel was an underwater mountain with twin peaks called Ripple Rock. One of the peaks of this dangerous obstacle was a mere eight or nine feet below the surface. This route followed Discovery Passage, connected with another narrow waterway, the Johnson Strait, and then rounded the northern tip of Vancouver Island and reentered the sea.

Captain Sprague was taking the Pacific north toward an archipelago of large and small landmasses called the Queen Charlotte Islands. The more southern of these was a large island which, with a few smaller ones, was home to the Haida Nation. The Haida people called it "Xaadala Gwayee" meaning "islands at the boundary of the world". They had become important business partners to the Russian, British and America fur traders and whalers and seemed to be more interested in acquiring wealth than did other indigenous people living in what was now the Colony of British Columbia. Legend had it that a Haida man had set off the Queen Charlottes

Gold Rush of 1851 when he traded a 27 ounce gold nugget for 1,500 blankets.

Muybridge had petitioned the captain to stop on this first island so that he could photograph the native totem poles that he had observed along the shore. But the captain muttered something about smallpox and refused to stop. Indeed, smallpox had been introduced to the Haida in 1862 and, as in the all too familiar scenario of meetings between native and nonnative cultures, the Haida had had no resistance to the disease and were considerably decimated.

"We will stop for your totem poles," the captain told Muybridge, "but at Fort Tongass. There you'll see totem poles galore."

12

An Abundance of Totems

Excerpt from the journal of Reverend Anthony Kulver:

August 13, 1868. We have arrived at Fort Tongass. The trip through the islands presented us with a spectacular panorama of primitive and unspoiled beauty. High mountains richly forested with pine and cedar and hung with moss reminded me somewhat (except for the moss) of the shores of the Hudson River back home. Only here the mountains rise to loftier heights and are possessed of craggy granite peaks often spotted with snow. The fort is build next to an Indian village of about sixteen native houses built from rough-hewn planks which are richly decorated with fantastic figures. Some of these small houses are raised above ground level, perhaps to prevent flooding in the spring.

Little Wind had not been allowed off of the steamer at the port of Nanaimo so she had not seen Alaskan native artwork up close. The totem poles visible from the deck had looked like bare painted trees, their carved faces indistinct. A few canoes had gone by filled with fishermen wearing drab clothing and wide-brimmed hats that reminded her of those worn by the Chinese she had seen in San Francisco. But the designs carved and painted on the canoes escaped her notice.

Now she was standing on a little avenue that ran along the water front at Tongass where a row of houses were carved and painted with the bold designs of the Tlingit culture. Dark browns, blacks and reds predominated and mysterious looking faces peered at her from eyes that seemed to merge into other animal shapes. She recognized birds, fish, bears and other animals but these were twisted into strange symmetrical forms like puzzles never meant to be solved. They seemed to move and transform and replicate while drawing her in, hypnotizing her. It was not a frightening experience although she might someday remember it as such; in fact the images thrilled her, spoke to her of an oneness with nature that she had not felt since leaving her village near Shasta Mountain. She felt a kinship here, and an alien reality as well.

From a circular doorway of one of the houses a woman emerged, having to stoop to exit the small opening. She wore a dress of red and blue calico, was stout and, thought Little Wind, quite beautiful. The woman smiled at Little Wind and said something in a language the Wintu girl did not know. Seeing that she was not being understood, the woman switched to a kind of pigeon English. "You come with the Boston men?" she said. Little Wind nodded. "You hungry?"

This was Little Wind's first introduction to the culture of the native people of Alaska. Tongass had been a native village on this island long before the Europeans came or the Americans built their fort. Its Native Alaskan name was "Kut-tuk-wah." Tongass was established as a customs port for travelers bound from British Columbian waters to the Stikine River shortly after the Alaska Purchase.

Known to the Americans as the Tongass people, the Taant'a-wáan, or "Sea Lion Tribe," were part of a Tlingit society distributed all along the northwest coast of North America. The chief of the village was called Quack-ham, or Captain Ebbitts to the Americans. He was an old man now, but his totem pole told a story of greatness and courage. It told the story of Captain Ebbitt's life and it was not yet finished. When he died his ashes would be placed in a hollow section of the pole near the top.

The old woman beckoned for Little Wind to follow her into the house. Entering through the small doorway, a feature which had been incorporated into the abstract bear design that decorated the house, made her feel as though she were being swallowed. Inside it was quite bright due to several glass-paned and mullioned windows set into the walls. Noticing Little Wind's surprise at seeing European style windows in a native house the woman explained, "Trade seal skins for windows."

A rack made from slender twigs stood over an open fire. Several large salmon hung from the rack. Smoke rose from the fire and exited through a hole in the ceiling. "We smoke fish. Store good."

Yes, Little Wind thought to herself, we do that too. She half expected, as the woman had asked her if she were hungry, that she would be offered a bowl of acorn soup. But the woman brought a woven basket filled with small dried fish. Little Wind smiled and took one of the fish which she later learned were called candlefish because they were so oily they could be burned like a candle.

"You are not gus'k'ikwáan...of the Boston men," said the woman. Little Wind tried to explain who she was and where she had come from, but the words came out jumbled and the story was all out of order. The woman grinned widely and handed Little Wind another fish.

"There are many kwáan like you and me. From inland, from north islands. Many different kwáan. This is good." The woman helped herself to a candlefish and chewed noisily. Then she said, "You afraid of something?"

"I'm not afraid. It's just...living with those soldiers right on top of you. We have soldiers like that at home. They come and kill without mercy. Doesn't that worry you?"

"Many come in old days for trade. Russia man come. Spain man come. English man come. We give sealskins, they give many different things we need. All good times. Then Boston man come and build fort. Make rules. Not so good. But not kill."

"If there was gold here it would be different. They'd move you out, or just kill you."

"Gold? They come for gold two times. Not so much gold here. They leave then."

"You were lucky."

Excerpt from the journal of Reverend Anthony Kulver:

August 14, 1868. I spent the day talking to the chief here, a man named Captain Ebbitts. General Halleck had gone up to inspect the fort and took Muybridge with him to get photographs. My word, what a lot of equipment that man has to lug around! I sketched some of the native houses and some of the wood carvings. They are a very skilled people with wood and seem to use shells and sharp stones instead of knives to get marvelous effects. Their fondness for art, if developed, would bear good fruit. If ever we can establish good schools here in the north we should include the fine arts in the curriculum.

Captain Ebbitts is an intelligent and polite man and was most informative. The Tongass regularly trade with the tribes back in the interior and are exceedingly jealous of outside interference that might hurt this relationship. Thus they resent the white people who venture up river and this is interpreted by the army officers as a hostility that might flare up uncontrollably. There is occasional friction between the ordinary rank and file soldiers and the town's people when they mingle. I have a theory as to why this is.

Beside the "natural" animosity the white race feels toward anyone who is different, and the history of our encounters with "savage" Indians on the plains, there is an element so foreign to this splendid natural environment (yet essential, apparently, to the soldier) that has been imported here against all reason: liquor. Among the other goods we delivered here at Tongass, and which we will no doubt leave at the other forts as well, were cases of champagne, barrels of ale and whiskey and other such drink. The "good stuff," as the men call it, that is, the champagne and brandy and port, are reserved for the officers. There being only four such officers at this post, one wonders why such quantities are needed.

The post is within three hundred yards of the Indian village, the consequence of which is that you cannot visit one of these Indian villages without meeting some soldiers or sailors wandering about. Their presence tends to demoralize the Indians, and is nowise better for the soldiers. One or the other should be removed! As the Indians are the oldest settlers, and the post has been placed there only recently, and as the Indians are perfectly peaceable, I think the post, and not the Indian village, should be removed.

Late on August 15 the SS Pacific docked in the bay at Fort Wrangell, the next fort on the general's agenda. The fort had been established only four months ago when troops under General Charles H. Pierce and a battery of artillery evacuated another fort at Stellacoom and set out with 112 men, 5 officers, a dozen or so mules and oxen and a six-pounder field gun. April had seen them working at Fort Tongass and by May they were building a stockade, a hospital, officer's quarters, barracks and a guardhouse at Wrangell. The six-pounder was pointed at the native village like an accusing finger.

The village had 32 houses, similar to those found in Tongass, and just over 500 inhabitants. Reverend Kulver watched as ten barrels of ale and five of whiskey were unloaded from the boat. They were addressed to Leon Smith, post trader of the fort. The next day, the reverend visited the store to enquire about the uses of the liquor.

"Oh it's fer the express use of the soldiers," Smith told him. A directive from the U. S. Government required it to be supplied to them (ale for the enlisted men and whiskey and brandy for the officers).

"Does it ever find its way into the hands of the Indians?" Kulver asked.

"Oh no, Sir. But theys those that runs rum and such up the river in small boats. Some of that gets to 'em...somehow."

"I had heard that the Indians will part with an inordinate amount of skins in trade for whiskey."

"Wouldn't be knowin' about that, Sir."

Later that afternoon, Kulver heard that Leon Smith and two drunken soldiers had assaulted an Indian who was passing by the front of his store. Smith claimed the Indian had struck his little boy but later retracted his statement. The Indian was seized and brutally beaten. When he fell to the ground the soldiers stomped on him. None of the whites were ever arrested or tried for the crime.

Reverend Kulver later wrote in a letter to the Commissioner of Indians Affairs that the "ill effects of the near proximity of soldiers to the Indian Village" was worse here than in other countries because it was more needless. "The soldiers will have whiskey," he wrote, "and the Indians are equally fond of it. The free use of this by both soldiers and Indians, together with the other debaucheries between them, rapidly demoralizes both...." Just what the "debaucheries" were was not elaborated on by Reverend Kulver.

General Halleck, however, in his report to the Department of the Interior, made after the conclusion of his trip to Sitka, said that the native Alaskans, "...once their relations with the military is established, are almost invariably friendly. They are not cheated or ill-treated by the soldiers, and soon learn to respect the authority of the officers and the power of a well-armed and well-disciplined command." It was necessary, he went on to say to establish military posts in the vicinity of the larger tribes and villages. They would then learn that "...our government is able and ready to compel them to good conduct...." This, he maintained, would eliminate the necessity for additional troops to carry on a long and expensive Indian war.

No one had asked Little Wind what she felt.

Excerpt from the journal of Reverend Anthony Kulver:

August 18, 1868—Sitka, Alaska. This is the present headquarters of the Military Command in Alaska, and the former residence of the Russian governor. We were most cordially welcomed by General Davis, and every assistance which both himself and the officers of the department could be given to further the objects of our visit was extended toward us.

A large quantity (nine hundred gallons) of pure alcohol, marked "coal oil," and directed to the care of the post traders at Sitka, was landed at Sitka from our steamer. This fraud was detected by Inspector Andrew Keed, and the liquor was confiscated by Collector Kapus. Liquors thus confiscated are kept in the storehouse a certain length of time, advertised, and then sold at public auction by the collector of the port. I can't help but believe there is some sort of conspiracy at foot in this liquor business!

Passing up the street at Sitka (there is but one) I met a crowd collected around an Indian girl. She was moaning, in great pain, and lying uncared for on the sidewalk. I asked "why they did not take her to the hospital," and was informed that "there was no provision made for Indians at the hospital." General Davis happening to pass at that moment gave me permission, and, assisted by two Indians, I carried her to the United States hospital. She was placed in a wretched, tumble-down part of the building, and medicine given her. The next day General Davis humanely issued an order detailing Doctor J. G. Tonner to act as surgeon in charge of the Indians near the town. I'm beginning to feel I may have some influence here.

The SS Pacific had wound its way through the labyrinth of islands to Baranof Island where the village of Sitka sat at the foot of a mountain created by volcanic activity and carved by glaciers eons before the arrival of man. The Tlingit told that their ancestors were attracted to the area by the smoke and fire of the volcano, now called Mount Edgecumbe, 10,000 years ago.

Sitka was founded by Alexander Baranov who became the governor of Russian America in the year 1799. The Russian American Company was chartered by the Tsar Paul the First and, then called the Redoubt Saint Michael, went into the business of exploiting the rich resources of Alaska. Angered by this intrusion into their homeland, the Tlingit destroyed the Redoubt, killed most of its inhabitants and demanded a ransom of 10,000 rubles for the surviving settlers. The Russians retaliated, returning with a warship which bombarded the village and recaptured the settlement. Even after the acquisition of Alaska by the United States, the Russian influence in Sitka in particular, and along the Alaskan coast in general, was very prevalent.

The Cathedral of St. Michael, the seat of the Bishop of Kamchatka, the Kurile and Aleutian Islands, and Alaska, was built in Sitka in 1848. The Russian American Company had stockpiled several warehouses worth of goods in Sitka. It took a good year after the transfer of ownership of the territory before the goods were disposed of by shipping them to San Francisco and selling them off. Hundreds of Russian immigrants still remained in Alaska.

The old Russian cathedral had attracted Muybridge's attention; it seemed an appropriate subject for a stereo slide. With Edwin Selleck's help he had set up the sturdy tripod and double-lens camera in the street in front of St. Michael's. Little Wind had watched from a small park nearby. She wanted to talk to Edwin but was afraid he would abuse her verbally as usual. She put aside her fear and her animosity toward the flippant young man and approached him.

"Hello Edwin," she began.

"Oh, hello, Windy. Out for a morning stroll?"

The girl looked up at the high dome of the cathedral. It looked like a hat, or an upside-down onion, she thought.

"Have you walked through the village yet?" Little Wind asked the boy. "The carvings are wonderful. And the poles! One had a giant frog sitting on top of a bear, sitting on top of an eagle, sitting..."

"What do you want, Windy?"

"I want to ask you to tell your parents how happy they made me and thank them for looking after me."

"What? I don't understand."

"I've thought about this a lot. I've met many wonderful people here, people that are like me. The villagers are called the Sheet'ká-áan. That means the Outside Edge of a Branch Tribe. They live in harmony with the animals and the trees and the mountains and the sea. I'm going to stay here."

"Windy, I...I don't want you to stay. Come back with us to San Francisco."

"What? First you want me to go...now you don't?"

"I'm sorry I've been rude and treated you unfairly. I was jealous. I see that now...now that I might not ever see you again. And my parents...already they probably blame me for your absence."

"It's a little late to think about that, isn't it? Edwin, I wanted us to be friends. I will think of you after you've gone back to San Francisco. Will you become a photographer like Mr. Muybridge?"

The photographer, Edward Muybridge, had been listening. He considered whether or not to allow the young Wintu girl to stay here in Sitka. How would it reflect on him personally? But could he force her to leave with them? He knew her well enough to know the answer to that. He called to Edwin:

"Edwin! I'm ready now to do the interior of the church. Come help me with the equipment."

In the past few days Little Wind had followed a gravel walk the Russians had built along the beach and into the woods surrounding the town. The path led through tall spruce, hemlock and yellow cedar to the banks of a river overhung by old willows and carpeted with thick green moss. She had watched as elk came to drink, oblivious to her presence.

She had explored the village of the Outside Edge of a Branch Tribe which the whites called the Ranche. She found there the familiar square wooden houses decorated with painted carvings and saw friendly, easygoing people, many of whom spoke English. She had been invited into their homes and offered food. She had learned of their culture and life-style, how they fished and traded with other tribes for vegetables, how many went to the Russo Church, how others drank the white man's whiskey and gambled.

There were other native villages nearby, she learned. There were the Jilkáat Kwáan, called the Chikat people, and the Kéex̱'Kwáan which meant The Opening of the Day Tribe, or the Kake people. Some hunted sea lions for meat and skins, some grew vegetables and gathered currants and berries, some fished for salmon and shellfish, and some went after bigger game like deer or mountain goats. The different tribes traded together and there was little conflict between them.

She heard a story that concerned her greatly. It concerned a chief of the Chikat tribe who, on New Year's Day had been at the home of General Davis, the big chief of the soldiers at Fort Sitka. The general had been generous with his brandy and the Chikat chief became so intoxicated that he stumbled while leaving the stockade in the company of another Chikat and fell flat on his face. A sentry, seeing what he perceived was a sleeping Indian lying on the ground in a courtyard where Indians were typically not allowed, approached and began kicking the Chief to awaken him.

This brutal action by the sentry so incensed the other Chikat that he began struggling with the soldier and managed to wrench his rifle away from him. The two Indians fled back to the village with this firearm. The general ordered the sentry and an officer to pursue and arrest the Indians. Shots were fired back and forth and the soldiers were forced to retreat. General Davis then sent word that unless the men surrendered and returned the rifle the entire village would be destroyed by the firing of the artillery piece that was already aimed at the heart of the village.

Orders were issued to prevent any Indians from escaping from the village and joining with other tribes to declare war on the army. The Chikat chief and the other man then surrendered and were sent to the guardhouse to await trial. This greatly angered the Sitkan people. General Davis, satisfied that he had the situation under control lifted the ban on Indians leaving the village. The post commandant was drunk at the time and failed, either through incompetence or by design, to issue the new order and hence the troops believed the curfew was still in affect.

Two Indians, a Chikat and a Kake, set out in a canoe to fish and gather firewood. The guards at the wharf, believing the Indians were still restricted to the Ranche, fired upon them and killed them both. The Tlingit people had their own sense of justice. Whereas in white culture where there was a somewhat arbitrary hierarchy of punishment-fitting-crime protocols, the Indians simply followed one rule: an eye for an eye. The Kake tribe, seeking revenge, killed two white men.

A United States Navy ship, the side-wheeler sloop-of-war USS Saginaw, was anchored off the Kake village on nearby Kupreanof Island. General Davis requested its assistance. The Saginaw was commanded by Richard Worsam Meade III, known as "Junior." Meade was a career Naval Officer who had distinguished himself during the American Civil War in active combat and blockade enforcement and had participated in the suppression of the New York draft riots of 1863. He was cruising the Alaskan Inner Passage on a mapping expedition.

The Kake villagers refused to surrender the killers of the two white men and so General Davis gave the order to destroy the village. If Commander Meade spent any time at all in reconnaissance of his target or took any precautions to avoid the murder of women and children present in the homes, he did not elaborate upon this in his report. His casual mention of the shelling of four villages and two forts all within 48 hours (contrasted with the depths to which he analyzed the harbors) suggests a reluctance to document details of the disaster. He wrote in his journal:

>...*at 5.45 p. m. anchored in Saginaw Bay, off a Kuke or Kekou village of six houses, in seven and one-half fathoms (low water), soft bottom.*
>
>*The Indians who inhabit this locality are known as the Kakes, Kekis, or Kekoiis, the terms being indifferently applied; are very treacherous and hostile to whites, and our object in coming to Kou Island was to punish them for the murder of two white men under circumstances of great brutality.*
>
>*...after having burned all but one house in the settlement at Saginaw Bay, left the anchorage and proceeded to the main Kekon village on the northwest end of Kuprianoff Island. The entrance to the anchorage shows clear at low water, but it should be run with great caution and the lead kept going, as there are numerous rocks and reefs which cover at half tide. No one should undertake to approach the place without someone on board who is tolerably well acquainted with the channel.*
>
>*We anchored within five hundred yards of the village, which contained about twenty houses, some of them built with great care. The chief's house was lined with cedar boards. This village has been in existence a great many years, as shown by the numerous posts carved in grotesque shapes which stand near every chief's house and are hollowed out at the top to contain the ashes of his ancestors.*
>
>*Off Kekou Village we anchored in nine fathoms of water, sandy bottom, and having destroyed the village very completely, returned at 2.35 p. m. to Saginaw Bay, where, at 5.10 we anchored for the night. The weather was thick and rainy, with wind from east northeast, which would probably be a southeaster outside or in Chatliam Straits.*
>
>*At 8.45 a. m., weather cloudy, but dry. Left Saginaw Bay and steamed around to the next indentation to westward, which subsequently proved to be a largo and well-sheltered bay which, from its advantages, I named Security Bay, and the anchorage Snug Harbor.*
>
>*Our anchorage was about seven hundred yards from Tom's Ranch, which we burned, and during the afternoon I sent off an expedition of two boats with their crews, and seventeen soldiers from the garrison at Sitka, to destroy two fishing villages at the head of the bay, four and one-half miles distant. Midshipman Bridge found two stockaded forts and two villages, which he destroyed. He carried a depth of eight fathoms to within a mile of the head of the bay, where the water*

there shoals suddenly to two fathoms and less, (one-quarter flood, when soundings were taken).

After the destruction of the Kake villages the alleged murders were delivered into the hands of the military. What would become known as the Kake War then ended. In his report on the affair General Davis wrote, "The Indians within the last few days have exhibited some signs of growing trouble, but I think I have succeeded in checkmating them in their designs, at least for the present."

Excerpt from the journal of Reverend Anthony Kulver:

August 20, 1868, Sitka, Alaska. At midnight I witnessed the most gorgeous curtain aurora borealis any eye ever beheld. A rich green and purple undulating curtain seemed suspended in the sky as far south as twenty degrees, and forming a perfect arc. At the west end of the curtain were two perpendicular columns of light, which rapidly traversed the curtain from west to east, and vice versa, giving to view every possible shade of the two colors, and making the rays fairly dance in and by their own light. Such a celestial sight would alone compensate one for a trip to Alaska.

August 30, 1868. Homeward bound! Under a full head of steam, we went booming on our return trip to California. The air was chilly, and as we approached the volcanic mountains surrounding the harbor they loomed up ghostly white in snow through the thickening gray fog of the gathering storm. We anchored that night in the Snug Harbor, and the next morning was as clear and quiet as a May day at home, not a sign of fog or cloud remaining. Before midnight, however, the wind began to blow a gale. The storm lasted thirty-six hours, and cleared off as suddenly as it arose. Finally, we were under way.

13

All the Live-long Day

When Hu Qiang barked his orders at Zack and Tommy he sounded more like a yippy little canine than a ferocious roaring tiger; his voice was already high pitched and the phonetic peculiarities of spoken Mandarin, the tongue against palate and the rising and falling inflections, exaggerated the similarity of his frantic mandates to the whining of a wounded animal. Although Zack and Tommy didn't know the meaning of all Hu's shouted words they still understood his body language. And they had once seen the camp cook chase one of the men away from the cooking area with an ax handle. Thus, without complaining, they balanced the wooden pole from which hung a five gallon keg of freshly brewed tea between their shoulders and hobbled along up the line to where Chinese workers were busy grading the track bed.

Lee Shao and Fong Dun Shung were among the work gang filling mule-drawn wagons with dirt. They saw the boys and dropped their shovels. The two English-speaking Asians hurried to get a mug of tea and spend a few moments chatting. Two other workers, Ging Cui and Wong Fook accompanied them. The Irish foreman took notice of the four leaving their posts and made a show of looking at his pocket watch.

Zack had learned very few words of Mandarin but listened as the four men talked and tried to glean the gist of their conversation. Occasionally, an English word or phrase would be part of the exchange. He heard Wong Fook mention "One-Eyed-Bossy-Man," who, Zack knew, was James Harvey Strobridge, the head of construction for the Central Pacific Railroad. Strobridge was a stern but fair task master who had a bad temper (although it was mostly for show) and an impressive vocabulary of swear words. Most of the men were afraid of him.

Strobrdige had lost one of his eyes in a blasting accident near the Boomer Cut. The crews had been setting off black powder charges and one of their attempts to open up a seam in the granite had failed.

121

When this happened, water was poured into the seam to try to float the unexploded powder back up. One of the workers, welding a crowbar, struck it against a rock and accidentally ignited the powder. Besides destroying Strobridge's eye the blast blew two men through the air severely injuring them and killed the man holding the crowbar. After the accident Strobridge wore a black patch over his right eye which added to his fierce demeanor.

Lee Shao, seeing Zack's interest, explained in English that a wagon train had arrived at Winnemucca, the next town the grading and leveling crews would reach some ten or twelve miles ahead. It was common for small boom towns to spring up along the route and certain unsavory elements were typically present. This wagon train included, besides the usual gamblers and bar-keeps, an assortment of ladies of uncertain virtue (actually their virtue was fully understood by the men)—and One-Eyed-Bossy-Man was not pleased.

Strobridge, vehemently opposed to gambling, drinking and carousing, was known to ride ahead of the construction front bringing a few handpicked men with him for the purpose of running these sorts of evil interlopers out of town. What concerned Wong Fook, Lee told Zack, was that the ladies in question were said to be Daughters of Joy, that is, Asian girls, and most likely just off the boat. The Chinese were already held in low esteem by the Caucasian workers and this would seem to the whites to be more demoralizing evidence of the Celestial race's inferiority.

Fong Dun Shung related that he had placed a bet that One-Eyed-Bossy-Man wouldn't bother running off the girls since they were only Chinese—but the odds were not in his favor. In fact, Strobrige and his posse were on their way to Winnemucca at that very moment. As the four Chinese men sipped their tea, the foreman, an Irishman named Patty Farrell, appeared dangling his pocket watch in front of him. He pointed at the watch, then at the workers, then at the work site. Fong, Lee, Ging and Wong quickly returned to their work.

Farrrell couldn't resist tossing a taunt after the Asians, although he was unaware that two of them spoke English. "Say Johnny," he called, using the derogative "John Chinaman" often applied to Asians by whites, "have ya seen any snakes lately?" Farrell was referring to an incident which happened shortly after the CPRR had emerged from the Sierra Nevada into the great basin of Nevada. Some Paiute Indians had told the Chinese that the desert here contained giant snakes which could swallow a man whole. Some of the Chinese workers, imagining dragons roaming the basin, took off to return home. Strobridge had ordered his Irishmen to chase the escaping Asians and bring them back.

Tommy Wepa, who didn't like the foreman any more than he would have liked a giant snake, got one of his clever ideas: he dipped a tin cup into the barrel of tea and offered it to Patty Farrell, anticipating the inevitable reaction with a grin. Farrell swung out and knocked the cup out of Tommy's hand. "Damn yellow bastard," he cried. "None of your liquid opium for me! Get back to work." He stormed off.

"You probably shouldn't have done that," Zack told Tommy. "That man would kill you soon as look at you."

"He thinks we are Chinese, did you notice? That's a good thing. They don't pay Indians as much money."

"And when was the last time you got paid?"

Zack thought about the pocket watch that the foreman had dangled in front of their faces. It was a symbol of his authority, just as Zack's watch was a symbol of his search for his father and for his own identity in this crazy upside-down world where the lowest of men lorded over the most worthy (but most powerless) of men. The Chinese were appreciated by the railroad owners as being capable (and humble) workers—even One-Eyed-Bossy-Man had to admit that. But the non-Asian workers despised them. And as for the few Native Americans who worked for the railroad, their status was the lowest of all.

The Union Pacific, the other railroad company that was working its way west from Omaha, had no Chinese workman. There were some Indians used as scouts to warn the construction crews of hostile Plains Indians, but the majority of those working on the railroad were white. As the railroad inched its way through Indian lands, it slaughtered buffalo for food and some of the tribes starved during the winters because of this. Some of the Indians tried to stop the progress of the Union Pacific by attacking work crews; the owners asked the government for help. Thus the intrusion of the railroad into Indian lands was a major factor in escalating the war between the Plains Indians and the United States Army. But that's another story.

There were heroes on both sides of course. Kit Carson had been a trader, a scout and an Indian agent: a hero and an antihero of many conflicts. In 1864 he had led 8,000 Navajo men, women and children on a forced march from their homelands in Arizona to a reservation at Bosque Redondo in New Mexico, a distance of over 300 miles. Many had died. Carson had just died this May, but not of starvation like the Navajos. The Navajos had finally got their treaty and were now returning home after the Long Walk. There was much bitterness in their hearts.

Red Cloud, another hero, was a chief of the Oglala Lakota. In spite of overwhelming odds he had led his people against the forces of the United States Army, finally obtaining from the government a treaty known as the Second Treaty of Fort Laramie which guaranteed the Sioux rights to the Black Hills of Dakota and expanded their hunting lands beyond the reservation boundaries. The Army agreed to abandon its Forts Smith, Kearny and Reno along the Bozeman Trail while the Indians agreed to become, as the treaty put it, civilized. The Sioux would later be forced to leave the Black Hills.

Chief Black Kettle of the Southern Cheyenne had also fought against the relocation of his people from their homeland in Kansas to a reservation in Colorado but was unsuccessful in his efforts. They were moved. And then in 1864 the Third Colorado Cavalry perpetrated what became known as the Sand Creek Massacre against the Cheyenne living on that reservation. Black Kettle survived and negotiated the Treaty of Little Arkansas from the government guaranteeing what the government termed "perpetual peace," but this forced another relocation on the Cheyenne, this time to Indian Territory in what is now Oklahoma.

In November of 1868 Black Kettle and his wife, Medicine Woman, would be shot in the back by the 7th Cavalry under the command of Lieutenant Colonel George Armstrong Custer, newly reinstated after his court-martial for leaving his post without permission. Custer would claim to have slaughtered 103 warriors (although half of the actual number of 30 to 50 would be women or children) and he would fail to rescue a small detachment of men led by a Major Joel H. Elliot, resulting in their deaths. Custer would become a hero of the Indian Wars.

There were new heroes emerging from obscurity to fame by the advent of dime novels. There was, for instance, William F. Cody who had been a pony express rider as a teenager and now was an U. S. Army scout working part time for the Union Pacific Eastern Division killing buffalo, an occupation for which he acquired the name, "Buffalo Bill." While he did have several encounters with hostile Native Americans, his later representations to the press of those exploits were far more dramatic.

And there were unlikely and mostly unknown heroes like Sarah Winnemucca. Sarah's Paiute name was Tocmetone which meant Shell Flower. She was the daughter of Chief Winnemucca after whom the town on the railroad right-of-way was named. She was born in 1844 and unlike many Native American women she had traveled, received an education and had learned English. She spent her early years in Stockton, California, then later stayed at the Pyramid Lake Reservation in Nevada.

In 1859 two white men had kidnapped and raped two girls from the reservation and the Paiutes retaliated by killing them. This led to the Pyramid Lake War and Sarah's cousin, Young Winnemucca, became War Chief. The settlers found they were no match for the Indians and a truce ended the conflict. Sarah was gaining an insight into how dangerous the strife between her people and the whites could become—and at a moment's notice.

Sarah and her family had come to the attention of James W. Nye, the first governor of the new territory of Nevada during a tour of the reservation in the early 1860s. The family exemplified the Paiute "Royal Family" as her grandfather and her father had both been chiefs. Soon the Winnemucca family earned money by being exhibited at venues such as the Maguires Opera House in San Francisco and on stage in Virginia City, Nevada. They had somehow managed to transcend the image of the ignoble savage, perhaps piquing the curiosity of the white population less familiar with indigenous peoples.

But conflict returned to Pyramid Lake again in 1865 when persecution of the Paiutes escalated. The Nevada Volunteer Cavalry was on the move across the territory raiding Paiute camps as punishment for cattle theft or any other infraction the white settlers fancied. In March they reached Old Winnemucca's camp of mostly old men, women and children. Nearly all were massacred by the militia. Sarah and her father and brother had been away at the time and returned to find the tragic aftermath.

Sarah's brother and some other braves planned to retaliate by raiding a nearby ranch and killing the settlers. Sarah hurried to warn the ranchers to leave the area, hoping to avert another massive tragedy, certain that the militia would retaliate against the remaining Paiutes. It was her first deed of heroism but it would not be her last. Sarah was then influential in enlisting the help of the United States Army in intervening between the Paiutes and the volunteer militia.

She was now helping to move her people to Fort McDermitt on the Nevada-Oregon border and, at least temporarily, out of danger. She sat in her wagon in the newly organized railroad town that bore her family's name, Winnemucca. She was waiting for an older Paiute woman to collect her belongings and bring them to the wagon when she heard shots being fired. Fearing that the militia was attacking she urged the horse into an alley.

There was some sort of commotion taking place up the street but Sarah's view was obstructed by the buildings. The gunshots had ceased but shouting and the clattering of wagon wheels reached her ears. She waited until the sounds stopped. She was about to venture back out into the street when something bounced onto the wagon bed. She heard a rush of jumbled words but could understand only the pleading of its tone. A small form was burrowing under a blanket behind her as three men burst into the alley in front of Sarah's wagon.

The men stopped when they saw Sarah. Their guns were drawn. For one terrifying moment she thought they might shoot her but they simply looked at her, looked into the wagon, then walked away. Sarah realized she was holding her breath. She let the air escape her lungs in an audible sigh somewhat alleviating the shuddersome dread that had seized her at the sight of the three men. Still she shook.

The blanket moved and a mass of disheveled hair appeared. Dark eyes peered into Sarah's. A questioning expression was followed by another rush of incomprehensible (to Sarah) gibberish. Before her, half hidden by the blanket was a young Chinese girl. Sarah spoke to her in English, the only foreign language that she knew:

"Calm down. You are safe now. Tell me what happened."

The girl became quiet. A minute later she answered, "The railroad men come. Chase us away. Gambler man shoot at them. Not good idea, I think. Some people hurt. I run away. Hide here. That's all."

"I think I understand. Don't worry. I won't let them get at you. My name is Sarah. I'm on my way to Fort McDermitt where we are protected. What's your name?"

"My name Mei Lim. I come with you?"

Work on the railroad line stretched for miles from the sandy, sagebrushed plains past Wadsworth through the Humboldt sink where the alkali desert retarded the growth of all vegetation, even the hardy sage. Water from the Humboldt Lake caused foamed when boiled and was undrinkable; the crews dug deep artesian wells but struck salt water. Water had to be brought from Truckee in tank cars.

Telephone poles traced a line westward, parallel with the rails. A separate work gang raised poles and attached crossbars and strung wire between glass insulators. A car near the front was used as a telegraph office so news of the railroad's progress and requests for materials could be conveyed back to Sacramento.

Trains shuttled back and forth along the finished line, passing each other at sidings placed every eight or ten miles. Passenger trains came from Sacramento as far as Wadsworth and these were often filled with newspaper reporters who then hopped on construction trains and headed for the front. The process of construction was observed and described in narratives such as this one penned by Jordan Chariton for the Daily Alta:

Along the line stand the mules and horses that pull heavily laden wagons of spikes and ties and the fish-plates used to connect the rails. The advance men, called "pioneers," move out from the very apex of the right-of-way carrying shovels and rope to set ties properly aligned according to the surveyors' stakes. This path has already been graded by teams of Orientals in baggy blue trousers and pan-shaped hats. Following the pioneers are spikers and bolters and the wagonloads of materials.

A train arrives near to the end of the completed track and rails are thrown off. These are loaded onto a horse-drawn car and brought to the end of the track where two men drag a rail from the car and four more help to maneuver it into position on the ties. How expertly they align that shining metal with all those others running in an unbroken line over mountains, through mountain tunnels, across deep gorges on trestles all the way to Sacramento!

The rail is attached to each tie by two spikes—hammers flash in the sun: clang, clang, clang, and the spike is driven home! 3 strokes to the spike, 10 spikes to a rail, 400 rails to a mile—how many times will the hammers swing until this awesome railway is completed? Another gang of workers follows and the level of the bed is corrected by adding ballast and tamping with long metal bars. Now the process is repeated and the line progresses by miles each day.

But the dust! It fills the air and covers our clothes. It is sun-dried and looks like nothing other than pure fine salt. It is from the alkali which accumulates in circular spots that appear to be pools of shining silver water, silently marking the landscape, a barren space where nothing will ever grow or foster. Will cities ever rise out here in this depressing and dull-gray plain?

Close to the end of the finished track stood a collection of special railcars, a sort of main street on wheels. These were dormitories for the white laborers, a kitchen and restaurant, an infirmary, a blacksmith shop, the car occupied by General Superintendent Menkier, Mr. Vandenburg, the Telegraph Superintendent, and some of the other overseers, and the railcar where James Harvey Strobridge, head of construction for the Central Pacific, his wife Hanna Maria and their two adopted children lived. Hanna had added a small porch to the back of their car, placed a colorful awning over it and during good weather hung out pots of red geraniums and the gilded cage in which she kept a yellow canary.

One-Eyed-Bossy-Man was pacing up and down alongside of the railcar, expelled from the living quarters by Hanna as he was swearing and ranting in a manner inappropriate for the children's ears. The excursion to Winnemucca had gone badly. Although he and his men had driven the liquor venders and the prostitutes from town, a skirmish had occurred resulting in one of Strobridge's men being wounded. The man now lay on a cot in the infirmary.

"Infernal damnation! Grifters and bamboozlers, scrubbers, trollops and dratted corn-juice peddling bastards!" said Strobridge although no one was within hearing range. "Tarnation swamp me if I don't kick the cussed scalawags into the next county!"

Strobridge walked to the railcar used as an infirmary to check on the condition of the wounded man. The doctor traveling with the construction company looked grim. The bullet had not severed any arteries nor had it pierced any vital organs but infection, the doctor said, was almost certain to set in. Being a chest wound rather than one on a limb the doctor would be unable to amputate (he was a veteran of the civil war and much experienced with the treatment for gangrenous wounds). All they could do now was to wait.

Zack and Tommy had taken to wearing the blue shirts and trousers and the wide hats common to the Chinese. Their disguise was now complete—but to what avail? They could pass for Chinese, but this was only a miniscule step above the status of Indians in the eyes of the white overlords. Still, they felt comfortable living with the Asian workforce. Some supplies had arrived recently and the meals now included sea foods: oysters and abalone, shrimp and dried fish. They enjoyed working under Hu Qiang although the camp cook was becoming increasingly cantankerous. Yesterday he had hurled a large metal pan called a wok at one of the men.

The front had moved several miles beyond Winnemucca where the confrontation resulting in the wounding of the man had taken place. The man, named George Calvin, was worsening. The doctor had changed the bandage and noted the purplish skin around the wound as he cleaned away puss and dried blood. He shook his head.

Zack intercepted Fong Dun Shung on his way to the tradition fan-tan game after dinner. He wanted news of the encounter in Winnemucca and wished to know the fate of the Daughters of Joy. A peculiar sense of anxiety and concern had descended upon him although he could not account for this. Fong related what details he had gleaned from gossip and his observation that someone was being treated in the infirmary. But as to what may have transpired concerning the Chinese girls he had no information.

"I'm curious," said Zack. "Why, if old One-Eyed-Bossy-Man hates gamblers so much, does he allow your fan-tan games?"

"Yes, it is curious. You know also that some smoke opium on Saturday nights? Is allowed for the reason, I believe, that we are not considered human beings."

"So we can't be corrupted by the vices of drink or..."

"Yes. I believe it is so. Now excuse please. I have game to attend."

The following day, as Zack and Tommy toted their tea barrel up the line very near the front, they saw a white man wandering aimlessly through the dusty desert near where the tracks were being laid. Was he drunk or crazy? They saw him at a distance now and could only just ascertain that the man was injured and stumbling. They set down the barrel and rushed to the man's aid.

Seeing a bloodstained bandage wrapped around the man's chest, Zack deduced that this was the man from the infirmary. Indeed, it was George Calvin who, in his delirium and sweating from fever had struggled from his bed and walked from the infirmary railcar out into the desert, perhaps trying to escape from some imaginary demons.

"Wait with him while I get Fong," said Tommy.

Zack tried to steady the man who was weaving about, clearly hallucinating and taking no notice of the boys. By the time Fong arrived with Ging Cui the man had collapsed and Zack was holding his Chinese hat above the man's head trying to shade him from the sun.

"Make stretcher and carry," said Fong. Ging Cui had procured a blanket from the nearby tent camp of the Asian workers and this was spread on the ground next to George Calvin. They rolled him onto the blanket as gently as they could and lifted him. "To tent of my sleeping place," instructed Fong.

In the tent Fong peeled back the bandages. "Look. Ignorant white doctor has done nothing to treat wound," he said. He opened his medicine box and retrieved a small jar of ointment. He dipped two fingers into the jar and smeared some of its contents on the man's wound. "Get boiling water. Bring clean cloth too."

Fong had dissolved a powder in the boiling water and soaked the clean cloth in it. Allowing it to cool for a moment he then draped the cloth across the man's face. Immediately George Calvin began to breathe more slowly and deliberately. He seemed almost peaceful as he lay on the bedroll in Fong's tent.

Suddenly another white man entered the tent. Patty Farrell, foreman of the work gang Fong and the others belonged to stood gapping at the scene before him: two Chinese men and two boys surrounding an injured white man lying on the tent floor. He burst into a rage shouting:

"What in tarnation is going on here? Why aren't you at your jobs? Who is that on the blanket? Oh crap! Why don't you learn English so I can communicate with you...you yellow bastards?"

Fong Dun Shung, yet knowing that it was to his advantage to keep his knowledge of English a secret, had to respond to the foreman in order to alleviate any possible misunderstanding of the situation. He chose to use the sort of pigeon English some of the Asian men had picked up.

"Lookee, Meesta Bossman. Him sick. Fong helpee. You likee?"

"Oh God, Johnny. What have you done to him? My God! Wait here while I get the doc. The rest of you…back to work!" Farrell waved his arms to indicate to Ging Cui, Zack and Tommy that they should return to the work site. He turned and hurried off to find the doctor.

"Oh now we're in for it," said Tommy after Farrell had gone.

The doctor was bending over George Calvin, holding his wrist in one hand and inspecting a gold watch which he held in the other.

"See Doc? That's what I was sayin'. Them yellow devils are tryin' ta smother the man." This retort came, of course, from Patty Farrell.

"Hmm…. His heart rate has dropped to normal and he seems to be breathing more slowly and steadily. Interesting. You there," said the doctor to Fong who was standing nearby, "what did you put on this man's wound?"

"Salve from old country. Very good. Stops bleeding and corruption. Also give herb to make breathe better."

"I see. Well, we'd better get this man back to the infirmary. Farrell? Help by grabbing an end of this blanket. You…what's your name?"

"Fong Dun Shung. I no doctor…just know herbs. Glad to help."

"Well, Fong Dun Shung I have to say I'm amazed, but very pleased. I'll have to come back and look at some of the herbs you have there. Come along, Farrell. Let's go."

"Meesta Doctor, you take salve with you. Put on man two more days. He better soon."

Zack, who had come back into the tent when the doctor arrived, had been fascinated by the doctor's ability to diagnose his patient only by holding onto his wrist and looking at a watch. And what a watch! It made his own non-ticking device seem humble by comparison. Perhaps because it was made from the shiny metal white people insisted on digging out of the ground it had some sort of magical properties. He believed, however, that if he ever needed medical attention, if he caught a disease or was bitten by some animal, he would not go to *that* doctor. No. He would seek out Fong Dun Shung.

14

Mei Lim

Her friends, the two Indian boys, had left Ah Toy's establishment on Pike Street in San Francisco's Chinatown only moments ago. Mei Lim had been dragged into the back room, a dark and depressing place where the wallpaper smelled of mold. All during their journey from Sacramento Mei Lim had been envisioning a new life in a luxurious salon, dressed in fine silks and jewels, and entertaining an exclusive clientele composed of only the richest and most influential Chinese men. But now she could hear Ah Toy talking to her bodyguards in the front room about taking the girl (meaning Mei Lim) to the Queen's Chamber. That had an ominous sound to it!

She waited in a windowless antechamber, its only illumination coming from a barely glowing oil lamp suspended from the ceiling like a gilded spider. Finally, Madame Ah Toy entered and stood studying Mei Lim for several minutes, minutes during which Mei Lim's skin began to crawl. Madame Ah Toy's pencil-thin eyebrows arching over her dark, piercing eyes gave her countenance a curious combination of beauty and menace.

San Francisco's most famous madam, one of the earliest sojourners to the Golden Mountain from the Far East, one of the richest and most independent and most powerful in this vice-ridden Chinatown, Madame Ah Toy began to interrogate the trembling girl standing before her. In response Mei Lim narrated her story, one familiar to Ah Toy as it duplicated that of so many young females from China: the poverty-stricken parents in the small village reluctantly selling their only daughter, the long sea voyage in the dark, rat-infested hold of a slow steamer, the overland trip to Sacramento squeezed together with dozens like her in a rickety old wagon. The indoctrination into the life of a prostitute.

Did the bossman of the underground brothel where Mei Lim had worked belong to any Tongs, Ah Toy wanted to know. Mei Lim didn't think so. This was important because although Ah Toy was respected in Big City she was also vulnerable to attacks, political, financial or even physical, from members of some of the Tongs who themselves ran criminal enterprises. If she were to be seen stealing girls from another brothel and its owner was a member of the Hongmen (also known as the Hong Gate or the Vast Family, and later as the Chee Kung Tong or the Hall of Universal Justice) —well, the consequences could be dire.

Had she ever entertained any of the white aristocracy, any government officials, bankers or rich merchants? Had anyone taken a special interest in her, offered to keep her exclusively? Mei Lim replied negatively to these and other questions put to her by this powerful woman who was obviously determining her immediate fate. Mei Lim decided to be honest and humble and to hope Madame Ah Toy would see something of value in her and not send her to the Queen's Chamber, whatever that was.

"You are pretty enough," said Ah Toy. "And you are experienced. I won't have to train you, will I? No? Then perhaps…"

"I'm very good, mistress. And I won't be any trouble. Please don't place me in a crib on the street. And don't auction me off. I'll make you good money, you'll see."

"Very well. We'll put you upstairs. See how you do. I may not be in this city for long anyway. I have some property in Santa Clara County. I may retire soon…oh, why am I telling you this? Well, we'll get some rice powder on your checks, some nice clothes…you know the difference between gold dust and brass filings, I hope?"

"Oh yes, mistress."

"Good. There are some gentlemen associated with the railroad coming here tonight. You can entertain them. Now, off with you. Get fixed up."

Ah Toy was right to be concerned about her standing with the various benevolent societies in San Francisco. Besides the Six Companies, who were primarily concerned with promoting legitimate businesses and countermanding racial hatred from the whites, there were other organizations called Tongs (which means "meeting hall" or "group that meets in a hall") descended in part from a handful of secret societies originating in China perhaps as early as the seventeenth century. These early societies tended to have the number three as part of their names and so were collectively termed "Triads" by an English administrator in 1821.

The Triads, typified by the Tiandhui, or Heaven and Earth Society, were often composed of the lower ranks of Chinese society; hence issues of basic survival were paramount. Armed robbery and extortion were traditional practices during times of economic downturn and a criminal component evolved within some of the Triads. This carried over to some extent to the Tong Societies who appeared outside of China on the North American continent during the late nineteenth century. One of the earliest Tong societies was the Hong Shun Tong or Hongmen Society appearing in San Francisco and Barkerville, Canada, and in British Columbia.

That the Tongs had a propensity for violence might be exemplified in what historians call the Weaverville Tong War of 1854. Accounts vary, but what is known is that two opposing groups of Chinese miners quarreled over mining rights leaving 26 dead and 60 wounded. Members of the Sanyi, Siyi and Nigyung Associations fought against the Yanghe Association and both groups were cheered on by the white miners. Two years later the Sanyi battled the Kejoa, again over mining rights, at Chinese Camp. There only four died. But the nature of disparate Asian associations to go to war over sometimes trivial matters of commerce or philosophy became common knowledge to nineteenth century white Americans (informed by their newspapers) who then characterized the groups as "Tongs" and their conflicts as "Tong Wars."

Mei Lim's fate, had she been sent to the Queen's Chamber would have been to stand stripped naked as prospective buyers pinched and probed her and, for some strange reason, inspected her teeth as if she were a horse. She would most likely have been sold into the cribs. The cribs were small rooms whose doorways, covered with steel mesh opened onto the alleys in the worse parts of Chinatown. In these rooms there was a chair of rotting bamboo, a table with a wash basin and a hard bunk affixed to the wall like a shelf and covered by thin matting.

The girls who occupied these cribs were of the lowest class of prostitutes and attracted sailors, drunken laborers, low class Chinese men and teenage boys who could barely afford the 25 to 50 cents they were charged. The owners of the cribs cared little to oversee the aberrant and often violent behavior of the crib girls' clients. A girl's life expectancy in the cribs was about four years.

Having been selected by Madame Ah Toy for "upstairs work" Mei Lim was expecting to be visited only by prominent and wealthy Chinese men—a good prospect as she hated the vile, arrogant whites who treated her as if she were an animal. She was dismayed to learn that the railroad men coming for this evening's entertainment were white—important, wealthy, but still white. It would be of no use to plead with Madame Ah Toy to be relieved of this duty; in fact, it would be inviting peril to disobey her new mistress.

Upstairs Mei Lim was turned over to an older Chinese woman named Xin Ye. Xin Ye had been retired from active prostitution at the ancient age of twenty only two years ago. Her duties now were the training and upkeep of the younger, high-class girls. She immediately took Mei Lim under her wing and would prove to be a warm and caring mentor for the girl in sharp contrast to the cold and indifferent Ah Toy. Xin Ye saw to it that Mei Lim was bathed, dressed in elegant silk, her hair arranged and held in place by ivory pins, her body perfumed, her cheeks whitened with rice powder and her lips reddened with cosmetic paint.

Six Daughters of Joy sat on velvet-covered arm chairs in the salon's upstairs waiting room. Several men roamed the carpeted floor, drinks in hand, examining the fair Lotus Flowers (as Ah Toy called her girls) that adorned the room. One by one the men paired off with a girl and slipped away through curtained doorways to private chambers along a dimly lit hallway. Mei Lim found herself in conjugal quarters with a stocky middle-aged man with a balding pate who puffed and wheezed as if the short journey down the hallway had been akin to climbing a steep hillside.

The man collapsed into a chair. Mei Lim sat on the cot that served as a bed. She studied her new client: well-dressed in tweed with a gold watch chain dangling from a vest-pocket, well-trimmed moustache but no other facial hair, a ruddy complexion (his noisy breathing had subsided now) and a soft smile and pair of gray-green eyes that shown with a kindly regard.

"What can Mei Lim do for gentleman?" she asked, having prepared herself mentally for just about any exigency that might occur.

"Mei Lim...I like that. Very pretty name. Well, Mei Lim, you can call me Mr. M. That's all you need to know right now. And to answer your question, for the time being, if you'll just sit there where you are, everything will be very delightful."

"I don't understand. Doesn't Mr. M want..."

"No, no, my dear girl. I would just like to sit and talk to you for a while. You see, I need someone who can listen. Is that satisfactory?"

"Oh yes...Mei Lim very good at listen."

That was Mei Lim's first meeting with Mr. M. She had found her very own Gold Mountain in the mysteriously polite, undemanding and soft-spoken man. Mr. M paid extra for Mei Lim's exclusive attentions, a situation which pleased Ah Toy nearly as much as it did Mei Lim. During the next month Mr. M came to see Mei Lim three times a week, always arriving at eight PM and leaving before midnight. Always only engaging in talk.

At first Mr. M's conversations with Mei Lim were soliloquies, fraught with vague desperation but containing meager information with which Mei Lim could decipher the man's angst. She learned he was a successful financier, family man, major stockholder in the new railroad which was being built to span the continent, well-liked by his peers and trusted by his wife—nothing indicating remorse or fearfulness. But a timbre of self-loathing accompanied each syllable, a tinge of guilt colored every word. What was this man's secret which he so ardently concealed but so obvious needed to reveal?

She began to interact, raising questions but being careful not to probe too deeply. This led her to no conclusions at all. She conferred with Xin Ye who cautioned her to refrain from intimacy with clients of any kind other than the physical. She recognized the danger and was grateful for Xin Ye's insights. But she realized she was worried about this man; indeed, she *cared* for him.

Then one evening, as Mei Lim sat cross-legged on the cot listening as Mr. M began to relate his day's activities, a trip to Woodward's Gardens with the children to see the exotic animals and stroll the winding paths, he suddenly stopped in midsentence. He face became a mask of dread. Moments later a slight flush of pink chased away the pallor, a weak smile unfurled his tightly pursed lips and the once familiar sparkle again appeared in his eyes.

"I'm sorry, my dear. What was I saying?"

"You were telling me about the fishes in the aquarium."

"Oh yes. We walked down a dark passageway built to look like a cave, with stalactites hanging from the ceiling—very authentic. Then we came to the tanks which have walls of glass at the level of the passageway. We came eyeball to eyeball with all manner of swimming things: sunfish, marlins, octopi, jellyfish, sharks, swordfish…"

Mr. M had frozen again, the gray cast to his cheeks had returned. He stared vacantly at Mei Lim who could now no longer contain her composure. She sprang from the cot.

"Mr. M! Tell me… tell me about the fish. What is it about the fish?" Her hands rose up to cradle his face.

Mr. M pulled away sharply from the girl's touch. He seemed to recover some degree of constancy. He lowered his eyes, drooped his chin nearly to his chest. Mei Lim again clutched his face between her hands, raised it.

"Tell me," she said again.

"The lady's name was…never mind that. Suffice it to say that she was other than my devoted wife. She was the most beautiful and delicate flower that ever bloomed."

"You were married, though?"

"Yes. It was an indiscretion—no, much more than that. It was a love that I had never imagined could exist. My wife…she and I were good companions. Even during that time we were more than civil to each other."

"Did she know?"

"I don't think she knew. Maybe she suspected. It was of short duration."

"What happened to her, your girl like a flower?"

"I…we…one day we went to the docks and rented a small sailboat. It was sunny and mild that day with infrequent gusts of wind that yet blew our little boat far up the bay. We had dropped the sail to float and picnic and enjoy our time together—time we had to steal whenever we could manage. She was becoming everything to me. I was contemplating leaving my wife and children for her. Running away to somewhere we could have a life together without shame. I told her this."

"What did she say?"

"She laughed. Not a joyful laugh. One of ridicule. I was not the love of her life, she told me. There was another. She liked me, liked the things I did for her, bought for her. But never could she spend her life with me the way I envisioned it. Then she told me I was fat, ugly, and it was just a good thing I was rich."

"How awful. Were you very hurt?"

"I was angry. Hurt, yes. But furious at her deception. She loved another! Oh, it was impossible to endure. I shook her. I would have struck her but she backed away from me and fell over the side of the boat. At that moment I lost my anger and feared for her safety but my heart began beating so hard I was forced to collapse onto the deck.

"It was some moments before I could catch my breath and stand to look over the rail into the dark water where she had disappeared— hoping to see her swimming back to the boat. Hoping even to see her struggling in the water, her dress soaked, her hair unraveled—but alive and making her way to my outstretched arms. There was nothing. Not a ripple on the black water to mark her passing. It was hopeless for, you see, I cannot swim and would not have been able to jump valiantly into the bay and pluck her from that tragic fate."

Mei Lim was stunned. She held him and began to sob. She had broken a cardinal rule of her profession: she had become involved with a client. However much tragedy and sorrow she had experienced in her short years as a Daughter of Joy, she had not been prepared for such pathos as now assailed her. She could not disengage her own feelings, her empathy for this wretched, suffering man.

Things were about to change dramatically for Mei Lim. Mr. M had stopped coming for their evening meetings. She stood night after night at the door of Ah Toy's salon looking up Pike Street toward the Ten How Mue Guy temple but Mr. M's familiar form failed to appear walking down his normal route. Madame Ah Toy was insisting that Mei Lim start taking new clients. Mei Lim stalled. Then a strange silence descended upon the salon. It was unusually deserted even at peek times when Chinese merchants liked to visit or when the few white men allowed upstairs came to drink and carouse. Mei Lim went to Xin Ye.

"This is so strange. Where is everybody? What is happening?" Mei Lim asked.

"Madame is closing the salon," Xin Ye explained. "She is marrying and moving to her country house. The girls will be sold to the highest bidders."

The highest bidders! If only she knew how to contact Mr. M. Perhaps he could be persuaded to buy her contract. But she didn't even know his real name. Two days later Xin Ye came to Mei Lim to tell her that all six upstairs girls had been purchased by a man named Cheng Fu who had been a competitor of Madame Ah Toy's. Cheng Fu was establishing a sort of traveling brothel with which he would visit the various boom towns that had sprung up along the railroad. He would be collecting his merchandise tomorrow. Xin Ye warned Mei Lim against any thoughts she might have of running away. If caught she would be tortured.

Cheng Fu had purchased two second-hand prairie schooners from overlanders who had recently arrived hoping to strike it rich in the gold fields of Northern California. The wagons' red and green paint had long since faded exposing weathered wood stained by mud and alkali dust. The canvas tops, except for a tear or two, were in good condition and the oxen had pastured for several weeks, rejuvenating their already substantial stamina. Cheng loaded supplies into one wagon and piled his regiment of Daughters of Joy into the other, repeating his admonishment against escape. The journey would be exciting and the rewards high, he told them (although none of the girls expected to ever see any part of the rewards).

Each wagon had a bullwhacker walking next to the point team, the second or middle pair of the six oxen, and just behind the lead ox called the Broad. A twenty-foot long whip with a wooden handle and a braided popper allowed the bullwhackers to apply encouragement to any of the team as needed. These were experienced men hired by Cheng Fu through the Sam Yup, one of the Six Companies. Onlookers on the streets of San Francisco may have wondered at the wagons passing out of the city driven by Oriental men wearing pointed, dish-like hats.

The trip from San Francisco to Sacramento was uneventful; although Mei Lim became apprehensive during the brief time they passed through the Second City, remembering her tenure in its underground. The wagons headed toward the Dutch Flats and Donner Lake Road, a preferred route for the crossing of the Sierra Nevada. The road had been built as a temporary wagon trail along the surveyed alignment for the Central Pacific Railroad in order to bring supplies, equipment and men to the construction sites in the mountains. It was smooth with few steep grades and wide enough for wagons to pass going both directions. Now it was used by stagecoach companies who bragged they could travel the 130 miles to Virginia City in only 17 hours.

From the summit the road descended on leveled granite between towering peaks given the name of The Silver Gate by travelers awestruck by the beauty of the vista around and below them. This was the road's steepest incline and Mei Lim and the other woman slid forward inside the tilting wagon. The resulting heap of Daughters of Joy, pressed down and shaken together like grapes in a winemaker's barrel broke into laughter—the first light-heartedness they had felt collectively—ever.

The wagons stopped at Donner Lake. A midday meal was prepared and the Daughters of Joy, their master, Cheng Fu, and four other men including the two bullwhackers ate along the banks of the peaceful lake. Its waters teamed with fish and with the new road being in excellent condition, it was now attracting tourists. There was an Inn on the road at the lake but of course the Chinese were not welcome there.

Just east of the lake was the town of Truckee, named for Chief Tru-ki-zo, the father of Chief Winnemucca and the grandfather of Sarah Winnemucca. The railroad descended from the summit and entered the town of Truckee, then proceeded to follow the valley along the Truckee River. Cheng Fu's route now paralleled the railroad. By the next morning the small wagon train arrived at Reno.

Cheng was disappointed. He had expected a bustling railroad town where he could set up his tents for the girls but there was little activity on the street; it looked dismal and vacant. He struck up a conversation with a white man leaning against a buckboard. The man was dressed too well to be a roustabout or a cowboy.

"The front's way gone now, up almost to Wadsworth," the man told Cheng, referring to the farthest point of construction of the railroad. "I've got faro and twenty-one and a little wheel game all packed and ready to go. Just waitin' for my boyos to wake up and I'm off. Boom town? You want to get out ahead of the front. Go way past Wadsworth to whatever the next town might be and set up there. Wait for 'em to come to you."

Cheng saw to it that the bullwhackers got the oxen watered for there was no telling where they might find anything drinkable out in the desert. As an afterthought he let the girls have a quick breakfast.

The wagons rolled off up the road to outdistance the construction crews and soon the only thing ahead of Cheng's wagons was a dust cloud kicked up by the gambler's buckboard. The next town past Wadsworth was Winnemucca. The gambler reached Winnemucca first, Cheng arrived a few hours later and started looking for a logical spot to pitch his tents. The girls, happy to escape from the close quarters of the wagon, sat side by side on the boardwalk like a row of China dolls waiting for a child's playful antics.

James Harvey Strobridge and five rugged, dust-covered, mean-spirited railroad men rode into town just as the gambler and his companions finished attaching a wooden sign to their tent advertising the games of chance they offered. Strobridge fumed. He rode up to the gambler's tent and accosted the man with dire threats concerning his fate should he decide not to hightail it out of town. The gambler, undaunted by Strobridge, reached into the pocket of his silk vest and extracted a small derringer pistol. This he cocked and aimed at Strobridge saying, "Like Hell we will!"

Cheng Fu, observing the confrontation taking place nearby hurried to collect the girls and usher them back into the wagon. Just then a shot rang out. The girls jumped up and scattered in all directions. Another shot and another, and pandemonium was reigning in the streets of Winnemucca.

When Strobridge's men had seen the gambler threaten their boss with a pistol they had all drawn their own weapons. The gambler's companions, two well-seasoned veterans (not only of the Civil War but of what the dime novels called the "Wild West") also drew their guns, army-issued Colts. Horses snorted and stomped hooves against the dirt. Eyes were locked in arrogant stares.

The stand-off didn't last long. One of Strobridge's men squeezed off a shot, whether by accident or by design, non-the-less effective in precipitating a sortie. Two more guns roared.

The gambler was outnumbered and at a disadvantage since Strobridge and his men were mounted on horses. He saw the wisdom of a quick surrender and did so, but not before one man had slumped over on his horse, blood gushing from a chest wound. This, thought the gambler, is not worth dying for.

Noticing the Chinese women running helter-skelter through the streets, some of Strobrodge's men began a somewhat dubious pursuit. They dismounted and ran after the one or two that hadn't disappeared into alleys or under wagons or behind the ramshackle sheds around back of main street.

Mei Lim ran down an alley. In the alley was a buckboard on which sat an Indian woman. Mei Lim could hear the sound of someone running down the street after her. Without hesitation she climbed into wagon and crawled under a blanket, her heart pounding and her breathing coming in short gasps. She tried to lie quietly, to control her breathing, yet she was certain her pursuers would hear the loud lub-dubbing of her heart.

After a time, when nothing had occurred, Mei Lim found the courage to peek out from under the blanket. No one was in the alley, only the Indian woman who now said something to her in a strange language. Mei Lim started to talk excitedly but neither woman could comprehend what the other was saying. Then the Indian woman tried English.

"Calm down. You are safe now. Tell me what happened," said the Indian woman.

"The railroad men come. Chase us away. Gambler man shoot at them. Not good idea, I think. Some people hurt. I run away. Hide here. That's all."

"I think I understand. Don't worry. I won't let them get at you. My name is Sarah. I'm on my way to Fort McDermitt where we are protected. What's your name?"

"My name Mei Lim. I come with you?"

"Mei Lim, of course you can."

15

Winter's Displeasures

Near the end of November a light dusting of powdery snow gave brilliance to the desert's blankness as the morning's red-eyed sun peeked over the horizon. During the shortened days a persistent chill penetrated even the fine weave of quilted Chinese jackets. Evening's errant coyotes sang a dolorous anthem of regret for the coming of winter, for the impending hibernation of hares and pack rats.

The railroad's progress would now be slowed by the cold. Snowdrifts in the Sierra Nevada would impede the supply trains. Soon the thin tents of the Chinese would be sparse protection against howling winds. The Celestials would build shacks of discarded wood or dig into the sides of hills for shelter.

In December the earth froze. Grading crews resorted to black powder to blast away dirt hard as granite. Frostbite was common. Fong Dun Shung kept busy applying salves and ointments and dispensing evil tasting teas made from herbs designed to battle colds and flu. Hu Qiang came down with fever, a serious situation since Hu was the cook for their work gang. Consequently, Zack and Tommy were given the task of preparing meals. As Hu Qiang had been reluctant to share his culinary secrets with the boys, the results of their cooking were less than appetizing in appearance, and sometimes tasted both scorched and raw simultaneously.

Hanna Maria Strobridge had long since moved her canary and houseplants into the railcar residence. In the close quarters her husband's ranting was inescapable. She was privy to every indignant harangue James Harvey Strobridge could summon when workers laying rails or pounding spikes proceeded at an inferior pace to his grand expectations. The children still played outside but Hanna Maria would soon limit their exposure to the winter's potentially dangerous temperatures.

Patty Farrell, the foreman, continued to harass Lee Shao and Fong Dun Shung. For some untold reason he had taken an extreme dislike to these two men. Fong would often be administering to a sick laborer and his absence from the work site seemed to hike Farrell's rancor. One day he ordered Fong to leave the tent of the ailing Hu Qiang and join the rest of the crew. Fong refused. Farrell began to beat the herbalist with a leather strap he carried for just such an occasion.

This altercation was observed by another white man who, once he recognized the mistreated Chinese man as Fong Dun Shung, rushed to prevent further calamity. George Calvin, the man wounded at Winnemucca and who Fong had nursed back to health, latched onto Farrell's shoulder and swung him around.

"Hold on there," Calvin cried. "Stop this beating or you'll receive a good measure of it to your own self!"

"Stay out of this, Calvin," Farrell said, pulling at Calvin's hand, still clamped tightly on his shoulder. "It's none of your business."

" 'Tis me business. This man is under my protection from this day on and you'd better understand that. Would you like to be taking it up with Mr. Strobridge, then?"

Farrell growled and grimaced and, once released from Calvin's grip, turned on his heel and slunk away like a wounded dog. In his own mind, however, Farrell hadn't groveled; he was merely backing off to wait for another time when he could repay both that yellow bastard and his champion.

The evening chores were finished and the boys sat in the dugout hillside they now occupied. The wind whistled past the enclosure and sent the canvas door flapping and their single candle flickering. Tommy was restless and mulling an idea over in his mind. He looked Zack up and down, a long, hard look as if he were a tailor sizing him up for a new suit of clothes. "You are my best friend," he told Zack.

"Yes, of course. We are like brothers, are we not?"

"Zack, I am thinking. We have been at this a long time…this quest to find your father and his family."

"You would like to go home?"

"I'm not saying that. Only, it's…cold! Maybe…maybe there's a better way to get to El-Ya-Noy. Maybe the boat was a better idea."

"You may be right. But here we are. We can't go back now."

"We could. We could get on the supply train that goes back to pick up more rails and things. We're owed some money for the work we do. It would be enough to pay for passage on a boat. At least I think so."

"It still seems like the long way around to me. If you are getting fainthearted and want to quit…"

"No, don't say that. I'll stick with you, of course. I'm with you through to the end. Whenever that will be."

"I wouldn't blame you if you went back." Zack slumped back onto his bedroll. He was troubled. Deep down he felt Tommy was right: this was a foolish quest and although Tommy hadn't said it out loud, Zack could tell he was thinking it. His hand found the watch he kept in his pocket. Somehow the feel of it gave him confidence at moments like this one when doubt darkened the threshold of his emotions. Could he even consider continuing if Tommy wasn't alongside of him?

By January, under One-Eyed-Bossy-Man's constant prodding, the Central Pacific was averaging almost one mile per day. They had reached the basin of the Great Salt Lake and to their east, the Union Pacific, proceeding with less vehemence, was only just emerging from the mountains. The competition between the two companies was about to intensify, each desiring to log greater mileage than the other and therefore to reap the financial benefits of government grants.

Hu Qiang had recovered sufficiently to return to his post as cook, to the great relief of most of the work gang. Zack and Tommy were reassigned by Patty Farrell to help with the grading at the front, now many miles beyond the new railroad town of Elko where the Chinese camp was still situated.

Elko had been founded on the site of a Shoshone Indian settlement called Natakkoa, or "Rocks Piled on One Another." Naming the new towns was an honor reserved for officials of the railroad. In this case, Superintendent Charles Crocker had named Elko after one of his favorite animals, the elk, and then added the "o" just to make it unique. In the future, when her husband supervised the Southern Pacific route, Hanna Maria Strobridge would name towns after her favorite literary figures such as Emerson, Dryden and Longfellow.

As the grading gang blasted, dug, carried away debris and flattened the road bed, the rail laying gang followed in their wake. Ties went down, carefully measured from the survey string. Rails were laid and straightened, then spikes were driven to the tune of clanking hammers. Occasionally a miss-swung hammer sent up sparks eliciting sharp curses from the foremen.

The supply train, positioned close to the end of the finished track had been unloaded. Zack looked up from the wheelbarrow he was pushing to see Tommy standing alongside of the empty flatcar—standing motionless as if transfixed by something. Zack returned to his work hauling excavated earth. The engine was puffing great white clouds of vaporous smoke and seemed to be straining its wheels against the newly-laid rails. A whistle blew; the engine shuttered and slowly inched backwards. As the train began picking up speed on its journey westward, Zack again looked over his shoulder at the spot where he had just seen Tommy. Tommy was gone.

The railroad men fighting the severe cold in Nevada would have been surprised to learn that the temperature in Sitka, Alaska, hovered at 40 degrees in January. Situated in the midst of a temperate rain forest, Sitka's climate was mild and humid. Fishing continued year round and the fish packing plant was one of the busiest enterprises on the island. A young Wintu girl now worked at the plant, cleaning fish and sorting the heads and entrails into one barrel and the cleaned fillets into another. Little Wind was now helping to support her new foster family, an elderly man and woman known as Old Payuk and Mama Takgrook.

Sitka was a divided city comprised of the army fort, the Indian village and the town itself in which the nonnative population endeavored to establish the kind of American frontier town that flourished in other territories. This effort was faltering as the Americans came, looked, and eventually left Alaska, disappointed by its poor economic potential and apparently unmoved by its natural beauty. The town was home to only about 50 Americans and 800 Creoles and Russians. Soldiers numbered 250; Sitka natives numbered 1,250.

Little Wind had washed the blood and mangled fish guts from her hands and returned to the village just as the soldiers were closing the gates of the stockade that isolated the Indians from the rest of Sitka. Mama Takgrook was rocking in an American-made rocking chair, a gift presented to the old couple by General Davis himself in appreciation for Old Payuk's leadership in his community—a leadership due more to veneration for his age than to any political position he held in the tribe.

"Situation is worsening," Mama Takgrook told Little Wind. "Hot head name of Scutdoo is talking about revenge. Could lead to war again."

Little Wind cringed at the thought. What was it about men, she wondered, that every response to injustice resulted in violence? The situation that Mama Takgrook referred to had begun, as usual, with liquor, that most vile gift of the white man to the Indian. A native man named Lowan had been celebrating with whiskey which had been smuggled into the village by white traders. He had stumbled through town making a nuisance of himself, visiting several saloons where he was turned away, as Indians were not allowed in drinking establishments. He had encountered a white woman exiting the bakery with a basket of bread. The woman was the laundress at the army post.

Lowan asked for a piece of bread. When he was refused even a scrap he reached for a loaf but the woman grabbed his arm. In a drunken rage, Lowan clamped his teeth on the woman's hand; she screamed as blood spurted from the stump of her finger the rest of which now dangled from Lowan's mouth.

Soldiers pursued Lowan who had fled up the Indian River and was making for the dense forest. They overtook him at a narrow bend where willows dipped their branches into the rush of crystal clear water—water that would wash away the crimson plumes that spread from his bullet-riddled body as it rolled in the torrent. The death, not being equal to a mere dismemberment, angered many of the Sitkan Indians. Retribution was called for.

One evening some weeks later, Scutdoo, the man Mama Takgrook had called a hot head, knocked at the door asking for Old Payuk. Little Wind, curled up in her sleeping loft above the main room was awakened by voices: Old Payuk and another man were talking loudly and rapidly in Tlingit. Mama Takgrook then entered the discussion. Little Wind had yet to learn enough Tlingit to follow what was being said but the next day Mama Takgrook spoke to her about what "hot head" had done.

Scutdoo had snuck into the fort and killed the post's trader in retaliation for the murder of Lowan. He wanted Old Payuk to hide him, but Mama Takgrook had intervened, telling him to be gone from their house by morning. Now it was morning but Scutdoo remained cowering in a corner of the room wrapped in a decorated blanket for which Mama Takgrook had traded many fish. Mama Takgrook was not pleased.

Little Wind watched Scutdoo's expression as Mama Takgrook began to badger the man in an effort to expel him from the house. She couldn't help feeling sympathy for this poor, frightened soul who was obviously as mortified about the taking of another man's life as he was about the doom he himself might soon face. Old Payuk had taken Scutdoo's side in the matter of sanctuary but was beginning to see the logic of Mama Takgrook's argument: did he want their village burned to the ground because of this fool, she asked?

The following days brought a resolution to the problem of Scutdoo's evasion of the white man's justice. General Davis had learned that someone in the village was harboring the fugitive. He made it known that he was prepared to shell the Indian village using the large artillery piece already aimed directly at them. Village elders met. It was with great sadness that Scutdoo was turned over to the soldiers. There was a trial. Scutdoo was found guilty and two days later was hanged.

Little Wind stood on the waterfront where the Indian River emptied to the bay. Sea birds squawked and circled around the boats of fishermen venturing out against the early morning's fog. The pungent smell of ocean life mingled with the acrid odor of steamboat fumes as several oceangoing vessels got fires stoked and boilers boiling. At least one of the five ships moored in the bay was a Navy man-of-war; the rest were traders being loaded with barrels of fish, seal oil and furs.

Water slurped and slashed at the pilings. Little Wind thought about her conversation with Mama Takgrook earlier that morning:

"Something is troubling you child. What is it?" the old woman had said, rocking in her chair and poking a needle through a tanned sheet of moose hide, soon to become one of a pair of mukluks she would sell at the trading post.

"I'm a little sad. I was thinking about my mother, so faraway. I worry about her." Little Wind crouched on the floor next to Mama Takgrook, watching the needle punching through the hide.

"What you have told me of California makes me also worry. Your whites are opposed to your people."

"It's because of the gold. Here you have no gold so the whites don't take your land away, kill you for it. But that man...Scutdoo...they took him and..."

"The whites have their idea of law. It is fair, although it sometimes seems crazy. If they knew Scutdoo had killed that man, why they had to talk about it for days, I certainly don't know!" Mama Takgrook stopped sewing, her attention now turned to the girl.

"I do think they are all crazy. But I have white blood in my veins. I worry I am crazy too," Little Wind told her.

"Ah sweet child, you are perfect girl. So good to work in fish packing place. So kind to be concerned about hot head like Scutdoo. And by the way, there *is* gold here. We do not tell the whites or let them look for it. It should remain in the ground for that is the way of our fathers."

"Now I *am* worried for you."

A flat-bottomed skiff was tied to the pilings near where Little Wind stood dreamily gazing out toward the big ships. A young man, a boy really, struggled with a bundle of sea lion hides and nearly tumbled into the bay for his efforts. Little Wind laughed.

"What's so funny," growled the boy.

"You are. Want me to help you with that burden?"

"Heck no. I don't need no help. You just watch."

Spurned on by male pride the lad deftly lifted the hides above his head, teetered, dropped the hides which hit the side of the boat, balanced for a second, then slid into the water as if the spirits of the dead sea lions were calling them back to their ocean home.

"Oh Gawd, no!" said the boy. "They'll skin me alive for this."

"Here, we can get it," Little Wind offered. They reached down, finding the water quite shallow and grabbed onto the bundle of hides. Tugging and pulling they managed to drag the soaking bundle up on shore.

"There now, that's not so bad, is it? What's your name?"

"Freddie. Freddie Barton, ordinary seaman of the schooner Luella, out of Victoria. Headed for San Francisco. And who are you? You a native?"

"I am called Little Wind. I'm not Tlingit. I'm of the Wintu, from California."

"What are you doing up here?"

"I was traveling. With a photographer. I stayed behind to live with these people. But now…"

"Now I have to get these hides on board. Can you give me a hand again?"

Little Wind and Freddie Barton tumbled the bundle of sea lion hides into the skiff. Freddie jumped into the boat and was about to shove off when he felt the boat rock. Looking around he saw that Little Wind had jumped into the boat right behind him.

"You're going to San Francisco? I'm coming with you," said Little Wind.

★ ★ ★

Camp McDermitt was established in 1865 by Lieutenant Colonel Charles McDermitt, commander of the Nevada Territory Military District. Its purpose was to protect travelers along the stagecoach routes between Boise and Virginia City from Indian attacks and to further protect the local Indians from retaliatory actions by white settlers. A majority of the troops stationed at the camp were from Troop M of the Eighth Cavalry under the command of a Colonel McElroy. They had enlisted two years ago at Angel Island in California where they had previously been engaged in gold mining activities during the gold rush of the 1850s. They were a rough, adventure-seeking bunch who had little affinity toward military discipline but relished frontier life. And they didn't particularly like Indians.

The camp, originally called the Quinn River Station, had been located on the ancestral lands of the Atsa-Kudok-Wa, a nomadic Northern Paiute tribe. Lt. Col. McDermitt was killed that same year in an ambush by either the Paiutes or the Shoshone, although no documentation of that event exists. The camp was renamed Fort McDermitt in honor of its fallen commander.

The fort had a large rectangular parade grounds around which adobe and stone buildings had been erected including officers' quarters, barracks, a hospital, stables and storehouses. Indians came to stay next to the fort and by the time that Sarah Winnemucca had come to live there, close to 500 Paiutes had established their camp under the protection of the army. Heads of families were given blankets, an army issue tent and daily rations of a pound and a half of meat and freshly baked bread. Sarah helped to distribute the food keeping a record of monthly allowances of beans, rice, coffee, sugar and salt and pepper.

Colonel McElroy had come to depend on Sarah. She had been made interpreter to the Shoshone peoples who also lived by the fort. The colonel had given her wagons with which to transport as many Paiutes as she could back to the fort for protection. That first year of the arrival of the Pauite people to Fort McDermitt Sarah had gone to the colonel with a request:

"Colonel, I am here all alone with so many men, I am afraid. I want your protection. I want you to protect me against your soldiers, and I want you to protect my people also."

"I will do my best, good woman," replied Colonel McELroy.

"I want you to give your orders to your soldiers not to go to my people's camp at any time, and also issue the same order to the citizens."

"The men will obey my commands, though I cannot guarantee the behavior of the settlers."

Orders were given and the soldiers obeyed them having little interest in the daily lives of the Indians. But one night a civilian by the name of Joe Lindsay, having drunk too much whiskey, came into the Indian camp looking for female companionship. He tried to enter one of the tents but was observed by some of the Paiute men who promptly chased him away. They reported his behavior the next day to the post commander and Lindsay was arrested and thrown into the guardhouse for the night. He was released the next day on the condition that he leave Fort McDermitt and not return.

Now it was February of 1869. Sarah and Mei Lim had come to the post trading store to look at bolts of cloth. Three white men were present. They were clearly not soldiers for their garments were not the dark blue of the army uniform, but dirty, ragged wool shirts and trousers of battered buckskin worn thin at the knees. They laughed and joked, making fun of the Indians in the store. These were only Sarah, Mei Lim (who they mistook for an Indian), and a Paiute man who was examining a bowie knife in a case at the front of the store.

The Paiute man spoke no English and so got none of the gist of the white men's crude comments. Sarah and Mei Lim were disgusted by the intolerant and rude manner of the traders. Sarah became alarmed when one of the white men was addressed as "Lindsay." Was this the Joe Lindsay who had been ordered away from the fort? Then Lindsay said something that made Sarah very afraid:

"I wonder if that there redskin is the one that turned me in. Whadda ya think?"

"Well Joe, I think he's a *good* injun. You know what they say about good injuns," said another of the white men.

"Yup, I shore do. Only good injun's a *dead* injun. Say, think I could shoot his eye out? I'll bet whiskey for the crowd I can."

"I'll take that bet," said another man.

Lindsay raised his pistol and fired, hitting the Indian just below the right eye.

"Damn!" said Lindsay. With a cool disregard for the human life he had just snuffed out, Lindsay took a knife and scalped the dead Paiute. Mei Lim and Sarah Winnemucca looked on in horror as Lindsay put the bloody scalp into his pocket and fled out the door. The other two men dragged the dead Pauite outside by his feet leaving a trail of gore behind them. They threw the body into a wagon and drove away thinking to hide it, but drops of blood left a path on the fresh new snow.

Soldiers apprehended Joe Lindsay in a bar in Winnemucca where he was attempting to pay for drinks with the Pauite scalp. This was good because Sarah had been unable to quiet the war talk of the men of her camp. However, army justice was once again a watered-down elixir that cured none of the tribe's anger and outrage as Lindsay and his friends were merely ordered out of the territory of Nevada under penalty of trial and imprisonment. At least the soldiers had torn down the men's cabin so that they could not stay. Destroying property was something the Armed Forces were good at.

Sarah and her younger brother, who was called Nevada, set out to follow the blood trail and retrieve the body of the murdered man. Mei Lim begged to accompany them, feeling a sense of duty stemming from the witnessing of the death and having a curiosity about the burial customs of the Indians. They found the body where it had been unceremoniously dumped along the side of the road.

Nevada and Sarah talked quietly in their own language as the wagon carrying the body of the scalped man slogged through slushy melting snow on its way back to the camp. The ground was still frozen or the wagon would have stuck in muck that the horses would have been unable to negotiate.

"I hope," said Sarah, "that we won't find that the men have gone to war when we get back."

"Don't worry, Sister. You know they would wait for me as war chief to lead them."

"You think very large of yourself, Nevada. But you are probably right. Fools need a bigger fool to lead them." Switching to English, Sarah addressed Mei Lim who was sitting wrapped in a blanket next to the corpse:

"I thank you for the respect you show to our dead, Little Sister."

"You have been so kind to me," Mei Lim answered, "allowing me to stay in your village as if I were one of you. Of course I want to help. But tell me, why do you trust the soldiers? They don't like you very much even though they do give you food and shelter."

"My father once said, 'these white people must be a great nation as they have houses that move. Yet you fear we will suffer by their coming to our country for they do not seem to think as we do. Yet maybe you are wrong—I am sure they have minds like us and do think as we do.'

"And he went on to say, 'I think they knew they were doing wrong when they set fire to our winter supplies. They think we are savages, without morals.' This made me realize that neither side, we, the inheritor of the land nor they, the invader, was always right or always wrong. That if we could just talk…'"

"While you talk to the Big Brother Soldier at the fort the Great White Father in Washington sends more men with more rifles to sweep across our land and litter their path with the blood and bones of our warriors and the tears of our women," said Nevada giving his own answer to his sister's plea for mutual understanding between the races. Then to Mei Lim he said:

"You must know about abuse at the hands of the white men. Certainly you came to us fearful of the 'Owl People,' with their white faces that lie and enslave."

"It wasn't the whites who abused me," answered Mei Lim. "It was my own people."

At a crossroads they came to a stagecoach station. They stopped to let the horse rest and obtain fresh water. As they sat in the wagon a man rode up on horseback: a Chinese man dressed in European clothing but wearing a red bandana tied around his forehead. He looked into the wagon at the corpse and then his eyes fell upon Mei Lim. He yelled something at her in Mandarin but Mei Lim didn't fully understand the dialect he used. Sarah questioned the man in English:

"What do you want? Who are you?" she asked.

The man ignored Sarah and reached to grab Mei Lim by the arm. He pulled back the sleeve of her jacket, exposing the red tattoo on her arm. "Ha!" he exclaimed.

"What is it? What does he want?" Sarah asked Mei Lim. Mei Lim ventured a few words of the Chinese dialect more common to her old home in Guangdong province. After a brief exchange in which several words where repeated and some gestures substituted for dialog, Mei Lim was sure she now understood the situation.

"This man," she explained in English, "is called Lu Zan Zhong. He is Hip-Yee Tong soldier seeking those girls who are missing from Cheng Fu's caravan. The mark on my arm identifies me as one of Cheng Fu's concubines. He wants to take me with him back to San Francisco."

"We won't let that happen, Mei Lim," said Sarah. She gave her brother a stern look as if to say "Do something!"

Nevada leaped from the wagon knocking Lu Zan Zhong to the ground. Mei Lim gasped. The two men rolled and tumbled in the snow, neither gaining much of an advantage over the other. Lu Zan Zhong's hand went to his belt where a long ugly knife hung in a red and gold scabbard. He pulled the knife and slashed at Nevada, cutting a gash across his forearm. Nevada had his own knife out and quickly plunged it into the Asian's belly. Blood spurted staining the snow scarlet.

The fight was over but now a possible destiny of fatal circumstances hovered over Mei Lim: the death of the Tong soldier would precipitate a more intense search for her by other members of the Tong. This would no longer be just about a financial debt; it would be one of blood vengeance.

"Hide the body," Mei Lim said to Sarah Winnemucca. She gave the older woman a lingering, remorseful look, then jumped from the wagon. She mounted the horse that had belonged to the Tong soldier, kicked her heels against its sides and rode away, tears in her eyes but with the certain knowledge that her presence at the Indian camp would mean more violence and death for her friends.

16

Tong War!

March 15, 1869. Jordan Chariton for the Daily Alta:

On the dry flats of the Utah desert this Monday morning two factions of Chinese met in heated battle. The See Yup and the Yung Wo are at it again! Bitter political rivals from the old country, these two clans seem to take almost any excuse to get into an altercation—our older readers will no doubt remember the Weaverville Tong war of 1854 which was started by a mere insult. This time, it seems, the fracas was precipitated over a young girl whose guardianship was claimed by both parties.

My sources within the Central Pacific Railroad's Chinese labor community further tell me that the girl was escaping from indentured servitude to one of the San Francisco Tongs. The Tong men had been run off by Superintendent James Strobridge and his guards, several stout Irish fellows who safeguard the workers' camp and by no means indulge any monkey business from outside influences.

The See Yup and the Yung Wo both wanted to take care of the girl—ah, these noble Celestials cherish their woman folk so greatly—or maybe there were another, not so chivalrous reason? An argument ensued and soon grew heated and in no time several hundred workers faced off in what might have been a "Chinese standoff" had not the leaders of the two groups given a signal to advance.

Both parties sailed in, armed with every conceivable weapon. Spades and crowbars, spikes, picks, and infernal machines were hurled between the ranks of the contestants. Then shots rang out and a Yung Wo man fell to the ground mortally wounded. Strobridge and his men arrived to quell the brouhaha and an order of a sort was restored. Cuts and bruises and a few broken bones were seen to. The young girl? Apparently she has settled in with some people from her old province, members of neither of the two groups who fought so diligently in her defense.

Fong Dun Shung had his hands full applying ointments, bandaging abrasions, setting bones. He was one of several Chinese herbalists helping the railroad's doctor to treat the wounded men. Hanna Maria Strobridge was also on the scene lending a hand. She carried a basin of cool water and a rag with which she mopped brows and cleaned dried blood from the barely conscious and the delirious. She moved from bedroll to bedroll inside the large tent which had been converted from a dining hall into a makeshift hospital. Zack Grosh lay on one of the bedrolls.

Zack felt the cool rag on his forehead. He ached all over and his head felt like a watermelon split open with its sugary juices dribbling out. He tried to focus his eyes but the tent was spinning too fast for him to fix on any particular object. His lids lowered; a galaxy of sparkling points of light spun around him as he sank deeper into darkness and blessed oblivion.

When he woke the sound of muffled voices was barely discernable against the ringing in his ears. The tent no longer rotated and two tall shapes, although blurred, resolved into human forms which seemed to bend over him like vultures picking at carrion. I have died, he thought. My flesh will rot and my bones bleach under this horrible burning sun.

The brightness scorching his vision emanated from an oil lamp held high by Fong Dun Shung. The herbalist leaned closer to Zack's face and sniffed.

"He wakes. Breath has hopeful odor of recovery. Give water with pinch of ginseng."

Zack lapsed into insensibility. He would sleep deeply without dreaming, a silent, timeless slumber that mimicked the peacefulness of death. He would wake with little memory of trauma or strife. He would wake with renewed acuity—the power to form those spots of light and dark into a vision of sparkly eyes, smiling lips, ebony tresses framing an enduring semblance—I know that face, he thought. I know who that is.

"Mei Lim!" he said, struggling to rise but collapsing in weakness and disorientation.

"No, lad, it is only I, Mrs. Strobridge. Rest now. Try to rest." Hanna Maria plunged the rag into the basin and rung it out. Water dripped like a miniature waterfall into the basin. She laid the wet rag over Zack's forehead and gently stroked his cheek. "Rest now," she repeated.

When he woke again the railroad's doctor was holding Zack's wrist and studying his watch. "Much improved," the doctor clucked like a mother hen among her chicks. "Very good. You'll be up and around in no time."

Zack was ready to be up and around immediately if he had anything to say about it, which, apparently, he didn't. Another figure entered his field of vision: Mrs. Strobridge, armed with a bowl of soup and a long-handled spoon. "Here now, how would we like a little nourishment?" she said. It was not a question.

Zack began to remember. With each sip of chicken soup came another snippet of the recent past. The rumors about a runaway Joy Daughter hiding out in the camp. How he searched for days, asking with the few Chinese words he knew but getting only blank looks, nervous shakes of the head, angry snubs. The arrival of riders: three Chinese men armed with daggers and swords, lacking only the medieval costumes of Mongol warriors to place them in another time and place. The fear these riders instilled in the camp as they moved through it, entering tents and shacks.

Zack had run to Lee Shao, desperate for information. Who are they? Why are they here? Do you know of a girl? He spit out questions in rapid succession. Lee Shao let the flood subside before answering.

"I can tell you this: we are in danger from these men and from what they may instigate," said Lee. "These men are from a tong that punishes for profit. This girl, whoever she is, is being sought. She hides here. But if they find her…"

"What will they do?"

"They may only return her to her owner…or…they may torture her and eventually kill her. Not to mention those that are aiding her in her escape! This is what I fear most of all."

"What can I…we do? We must help her!"

"You know this girl?"

"I don't know. I think…I hope it is not the one I know, but all the same it is not right she should suffer."

"I tell you what. We go to see One-Eyed-Bossy-Man."

Strobridge's men dismounted and moved cautiously through the Chinese camp. Three horses were tethered to the side of an abandoned wagon near a cluster of tents. Seeing the men approach, the horses began to shuffle and whinny. The flap of a tent flew open and the Tong men stood in the entrance appraising the scene: six rugged white men armed with rifles and handguns formed a semicircle blocking the escape route to the horses. The Tong men glanced at each other, seemed to agree on some unspoken stratagem and moved slowly into the open, fanning apart.

Now each Tong man faced only one pair of opponents. Strobrodge's men hesitated, a bit unnerved by the sight of three Celestial warriors so obviously unaffected by the uneven odds or the superior weapons of their enemy. Slowly, confidently, each Tong man reached over his shoulder to grip the handle of the sword that was strapped to his back. The sound of metal pulled along metal and the singing of blades slicing into the dry desert air gave Strobridge's men further cause for alarm.

The three Asian swordsmen each took a stance with their sword, a light, razor-sharp straight sword called a Jian. This they held horizontally above their heads with tip pointing toward their intended victim. With their left arms extended they pointed with two fingers at the white men. It was a frightening sight.

George Calvin, one of the Strobridge guards on this occasion, turned and ran back toward his horse. Before any of his companions could complain about this seemingly cowardly act, he had returned holding his army-issued cavalry saber, a weapon that he had used effectively during the War Between the States. This he pulled from its scabbard with a zinging noise that rivaled that made earlier by the Jians.

"I think this should be adequate against those little pigstickers," Calvin said.

The Tong man closest to Calvin advanced swinging his sword in an arc from overhead, backwards and down, then cutting upward toward Calvin's belly. Calvin reacted quickly, bringing the heavy saber down against the Jian, narrowly escaping being disemboweled. The Tong man used the momentum of the saber's strike to swing his sword back into play, this time arcing upward and around on a direct line toward Calvin's neck. But Calvin brought his own blade up and blocked the blow, ducking at the same time.

The lethal ballet of the two swordsmen continued. The other two Tong men still stood staring down the white men. One of the Strobridge men took aim with his rifle. Instantly both tong men rushed forward, swinging their swords and letting out a yell the likes of which hadn't been heard since the Rebels rallied at the Second

Battle of Bull Run. Even at close range the onrushing targets were difficult to hit and so bullets struck and sprayed festoons of dirt or whizzed through tent canvas like angry bees. One bullet struck home, toppling a Tong man. One blade found its mark, slicing through flesh and nearly taking off the arm of a Strobridge man.

At the end of the skirmish a Tong man lay dead, a Strobridge man was grasping a gushing wound, Calvin had vanquished his dueling partner with a blow on the head with the flat of his blade, and the third Tong man had escaped on his horse. The unconscious Tong and the wounded man were hurried to the doctor's infirmary. It seemed as if the crises had been averted. But there had been spectators; there was a milling and a debate and factions had arisen with opposing views among the Chinese onlookers.

One group was satisfied that the Tong men had been driven off. The Strobrdige men would keep them away. The other group, perhaps having some members with associations to the Tong attackers, wanted to turn the girl over to the Tong. The Tongs most certainly would return, they argued. The argument lasted for most of the next day with men taking sides according to their affiliations with this or that branch of the Six Companies. In the end the See Yup and Yung Wo, the two most militant groups, faced each other with murderous looks.

Ironically, the girl, the object of contention, had been slipping from tent to tent during the confrontation and neither group was aware of her location. Zack also went from tent to tent, intent on finding the missing girl. Could it be Mei Lim, he wondered? He had no reason to believe it was she—no reason, only a faint hope born of loneliness. Since Tommy had left, Zack had no one. The two Chinese men, Lee Shao and Fong Dun Shung were good companions but Zack never felt he could confide his innermost thoughts and emotions to them. He entertained a vague assumption, however, that Mei Lim would understand his doubts and fears and his needs.

Into a tent he popped his head, straining in the dim light for any sign of a hidden girl: a lump of blankets piled too high, a curtain hung against an interior wall with toes of sequined slippers protruding—anything that indicated the presence of a purloined maiden. Maiden? Well, she would always be such to Zack in spite of her past history. For in his eyes she was innocent of the crimes perpetrated against her and her gender. And she needed protecting.

In the next tent Zack found an old woman sitting cross-legged before a low wooden table. A teapot and two cups were in front of her which seemed to suggest that she was not alone. Zack asked if she knew the whereabouts of a young girl: "Niū? Xíngzōng nǔláng?" But the woman only shook her head. Zack tried to remember the word for "friend" and failing, attempted sign language.

"You the boy that speaks the English, are you not?" asked the woman.

"Yes, Grandmother, I do. I want you to know that I am a good friend to the girl."

"How do you know this girl?"

"We traveled together...that is, if it is the same person."

"You have name for girl?"

"Mei Lim," answered Zack, hoping that he had convinced the woman of his utter sincerity. He shuffled his feet unconsciously, as much from his nervousness as from his impatience.

"Sit. Have tea. We talk," said the old woman.

The sound of conflict drifted across the camp reaching the tent where Zack sat sipping green tea from a china bowl. He started to rise but the woman motioned for him to stay seated. She herself rose and peeked through the tent flap.

"Fighting," she explained and sat back in her place calmly lifting her tea bowl to her lips. Then she said, "Girl is hiding. Tong men looking for her."

"But the One-Eyed-Bossy-Man chased them away. It's safe for her to come out now."

"Not so. See Yup men want her now. Fighting. Must wait and see what happens. Must have caution...and much patience. Be like Buddha. Wait quietly."

It was too much to ask of a young boy whose personal gods were nothing like the Buddha. Had he waited as the woman instructed, he might have learned the whereabouts of the girl and if she was, indeed, Mei Lim. But Zack sprinted from the tent out and into the center of the conflict that had erupted between the See Yup and the Yung Wo men. He had no idea even which group was which, nor was he anxious to engage in fisticuffs, yet the battle seemed to him to be the only avenue that might lead to Mei Lim.

He stood motionless for a moment in the midst of a melee in which men swung metal pikes at each other's heads or flung rocks and railroad spikes. Which side knew where she was, he wondered? He edged his way across the battlefield toward a small crowd of spectators who were not as yet engaged in fighting. Perhaps they knew. As he approached someone grabbed him around the waist.

The next thing he knew, Mrs. Strobridge was spooning chicken soup into his mouth.

It had started simply enough. The talk of the workday had been the escaped Daughter of Joy and the attempt by the Hip-Yee Tong to recapture her. With the Tong men defeated there was still the problem of the girl: should they force her out, give her to the Tong men when (not if) they returned, hide her at the risk of retribution, or perhaps terminate her? In the brothels when a girl was no longer attractive and productive she would be locked in a room and given only water—until she died! But that was an extreme solution for which there was little if any avocation.

No, it boiled down to two choices: give her to the Tong or keep her hidden. After an entire day of heated argument the issue was still unsettled. Early Monday morning, before the work crews assembled, there was an assembly of another sort. The See Yup clan and the men of the Yung Wo stood in two long lines exchanging insults. The signal was given and the men ran at each other brandishing whatever makeshift weapon they could find.

Someone ran to tell One-Eyed-Bossy-Man. The white, mostly Irish born laborers who were within ear range heard the shouting and congregated to watch the battle. They cheered and placed bets as the two factions assailed each other brutally. There was a sound of bones cracking as steel bars connected with limbs. There were angry taunts and the cries of men wounded by sharp objects like picks or the edges of shovels. It was a bloody battle, but a short one.

Strobridge's men arrived just about the time that Zack had been pulled into the fray. Rifles were aimed into the air above the heads of the combatants and a volley of reports brought the fighting to a swift halt. But one man lay bleeding from a bullet wound. No one could say exactly how he had been shot; no one would ask for an explanation. All that mattered was that the war was over. No one had won.

"What happened to me?" Zack asked Lee Shao who had come to his bedside for a visit. He had been in the makeshift hospital for three days now. Lee and Fong had come to see him regularly.

"I saw you working your way through the fight. I tried to get to you but you were pulled into a group of men that fought with bare fists. You struggled and threw a few punches yourself. You can take care of yourself pretty well for a youngster."

"Youngster! So I fought back?"

"Well, you tried. Then someone struck you with…I think it was a shovel. Cold-cocked you and you fell. You lay there and were kicked all about. When we finally got to you, you were bleeding and you looked like a train had run over you."

"Well, thank you for helping me. I don't know why I got into that battle. Oh! I was looking for Mei Lim, the girl that was hiding."

"She is not to be found, I have heard. Perhaps she has left the camp."

"Lee, there is an old woman. She lives in one of those tents near the south end of the camp. I believe she knows where Mei Lim is. She may be hiding her, in fact. Could you…?"

"I'll see what I can do. I promise nothing. You also must realize the risk…to her, and to you."

That evening Hanna Maria Strobridge had brought food for the few patients still in the hospital tent. Zack was not the worst of the lot and one or two were still being spoon-fed. Hanna Maria, through her ministrations to the injured and for many other acts of kindness had endeared herself to the Chinese people on the railroad. She was in the tent when Lee Shao arrived accompanied by a young Chinese girl.

"Zack," said Lee, "there is someone here to see you."

Zack had been dozing and lifted his swollen eye lids gingerly. "Mei Lim! I knew it had to be you!"

"Hello, Zack, my friend. How are you feeling?"

"Now I feel wonderful! It is you. I was so worried…"

"You were brave to look for me. I feel awful about the bloodshed…over me!"

"Not entirely over you," said Lee Shao. "Those clans have probably forgotten what started the fight already. They were so intent on killing one another; you were just a good excuse."

"Yes, but I think it is time for me to leave before there is more trouble. I just had to see Zack first."

"Mei Lim," Zack said, reaching for her arm and grasping it. "You can't leave me now that I've found you. You can stay with me. I'll protect you from the See Yups and the Tong men. Please don't think of leaving!"

"No, Zack. It is right for me to go. It is too dangerous for all of you."

Hanna Maria Strobridge had been listening. She set down the tray of food she carried and came to Zack's bedside. "Hello," she said to Mei Lim. "I'm Mrs. Strobridge."

"Hello. I am Mei Lim. I...I shouldn't be here. I'm so sorry."

"Dear girl, I know your story. Word gets around to us more than you might imagine it could. I don't think it is wise for you to venture out into this desert alone with those Tong men lurking about. We can protect you here."

"But the See Yup men..."

"I have a solution, one that I think all of us will like. Your friends will be blameless as far as the See Yup are concerned and the Tongs will not dare come near you. You will come to stay with me in the railcar. There is plenty of room and you can help out with the children."

"Won't One-Eyed-Bossy-Man mind? Oh! I didn't mean..."

"That's alright, child. We know he's called that. He's a good man. He will be happy to be saving you from an evil life, if you see what I mean."

"Mei Lim," said Zack, "please stay with Mrs. Strobridge. At least until we can think of what to do."

Zack recovered from his injuries and returned to working for Hu Qiang, the cook. Mei Lim moved in with the Strobridges and from time to time came to Zack's tent in the early evening hours. She was careful to return to the Strobridge's before it got late and before they became concerned for her safety (and for the sake of propriety). The last thing she wanted to do was to offend these kind people who were providing her with sanctuary. The fact that they intended to also save her from her life of sin was of secondary concern. She was, in fact, enjoying her new role as nanny to the Strobridge children.

The railroad was advancing now faster than ever. The one-mile-a-day rate of laying track had increased, partly because the terrain was more forgiving, and partly because their competitor, the Union Pacific Railroad, was doubling their own efforts to reach the connection point before them. It was now April and the lines were getting closer and closer.

The UPRR would lay three miles in a day and the CPRR would counter by laying four. Four would be met with five and soon both railroad companies were advancing at the rate of six miles a day. It didn't seem possible to surpass that. The big difficulty now was that the actual junction, the point at which the two railroads would come together, had not yet been chosen. Each company would continue laying track and would pass each other creating parallel roadways that seemed to stretch forever into the desert.

Officials from the Central Pacific's offices in Sacramento rode the passenger lines that ran most of the way now, and then transferred to work trains to arrive at the construction site in order to inspect the progress for themselves. Of the "Big Four," the founders of the CPRR, only Charles Crocker had worked at the front hand in hand with engineers and surveyors. The three other men, Mark Hopkins, Collis Huntington and Leland Stanford would now make periodic visits.

One day in late April Leland Stanford and an entourage of investors and important figures from California arrived at the work site. Hanna Maria Strobridge entertained the party. Mei Lim was drafted to wait on the officials and this she did happily. But as she carried the soup terrine serving each person seated at the long table she stopped suddenly, nearly spilling the soup. Before her, filling the chair with no room to spare was a man whose round face, well-trimmed mustaches and balding cranium were all too recognizable. She had nearly spilled soup onto the ample lap of Mr. M!

17

Ten Miles in One Day!

"Mortimer, you look like you've seen a ghost," said Leland Stanford, stirring his soup with a silver spoon decorated with the monogram, "JS". The man he called Mortimer did, indeed, seem a bit pale.

"Ah, train journeys always make me a little sea sick, Lee," the man replied, forcing a smile and hoping that the slight blush he felt creep across his brow would cancel out the pasty complexion so astutely observed by Leland Stanford. Yes, he had seen something like a ghost—someone he never expected to see again. Traveling a thousand miles to be face-to-face with your former mistress was…well, it was unnerving. Unnerving, but not necessarily unpleasant. A conundrum, certainly, because how was he to reconnect with his pretty young confidant but remain incognito in the process?

Was there a chance she hadn't recognized him? A snowball's chance in hell, he thought! No, he could see the change in her body language, the nervousness with which she ladled soup and cleared plates. He wasn't, after all, an ordinary looking man. Not handsome perhaps, but distinctive, classy, important in stature and expert in social decorum. How could she not recognize Herman P. Mortimer, the mysterious Mr. M?

At least she hadn't given away the fact that they knew each other. In this company, with officials of the new railroad, politicians and businessmen of importance present, it would be tantamount to financial and social suicide even though, and this he was sure of, a good percentage of those seated at the long table had mistresses or visited brothels regularly themselves. It just wasn't something you wanted out in the open.

Leland Stanford turned his attention to Charles Crocker. "Your pets, Charles, seem to be doing wonders," he commented. The Chinese railroad workers were often referred to as "Crocker's Pets," especially by those who stood in envy of Crocker's brilliance in his utilization of the Celestial workforce. These would-be pundits usually forgot that Crocker initially hadn't wanted to employ the Chinese and that he himself had needed convincing.

"Yes, we are racking up the miles faster than ever. Helps to be out of the mountains, of course. When you think that the Union Pacific was originally supposed to meet us at the California border!"

"We could have built this road all the way to Pittsburgh before they got to California." There was laughter among the dinner guests. Mei Lim was returning with a platter of meats and boiled potatoes, averting her eyes from Mr. M as she began to serve the food.

Mark Hopkins, one of the "Big Four" founders of the CPRR was seated next to Arthur Brown. Brown was Superintendent of Bridges and Buildings and had engineered the miles and miles of snow sheds and bridges in the Sierra Nevada. Hopkins leaned closer to Brown and said surreptitiously in a low voice:

"Art, I understand there's been some trouble with the Union Pacific. Is that true?"

"You know that the beds run parallel now as the terminus hasn't been selected and no one is willing to stop building. Well, sometimes the Union Pacific crews set off their dynamite without warning our people. There have been some injuries. We think they do that on purpose."

"That's unfortunate. Can't anyone complain to Durant or his superintendents?"

"Just between you and me, I think Durant condones such behavior. Why, there was a rumor that the Union crews were going to march on us and clean out our Chinese! Can you imagine?"

James Strobridge had overheard the conversation between Hopkins and Brown. "Rest assured, Gentlemen," he interjected, "that no such occurrence will be tolerated on my watch! And let me say this about Thomas Durant. He has shown great initiative as vice president of the Union Pacific. He's been right on the scene, much as our Charles Crocker here has and it's to his credit that the Union Pacific is in Utah at all."

"Here, here!" Several voices raised the cheer. This laudation was perhaps due less to an appreciation for the prowess of the competition than to a jubilation born of the potency of the wine.

Mei Lim was clearing plates from the table as brandy was poured and cigars were drawn from vest pockets, their tips bitten off and their aromas sampled by noses big, small, long and hooked or round, bulbous and puffy. Of course she had recognized Mr. M. She still retained a modicum of sympathy for the man, remembering his tragic story of lost love and irreconcilable guilt. But he had stopped coming to see her at Ah Toy's salon. He might have taken her away with him, saved her from the ordeals that followed. But he had not. What now was she to think?

She brushed softly against Mr. M as she reached to clear away his plate. "Is Mister done with his plate, please?" she said, looking directly into his eyes.

Mortimer found he was tongue-tied and could only nod in response. His face reddening and his breathing abrupt and irregular, he hoped no one would take notice. But Leland Stanford had noticed.

"Are you all right, Herman? Do you need to lie down for a bit?"

"No, no, Lee, Thank you, but I'm fine. I get these spells sometimes. They pass quickly." He raised his glass. "Here's to greater and greater mileage. And to the government subsidy of $32,000 per finished mile!"

They cheered, they drank, they exhaled clouds of cigar smoke, and Charles Crocker, inspired by the enthusiasm, clanged on his glass with a spoon.

"Gentlemen," Crocker began, "I wish to announce that tomorrow—and I hope you all will be present to witness it—we will put down *ten miles of track*!"

"Ten miles! Ten miles—how can you do that?"

"It's never been done! It's amazing—*can* you do it?"

"What an achievement! Crocker, you're a genius if you pull it off!"

"Here, here! Let us drink to the success of the ten miles!"

There were further kudos and hurrahs and expressions of astonishment. And of course, more toasts. When the brandy was all gone the celebrants retired to their quarters in the Silver Palace Sleeping Car in which they had arrived. Mr. M, Herman P. Mortimer, lurked momentarily outside the Strobridges' railcar in the hopes that Mei Lim would appear. He was disappointed.

Charles Crocker's boast that he could complete ten miles in one day was not just drunken bravado. He and James Strobridge had been planning it for days. The record, held by the Union Pacific, now stood at eight and one half miles and Thomas Durant had bet Charles Crocker $10,000 that he could not exceed it. The way had already been partially graded by the Chinese and ties had been laid out in neat piles spaced at intervals along the route; Crocker was ready to start.

On the first day of the attempt, April 27, 1869, a work train jumped the track. Crocker was forced to postpone until the following day. Early the next morning, with reporters and a few officials from the Union Pacific to act as witnesses, he gave the signal and a swarm of Crocker's Pets began the impossible task.

Crocker had hand-picked eight of his Irish workers to lay the rails: Michael Shay, Michael Kennedy, Michael Sullivan, Patrick Joyce, Thomas Dailey, George Wyatt, Edward Kioleen, and Fred McNamara. They alone would carry the 560 pound rails and place them on the road bed—3500 of them!

Four thousand men, all but a few hundred being Chinese, were arrayed along the line. Crocker had managed to work the usually calm Celestials to feverish excitement over the project. Hundreds of horses, mules and oxen were employed to cart supplies. There was a trainload of rails and materials waiting at the finished end of the tracks to be distributed up the line.

Men tossed kegs of bolts, spikes and fish-plates from the train. These were loaded onto handcarts and horse-drawn wagons. Next came the rails: 16 to a specially built car that ran on the rails and was pulled by a single horse. Once unloaded, the train backed off and another was brought up. The men working at the front never had to wait for supplies.

Three men, the so-called "pioneers," moved swiftly setting the ties. The rails were brought up as close to the railhead as possible; the rails had to be spiked and leveled before the roadbed could withstand the weight of the car. The transition from car to road-bed was fast and fluid. Four men lifted a rail from one side of the car while another four did the same on the opposite side.

Crocker had informed the foremen how to streamline the process of fixing the rails to the ties. He told them:

"…you are going to have your men to spike: the first man drives one particular spike and does not stop for another; he walks past that rail and drives the same spike in the next rail. Here another man follows him and drives the next spike to that in the same rail; and another follows him and so on. You must have spikes enough so that no man stops or passes another...."

Spikers, bolters, straighteners, tampers, men with crowbars raising the rails while men with shovels filled in the ballast, men pulling handcarts full of spikes and bolts, horses pulling wagons full of gravel, men and boys with long poles from which hung buckets of lukewarm tea—a line two miles long advancing at the rate of one mile each hour.

At 1:30 p.m. they had laid six miles of track. Crocker knew their goal of ten was now within their grasp and so he called for a lunch break for everyone. He dubbed the site "Camp Victory." Some of the Union Pacific observers lunched with Crocker, Stanford and the others. Their initial skepticism had eroded; they were quite ready to offer their congratulations. "Your Chinese," said a Union Pacific man, "can we borrow them?"

Jordan Chariton, reporter for the Daily Alta, used his watch to time the tracklayers. He found they could lay 240 feet of track in less than one minute and twenty seconds, as fast as someone on a brisk walk. Twelve hours from the start of the workday, ten miles and 56 feet of new track had been laid, enabling the CPRR to run a locomotive over it at forty miles per hour.

The celebration that evening at the Strobridges' railcar included the eight Irish rail-layers. A special tent had been set up to accommodate the crowd. The Union Pacific officials had sent over a case of champagne and a congratulatory note which read, "Wouldn't have believed it if we hadn't seen it with our own eyes. Good job!" and which was signed by Thomas Durant.

"If the landscape here had been level," Crocker said, "we could have built for fifteen miles easily."

"The ends of the two railroads are so close together now," added Strobridge, "that the Union Pacific couldn't break our new record even if they tried!"

"Is Congress ever going to make up their minds as to where the rails will meet?" someone asked.

"I heard it would be at Ogden," said another.

"I have it on good authority," offered Crocker, "that Promontory Summit will be selected. Not Promontory Point which is a peninsula sticking out into the Great Salt Lake, but some nasty little hill of dirt where nobody ever goes. What do you think of that?"

"I don't get it. Why not Ogden? It would be a logical connection with Salt Lake City."

"The Mormons aren't too happy that the Transcontinental Railroad is passing so close to their private Mecca," answered Crocker.

"I have a solution to that," said Leland Stanford. "I'm going to contract with Brigham Young to use Mormon labor to build more roadbeds through Utah. That should change his mind!"

"Well, here's to our good Sons of Erin," said Crocker, raising his glass to toast the eight Irishmen. Even James Strobridge, who detested alcohol and spent a good deal of his time trying to rid the camp of it, raised his glass of champagne in tribute. He touched lips to the glass but did not drink.

"I'm going to take you boys back to Sacramento and organize a parade in your honor," said Stanford. "You deserve a little vacation!"

"We should do something for the Chinese as well, Lee," said Strobridge.

"Kind of a lot of 'em, aren't there?"

"You know," said Michael Shay, "at first we were put off by the yellow heathens—felt they were takin' away our jobs. But they work like the devil out there. They's good people, it's a fact."

"I echo yer sentiments," said Fred McNamara."

"Aye, and count me in on that," added Michael Sullivan. The others nodded in agreement. Strobridge was skeptical of the sudden appreciation these hardened men were showing for the Celestials, but he welcomed it. Perhaps it would spread.

The Silver Palace Sleeping Car stood ready for its return trip to Sacramento. Eight Irishmen were already seated in the luxurious interior with its crystal chandeliers and richly patterned carpeting. The other men who had traveled to the front were boarding, stepping up the stairs of the rear platform to pause momentarily and wave, proud and elated at their experience of the previous day.

Herman P. Mortimer moved to the back of the line, lingering and scanning the faces of the small crowd who had gathered to see off the investors and Railroad officials and the eight heroes of the "day of the ten miles." When Mei Lim appeared near the rear of the assembled well-wishers Mortimer could not restrain himself from rushing to her side.

"Mei Lim!" he called. The girl saw him coming and looked from side to side for an avenue of retreat. He reached her before she could manage to avoid him and so she stood passively, awaiting the inevitable encounter.

"Come with me back to Sacramento," said Mortimer, oblivious to the surrounding onlookers. "I'll set you up in an apartment of your own."

Hanna Maria Strobridge, standing within earshot, was shocked. Such behavior by a prominent businessman, an investor in the railroad, was unconscionable. She was aware of Mei Lim's past, and the male propensity toward double standards did not surprise her either. However, witnessing the reality of an unwholesome proposition such as the one Herman P. Mortimer had just blurted out—in public!—was just too much.

"Too late, Mr. M," answered Mei Lim. "Too late for arrangement. I am no longer Daughter of Joy. I have new life. I thank you anyway. You very kind man."

Mortimer flushed and began to breathe hard and irregularly. His hand went to his chest. This is it, he thought. This is how I die—from a broken heart! But it was not Herman P. Mortimer's time to die on that morning. Not on *that* morning.

"Mr. Mortimer," said Hanna Maria Strobridge, "your train is waiting."

The engine had been rotated on a wooden turntable, one of many placed up and down the line. She was a veteran of numerous trips across the mountains and her name, stenciled in garish red and gold letters on her black iron belly, was Dinah. Her whistle sounded and smoke rose from her funnel, a gray-black issuance of acrid vapor that chased the very birds from the sky. The train with all its passengers, including the ailing Mr. M, pulled away from Camp Victory, the spot where Strobridge had halted construction of the ten miles to break for lunch on the previous day.

As night fell the passengers unlatched the moveable seats which converted into sleeping berths, an ingenious invention added to the car by T. T. Woodruff & Company, supplier of the car to the CPRR. Woodruff would later spare with George Pullman over the patent. In Woodruff's version, the lower berths were made by pivoting the seat cushions downward and forward while the upper sleeping platforms unfolded from the walls on hinges.

Back at the camp lanterns were blinking out one by one inside canvas tents like so many fireflies surrendering to the blackness of the night. Lying in the darkness Zack pulled his blanket up around his neck. The days may have been hot but the desert night was always frigid. His mind was filled with the events of the past few days; the energy generated by the big push still vibrated through him. Just as he was drifting off to sleep a soft voice said: "Move over. Let me in. It's cold out here!"

Zack was wide awake now as Mei Lim crawled under the blanket and wrapped her arms around him. She had never done this before on any of her frequent visits to his tent. Usually they sat and talked and then she left early in the evening, even before the stars came out. Something about tonight was different—different and very pleasant!

"No sex. We just hold each other. Talk now," said Mei Lim. In spite of the admonishment, Zack was feeling somewhat excited. He forced himself to think of something dull and ordinary. Like fishing or gathering wood or—and this seemed to have the required affect—his mother's smile.

"I have heard the railroad work is nearly finished," Mei Lim told Zack. "The rails will meet and all workers will be dismissed. This will be soon."

"This is a good thing?"

"Perhaps. But what will you do when the work is over and you must leave? Where do you go?"

"You know where, Mei Lim. I am going to El-Ya-Noy to seek my father's family. That's where I've been headed all along."

"I ask Missy-One-Eyed about this El-Ya-Noy. She say it still very faraway. How you get there?"

Zack stirred, shook the beginnings of a cramp from his leg. Why did women always have to be so practical, he wondered? "I don't know," he answered.

"I tell you how. Missy-One-Eyed say you take other railroad to a place called Oh-Ma-Ha. Then you go on boat or maybe another train. Takes many days. And money."

"I'll have money. Our pay is due. Mei Lim, I can do this. I've had doubts, but now I'm sure I'll get there." Zack hugged Mei Lim more tightly, raised her face to his and kissed her.

"I go with you," she said. "Okay?"

It wasn't the grandest parade Sacramento had ever seen. Certainly it hadn't rivaled the day the Grand Army of the Republic had marched through the muddied streets—those brass bands, those thousands lining the avenues with flags held high, those charming, dressed-to-the-hilt society ladies throwing garlands. And it hadn't held a candle to that other procession that had wound its way up to cemetery hill to honor the soldiers that fell in the War Against the Rebellion, although it was considerably more jubilant than that solemn affair had been. Nor was it as spectacular as the Dragon Dances in Chinatown at Chinese New Year with the crackle of sparkling fireworks and the blur of swinging red lanterns and the galumphing of many sandaled feet beneath the cavorting paper dragon.

But it was a good parade. A band playing the "Stars and Stripes" led it through the streets of the financial district. In the first carriage waving to the onlookers were Leland Stanford, Mark Hopkins and Colin Huntington, three of the Big Four. Following them rode Edward Kioleen, Michael Sullivan, George Wyatt and Michael Shay, four of the eight Irishmen. In the third carriage were the other four, Michael Kennedy, Fred McNamara, Patrick Joyce and Thomas Dailey.

Banners with the words "Central Pacific Railroad" and "Ten Miles in One Day" adorned the open carriages. Women threw bundles of flowers and spectators cheered. Children ran alongside of the carriages waving American flags made of paper. Leland Stanford had alerted the Sacramento newspapers of their achievement and instructed them as to when and where the parade was to be held. The power of the press had responded to the power of the railroad mogul; a crowd was manifested to suit the occasion.

A small group had followed behind the carriages as the parade's pageantry wound down in front of the headquarters of the Central Pacific Railroad at the foot of K Street. As the parade ended the crowd began to drift away. Among them were two young Native Americans, a boy and girl. Tommy Wepa was still dressed in his Chinese workman's clothing while Little Wind had retained the traditional Tlingit costume she had adopted while living in Sitka.

Their appearance caused some heads to turn but no one thought to challenge their right to be on the streets for the festivities.

"I think I recognize that one with the long beard from the day I first met the photographer," said Little Wind to Tommy Wepa. "I think he is a big chief of the railroad."

"That's good. Now all we have to do is get in to talk to him."

They followed as the men left their carriages and entered the building. The entourage walked down a long hallway and filed through a door with an opaque glass window sporting bright gold lettering which neither of the teenagers could read. They hesitated, uncertain whether their plan would succeed or result in them being sent back to the reservation. Tommy then pulled open the door and they crept into the office.

"Hold on there, you two," shouted a voice. "Where do you think you are going?" A man, dressed in a guard's uniform, stood in the large space that served as the waiting room for the railroad offices. The guard examined the two strangely dressed young people, shook his head and waited for a reply.

"Please, we wish to see headman of railroad."

"Oh you do, do you? I think you will see the back of me hand in a minute if you don't be on your way out of here!"

Just at that moment Leland Stanford came from his inner office into the waiting room. "George," he said to the guard, "we'll need some coffee sent in." Then, noticing Little Wind and Tommy, Stanford demanded, "What's going on here?"

"Sir, these two urchins got in here somehow. I'll send them away," answered the guard.

"Wait. Please, can we talk to you, Sir?" Tommy pleaded. "We have to get to the front."

"The front, is it? And what would you be knowing about the front?"

"I worked there. I came home to visit my mother, but now I want to go back."

"Go down to the depot and talk to the foreman there. Why are you bothering me? Can't you see I'm a busy man?"

"Sir, we did that. They say no one is to be hired any more. The work is almost finished."

"Ha! So you thought you'd go over their heads! I like your enthusiasm. But why is it so important to you? And you, young lady, what is your interest in all this?"

"My brother is out there somewhere," answered Little Wind. "Tommy and I must go to him. Bring him home. My mother, you see, is…dying. Oh please…we'll work hard. Let us go to this front, wherever it is."

Stanford was touched. "You two, you're not Chinese, are you? No, I didn't think so. Indian? Tell you what. We are going to be joining the lines together in a few days. Big ceremony. I could use some extra hands to help out. You'll come along in my private car. But you'll work for your passage. Serving food. Cleaning. Whatever we need. Does that suit you?"

18

The Golden Spike

Promontory Summit, May 10, 1869 — 12 noon.

To his Excellency General U.S. Grant President of the United States, Washington, D.C.:

Sir: We have the honor to report that the last rail is laid, the last spike is driven, the Pacific Railroad is finished.

LELAND STANFORD.
President Central Pacific Railroad Co.

DR. DURANT
Vice-President Union Pacific Railroad Co.

Standing at the top of a telegraph pole, just beneath the windblown American flag at Promontory Summit, the site of the junction of the two railroad companies, was a tall man, a Mr. Amos L. Bowsher, the general foreman for the Union Pacific Railroad in charge of telegraph construction. Bowsher had overseen the connections between the Central Pacific's telegraph wires and those of the Union Pacific, creating, for the first time, a direct line between the east and west coasts. He had directed that wires be run to a copper plate attached to a sledgehammer and to an ordinary iron spike. If the spike were hit by the sledge a signal would be transmitted across the continent.

In San Francisco, at 11:47 A.M., on May 10, 1869, the telegraph wire surged with three electrical pulses. A fifteen-inch gun at Fort Point was fired by the first pulse. At the Fire Department tower all the fire bells were rung by the subsequent electrical signals. At Washington, D.C. a ball dropped which had been suspended outside of the Capitol Building. Bells in the capitol dome rang once for each of the three times the electrified sledge hit the iron spike.

In New York City, Mayor Hall ordered a salute of one hundred cannons in the City Hall Park. He had received a telegram from Mayor Brown of San Francisco informing him of the driving of the last spike only five minutes before. In Chicago there would be a parade of bands and marchers spread out over the astounding length of seven miles.

Simultaneous celebrations took place in Philadelphia, where bells sounded out from Independence Hall and all the fire stations, and the din was supplemented by the sirens of fire engines, and in Buffalo, New York, where the telegraph wire was attached to a large gong at the Board of Trade Building, and in Scranton, Pennsylvania, where cannon fire, bell ringing and train whistles combined to herald in the New Age. There was, of course, pandemonium in Sacramento, birthplace of the Central Pacific.

At Promontory Summit Leland Stanford had given the last spike a few gentle taps with the wired sledge. That was all that was needed to generate the signal. He then passed the sledge to James Strobridge's wife, Hanna Maria, who also took a swing at it. Others then got in on the act. This was truly the last spike that now connected the two railroads—and thus, the continental United States.

Moments before, a brief ceremony had taken place in which a golden spike had been driven using a silver sledge by Stanford and Thomas Durant. The golden spike had been presented to Stanford by David Hewes of San Francisco. It weighed nine and a half pounds and, as it consisted of 17.6 carats, it was valued at $200. A hole had been augured into a ceremonial tie made of California laurel. The golden spike was placed into the hole and both Stanford and Durant took turns swinging the silver sledge—both men missing it completely on their first attempts, delighting the railroad workers who were present.

Besides the Hewes spike there was the Nevada Silver Spike which had been rushed to the ceremonies at the last minute, having been ordered early in May and produced quickly in Virginia City. It was made from 25 ounces of silver. And there was the Arizona Iron-Silver-Gold Spike which was "ribbed with iron, clad in silver and crowned with gold." And there was a second gold spike, made at the same time as the one pounded into the laurel tie. This was presented to Leland Stanford by Frank Marriott, proprietor of the San

Francisco News Letter. Unlike the first golden spike, this one would survive intact.

Before the driving of the gold and silver spikes there had been the prayers and the speeches. Leland Stanford praised the symbolic spikes and added, "...allow me to express the hope that the great importance which you are pleased to attach to our undertaking may be in all respects fully realized. This line of rails connecting the Atlantic and Pacific, and affording to commerce a new transit, will prove, we trust, the speedy forerunner of increased facilities." He was setting the stage for future railroad construction throughout the west—by his own company, of course.

General Grenville Dodge, the chief engineer for the Union Pacific said, "The great Benton prophesied that some day a granite statue would be erected on the highest peak of the Rocky Mountains pointing westward, denoting the great route across the Continent. You have made the prophecy today a fact." He was referring to the politician, Thomas Hart Benton, United States Senator from Missouri in the early part of the century and father of the famous painter of the same name, who had promoted western expansionism in the spirit of the country's Manifest Destiny. Who the predicted statue might represent, he had not said.

The laurel tie was brought up and James Strobridge and his counterpart from the Union Pacific, Samuel Reed, slid the ceremonial Last Tie beneath the rails. The tie had been polished to a fine shine and at its center was placed a silver plaque proclaiming it as "The last tie laid on the completion of the Pacific Railroad, May 10, 1869." Names of the directors and officers of the two railroads were listed on the plaque. Holes had been drilled to accommodate the gold and silver spikes.

Music was supplied by a military band from Fort Douglas and the 10th Ward Band from Salt Lake City. A brigade of the 21st United States Infantry under the command of Major Milton Cogswell had happened to have been traveling to the Presidio at San Francisco and had stopped to line up along the north side of the tracks, adding more even more pomp and pageantry to the proceedings. Brigham Young, president of The Church of Jesus Christ of the Latter Day Saints, sent Bishop John Sharp to represent the Mormon Church. At least 15 newspaper reporters and three photographers helped swell the crowd of 500 onlookers.

There was a pause in the program as photographer Alfred A. Hart, perched atop the cowcatcher of the Central Pacific locomotive, The Jupiter, took a picture of the group poised to begin pounding the spikes. A large crowd of spectators lined both sides of the newly positioned rails. Standing on the roadbed holding the silver sledge was Leland Stanford. Next to him was Union Pacific vice president Thomas Durant. Two officials of the UPRR, John Duff and Sydney Dillon, held up the golden spikes. Arizona Governor Anson Safford held the Arizona spike.

The surrounding crowd was asked to step back to clear an area so that additional photographs could be taken. Photographers Andrew J. Russell and Charles R. Savage had set up on the south side of the joined rails. Watching them work was a young Wintu girl who mused to herself that it was a shame that her friend and photographer, Edward Muybridge, wasn't also there to document the historic event.

Earlier that morning the last rails had been laid in place. One rail was positioned by a team of Union Pacific men. The other was placed by eight Chinese workers from the Central Pacific. Among them were Lee Shao, Wong Fook and Ging Cui. The two Native American boys, Tommy Wepa and Zack Grosh, watched with pride as the rail was lowered by their comrades. The photographer, Andrew J. Russell took a picture documenting the moment. It was one of the few photographs that would show Chinese or Native American men at the ceremony.

Each railroad company had brought an engine close to the point where the rails joined. The Union Pacific's engine, Number 119, was a standard American locomotive with the configuration of 4-4-0, that is, it had four wheels on the leading truck and four driving wheels, with no trailing truck. It had a tall, slender smokestack and a triangular cowcatcher called a pilot, on the front. Facing the 119 from the west was the Central Pacific's Jupiter, also a 4-4-0. She had the large, diamond-shaped funnel that characterized many of the locomotives of the day.

The actual first meeting of the competing railroads' locomotives had taken place on May 7, when the Union Pacific's Number 60 had come pilot to pilot with the Central Pacific's Whirlwind. The Whirlwind and Number 60 were originally going to be used in the track-joining ceremony but at the last moment the Jupiter and Number 119 were substituted.

The last mile of track had just been laid leaving a short, unfinished section where the festivities would take place. The event was scheduled for May 8, but it would be delayed. On May 7, a blustery, overcast day that threatened to dump buckets of rain on Promontory, Utah, Leland Stanford's special train arrived carrying Stanford himself, the usual directors, officers and local Sacramento businessmen, as well as all the ceremonial accoutrements, banners, the gold and silver spikes, laurel tie and the silver sledge. Tommy Wepa and Little Wind had worked on the train as waiters serving the dignitaries. Of the CPRR officials, only Stanford, Strobridge, Gray and Montague would be present at the ceremony. Huntington, Hopkins, and Crocker would not be in attendance.

A special train coming from the east carrying Union Pacific officials including Thomas Durant and Sidney Dillon had reached Piedmont, Wyoming on May 6. A gang of striking Union Pacific workers waylaid the train. They numbered nearly 500. The issue precipitating the attack was that back wages had been owed to them for much too long a time. They intended to collect and collect immediately.

They accosted Durant's private car, uncoupling it when the train attempted to move away from the station. They then chained the wheels to the tracks and informed the railroad vice president that he would remain a prisoner of his own railway until their moneys were paid. Durant finally relented and wired for funds, paid off the workers and set off again for Promontory Summit. He would not arrive until May 10. Durant, Dillon, Duff, Dodge and Reed would represent the UPRR. Oakes and Ames, two of that railroad company's most important men would be absent.

Promontory, fast becoming a rugged rail town like so many "Hell on wheels" boomtowns that had sprung up along the route, was situated in a valley three miles wide. The ground was level and well suited for the junction of the two railroads. There ran the parallel tracks of the two railroads. There the CPRR waited for the UPRR to finish its work on the last trestle. There they would finally connect these two great engineering marvels of the century.

Camps of the Union Pacific sprawled across the valley and up the eastern slopes. They had names reminiscent of western mining camps: Deadfall, Murder Gulch, Last Chance. Tents of the Central Pacific's Chinese workers stretched westward for miles. There were many more men occupying the valley than were required for finishing the work so by May 3 they were being dismissed in droves.

Many of the out-of-work men lingered, drank, gambled, and visited the saloons and houses of prostitution that constituted the majority of the town's businesses. There were fistfights, shootings, and a general rowdiness that pervaded the community, an enveloping headache for the foremen and particularly for James Strobridge. Given the history of strife between the workers of the two railroads, the clash of cultures, the rivalries and jealousies, Strobridge was fearful that an all-out war would develop.

On May 5 the Union Pacific drove the last spike into the Big Trestle and blasted through Carmichael's Cut, completing another trestle across Clark's Cut on the following day. They rapidly laid the few thousand feet remaining to the sidings that had been constructed earlier at the Summit, and the work was finished. Only one section of track the length of a single rail lay between the Central Pacific Railroad and the Union Pacific Railroad, between the Western United States and the Eastern United States. Now they waited for the dignitaries to arrive.

Leland Stanford's special train had descended from the Sierra Nevada onto the Great Basin of Nevada and was speeding toward its appointment with history. Little Wind, dressed in a white frock with the insignia of the Central Pacific Railroad embroidered in blue, carried a tray with two steaming bowls of soup down the swaying aisle of the dining car. Her mind drifted; she thought of her mother on the reservation and of how she had lied to Leland Stanford about her mother dying. It was not good to tell lies, she knew, but she had been desperate to travel to see her brother; an impending death in the family was a persuasive argument. Besides, many of her people on that reservation *had* died recently—from the white man's disease: smallpox.

A barren landscape flew by the windows of the railcar. Little Wind had never traveled this fast before; the speed made her dizzy if she looked out the window. She steadied the tray against a table on which was a white linen cloth and a single red rose in a slender glass vase. As she served soup to the two gentlemen seated there the train took a sudden turn, jostling passengers, waitress and soup bowls. A deluge of creamy bisque bounced out of the bowl and onto the lap of one of the men. He let out an oath as he brushed bits of lobster from his trousers.

"You clumsy girl," shouted the soup-drenched man's companion. "Mortimer, you should report her."

Herman Mortimer raised his hand to quiet his friend, then thought to lick the lobster bisque from his fingers. "It's all right, Potter. Accidents happen. Accidents will be part and parcel of this new modern age, I expect."

"I am so sorry," said Little Wind, mortified that she had spilled soup all over this man. "I'll bring a towel. And more soup."

"You do that, my dear." Then as Little Wind hurried to fetch the towel, Mortimer said, "Cute little gal, isn't she? I wonder, is she Mexican?"

When Stanford's train arrived at Promontory Summit the sky was overcast and rain clouds began to roll over the Promontory Mountains. The gloom was heightened by the news that the Union Pacific officials were delayed and the ceremony would have to be postponed. Little Wind and Tommy Wepa wanted to set out to locate Zack, but they were confronted with a virtual city of tents, nearly 275 of them. To make matters worse, the Stanford group, facing the prospect of a weekend in the rain and mud in the middle of nowhere, had consented to a proposition made by Jack Casement, the construction leader for the Union Pacific and their host at Promontory, to follow him on a sightseeing tour. Little Wind and Tommy were instructed to accompany the CPRR group to assist in pouring the champagne.

Jack Casement had been a Union Brigadier General during the Civil War. He had previous railroad experience which had prompted Grenville Dodge to hire Casement to lead the construction of the Union Pacific line. Now he assembled an excursion train complete with an assortment of scrumptious edibles and heady refreshment, herded the Stanford congregation into the railcar and headed out for a picnic on the banks of the Weber River at Taylor's Mill.

It was a pleasant spot, the shallow river running clear and brisk over water-rounded rocks, cutthroat trout clustered together in shady pools along banks thick with cedar and pine. They spread tablecloths on the dried mud flats near a spring-fed creek that emptied into the river. China plates and crystal goblets were produced from wicker baskets and the champagne flowed and sparkled in harmony with the ebullience of the river. Gaiety prevailed and the knowledge that storm clouds just barely visible above the mountains to their north meant an inundation of inclement weather, standing water and sticky muck back at the junction site did nothing to dampen their merriment.

Little Wind was careful not to spill a drop of the sparkling wine, especially when she refilled Herman Mortimer's glass. Mortimer watched her intently as she moved through the picnic area. The man called Potter noticed Mortimer's obvious interest in the girl.

"You always did have an eye for the young ones, Mortimer," Potter said.

"No, no, Daniel. It's not that at all. I just find that young people are so...young! They have an innocence and an enthusiasm for life that older women have lost. Mature women have become jaded and cynical and have no appreciation for older men as the young do. And the young...they are such good listeners!"

"Good listeners, huh? Have it your way, Mortimer. Have it your way."

After lunch the party hiked partway up Weber canyon to watch for eagles and take in the spectacular view. Back at the picnic area Little Wind and Tommy helped load dishes and glassware into the wicker baskets.

"That old man has been watching you again," Tommy told Little Wind. "I don't like him."

"He's just a nice old man. He didn't complain when I spilled soup all over his friend. He just likes me, that's all."

"He better not try anything. I still have my hunting knife, you know. I'll skin him like a beaver if..."

"Oh, Tommy. You don't have to worry about that old man. He doesn't mean anything by looking at me. I kind of like it."

"You do? Oh...I...I don't. That's all."

Hiking up the canyon, the group followed a little stream. The terrain was rocky and steep with occasional sharp outcroppings that necessitated the climbing skills of a mountain goat. Herman Mortimer, also known as Mr. M, whose constitution was shaky even during an evening's brisk walk around the block, was struggling. He panted and sat down hard on a boulder.

"Herman, perhaps you'd better go back," Potter said to him.

"Yes, yes…I think that best. Only, could you come with me? I'm afraid I won't find my way very well."

"Of course I will. Rest for a bit and we'll start back."

When the hikers returned they found Herman Mortimer propped against a tree truck, his face a pale mask and his eyes glassy. Potter said to Leland Stanford, "I think he may be having a stroke, Lee. We should get him to a doctor."

The excursion train was packed and headed for Ogden, the largest and the closest previously-settled town near Promontory. Jack Casement had planned to spend the night in Ogden anyway. Ogden was next in population only to Salt Lake City and had been the favored spot for the railroad junction until Promontory had been selected. It was an obvious hub. The Central Pacific would later purchase from the Union Pacific for 2.8 million dollars the forty-seven and a half miles of the track from Promontory to Ogden in order to establish the terminus of their part of the Transcontinental Railway there.

It was a good place to die. Herman P. Mortimer, also known as Mr. M, didn't survive to be a witness to the joining of the rails and the driving of the last spike. He lingered only a few days. His body was shipped in a hastily built coffin to his wife in San Francisco where he was buried under the shade of an ancient oak tree. Mei Lim, had she been aware of the death of Mr. M, would surely have mourned the man. Most of the other visiting dignitaries barely noticed his absence.

The excursion train returned to Promontory that Sunday. By then the rain had stopped and only a few muddied puddles remained as evidence of the storm. Little Wind and Tommy, now relieved of any immediate duties, were free to search for Zack. Tommy inquired at the Chinese camp's cooking facilities. There, one of the railroad's cooks who understood English directed Tommy to the tent of his old boss, Hu Qiang. Hu Qiang, seeing Tommy's face appear at the door flap of his tent, jumped and shouted and flailed his arms. By the angry tone of his voice Tommy knew the camp cook had remembered him. Through sign language and the few words of Chinese that Tommy knew he managed to calm Hu Qiang and at last discovered that Zack lived in a tent that was not faraway.

"Zack? Are you in there?" Tommy called. The canvas tent rustled in the wind as the door flap opened and a familiar face peered out.

"Who? Tommy!" said Zack, surprised by the sudden appearance of his friend. Then he saw his sister, Little Wind standing right behind Tommy. He ran to her and embraced her. Tears of joy flowed freely on the faces of all three.

"How? Why are you here? It's so good to see you," said Zack.

"I owe it all to Tommy," said Little Wind. "He found me at the reservation. I had returned to be with mother. He explained where you were. I just had to be with you again."

"Returned to be with mother? Where were you?"

"That's a long story. I'll tell it later, when we're settled."

"And you, Tommy? Why did you come back? For that matter, why did you go away?"

"I told you I wouldn't abandon you, Zack. It may have seemed that way when I jumped on that train. But I was homesick. I wanted to see my own mother. I knew I'd come back...and look! I've brought your sister with me. Don't be angry."

"And...White Cloud? Zack? Who are you, anyway?" Little Wind asked, not knowing her brother had been going by his white person name. "I'm coming with you," she added, as if that were a foregone conclusion.

Zack rubbed his hands together, a quirky habit that surfaced whenever he needed to take a moment to think things through. "I don't know, Little Wind. I think maybe you should go back."

"You should know me better than that. You go to El-Ya-Noy, I go to El-Ya-Noy too."

"And me too," said Tommy.

"Well, that makes four of us now," Zack said.

"I don't understand," said Little Wind. "Four? Who is...?"

"Her name is Mei Lim. She's been a good friend. She also says she is coming, even if I say no. You have a lot in common."

"Mei Lim? That's not a Wintu name. What tribe is she?"

Zack and Tommy exchanged looks. This was going to take some explaining. "We'll tell the story later. When you tell me your's. For right now, let's go see what is happening at the rail junction. There's going to be a big celebration once the Union Pacific men get here. There are bands and soldiers and everything."

"Zack," said Tommy, "it almost seems like you've become a real railroad man."

"I sometimes feel like I built this whole thing all by myself."

The speeches were over. The band had played. Leland Stanford had pummeled the golden spike with his silver sledge. The spike had been struck seven times by various people and, being solid gold, was now mutilated beyond recognition. It was summarily extracted from the laurel tie and sawed in half, given in equal portions to Sidney Dillon and General Dodge as tokens of the importance of the day. The broken spike was perhaps symbolic of the fractured relationship between the officials of the two railroads.

James Strobridge invited the eight Chinese men who had laid the last rail for the Central Pacific to join him in his railcar for a congratulatory meal. He praised the men and their countrymen who had been the bulk of the workforce during the building of the railroad. As they supped, military officers were taking their turns striking token blows at the ordinary iron spikes that had replaced the gold and silver ones. The crowd was again asked to step back so that photographs could be taken. The two engines were brought forward and were now nearly touching as Andrew J. Russell took the official picture—one in which no Asians would be present.

19

By Rail to Om-Ah-Ha

Mei Lim had appealed to Mrs. Strobridge; Hanna Maria Strobridge had persuaded her husband; James Harvey Strobridge had persuaded Jack Casement; "General Jack" had persuaded Thomas Durant and so four rail passes had been issued for travel on the Union Pacific Railway between Promontory and Omaha. Four happy adventurers climbed aboard the first passenger train to make the journey eastward since the joining of the rails and the pounding of the last spike.

The Central Pacific had a policy of allowing the Native Americans, through whose territories the railroad had been built, to ride for free. Except for a few Pawnee, the Union Pacific didn't extend such a perk to any Indians. The UPRR had a long history of confrontations with the Plains Indians who in turn resented the intrusion of the railroad across their lands. The only exception was the Pawnees who had always been friendly to the United States government and acted as scouts for the army. Grenville Dodge recruited members of this tribe to act as protection against the more belligerent Lakota Sioux, the Arapahoe and the Cheyenne who threatened the railroad workers.

Indeed, the die of racial hatred had been cast years before the railroad laid the first tie in Nebraska. The Union Pacific's chief engineer, Grenville Dodge was a Brigadier General and Union Civil War veteran, who, after the war was over, had led Army troops in battles against these same tribes from Nebraska to Kansas, Colorado and Wyoming. In 1865 Dodge had sent an expedition of soldiers to stop Indian attacks against settlers along what was known as the Bozeman Trail which ran north from Fort Laramie through the Powder River hunting grounds of the Lakota. An Arapahoe village was subsequently destroyed.

This conflict and others, and the establishment of forts along the Bozeman Trail by the U.S. Army, led to what would come to be called Red Cloud's War, so named after the Lakota chief who had been instrumental in attempted negotiations with the government. The war would rage until the advent of the Treaty of Fort Laramie in 1868. This treaty created the Sioux Reservation in South Dakota which included the Black Hills. Red Cloud had insisted that the treaty specify that no white persons would be permitted to settle upon or occupy any portion of the Powder River country without the Indians' explicit consent. Later, gold would be discovered in the Black Hills. The treaty would evaporate.

The railroad had actually hired Indians to work for it as early as 1863 when there was a shortage of white workman during the Civil War. These crews included Native American women who were paid 15 cents per day as opposed to the dollar a day the white male workers got. They were Pawnee and Shoshone, known to be "friendly Indians" whose treaty with the government had mentioned the possibility of a railroad being built through their territory. The repercussions of this possibility must have been a concept which evaded the Indians.

Dodge came to work for the Union Pacific in 1865. By then the situation with the Plains Indians had worsened. The Union Pacific was given a small detachment of U.S. troops to help protect the railroad but they needed more. A regiment of Pawnee scouts was formed for added security. Not only were raids on the railroad workers by the Sioux and Arapaho and others a problem, but public opinion was turning against the railroad because of the perception that travel on it would be dangerous.

In 1866 Thomas Durant had a plan to counter the bad publicity. He decided to bring a group of influential investors and their families on a rail trip as far as the line had been built—across the plains where the Indians dwelt. He hired the Pawnee to put on a show for the dignitaries. The train stopped for the night and the guests got to watch as the Pawnee staged a war dance complete with a bonfire with flames licking up toward the star-filled sky. Some of the guests were frightened when an Indian jumped out at them, but Durant assured his audience that it was just a show.

The following morning the Pawnee staged a raid on the train, whooping and hollering and waving tomahawks and again the guests needed to be told that it was just an act and that these were friendly Indians. Durant's plan seemed to be backfiring on him. Then, as the train rumbled along the rails, the passengers gazed out the windows at an extraordinary sight: there on the plains a battle was taking place between (they were told) the Pawnee and the Sioux. Arrows flew through the air and shots rang out and blood curdling screams could be heard over the rattling of the wheels against the cold iron rails. Fears dissolved into fascination and enthrallment.

The Pawnee had played both roles in the exhibition of the battle, some dressed as Sioux warriors, some as Pawnee. There were no actual casualties. The excitement of seeing what most of the passengers had only read about in the pulp fiction publications was something they would tell their friends about for years to come; they were thrilled. Ironically, the Union Pacific gained even more investors that day. Another scout hired to work on the railroad's south branch, a white man named William Cody, heard about the Pawnee's pretend battle and the favorable reaction it had gotten. It would inspire him in later years to add Indian battles to his "Buffalo Bill's Wild West Show."

Zack, Tommy, Little Wind and Mei Lim had not been allowed in any of the Silver Palace Sleeping Cars where paying customers enjoyed comfortable accommodations in luxurious surroundings. Instead they were relegated to a car called The Emigrant Car where a few Pawnee and some of the Irish laborers rode on hard wooden benches and where they would sleep sitting up. Tommy of course complained of the close quarters. This resulted in Mei Lim recounting her ocean voyage to America as a young girl, wedged into the dark hold of the ship along with what must have been hundreds of other Chinese men and women, wet, stinking, and wailing in fear and bewilderment at their plight.

"Not so crowded," she told Tommy. "You don't know crowded!"

The train passed along Weber Canyon, past the Thousand Mile Tree, a tall pine so called because it stood at the point where construction of the roadbed had reached that distance from Omaha. Passengers could then gape out the windows at two vertical limestone ridges dropping off toward the canyon floor named, appropriately, the Devil's Slide. The tracks then followed through the Wilhemina Pass, another picturesque feature of the trip out of Utah. It promised to be a pleasant journey. But promises are like will o wisps: they tend to dissipate at the morning's first light.

"You didn't finish your story," Zack said to Little Wind. "How did you get from Alaska to back home?"

"There was this sweet boy, Freddie, who let me go on a cargo ship that was sailing for San Francisco."

Tommy Wepa wrinkled his face at the phrase, "sweet boy." He was about to interrupt Little Wind's narrative but thought better of it. He was unable, however, to suppress a sigh which did not go unnoticed by Little Wind.

"Yes, Freddie was a sailor on the Luella. He smuggled me onto the schooner when no one was looking. Otherwise I'd of never made it back. I had to hide down in the hold with a lot of smelly cargo and Freddie brought me food when he could."

"I wonder why he decided to help you," said Tommy. "Was the 'sweet boy' sweet on you, do you think?"

"Oh, Tommy. Some people are just nice. Even white people sometimes."

"Well, that was fortunate," Zack interjected. "Then you arrived in San Francisco and...?"

"I had to get back up to Nome Cult Farm somehow and I couldn't risk going near the Wood Farm where I was technically indentured. I went back to the Sellecks, looking for Edwin."

"But I thought Edwin Selleck was mean to you. Why would he help you?"

"People can be one thing on the outside and another altogether different thing on the inside. Edwin was like that. For all his gruff and huffing he actually cared enough about me to help." Little Wind looked at Tommy, thoroughly expecting him to comment, but he simply frowned.

"Edwin was working for Mr. Muybridge, the photographer I told you about. He took me to his studio and we talked for a long time about Alaska and my experiences there. I told Mr. Muybridge how I wanted to visit Mother at the West Place. He was so nice...he offered to take me there on his next photographing trip which was to make pictures of those lighthouse things they build to protect boats. Lucky for me there was one out on the bay not so far from the reservation. So it wasn't long before I got back and saw Mother."

"How is she? Was she worried about us? Oh, of course she would have been. I'm so glad..."

"Yes. You are glad I finally managed to deliver your message. A little late. And yes, she was worried. She thought we were both dead or in a lot of trouble somewhere. Then when Tommy showed up, we could tell her the whole story. She wouldn't want me to admit this to you, but I think she was very proud of you."

Mei Lim, former Lotus Flower, marveled at the familial bonding that lay at the center of each of her companion's stories. Happiness bloomed in her, nourished by a vicarious unconditional regard for these, the loved ones of others she had never met. Still, she was rooted in a mixture of jealousy and chronic despondency as she tried to imagine herself traveling so many miles to be with her own parents—parents to whom she was a commodity, a sacrificial means to an endless struggle against starvation—but parents who were perhaps broken-hearted to relinquish their only daughter to the skin trade—or perhaps were not.

As a very little girl in the village of Humen Town in Guangdong Province, Mei Lim had never been particularly happy or carefree. Her country had been embroiled in a brutal civil war, the Taiping Rebellion, since before she had been born. Brothers, uncles, and cousins had disappeared during the conflict; whole towns in nearby provinces had been totally destroyed.

And before that, in 1839, Humen had been the site of the destruction of over one thousand tons of British opium seized by the Imperial Commissioner, Lin Zexu. It was an incident that led to the First Opium War with Great Britain. So it seemed that her people were forever battling foreigners or fighting among themselves over trade, religion, land or power. Yes, the Qing Dynasty was riding on a turbulent wave of blood towards eventual destruction and Guangdong Province sat in the middle of the maelstrom.

Mei Lim's only pleasant childhood memory was a trip to visit Keyuan Gardens. The name meant "a garden not too bad for visiting" but to a little girl used to dirt streets and ramshackle wooden houses, it was heaven on earth. Built of blue bricks by a retired Qing officer named Zhang Jingxiu in 1850 as a peaceful place where he could pursue poetry and painting, it was open to scholars and poets and artists and it quickly became the cultural center of the province.

Mei Lim had been lucky enough to travel up along the Pearl River to Keyuan with an elderly uncle who had been invited by Zhang as an expert to teach calligraphy. Now as she closed her eyes she could evoke the images of that garden: a triangular area with buildings and pavilions surrounding serene pools where elegant bridges of classical design and the drooping tendrils of delicate willows were reflected in the shimmering water. The bricks of the walkways and buildings flowed blue and bright in the sunlight as if they were dabs of an artist's brush on a canvas made of orchids and wisteria. There was nothing else in her experience, not the Gilded Age mansions of San Francisco nor the magnificent machinery of the railroad locomotives to compare with the architecture and design of the Keyuan Gardens.

This was her happiest memory, but one shattered as the uncle explained why he had brought her to see the gardens: "You must remember that we have beauty to contemplate even in the midst of strife. You must realize that men are not all violent and self-absorbed; they also are creative and love nature. You must fix this place in your heart because you will leave it soon." It was then that Mei Lim learned that her parents had sold her into servitude.

They slept. Iron wheels rolled over the newly laid rails. The work had been rushed, and in many places would need repair, but for now it sufficed. The click-ity-click-ity-click-ity that had lulled them to sleep was the heartbeat of a new-born babe—of a new era of expansion and exploitation; of the rape, the robbery and the genocide of an indigenous people; of the rush toward unfathomable wealth and unimaginable poverty and the evolution of class war—in short, the palpitating heartbeat of the Gilded Age.

Zack woke. The train had stopped for water. He looked out the window, eyes blurred and window glass coated with soot and dust, and he saw indistinctly two figures outside near the roadbed. The two figures seemed to be quarreling, the larger pulling at the smaller, the smaller pushing at the larger. Zack tried to blink the sleep away, wiped at the window pane (but of course the grime was on the outside) and glanced at his companions. Tommy and Little Wind were still asleep, huddled together in what must have been uncomfortable positions. Where was Mei Lim!

"Tommy! Wake up!" Zack shook Tommy. "Come. Mei Lim is in trouble!"

Together the boys ran to the door and leaped from the train. Mei Lim was shouting something in Chinese. The man who was accosting her, a stout Asian man wearing a red headband, shouted back and grabbed at her. Zack threw himself at the man, his momentum momentarily staggering the assailant and breaking his grip on the girl. But now the man drew a dagger from his belt and faced the would-be rescuer with an expression that reminded Zack of a mad dog he had once seen back on the reservation.

"He's Tong," yelled Mei Lim. "Watch out!"

Tommy looked for some sort of a weapon: a stick or a large rock, but found nothing within reach. He and Zack now stood shoulder to shoulder as a human barricade between Mei Lim and the Tong man. How, he wondered, had the Tong man found Mei Lim?

As if she had read his thoughts, Mei Lim answered, "He has been on the train watching me. Waiting for the moment when he could take me. They will never stop!"

"This one will stop right now," said Zack. "I'll go for the knife," he said to Tommy. "You hit him as hard as you can."

They rushed at the Tong man. Zack grabbed the man's knife arm and forced it backwards as Tommy crashed against the man's chest and swung with all his strength at his face. Then they were on the ground, grappling and rolling, the knife still clutched by the Tong man, but his arm was now pinned under Zack's weight and therefore immobile.

There were faces now at the windows, peering out at the tussle. No one, however, seemed willing to intervene. Mei Lim tried to wrench the knife from the man but only succeeded in receiving a long cut across her palm. She then tried kicking at it but the Tong man held tight to his one advantage and waited for just the right time when his arm would become free. Then he would strike: he would kill these two unworthy opponents. Then he would kill the girl.

Tommy landed several punches on the man's chin and neck but the Tong man seemed to be made of solid steel. The Tong man twisted and rolled and was working his way out from under the boys. With a sudden effort the Tong man shook them off and gained his feet. He stood, brandishing the knife, a sardonic smile spreading across his face like a gash. The boys struggled to stand up, aching from bruises and gasping for breath. What now?

The Tong man crept slowly toward Zack and Tommy. His knife was poised and it seemed certain that one or the other of the boys would be the first to feel it ripping into the flesh of their stomachs or slashing across their throats. Suddenly the Tong man let out a scream and pitched forward. He fell to the ground in front of Zack and Tommy, an arrow sticking out of his back.

A small party of Sioux had decided to attack the train as it stood at the water tower. Although there wasn't much point to the attack, the Sioux would take every opportunity to inflict whatever damage they could on the railroad. During its building they had raided work gangs and destroyed bridges. The coming of the railroad had been inevitable, unstoppable, and devastating. Now they attacked from frustration more than purpose.

"Oh my," said Zack. "Wild Indians!"

The rail siding onto which the train had pulled was on a slight rise. Arrows clattered against the railcars as the Sioux sent them arching through the air like angry mosquitoes hungry for blood. Zack, Tommy and Mei Lim ran for their car just as the sound of gunfire came from a railcar further up. Windows had been lowered and muskets bristled from the Silver Palace Sleeping Car as the passengers fought back. Perhaps some thought popping off a redskin was great sport; as entertaining as shooting buffalo from a moving train.

And the train did move. It left the raiders in a cloud of wood smoke and road dust. It rolled through the Wyoming Territory, past Green River, Point Of Rocks, Bitter Creek, Rawlins, Sinclair, Granville, Fort Steele, Medicine Bow, Cooper Lake and Benton without further incidents. Early the next morning the train pulled into Laramie, not quite halfway to Omaha.

Laramie had been little more than a tent city on the Overland Stage Line route before the railroad came. In 1868 it became the western terminus of the Union Pacific and a destination for entrepreneurs and outlaws alike. Now the streets of Laramie were lined with permanent buildings fashioned from local stone. They housed stores, a school, a church, and a number of saloons. The most notorious of the drinking and gambling establishments was Big Steve Long's Bucket of Blood.

Big Steve had been the town's first marshal. He and his two half brothers, the Moyers, terrorized the townspeople forcing them to sign over the deeds to their lands. Long and the Moyers were the quintessential western gun slingers; gunfights involving them and their victims were a common sight on the streets of Laramie. Long himself killed 13 people. But as the Wild West had its villains, it also had its heroes. The county sheriff, a man named N. K. Boswell, became tired of the reign of terror of the three outlaws. Together with a Vigilance Committee he had hurriedly organized, Boswell marched into the Bucket of Blood and arrested Long and the Moyers. Within the hour their bodies swung from a tree limb just down the street from their saloon.

"Ten minutes! Ten minutes to stretch your legs," called the conductor.

Across from the train depot stood a row of storefronts. Zack and Mei Lim strolled along the boardwalk, peering into windows. Laramie could have been any frontier town: carriages and wagons lumbered up and down its dirt-blown streets; a herd of six oxen were being led out of a corral by a boy, barefoot and brandishing a long whip; music leaked from between swinging doors at a saloon; soldiers from the fort south of town paraded gallantly up the boardwalk toward the nearest brothel—there was nothing to indicate that the town had sprung to life only one year ago.

Pausing before a plate glass window to an emporium, Zack studied the various advertising signs and displays of merchandise. He was unable to read the signs, but then, many of the townsfolk were illiterate as well so the advertising utilized graphic illustrations to lure customers from the streets. A sign depicting a man bending over a pocket watch with a small screwdriver in his hand caught Zack's eye.

"Mei Lim," he said, "I'm going in here. Maybe I can get them to wind my watch for me."

"Zack…Zack…that always gets you in trouble," Mei Lim answered.

"No, wait. You'll see." Zack entered the emporium and approached the clerk. "Excuse me please, Sir. I have this watch, and…"

"Boy, what are you doing in here? We don't allow your kind in here." But then the man saw the pocket watch in Zack's outstretched hand. "Ah hah! Where did you steal that?"

"No, Sir. It's mine. I need to ask you…I have no winding key. Could you wind it for me? Or sell me a winding key?"

"What? You aren't trying to sell me the watch? Just want it wound up, eh. Think you know how to tell time, do you?"

"Sir, it's important. If I can get it to work…well, it might mean my father is still alive."

"I'm not sure I understand that. But give it here a minute." The man opened a drawer and fumbled for a few seconds, then retrieved several winding keys. He proceeded to try each key on the watch. At last, one fit. He turned it a few turns and the hands on the watch started to move.

"Oh, thank you. Thank you," said Zack.

"Wait just a minute, now. You want to buy this key so you can keep the watch wound? Do you have a dollar?"

"A dollar! That's awfully expensive for a key, isn't it?"

"Do you want it or not?"

Zack reached into his pocket. "I have this script from the railroad," he told the man. "It's good for getting gold money from a bank. You have one here, don't you?"

The man examined the promissory note Zack held out to him. It was for three hundred dollars: all the money Zack had earned working for the railroad. It was drawn on a bank in Sacramento but would probably be honored even at the bank in Laramie. He hesitated.

"Son," the man said, "I don't want to cheat you. Oh, it's tempting all right. But I'm just not that dishonest. This note is worth three hundred dollars. You didn't know that, did you?"

"I can't read, Sir."

A whistle was blowing frantically across the street at the depot. Mei Lim rushed into the store shouting, "Zack! Come now. Train is leaving!"

The man returned the watch to Zack with the key still stuck in it. "Good luck, boy. I hope your father is alive and your watch keeps good time."

20

Holy City of the Cow

The train climbed a gradual incline. They were now nearly twenty miles west of Laramie at the Dale Creek crossing. The UPRR had constructed their longest, highest, most impressive trestle at Dale Creek. It spanned 450 feet of gorge and was itself 750 feet long. The two abutments at either end of the gorge were built from local hand-dressed stone. The trestle was a spindly grid of wooden timbers which required steel guy wires to prevent it from swaying in the wind. The creek was 150 feet below.

The tiny hamlet of Sherman lay two miles east of the trestle at a feature of the Black Hills called Evans Pass. Evans Pass, first called Lone Tree Pass, was a rolling plain speckled with crags and rocky outcroppings. It rose to the highest elevation that the railroad—that any railroad in the world of 1869 would reach: 8,262 feet above sea level. The town of Sherman had little to offer other than the view. It was the location of one of the railroad's machine shops, of a Wells Fargo office, two hotels, a newspaper, a store and, of course, a saloon. This train would not stop at Sherman; it clattered on.

From the windows of the Emigrant Car the passengers could see distant mountain peaks: Long's Peak, Pike's Peak, Elk Mountain and others miles away in the Colorado Rockies. Many years later, in 1882, the Union Pacific Railroad's board of directors commemorated this, the highest spot on the line, by erecting a monument of rough-hewn granite in the shape of a small pyramid. They dedicated it to Oakes Ames and his brother, Oliver.

Oakes Ames was a congressman from Massachusetts. He had obtained major financial support for the railroad although he achieved this, it was said, through underhanded practices and skimmed a fair amount for himself. His brother, Oliver Ames was President of the Union Pacific during the construction years and a fellow grafter. The two brothers are remembered, not for their pile of rocks on high, but as two great swindlers who embroiled the Union Pacific in scandal and bribery. Their financial shenanigans reached as

201

high as Schuyler Colfax, then Vice President of the United States, James Blain, the Speaker of the House of Representatives, Harry Wilson, the Republican candidate for vice president, and future president James A. Garfield. The pyramid, like those of ancient Egypt, built by slave labor for the adoration of kings, was an apt symbol for the greed and corruption that plagued the railroad, although the directors probably missed that obvious irony.

The train now began the descent from Sherman Hill. Zack and Mei Lim had taken the bench seat furthest back in the car. Tommy and Little Wind sat a few rows ahead. It seemed that both couples needed time alone for intimate conversation—or mutual meditation—or just a little distance from each other.

"What did he mean...that man...that he wished your father were alive?" Mei Lim asked Zack.

"I told him that if the watch ran it meant Father was still alive."

"You think this watch is an object of magic?"

"I saw how a white doctor used his watch to try to cure a wounded man. And I remember the sign above the watch shop...it had eyes that looked down at you. There must be something..."

"Oh, Zack, if only you are right. It is possible. In my country there were those who pursued magic elixirs to get immortality. There were stories of monks who lived for 900 years. But I don't know..."

"The shaman would be able to tell me. If I were at home. Why didn't I go to him? It was foolish to go off on my own."

"You aren't alone, Zack. You have Tommy."

"And you, Mei Lim. I have you."

"Zack...I am thinking...I must part from you again."

"What? Why?"

"I only bring trouble to you. These men, the Tongs, they are everywhere. They see me and try to take me."

"The mark on your arm. Can't we cover it up somehow?"

"It would do no good. Every Chinese girl is the same to them. An object to use."

"All the more reason to stay with me. I can protect you."

Mei Lim was silent. A tear attempted to escape from her eye as she gazed at Zack. She sniffed it back. "Oh, look out the window," she managed to say. "What wonderful snow-covered mountains!"

From Sherman the train followed a natural land bridge which was called the Gangplank. The railroad engineers had found an easy way up this narrow ramp where sedimentary rock had failed to erode during the formation of the mountains. They could thus avoid following the Overland Trail which was suited only for oxen and wagons and would require extensive modification. The Gangplank had been a major criterion in the planning of the route.

The peaks were harder to see as the train descended toward the high plains ahead: a ring of unbroken mountain ranges surrounded them masking the horizon. They had lost 2000 feet of altitude as they approach Cheyenne, Wyoming, the Miracle City of the Plains, the Holy City of the Cow.

Grenville Dodge had laid out the streets of Cheyenne in 1867 as a staging point before ascending the Gangplank toward the summit of the Laramie Mountains. He had been attacked by Indians as he drew lines in the dirt for streets; three men were killed. The first finished plot in town was a cemetery.

Entrepreneurs of all sorts quickly arrived just as they had at all the towns, those "Hell on wheels" towns created as the railroad stretched across the wilderness. Essential to the construction of the railroad was nourishment for its workers and now, as they entered the mountains, they would not be able to rely on the abundance of buffalo as they had in Nebraska. Thus a cattle ranch sprang up a few miles from town along the Crow Creek. Cheyenne became the northern terminus of the Goodnight-Loving Trail along which herds of Texas cattle made their final journey to the dining tents of the Union Pacific. They were corralled at the Holy City of the Cow.

"Quite a difference in two short years," said a man who had just stepped from the Silver Place Sleeping Car onto the platform. The man who had spoken was conversing with another man who was wearing a cleric's collar.

The layover at Cheyenne would be a whole half hour and Zack and his party had quickly descended from the Emigrant car eager to breathe fresh air and see the town. This was also the first opportunity they had had to observe any of the passengers who had been riding in the first class carriage. Some were of the group of dignitaries that had been at Promontory.

"Look," said Zack, pointing at the man with the cleric's collar. "Isn't that one of the Franciscan brothers?"

It was not. It was, in fact, the Reverend Doctor Montgomery Peters, Rector of Saint John the Baptist's in Newark, New Jersey, who had attended the Last Spike ceremony with three ecclesiastics from the Trinity Church in New York City: the Reverend Doctor Morgan Dix, the Reverend Doctor Vinton and the Reverend Doctor Ogilvie.

The reverends had all made speeches or said prayers at the ceremony.

"You were here in Cheyenne when the railroad first arrived?" the good reverend asked the other man.

"Oh, indeed I was. Quite a wild place! The Big Tent stood over there near where that hotel is now. The Big Tent was…well, Reverend, you don't want to know what went on in the Big Tent. Yes, and if it wasn't gamblers or laid-off railroaders roaming the streets it was drunken cowboys."

"Cowboys? You mean trail riders?"

"Mollie Goodnight, that's Charlie's wife, always called the hands her 'boys.' That's where the term 'cowboy' comes from. If you read any of the pulps you'd know about that."

"Really, Sir!"

"Sorry, Reverend. Anyway, look at the town now. I hear tell the hotel holds fifty people and they can feed 400 at a crack. There's two churches…"

"And I can see six saloons from right here. How many live here?"

"About five thousand, I think. And look at the size of that windmill! It must be 75 feet tall. The blades are 25 feet long, I'll wager."

"Well, if you want to wager, I'm sure you can find some entertainment up the avenue," commented Reverend Peters, not disguising the sarcasm in his voice.

Zack, Tommy, Mei Lim and Little Wind ambled up the broad street examining the storefronts. These were wood framed buildings with flat roofs. Near the tracks stood one of the few stone buildings, a machine shop constructed from native sandstone. Ahead of them rose a large two-story building with a portico: the Cheyenne Hotel which was operated by the railroad. Next door to this was a saloon with the dubious name of The Cottage of Content Saloon.

Cheyenne had been the winter quarters for the railroad workers only two years ago and a smattering of crude sod houses and dilapidated canvas tents still remained here and there among the newer wooden structures. But Cheyenne had not disappeared like so many of the railroad boomtowns. The Sweetwater gold mines to the northwest created a need for supplies and many a miner trekked to Cheyenne for their needs. The cattle drives continued up the Goodnight-Loving Trail and the railroad became an important purveyor of Texas beef to the east.

Not only was Cheyenne becoming a hub of western commerce it was also the capital of the new Territory of Wyoming. There was no capitol building, however, and the two houses of the legislature met in rented rooms just down the block from Luke Murrin's Wholesale Liquor House where the congressmen could visit the sample room in the rear of that establishment. But in spite of its rough edges, the government of Wyoming led the country in liberal thinking and action. In December of 1869, Governor John Allen Campbell extended the right to vote to women, making Wyoming the first territory or state to do so.

Now Zack and his companions turned a corner and strolled up 17th street. They met the four reverends, Peters, Dix, Vinton and Ogilvie coming from the other direction. The four were scurrying like frightened penguins running from a polar bear. When Peters saw the young travelers he blurted:

"Go back, young people. You don't want to see what is ahead of you."

Which, of course, they did. Ignoring the good reverend's admonishment they continued up the street until they reached an alleyway leading off to their right. At the end of the alley stood a crudely-made gallows. From the gallows a body turned slowly like a broken compass as it dangled from a rotting rope. The rope, being only two feet in length, had failed to snap the man's neck properly resulting in a slow death by strangulation, the evidence of which showed on the distorted features of his bloated blue face.

"Now I've seen many white men—those that they call the 'ghost people' because they are so pale," said Tommy as they stood looking at the corpse on the gallows, "and I've heard that Mei Lim's people are called the 'yellow ant people,' and we are known as 'redmen' although none of us are anywhere near that color, and then there are the 'blacks' of course, although I've seen only a few of them, but— and this is the truth—I never heard of a 'blue man'—no, never!"

"Tommy...," Zack began but immediately realized an explanation would be pointless. As they stood contemplating the deceased man the four reverends had followed them back into the alley. Reverend Vinton now spoke:

"Children, come away from there. The corpse may carry disease for all you know."

"Children!" said Tommy, enraged as usual by the disparagement of older people. Before he could say more, Zack interceded with:

"I recognize you. You were the father that talked so long at the spike driving."

Reverend Vinton was taken back by this factual, but slightly insulting observation. "You were at the Last Spike Ceremony?" he asked.

"We helped build the railroad," Zack answered, proudly.

"And you thought my comments were a bit long-winded, did you?"

"Oh no," said Zack, shuffling his feet. "I liked your talk. I liked how you said the meeting of the rails was a great victory for peace and that people could now travel from ocean to ocean. I don't understand that entirely, but I like the idea of it."

"You *did* listen to me. That's remarkable for one so young."

"You think we are children, Father. But we are not. And another thing I didn't understand...you said it was a triumph of commerce— that means buying and selling things, right? You said that the triumph of commerce meant that free trade would be the law of the future of our nation. I don't understand—is it buying and selling or trading things for free that is the future?"

"No, it means that...free trade means...oh, Doctor Peters, will you explain it to the boy?"

"I don't think you should be calling him a 'boy,' Doctor Vinton. He seems to have grasped the gist of your homily," said Reverend Peters.

"But there was so much more to my speech. I said, and I can quote myself exactly because I am adept at memorizing sermons, '...this Pacific Railway is a means, under Divine Providence, for propagating the Church and the Gospel from this, the youngest Christian nation, to the oldest land in the Orient, now sunk in Paganism and idolatry, and so will revive the worship of the Triune God—the God of our salvation—in the farther East, the birthplace of Christianity.' That was the meaning behind my words."

Mei Lim had cringed at the phrase, "the Orient, now sunk in Paganism and idolatry." Reverend Vinton saw the expression on her face and addressed her:

"No, my dear, I meant the *Middle* East. Palestine and Jerusalem. We are aware of and glad of the number of Christians now in China and are hopeful for the final total conversion. It's the Jews and the Muslims that are our concern."

"Doctors and young people, I think it is time," said Reverend Peters, "to be on our way back to the train. I think I hear the whistle blowing."

"Yes, I concur," added Reverend Ogilvie who had until now been silent, watching and listening to his colleagues with veiled amusement. "Jerusalem will still be there when we get back but the train will wait for nobody." Reverend Dix nodded in agreement.

As the group returned to the depot they passed the offices of the Cheyenne Argus, one of three newspapers in the town. In the window was a broadsheet from a recent edition. The headline read, "LOCAL MAN LYNCHED!" Reverend Dix stopped to read the article which followed.

"Charles Martin," Dix read, "co-owner and proprietor of the Keystone Dance Hall shot and killed his partner, Andy Harris, late Thursday afternoon outside their establishment. It was rumored that the partners had financed the purchase of the hall with the proceeds from an armed robbery; at least that is how local lore would have it. Martin and Harris were seen arguing earlier and although no one witnessed the shooting, Martin was swiftly arrested and tried for the murder. He was acquitted of the crime for lack of evidence and so he returned to the Keystone last night where he began to celebrate by dancing and drinking to his heart's content. Soon four or five men in black hoods stormed into the dance hall and seized on Martin, dragging him into the alley where they proceeded to tie a rope around his neck and throw the loose end over a post. They strung the fellow up and although this editor distains vigilantism, we have to say that in this case, justice was adequately served."

They returned to the railway platform and prepared to board their respective cars: the four reverends would be mounting the steps of the Silver Palace Sleeping Car and Zack and his party would climb into the Emigrant Car. As they parted, Reverend Peters pulled Zack to one side. "Son," he said, "if you have any questions or concerns about anything you saw or heard today, I am always available to talk to."

"Thank you, but I can't go into your car. It's not allowed," said Zack.

"Hmm…I see, Well, I can come to you. If you wish me to."

"That's very kind of you, and there *are* certain things I don't understand. But…"

"But nothing. Later this evening, after the meal, I'll come back and we can have a talk. Just you and me. Would that be satisfactory?"

What am I getting myself into now, thought Zack? He remembered the Franciscan fathers at the reservation all too well. They always wanted to talk. Talk always got around to how you should love Jesus. Zack never really warmed up to that notion. After all, Jesus got himself killed. What kind of a role model was that? His words were good though. But somehow it seemed to Zack that Jesus-loving white people always were the first to steal, kill and enslave others. And there were other considerations.

He remembered one day when he was very young. He was at the school at the reservation and classes were over for the day. Father Angelo had told him to stay for a while. To talk things over. To talk about Jesus. He complied, of course. Father Angelo was always kind, always smiled at Zack and the other children. Never yelled at them or whipped them as he had seen the other white people who were in charge at the reservation do.

But something wasn't quite right. Father Angelo waited until all the other children had left the schoolroom. He motioned for Zack to come closer. Closer so I can embrace you with the love of our Savior he had said, or something similar—Zack had repressed most of the memory.

He did remember having a sensation as if he were suddenly awakening from a dream. Father Angelo was holding him tightly against his own body—not the kind of embrace Zack had gotten from his mother or his father—something different—something that scared him. He remembered pulling away and running from the room, afraid of what Father Angelo might say, but more afraid of that embrace.

The incident was never repeated. Zack's opinion of the Franciscan fathers was that they were, for the most part, good, caring men who desired to help the "savage" Indian children. Yes, help them by tearing them away from their beliefs and substituting the stern, demanding Christian God for the animal spirits Zack had been brought up to trust, to believe in, to respect. But that was all in the past now. Or was it?

Later, as the train had left Cheyenne and rumbled into Nebraska, Zack sat with Mei Lim at the back of the Emigrant Car. He told her the story of Father Angelo and of his fears about Reverend Peters.

"You right to be careful," Mei Lim told him. At Madame Ah Toy's were not just girls. She had boys for special customers."

"You mean…"

"Yes. I don't remember if religious men visited, but I not doubt it. Men all alike whether they visit girls or boys. Men all the lowest of animals—below pigs and rats."

"Then why did you…oh, never mind. What should I do if he comes tonight?"

"Maybe you hide somewhere. Somewhere he not look."

After the sun had set, lanterns were lit which cast a soft flicker of golden light across the long, narrow interior of the Emigrant Car. The gentle rocking of the car and the monotonous rhythm of the rails combined to ease the travelers into deep slumber. Zack's head bobbed as he slept sitting up on the hard uncomfortable bench. Mei Lim had curled up next to him with her head on his lap. All around them people snored and coughed and made wheezing noises.

The Reverend Doctor Montgomery Peters made his way in the dim lantern light, swaying with the motion of the train. He squinted at dark silhouettes attempting to locate the object of his search, the Indian boy, the lost soul who needed salvation, needed comforting, needed the loving Christian concern he could offer. The crowding in the car, the smells that close quarters can generate, the discarded food boxes under foot, the empty whiskey bottle that nearly tripped the good reverend—it all disgusted Peters. These dregs of humanity of the lower classes were repellent to him; oh to be back in New Jersey where society was civilized!

I can bring the boy back to my car now that people are sleeping, the reverend thought to himself. If we are quiet and I draw the curtains no one will ever know. He began to hum one of his favorite hymns to himself, "Great is the Lord and Greatly to be Praised." The lanterns had been turned so low that the brightest illumination came from moonlight reflecting from the plains outside. Peters stumbled and caught himself on the shoulder of a snoring Pawnee, startling the man who let out a yell.

"Sorry...sorry," Peters whispered but as the commotion he caused had awakened half the car, his attempts at stealth were now pointless. Mei Lim had been roused and she shook Zack.

"Look. It's him," she said. "Now you hide."

"Hide where?" said Zack. "It's not like he's some monster coming to devour me. He's just a nice man that wants to talk about Jesus."

"Okay. You talk about Jesus. See what I care."

But Peters now thought better of his expedition into this world where these unfortunate castaways of civilization where packed together like sausages, where all those dark eyes were focused on him, the interloper. He turned and hurried out of the Emigrant Car, nearly slipping again on the empty whiskey bottle.

Later Zack said to Mei Lim, "You think I'm a low pig or a rat? I am a man too."

"I think you are Dragon Warrior. You save me many times. You never pig or rat."

"That's good. I think you are...worth saving."

What followed was the first kiss Zack had ever experienced, at least one full on the lips. The Dragon Warrior turned crimson with embarrassment but quickly lost his blush and returned the kiss with equal passion.

21

Connections

"May God continue the unity of our Country as this Railroad unites the two great Oceans of the world."
—inscription on the ceremonial golden spike presented by David Hewes of San Francisco to Leland Stanford.

Twenty-four hours after leaving Cheyenne, Wyoming, the four travelers stepped off the train in Omaha, Nebraska. The towns had slipped by like the fleeting images of a dream: Kimball, Sidney, Julesburg, Ogallala, North Platte, Cozad, Grand Island, Columbus, and Fremont. As they flew along the tracks the rolling plain had greened, prairie dogs standing erect along the roadbed became fewer, and here and there they saw new groves of young trees, nature's replacements for those stripped from the land for fuel by the railroad. From the summit at Sherman, Wyoming, to here at Omaha they had lost 6150 feet of altitude. Between San Francisco and Omaha they had traveled over 1770 miles by rail. They would travel another 470 miles more before they set foot in El-Ya-Noy.

Before the railroad came, this trip of a single day from the Rockies to the Missouri River had taken six days and nights by stagecoach and longer by wagon train. Three wagon trails had stretched across the open Nebraskan plains: the Oregon Trail, the California Trail and the Mormon Trail, the later funneling the majority of the Later Day Saints from Council Bluffs, Iowa, to Salt Lake City, Utah.

Council Bluffs, just across the river from Omaha, had seen the great influx of Mormons in 1846 and their great exodus in 1852. It had been the primary staging area for the Argonauts, the fortune seekers of the California gold rush of the 1850s. It would grow from a population of 2000 in 1860 to over 10,000 by the end of the decade. Eight different railroads would connect at Council Bluffs.

Illinois lawyer Abraham Lincoln was a visitor to Council Bluffs in 1859 during the time he campaigned for the presidency. Lincoln was there investigating for a lawsuit against the Mississippi and Missouri Railroad whose bridge had been struck by a steamboat. He had received 160 acres of land in Council Bluffs as collateral from an attorney for the M&M. While there he gave a speech at Palmer's Concert Hall and met with banking officials of the town. Later at the Pacific House Hotel he met Grenville Dodge and the two men talked over routes for the proposed Transcontinental Railroad. Dodge favored a route from Council Bluff along the Platte River.

During the first year of Lincoln's presidency in 1862 he had signed the Pacific Railroad Act into law. A variety of personages in the military, in business and government had vested interests in seeing the eastern terminus located at Council Bluffs including Dodge, who Lincoln now promoted to brigadier general, Thomas Durant, who had made a fortune manipulating stock in the M&M Railroad, John Blair, a railroad financier and friend of Oakes Ames, and Major-General Samuel Ryan Curtis, who had an interest in the Council Bluffs and Nebraska Ferry Company. Lincoln named Council Bluffs as the terminus and Thomas Durant's Union Pacific Railroad as the builder of the Transcontinental Railroad.

But now the great Pacific Railroad did not yet connect the two great oceans. There were no tracks between San Francisco and Sacramento. And there was no railroad bridge across the Missouri between the twin cities of Omaha and Council Bluffs. Connections to the east, which meant either Chicago or Saint Louis, could be made by train, once one crossed to the east of the river by ferry. The Cedar Rapids and Missouri River Railroad, then consolidated into the Chicago and North Western Railway had built down to Council Bluffs in 1867 but without a bridge there was no way to bring the Union Pacific trains across the river; the UPRR did attempt to cross over the frozen ice in winter, but quickly abandoned the idea. The Union Pacific Missouri River Bridge would not be built until 1873.

Omaha was a city of eight thousand people. The main part of town was three blocks of stores and warehouses, offices and houses. Brick structures accounted for half of the buildings, the rest being of wood assembled with varying degrees of carpentry skill. A hotel, a bank, a theater were expertly constructed with ornamental details and thick coats of paint; here and there were ramshackle houses of rough plank. At least the tents were now gone.

The main road was Farnham Street which connected the business district with the riverfront. Here were found restaurants and bars and the Herndon Hotel where celebratory meetings of Union Pacific Railroad officials had taken place at the onset of the Transcontinental Railway. From the river the landscape sloped gradually back toward a ring of low hills. Small houses and farms dotted the hillside. At the top, unique in size and architectural design, stood a grand pair of edifices: the Capitol Building and St. Mary's Church, sentinels of government and religion, overlooking the bustling city like two wizened old men.

Tommy had quizzed the stationmaster for information on reaching El-Ya-Noy. "You have to cross the river here or farther north," the stationmaster had told him. "You could cross up at Sioux City, but if you go over to Council Bluffs you can catch the train directly to Chicago."

"Chicago?" Tommy asked, looking puzzled.

"Chicago is a city in Illinois. That's where you want to go, isn't it? Take the Lone Tree Ferry across the river. You can then buy tickets at the depot for the Chicago and North Western Railway."

When Tommy returned to his waiting companions he said, "We'll need more money. We have to cash in the script the railroad paid us and get regular money for it."

"Let's see if we can find a bank," said Zack. The four travelers wandered down Farnham Street toward the river, examining the various office buildings to discover the purpose of each. Not being able to read was a distinct disadvantage. Eventually, at the prompting of the girls, they asked directions from people walking up the avenue and thus found their way to the offices of the Merchants' Exchange Bank and Trust Company.

They entered the bank which was housed in a handsome red brick building with large plate glass windows covered with gold leaf lettering. Tommy and Zack walked up to the cashier's window and presented the clerk with their scripts issued by the Central Pacific. "Please wait one moment," said the clerk who promptly disappeared from the cage. Several minutes later he returned in the company of another man, older, bewhiskered, stiff-collared and scowling like an annoyed old owl ready to swoop down on a frightened field mouse— or two.

"I am the bank manager, Mr. Owens," said the man in a dry voice and with post-straight posture which suggested that he expected the boys to genuflect or otherwise cow tow to his authority. "Where did you get these?" he asked, pointing to the scripts he now held in his hand.

"From the railroad, of course," answered Zack. "We worked for them."

"Do you have any proof of that?"

"We have the blisters," said Tommy. "We worked long and hard hours for many days to earn that money. It's owed to us."

The bank manager looked briefly at his clerk as if for some approval that he didn't really need. Then he said, "These are drawn on a Sacramento bank. You'll have to go to California to cash them in." He turned on his heel and left the cashier's cage.

The cashier returned the scripts to the boys. "Sorry," he said. "Maybe you could try the railroad offices. Their building is just down the street. Good luck to you." What chance, the clerk thought to himself, do these Indian boys have of getting their money? A snowball's chance in Hell!

They found out later at the Union Pacific office. After waiting for over an hour on hard benches in the lobby Tommy and Zack were ushered into the office of Mr. Jacob Daniels who worked in the financial division of the railroad. Here they waited again while his secretary, a Mrs. Skelly, according to her nameplate, pounded on a typing machine, a contraption that Zack thought was a confusing looking metal monstrosity designed only for making an annoying clattering noise.

When one waits in a place for a long time, one notices tiny details: corners of the floor not swept properly, smoke stains on wallpaper behind gaslights, a small crack across one corner of a window—not large enough to require replacing the pane, rings left on desktops by coffee cups. Eventually Daniels came out from his inner office. Mrs. Skelly explained the purpose for which the boys had come and Daniels examined the two scripts the boys had brought.

"These are the responsibility of the Central Pacific," he said. "Not our problem. Go see them. Say...you Indians? Yeah? Well go to..." Daniels left the room shutting his office door with a loud bang.

Mrs. Skelly, seeing the boys' discomfort, said, "Please don't pay any attention to Mr. Daniels. He has an attitude about Indians which...well, which comes from the fact that his son was with General Connor at Tongue River. He was wounded by an Arapaho tomahawk and died of his wounds soon after. Mr. Daniels seems to take it out on all Indians."

Neither Zack nor Tommy had heard of General Conner or of the Tongue River. General Patrick Edward Conner had been a Union General during the Civil War but had only seen action against Native Americans. He was a naturalized Irish immigrant who had been in and out the army, had fought against the Seminole Indians, fought Mexicans in Texas, gone to the gold rush and found himself in command of a California militia unit at the outbreak of the Civil War. His unit was absorbed into the California Volunteer Infantry and his regiment was ordered to Utah to protect overlanders from Indian attack and to thwart an expected Mormon uprising.

Connor wanted to fight Confederate soldiers and petitioned then general-in-chief Major General Henry Halleck (the same General Halleck who later was in charge of military operations in Alaska) to send his regiment east but Halleck, although a good friend of Connor, denied him that opportunity. Connor stayed in Utah.

In the early 1860s Connor had become aware of Indian attacks on settlers and miners in the Cache Valley. During the brutally cold January of 1863 he marched his regiment 140 miles to a Shoshone encampment along the Bear River. Connor was determined to exterminate all the hostile Indians he could find. Facing only minor resistance from arrows and tomahawks, the soldiers managed to destroy the Shoshone village killing nearly all its men, women and children, some 368 individuals. The resulting Bear River Massacre made Connor a hero to those persons who desired the eradication the Native American population.

After the end of the Civil War, Connor was made a brigadier general and assigned by General Grenville Dodge to cleanse the Great Plains of Indians for the coming of the Union Pacific Railroad. The undertaking was called the Powder River Expedition. General Connor issued his orders: "You will not receive overtures of peace or submission from Indians, but will attack and kill every male Indian over twelve years of age." Although his orders were countermanded,

Connor intended to use his massacring techniques on the Cheyenne, Arapaho and Sioux that apparently stood in the way of progress.

The Battle of the Tongue River took place in 1865. Connor and his troops attacked an Arapaho village and reportedly killed 63 of whom 35 were warriors and the rest women and children. Five soldiers died and two were wounded, including a boy named Jeffery Daniels, the son of the man Zack and Tommy were asking for help.

Mrs. Skelly studied the two young men (she would never have thought of them as children) who stood before her desk. She had a different opinion of Indians from that of her boss. Alice Skelly was 38, widowed and childless. Her prospects seemed to her to be as much of a dead end as did her job. The daughter of one of the original Mormon settlers at Winter Quarters on the Missouri River, she and her husband had stayed in Council Bluffs when the majority of the Later Day Saints had left for Utah. She had taken the job in Omaha after her husband's untimely death from smallpox.

Alice possessed a greater affinity toward Native Americans than most of own her race living at that time in Nebraska's "Gateway to the West". She had befriended many of the local Pottawattamie and had seen them pushed further and further from their homelands and persecuted relentlessly during the inevitable onslaught of white westward migration. Here before her now were two Indians boys who needed help.

"Which bank did you go to?" she asked.

"Ah...it was down nearer the river," Zack answered.

"I have an idea," said Alice Skelly. "I can help you."

Alice Skelly's husband, Arthur, had been in the meatpacking business with his brother, Howard. The brothers had been successful enough in their enterprise to warrant the respect of the local business professionals on both sides of the river. Alice still had a good relationship with her late husband's brother and he, in turn, had excellent credit at the bank—the other bank, the one not near the river. Alice Skelly brought stationery from a drawer in her desk and began to write.

"Take this letter," she told the boys, "to the Nebraska National Bank on 2nd Avenue. That's three blocks north of here. Ask for Mr. Partridge and tell him Alice Skelly sent you. He will cash your scripts for you without any trouble. Quickly now, before the bank closes for the day!"

The mannequin in the store window a few doors down had attracted the girls as they waited in the street outside the bank. It was dressed in an elliptical-shaped skirt with a high waist and an overstated bustle. The neck-line was square and the fabric was some brilliant green silky material that that seemed lit from within. The slim figure of the mannequin suggested that the old-fashioned, massive crinoline was absent as a form-crafting device; the bustle would suffice. Little Wind stared at it, fascinated.

"Would you wear that?" Little Wind asked Mei Lim.

"Well, I like the little hat, but, no…I don't think I would like all that weight hanging on me."

"The cloth is pretty."

"Some of the girls wore western clothing where I worked in Sacramento. It attracted certain men who wanted to pretend we weren't Asian."

Little Wind still wore the traditional Tlingit clothing she had brought back with her from Alaska. It was comfortable and she liked the colors and patterns. Her dress did, however, attract undue attention from passersby. Mei Lim had suggested that they both might blend in better by purchasing the kind of clothing the white frontier women wore. The high fashion dress in the store window, however, was itself a bit too flamboyant for their purposes.

They had entered the shop but had been turned away by the proprietress. There was nothing to do but wait for Zack and Tommy to return. Little Wind found herself studying the Chinese girl, looking for what, she did not know. She was curious, of course, about Mei Lim's former life. There was a worldliness about her that intrigued Little Wind—and frightened her.

"You and my brother," Little Wind said, "are you…?"

"We are friends. Good friends. I owe your brother much. And is always good plan to have regard for those who have talent in so many things. You not worry about Mei Lim corrupting Zack. Zack is a good boy."

"The way you look at each other sometimes…"

"There is old expression: a woman's heart is like a needle at the bottom of the sea—hard to grasp. And you? You and Tommy the Coyote? What goes on there?"

"Tommy...is...oh, he makes me so mad sometimes. Then sometimes he can be...so sweet."

"Ha! You perhaps yī jiàn zhōng qíng—means, upon first seeing, you love!"

Before the precise nature of these relationships could be sorted out to the satisfaction of the two young women, Zack and Tommy emerged from the bank building. Mei Lim explained that the girls needed new clothing. She also pointed out the difficulties in obtaining it.

"Don't you worry about that," said Tommy. "I am an expert at getting clothes. But for right now..."

"We need to get across the river before the ferry closes up for the night," Zack explained. "We have our money now. We'll buy train tickets for tomorrow morning. But..."

"We may need to sleep in the train depot," Tommy said, finally finishing the sentence.

The Chicago and North Western Railway Depot stood half-completed at 11th Street and Broadway, not close enough to Council Bluff's waterfront to facilitate bringing railcars across by ferry to connect with the Union Pacific. A spur line would soon be built for that purpose. When the building was finished it would resemble a stately Victorian palace with twin corbie- or crow-stepped pediments rising like peaked caps complete with arched Queen Anne windows, these providing a double row of all-seeing eyes for surveying the red brick platform below. A pentagonal turret with conical roof would climb skyward over a many-windowed porch.

Inside it was dusty, dim and depressing. Tommy had disappeared right after they purchased their tickets, a mischievous grin on his face. They waited and talked, telling each other stories from their more recent adventures or of their lost childhoods: Mei Lim's bittersweet girlhood in her village before her seizure by the flesh-peddlers; Little Wind's and Zack's contentment in their peaceful encampment under the shadow of Shasta before being wrenched away to the reservation.

Tommy returned with a bundle under his arm. His impish grin, if it were possible, was even wider and more infectious than before. "Clothes for my ladies," he said, unwrapping the bundle, "and some new pants for us men."

"Oh, Tommy, you didn't steal these did you?" Little Wind asked, fully knowing the answer and dreading its confirmation.

"They were hanging out on a wash line. I selected the best that looked like they would fit. And I left some money, so I guess it wasn't stealing."

"How did you know how much to leave?" asked Zack.

"You remember at the bank, how the man showed us which numbers were biggest and which were smallest? I left one each of the smallest, the straight up and down mark."

"I think we are going to have to learn to read the white man's marks," Little Wind told them. "If we are to live among them it will be necessary."

"Mei Lim," Tommy said, "do you know how to read the marks?"

"I know a few. Not all. It wasn't allowed to learn much, but I picked up a little knowledge. There's an old saying…"

"Let me guess. To know little is to know a lot of danger."

"Yes, something like that."

With morning the four travelers, dressed in their new clothes—Little Wind thought of them as "Christian clothing," simple, unadorned dresses of a dull gray color—waited eagerly on the platform as the train pulled to a stop in front of them. Clouds of white steam enveloped them. The clanging of the brass bell hurt their ears. The smell of smoke and cinders choked them. But a spark of excitement jumped through them, welded them together in anticipation of this, the final portion of their long journey, welded their destinies to this puffing, fuming metal monster.

Soon the Chicago and North Western Railway would add an express train between Chicago and Council Bluffs. The trip would take a mere 22 hours. This train, however, would make a fair amount of stops before it reached Chicago: Crescent Station, Honey Creek, Loveland, and across the Iowa plains to Denison, Carroll, Ames and beyond. Ames, Iowa, founded as a rail stop for the Cedar Rapids and Missouri Railroad, the C&NW's predecessor on these particular rails, was named for Oakes Ames, the same Oakes Ames who had financed the Union Pacific through bribes and influence peddling.

Zack had purchased coach tickets for the group; they would not need to suffer the inconvenience and crowding of the emigrant car on this trip. Seats were not reserved as they were in the first class sleeper cars, so passengers scrambled for the best seats as they boarded. The four travelers had entered one of the newer coaches which had seats upholstered in what looked like green velvet. The backs were hinged for adjustment and illumination was provided by gas lamps with crystal shades. There were brass luggage racks above the seats and men's and women's restrooms at the ends of the car. They found four seats together on the shady side of the train as it pulled out of Council Bluffs.

"Tick-kets! Ti-ic-kets!" called a man wearing a dark blue suit with gold buttons and a flat-topped, short-brimmed cap with a silver badge pinned to it. Tommy looked up with delight at the conductor, a man with deep dark brown skin and gray whiskers—a black man!

"Yo' happy ta see me, youngster?" asked the conductor, noticing Tommy's beaming smile.

"Yes Sir! Oh…I'm sorry if I'm being rude. It's just that…"

"It's jus' that I'm a black man wearin' a uniform. You surprised?"

"No Sir, I'm happy to meet you."

"I see you youngsters are also people of color. Where do you hail from?"

And so the introductions began, the short versions of life stories were told, and a friendship started that would last at least as long as the train ride. The conductor's name was Calvin Bellows. If not for his gray hair he could be taken for a much younger man—this due to the sprightly energy emanating from his bright brown eyes and his springy gate that matched the rocking of the railcar much as a seasoned sailor at sea might navigate the rolling deck of a ship in a gale.

Calvin Bellows was instantly drawn to the four youngsters, the only people of color within his conductor's purview. The kinship he felt was not without historical significance. Indeed, Calvin Bellows had had much experience conducting nonconforming or unacceptable or illegal wayfarers during the bad times: those bad times when Calvin Bellows, working as a porter on the Illinois Central between Cairo, Illinois, and Chicago, had aided escaping slaves who were following the tracks of the Underground Railroad.

In those years before the Civil War, before emancipation, Bellows was risking imprisonment or, even though he was technically a free Negro, being kidnapped and sold into slavery. By helping runaways who were following the drinking gourd, that many-tentacled path to freedom called the Underground Railroad, he was breaking the law. Although Illinois was a free state, it was illegal to bring a black man across its borders. The Fugitive Slave Act, part of the Compromise of 1850, required people living in free states to return runaway slaves to their owners.

And Illinois wasn't entirely free. The southern portion of the state, known colloquially as Egypt, still practiced indenturing blacks to work in its salt mines. Many were held in actual slavery at the infamous Hickory Hill Crenshaw Mansion near Cairo, Illinois. Crenshaw's slave house was a station on the Reverse Underground Railroad along which kidnapped blacks were shipped back to slave owners in the South.

Calvin Bellows sought every opportunity to sit across from Zack, Tommy, Little Wind and Mei Lim and trade stories. These were fleeting moments as the conductor's duties at each stop were crucial to the train's operation. He was like the captain of a ship, making sure passengers boarded or embarked safely and seeing to their needs. He signaled the engineer and the brakemen when it was time to pull away from the station. Only between stops had he the precious moments to converse with the four travelers.

He was quite interested in Little Wind's story of the ranch where she worked as a slave, and in Mei Lim's entire early life. He had outlined his days on the Illinois Central, sneaking black men and women onto the train at night and seeing them safely to Chicago where they could find passage across the Great Lakes to Canada. But there was more to his story. Much more.

"Yo' probably wonderin' hows I's got to conductin' on dat Underground Railroad. It bein' risky all right. Well see I's been hepped myself by folks run dat ting back in the day. Oh, I's freed of course, but some white folks dint care no how 'bout dat. We gets pass Cedar Rapids, theys a fair stretch of time between stops an' ma'be I tells yo' my story. Yas, I do tink I do dat."

Byron Grush

22

Following the Drinking Gourd

I think I here'd the angels say
Foller the drinkin' gou'd.
Stars in Heavin gonna show de way
Foller the drinkin' gou'd.

Zack had his Road of Stars, the great Milky Way that stretched across the heavens creating a shining path for his gods; Bellows, the black man who had become the boy's friend as rode this Iron Trail toward an uncertain future, had also looked to the night sky for guidance: *his* people called a certain formation of stars "The Drinking Gourd." It pointed northward.

He was thirteen when he was separated from his mother and sister. His father, Gerald Bellows was a white landowner in Burlingame, Mississippi, who had taken his mother, Teja Brown, a slave, into his household as a mistress, fathered two children by her, then died of pneumonia, declaring in his will that the mother, his legal property, was to be given her freedom along with her two children. The children, Calvin and Lisa, identified in legal documents with the last name of Bellows, and the mother, Teja Brown, were not to be transferred as property along with the other twenty-nine slaves Bellows owned in order to pay debts owed by his estate.

Gerald Bellows was of stout southern stock: of farmers who first broke the land up into cotton and corn or tobacco, who created a vast agricultural economy, and who were dependant upon the hard labor of a race of people stolen from their homelands and sold into slavery. Bellows was a decent, God-fearing man who never mistreated or abused his laborers by his own hand, but who, like many landowners of his ilk, observed the practice of hiring overseers whose expertise in keeping the slaves in line was crucial to maintaining an obedient and efficient workforce.

Teja Brown was a field slave, picking cotton when the bulbs were ripe or tilling and planting and pulling weeds until her fingers bled and her back ached as if lightning had crawled up her spine, hot and crackling like the Mississippi summer. She had caught the eye of the master by sheer accident. One morning when the field-workers were leaving their shacks and scurrying up the dirt road towards the cotton field, the master, Gerald Bellows, was driving his buggy into town to a meeting of the Knights of the Golden Circle. As his buggy passed the group on the dusty road Bellows noticed his overseer, a black man named Moses, bending over a woman. Moses had been elevated to the position of overseer by Bellows and he mercilessly abused his newfound power by punishing his fellow slaves for any infraction, no matter how small. Moses was beating a woman who had fallen into a ditch along the side of the road. The woman was Teja Brown.

Bellows pulled up his horse and jumped from the buggy to grab his overseer's arm as it descended, thick hickory switch in hand, toward the cowering Teja Brown. Moses was surprised and angered, but seeing that it was the Master who was aborting his corporeal punishment of the woman, he wisely decided to desist and he backed off apologizing. This incident instilled a hatred of Teja Brown in the overseer which would return to plague the woman in the days to come. Fortunately, Gerald Bellows was taken with the frail but comely young woman and thereafter often inquired as to her well-being. Eventually he attached her to the household staff where her close proximity increased his interest not only in her welfare, but also in the advancement his own his pleasure.

Bellows had married a distant cousin when both were quite young: he twenty and she sixteen. He had inherited the land he now farmed and the young couple had looked forward to many happy years of prosperity. But Bessie May Bellows was not destined to enjoy the fruits of the labor of the many slaves that worked on their cotton plantation. She was the victim of a yellow fever epidemic that coursed through the Mississippi delta lands one horrible summer leaving one of every tenth person dead in its wake. So it was that Teja Brown filled the void left to the lonely man by his wife's demise.

Teja had been brought from the west coast of Africa to America as a child and could barely remember a day when she had not been in servitude to a white man. Her time in the Big House as Bellow's mistress was, in sense, a blessing as it protected her from the brutal treatment Moses imposed on the other slaves. But it wasn't long before she was with child—a dangerous predicament for a house slave.

At first Bellows rejected the child. Certainly, fathering a biracial son or daughter was not uncommon among Southern landowners in those days. However it was never discussed or acknowledged and kept as secretive as possible. Slowly Gerald Bellows began to feel connected to his secret family; Teja held a special place in his heart and this child was part of her and of him—dark eyes and brown skin not withstanding. Soon the little family expanded as a second child was born. If Bellows didn't feel love (even that strange and unnatural love that a true Southern gentleman might feel for a slave) he did have a deep sense of responsibility and an unconditional regard for Teja and the children.

The children, Calvin and Lisa, were given advantages that very few Black children could aspire to—even free Black children. They grew up in the relative comfort of the slave quarters of the Big House and were treated to an adequate education by Bellows who wanted them to learn to read and write. This set them apart from the other slaves and as they were also isolated from white society, it was as if they had been marooned on a small island surrounded by a hostile social environment. Storms of prejudice threatened them from every direction. Even the other house slaves resented them. At least they were spared the overseer's whip.

When Gerald Bellows died, the lawyer who handled his estate, although reluctant to give the precious gift of freedom to Teja Brown and her children, still executed his duty and drew up the proper papers. In the days following the funeral the land and property of the deceased were put up for auction. The property, of course, included the slaves and was in fact valuable enough to pay off most of the debts Bellows had incurred. Moses, the overseer, was in charge of assembling the slaves for shipment to the auctioneer. Teja Brown had not yet been told of her good fortune: that she was now a free woman and that she and her children could now go their own way. Moses knew about the papers but his hatred of the woman was intense. She and the children were hustled off along with the other slaves and soon found themselves on the auction block.

Thus it was that Teja and her children were separated, each sold to different slave dealers and ultimately to landowners in different slave states. Calvin was never to see his mother or sister again. Calvin Bellows spent the next three years on a small plantation north of Mobile, Alabama, experiencing the harsh life of a field slave. He was thrown together with the younger boys and unmarried men in a crude cabin with a dirt floor and openings between its rough hewn planks that let in wind and rain and very little daylight. Meals consisted of an allowance of meal or corn and only rarely did they receive meat or fish. There was a tiny, poorly tended garden that provided a few vegetables for the entire encampment but the favored slaves, those that worked the hardest, had first pick of these.

The landowner, Coronel Samuel Howard, employed an overseer, an uneducated white man named Craig who carried a nine-foot long rawhide whip tipped with a leather thong with lead pellets braided into it. He would flail this against the backs and the legs of the slaves at will, needing no particular motivation other than that of his own sadistic nature. When more official punishment was rendered for an infraction such as arriving late to the field or wondering off, the slaves were stripped to the waist and their hands were tied in front of them with a rope which was passed over the limb of a tree. They were hauled up by the rope until they could barely stand on the tips of their toes. Then they were whipped until the lacerations ran red with blood and their screams stopped as they fainted from the pain.

Calvin had one consolation: his former overseer, Moses, had been among the group of slaves bought by Calvin's current owner, Coronel Howard. And Moses no longer had privileged status. In fact, Moses presented just the kind of uppity attitude that Craig loved to make an example of; Moses did not escape the lash. As it was common for the field slaves to be required to witness floggings, Calvin had to watch as red welts appeared on Moses' bare back. Calvin flinched with each brutal impact of the whip. Instead of feeling satisfaction in seeing the former overseer get his just rewards, Calvin took pity on him. At the end of it, Calvin rushed to the man's side and helped him to his cabin. He applied grease to ease the pain of his wounds and sponged his brow with cool water.

"You?" said Moses, coming out of the shock of the beating. "Why would you help me?"

"Yo' human, Moses. Tha' Mister Craig...he's not."

"I have to tell you something," Moses said after several moments of silence. He revealed to Calvin the fact that their former master had freed him and his mother and sister. That the lawyer had drawn up the papers but he, Moses, had seen to it that they were sent to the auction block anyway. It might have been either a forced smile or the grimace of pain that sat on Moses' clinched teeth, it was impossible to tell. Calvin continued to run the wet cloth across Moses' forehead and said nothing. The injury that had been done to him by this man was beyond comprehension, beyond any possible revenge he might conjure, beyond the scope of his suppressed anger.

One day a journeyman carpenter arrived at the plantation looking for work. As none of the slaves had his wood working skills he was hired on the spot for repairs needed up at the Big House. The man found time to chat with the house slaves when no one was looking. His name, he said, was Joe, and he was a former ship's carpenter. He had an injury which had forced him to seek work away from the sea: he had lost a leg and he now hobbled along on a wooden peg. The slaves he befriended called him Cap'n Joe or Peg Leg Joe or simply the Ole Man. They became very fond of him and his stories. Peg Leg Joe taught the house slaves a song and encouraged them to teach it to the field slaves as well. The song became known all across the plantations of Alabama and Mississippi. It was called "Follow the Drinking Gourd."

> *Foller the drinkin' gou'd,*
> *Foller the drinkin' gou'd;*
> *The ole man's awaitin'*
> *For to carry you to freedom;*
> *Foller the drinkin' gou'd.*

The slaves knew what the Master never suspected: the song was a coded message describing the route to freedom that a runaway should follow. The "Drinking Gourd" referred to the constellation in the sky called the Big Dipper. The two stars on the outside of the "bowl" of the dipper always pointed toward the North Star—a sure way to locate north. And the Ole Man? Peg Leg Joe was in fact an agent of the Underground Railroad. By spreading the song throughout the South he was enabling escaped slaves to find their way to the free states in the North.

Calvin was determined to escape. He was now 16 years of age and avoiding notice by Craig the overseer was getting to be more and more difficult. He had befriended another field slave named Chiko and together they formulated a plan. Peg Leg Joe's song gave them a sort of map to follow, and it was said that Peg Leg had marked certain trees along the way with his sign: a left shoe print and a round mark like that made by a peg leg applied with mud or charcoal. It was only necessary to wait for the proper time to go…and for darkness.

> *When the sun come back,*
> *When the firs' quail call,*
> *Then the time is come*
> *Foller the drinkin' gou'd.*

Calvin and Chiko waited. One spring night, the moon was barely a thin sliver. Stars shown brightly in the cloudless sky. The two young men slipped from the encampment with the clothes on their backs and a small bag of food. Above them, the Drinking Gourd and the North Star pointed the way.

> *The riva's bank am a very good road,*
> *The dead trees show the way,*
> *Lef' foot, peg foot goin' on,*
> *Foller the drinkin' gou'd.*

They followed the Tombigbee River, hiding in the brush during the day and traveling by night. Marsh and swamp, thicket and hillocks of brambles defied their traverse, but on they trudged. The Tombigbee's headwaters originated in northeastern Mississippi. When they reached the river's end they relied on trees marked with Peg Leg Joe's sign. At the juncture of roads they saw nails pounded into tree trucks indicating which turning to take. Woodall Mountain lay ahead, twin peaks beckoning them toward the next part of their journey.

> *The riva ends a-tween two hills,*
> *Foller the drinkin' gou'd;*
> *'Nuther riva on the other side*
> *Follers the drinkin' gou'd.*

North of Woodall Mountain they found the Tennessee River, its rushing waters arching southward back toward Alabama and northward toward the Ohio River. The next night was cloudy, the stars obscured. But they found moss growing on the north sides of trees and thus were able to make the correct choice of direction. All would have been lost had they followed the river south and returned to Alabama. They came to a small farm where a quilt was draped over a rail fence. Chiko recognized the pattern stitched onto the quilt: he called it "Log Cabin." Its yellow center meant this was a home friendly to escaping slaves. They slept in relative comfort in the barn that night.

As they followed the Tennessee through hills and dales there were more signs of people with links to the Underground Railroad. A quilt with squares broken up by triangles that looked like bow ties meant they had come to a home where they could exchange their slave clothing for those a free person of color might wear, making them less conspicuous. If they were seen by "Christian wolves," as the slave hunters were called, they would be sent back—or worse.

Wha the little riva
Meet the grea' big un,
The ole man's awaitin'
For to carry you to freedom;
Foller the drinkin' gou'd.

Where the Tennessee River flowed into the Ohio a thriving river town had emerged as an important transportation hub. Paducah, Kentucky, offered dry docks for steamboats and towboats, and so several barge companies had made their headquarters along its banks. There was access to coal and so foundries had started up to forge iron and steel components for the railroads. It was also one of four or five favored crossing points between the slave state of Kentucky and the free states of Illinois, Indiana and Ohio.

The Drinking Gourd song had led them to Paducah, but if they had expected to see Peg Leg Joe waiting for them with a river skiff, they were disappointed. A farmer had transported them hidden in a wagon of hay and hemp baskets into the city to a safe house, a church on Second Street. They found themselves clustered together with several other runaways, waiting in the darkness of the church's cellar for word of transport across the river and ultimately to Canada.

Their companions in hiding included a twenty-three year-old black man named Albert, whose master had often taken a shovel to his head and on other occasions had kicked him repeatedly. Another young man named Percy had only one usable eye; the other having been smashed by the handle of his mistress's riding crop for some minor infraction or other. Then there was Leo who had been concealed in close quarters for six months prior to his escape, in fear for his life. His master, a Mr. Belden, was in the habit of flogging his slaves regularly in order to keep them docile. Leo refused to cooperate and Belden promptly shot him in the head, wounding him badly. He was shot a second time a year later by the local sheriff who went after him with a squirrel gun for resisting some young white boys who had decided to beat him just for fun. Now recovered, he had decided to run. The only woman in the cellar was named Dory. She had tried and failed to escape from bondage several times. She finally succeeded after a long period of confinement hiding in a chicken coop by dressing in male attire. Once out on the street and blending into the crowd she reached members of the Underground Railroad who then moved her to the next station hidden in a shipping crate.

There were three major routes to Canada from Paducah, Kentucky. One could take a steamboat up the Wabash River through Indiana and enter Canada near Detroit. Alternately, one could steam down the Ohio and up the Mississippi to the town of Alton, Illinois, just upriver from Saint Louis, and go across the state to Chicago and Lake Michigan where another boat would provide transport to Canada and freedom. The third route was to Chicago by rail from Cairo, Illinois, the port town at the southernmost tip of Illinois. This was by far the most dangerous as Southern Illinois was rife with slave hunters.

The denizens of the church cellar were united in their ambition to follow the Wabash route. The only drawback, and this was also true of the Alton, Illinois route, was that passage on a steamer, which meant a dark and crowded corner of the engine room, cost $100. Certain members of Abolitionist groups would raise the necessary cash if they thought the escapee's plight was pitiful enough, say, having been beaten nearly to death or being minus an eye or a limb, but this took time. Hence the crowded basement.

Calvin decided on Cairo. It would be quick, cost nothing, and get him back outside and away from the sweat and the murmuring of the other runaways. The following evening just about dusk he was led to the waterfront where a man wearing a rubber fisherman's hat and boots and carrying fishing tackle placed him in the bottom of a dingy and covered him with a blanket. The night air brought a chill and water lapped over the sides of the dingy, drenching the blanket.

They floated down the river, past Cave-in-Rock where river pirates still lurked, past Shawneetown, past the wayside tavern on Pott's Hill where it was said unwary travelers often disappeared down a well, and past the Crenshaw slave house where forty men were chained in small rooms in the attic. They hadn't escaped notice as they approached the wharf at Cairo but the calls of "How's the fishing?" reassured Calvin that his concealment was secure.

Cairo sat at the confluence of the Mississippi and the Ohio and because of this prime location should have been of major importance to traffic on the river. It was a source of fuel for the steamships, but practices of charging high docking rates and the inherent corruption of city officials had stunted its growth as a port. The coming of the Illinois Central Railroad had saved it from extinction and that railroad would soon link Cairo, East Saint Louis, and Chicago with New Orleans, creating a fast and economic way to ship goods between major city centers.

There were tunnels along the Illinois Central Railroad embankment where a runaway could hide while waiting to jump a freight train, or so Calvin had been told. He was having trouble finding these as he walked up toward the freight yard in the early evening. Kerosene lanterns mounted on poles spilled pools of dim light over the cindered grounds. Although he kept to the shadows of boxcars his movements were detected by a guard. Soon he heard someone yelling. He ran, stumbling in the near darkness, disoriented and scared. A shot rang out and the zip and thud of a bullet hitting a nearby boxcar panicked him. He dove under the car as a second bullet sent fragments of rock flying toward him. A piece of rock struck and lodged in his shoulder. He suppressed a yell of pain by biting down on his lip. He scrambled out from under the car on the side opposite the shooter and ran for all his might.

"Here!" came a voice. "Jump up here!" A man stood on the rear platform of a caboose waving to him. Calvin suddenly realized that the train with the caboose and the man were moving, slipping rapidly away. The pain in his shoulder was intense but he ran as hard as he had ever been able to run. He barely reached the caboose before it was out of reach. The man latched onto Calvin's arms, sending arrows of pain shooting through them as he pulled him to safety. Calvin collapsed in a merciful faint.

"Mr. Bellows," said Tommy, "how come you didn't go all the way to Canada? You were on the train. The hard part was over."

"Over? Yes, I 'spose it over. But this am the best part of the story. See, this man, his name is William, he is treating my wound and lettin' me sleep in the caboose car—tha's illegal ya knows. So him is tellin' me all about how he always looks out fer fellas like me...the runned-a-ways. He's hepin' when he can. We talk and talk an' I gets me the idea that I'd like to hep other runned-a-ways like he do."

"But you were an escaped slave. They'd send you back."

"Well suh, here's de ting. He's tellin' me about his fudder that lives near the end of the line. How this is a smart man who mabe can hep me get my papers. He say, 'yo' gets off a Polo town an' ask for my fudder. Tell him I sent ya.' So I think mabe this is a good plan—better 'an goin' to Canada. An' William say when I legal he get me a job on the Illinois Central like he has. 'Course I wanna do this.

"His fudder, name of Isaac, he write to the court house down in Mississippi an' they sends my papers. I stayed wif him for a while until I heal up an' I hep on his farm. And then William get me job on the train. Now afta de war is over and we emancipated I no longer need hep runned-a-ways. Now I work on de Nor'western."

"Excuse me, Mr. Bellows," said Zack. "But what did you say the farmer's name was?"

"It be Isaac. Isaac Grosh. A fine man, him."

"Isaac Grosh...that's my name! They call me Zack, but it's Isaac. Could it be...?"

"Mr. Bellows," interrupted Tommy, "what can you tell us about this Isaac Grosh? Was he an old man? A young man? Did he have any other sons?"

"Funny you ask. He tell me he has two sons have left for the gold rush, just about a year fo' I show up. Tha's why he need hep on his farm."

"How can we find this Isaac Grosh?"

"This train don' go right to there. But close. You gets yerself off at Dixon. I'll tell you when dat stop comes up. Then you starts awalkin'. Walkin' north, jus' like you is follerin' the drinkin' gou'd." Bellows chuckled at his own joke. His eyes twinkled as if the chance to aid these wayfarers had returned a familiar but absent purpose to his life. "It not too far. You be askin' folks as you go. Somebody'll know Mr. Grosh, all right."

"Little Wind!" said Zack. "We're going home!"

Byron Grush

23

The Two Isaacs

Pine Creek Township, Illinois, May, 1869

Isaac Grosh wiped the sweat from his brow with a red kerchief that his new wife, Catherine, had stuffed into the front pocket of his overalls as he had left to work the fields that morning. Catherine was his second wife, joined with him in matrimony only last year and already expecting. She was 34 years his junior and a widow bringing three children, Mary Susan, Minnie May and Anna Alsamena who they called Elsie, to the marriage. Isaac's first wife had passed 18 years ago, a more than respectable period for mourning—and an interval destined to germinate a desire for renewal in this still viral and zoetic man of 67 years. After all, Isaac was a farmer, tilling and planting and affected by the natural cycles of life: a force of life dormant during winter's dreary solitude, then flourishing with spring's thriving abundance.

Isaac had been born in 1802 in Lancaster County in Pennsylvania, the grandson of a German immigrant settler. He had moved to the tree-covered, rock-strewn hills of the German Valley in Western Pennsylvania where he worked building barrels. He wanted to farm but the quality and availability of land made that nearly impossible; the lure of new, virgin lands farther west was compelling. Many of the Brethren Church, his spiritual community, were traveling to a place in the Rock River Valley of Northern Illinois to start new lives. So in 1846, Isaac, his wife and eight children, acquired a flatboat and set off along the canals, down the Ohio and up the Mississippi to settle in Pine Creek Township, in Ogle County, Illinois.

There he purchased 160 acres where the rolling prairie met the old-growth pine forest and a sparkling creek gave promise of nourishment for the crops he would plant and the animals he would raise. One by one his children were marrying and moving away. His oldest son, Philip had been the first to leave, only three years after the family had settled on the farm. Philip now taught school in a nearby town. William, the third oldest son had been next to move out. William had worked on the Illinois Central for a few years, then resettled in Iowa to begin his own farming career. John and James had gone prospecting for gold in California. John had returned to Illinois in 1860, married and purchased a farm just down the road from his father. James, Isaac believed, was dead.

The girls, Mary Jane, Elizabeth, Emma and Katy were all happily married and all except Katy lived close by. A constant parade of grandchildren gave Isaac the utmost pleasure, yet the emptiness left by the death of his first wife had persisted. There had been two more children born in Illinois: Harriet and David. Harriet had succumbed to scarlet fever 9 years ago. That left David as the only child still at home. Young David, now 19 years of age, wouldn't remain long on the farm, not with his current interest in Mary Ann Snyder—Isaac was certain that for himself, a dismal loneliness was inevitable. And there was that widow lady, that Catherine Lutz Eshleman, who had been on his own mind now for some time. Thus Isaac had remarried. The cycle of life had begun again.

But this second wife, a second Catherine—for that had been his first wife's name also—only made him miss the first Catherine more. Now as he stood in the field, watching the sun sink slowly behind the distant pines, his thoughts strayed back to those early years in Pennsylvania when they were young, in love and had their whole lives ahead of them. Lives full of happiness, adventure, and sometimes sorrow. A pang of guilt assailed him as he realized his reverie had the aspect of unfaithfulness. The new Catherine was his new soul mate now; young David was the cement that held them together. And yet...

Isaac returned to the house, his day's labor done. Catherine stood on the front porch waiting for him, her hands smoothing the white cotton apron she wore over her calico dress. The house had certainly changed over the years from the small log cabin they had constructed when the family first arrived in Pine Creek Township. Rooms had been added. A veranda with a low, overhanging roof now graced the exterior; wisteria climbed up and across it, purple blossoms fragrant in the springtime. It was a tranquil area where Isaac and Catherine often spent evenings, he on his rocker, she on her wicker chair. There they listened to the wind singing through the pine needles while the crickets and frogs and the occasional magpie contributed their voices to the night's symphony.

Catherine seemed uneasy as Isaac stepped up to the porch. He was able to read her temperament instantly from the four years he had known the woman before they married. Slight subtleties of expression and posture required his investigation; often he adopted an inquiring look, a tilting of the head, a raised eyebrow to aid his interpretation. Isaac paused as he came to her. He gave her a weak smile and a head tilt that asked an unspoken question: "Is everything all right?"

"We have visitors," she said.

Not unusual. But she might have said, "Elizabeth is here with the children," or "Sammy Funk's boy is here with the Polo Daily Reporter," or "Deacon Blecher has come to stay for dinner." The lack of qualification was unsettling. It hinted at some sort of unpleasant occurrence, one that was difficult for her to relate. Perhaps some cattle had hoof-and-mouth disease and the county man had come to dispose of them. Or a neighbor's barn had burned—but no, there hadn't been any smoke. Someone had died. There was to be another war. What kind of catastrophe could it be?

Isaac followed Catherine into the front parlor. Four young people were standing there in a straight row, almost as if at military attention. They stood stiffly, with no physical clues as to their dispositions or attitudes. They were not white, that was obvious; one was Asian, and Isaac guessed the others were Mexicans or Native Americans, but definitely not Negroes. Had they been Blacks, Isaac would not have been surprised. He had had quite a bit of experience before and during the war with the passage of Blacks through his household— travelers on the Underground Railroad. Now he looked to Catherine for an explanation.

"This is...let me see if I can remember your names correctly. White Cloud, Little Wind, Tommy Wepa, and..."

"Mei Lim," offered the Asian girl.

"They are...they are here because..."

Tommy stepped forward out of the ranks smiling. He had suggested to the others that he be the spokesperson, at least for the introductions. It wouldn't do, he had told Zack, to blunder up and say, "Hi, I'm your grandson!"

"How do you do, Sir? We are travelers, out to see the world. I am from the Maidu People, from the place you call California. White Cloud and Little Wind are from the Wintu People. Also from California. We met Mei Lim there...she is from China. As we journey across this vast land..." Here Zack gave Tommy a warning glance, an admonition not to get so flowery in his dialogue. Reluctantly, Tommy abandoned the speech he had memorized for this occasion. "Um...and we met a nice man, the porter on the train, who suggested we come to visit you and bring you his greetings. His name is Calvin Bellows."

Now Isaac was surprised. Finally he said, "Of course! Of course...Calvin was here several years ago. He has a good position on the railroad now? That's just fine. Just fine."

As Zack witnessed the old man's apparent good humor he let out an audible sign of relief. They weren't going to be chased away, at least not at this juncture.

"You'll stay for supper, yes? Catherine? Have we enough...of course. We always have enough."

Isaac's curiosity about the four travelers was now piqued. The connection to Calvin Bellows alleviated some of his apprehensions about them, but there were still unanswered questions. Questions that soon would be asked. Everyone seemed to relax a little: the steel-like rigidity of the foursome melted. They all filed out of the parlor and took seats around the long oak table where meals were eaten in the Grosh household. Catherine scurried away to fetch this evening's meal.

She had fed the younger children earlier and sent them off to play together for a while before their bedtime. Now she carried a large platter of roast beef, vegetables and potatoes and set it before Isaac to carve. She smiled sweetly at her guests as she sat at the end of the table. "Tell us more about your travels," she said. "You came all the way from California?"

Tommy offered a few anecdotes about riding on the Transcontinental Railroad. He reserved the information that he and Zack had worked building that railroad for later. As they sat, the conversation still not touching on anything but trivialities, a boy and girl burst into the room: Isaac's youngest son, David, and his girlfriend, Mary Ann Snyder.

Mary Ann, a slip of a thing, just seventeen and energetic as a kitten unraveling a ball of yarn, pounced down on an empty chair without waiting to be asked. David followed close behind and sat next to her. Isaac turned toward the couple with a frown. "Your hair is wet," he said.

"We were swimming at the pond at John's, Poppa," David answered.

"Hmph. You had swimming suits with you, I assume."

"Well, we...uh..."

"Never mind. I expected you to help with the hogs this afternoon."

"I'm sorry Poppa. You see..."

"These are our guests, friends of Calvin Bellows who worked here years ago. This is my son, David and his friend Mary Ann. Here we have..." Tommy interrupted, supplying their names. Isaac frowned; he had remembered their names—he was good at such things.

"Catherine?" said David—he called his stepmother by her given name because "Momma" was reserved for his real mother, albeit a mother he could scarcely remember having been only one year old when she had left the land of the living. "Why are these people here?"

"David! Don't be rude. Please forgive my stepson. He's just being curious."

Zack now entered the conversation, impatient with Tommy's formality and avoidance of the real issue. "We decided to go to work for the railroad. Joined up in Sacramento and worked until the joining of the rails. Now *that* was quite a ceremony! Crowds of people came to see it."

"We read about it in the newspaper," said Isaac. So you were there! They say that the railroad will change many things for this country. I remember when the Galena and Chicago Union was built through to Freeport. Made it easier to transport goods and people between the river and Chicago. Hurt some of the local people, though. Some of us can't afford the shipping charges. This one...all the way to the ocean! But...what brought you to my farm?"

"We said," Tommy interjected, "that we met Calvin Bellows. He suggested..."

"Yes, yes…but you were already headed this way. Why didn't you go back to California? California! You know, my sons…my son John was in California for the gold rush."

"And James, Papa," said David, interrupting his father. He was rewarded with such an earnest scowl from his father that he slumped quietly back onto his chair.

"They were miners along the Trinity River," Isaac continued. "You know this area?"

Zack spoke up. "Our villages were close to the place you speak of. In the shadow of the sacred mountain, the one they call Shasta."

"James…James was killed in an Indian attack. You know of the Medoc tribe?"

"They are enemies of the Wintu and the Maidu and the Shasta. Your son was killed…are you sure about this?"

Isaac tugged at his beard. "When I first saw you in my house I was afraid…afraid you might be of that tribe. I know you are too young to have been involved. But the wars between Indians and whites…it is so tragic! I haven't been able to hate…but I still can grieve."

In the short silence that followed, an exchange of meaningful glances circulated around the table. Catherine looked at David, her glare expressing her disappointment at his behavior. Tommy looked at Zack, his wide eyes cautioning him to be patient. Mei Lim looked at Isaac; she felt empathy for his loss and tried to project an understanding smile. Isaac looked at Zack and Little Wind, questioning in his own mind a certain familiarity about the two siblings. He had a vague feeling, something akin to what people termed déjà vu, the feeling that you are reliving something that happened before. He shook it off.

Mary Ann looked at Catherine. Mary Ann was fidgeting, a nervous habit she had when there was tension in the air. She decided to break through the mood with a change of subject. She asked Catherine, "When is your baby due, Mrs. Grosh?"

"Oh, I think September or October."

"Have you picked out a name? Or names, I mean? Do you want a boy or a girl?"

"We talked about Vernon if it's a boy. I think it will be. I had an uncle by that name. It could work for a girl too…Vernie."

"That's sweet. And I heard that your stepson John and his wife…aren't they expecting too?"

"Yes! As soon as July. It will be quite a year. An aunt or uncle and a niece or nephew…both the same age! They can play together."

Mei Lim was struck by the disparity in ages between Isaac and his wife. There had been a few old men in her hometown in China who had taken younger girls for wives—did that also happen here in America? Did they have multiple wives like the aristocrats in the Forbidden City? She hadn't thought so. Although back in Utah she had heard that the Mormons had multiple wives. Things weren't so different here after all.

Little Wind was intrigued by Mary Ann. Cocky and effervescent, the girl inserted herself into the order of things, not content to remain extraneous. Little Wind's experience with whites taught her about the importance they placed on the hierarchy of man, woman, boy-child, girl-child. But here was a young girl behaving as an equal and, it seemed, accepted as such by her elders! Maybe Zack's obsession with finding their father's family wasn't so crazy after all.

Tommy sat rotating his glass of cider in a slow circle. He was deep in thought. We've accomplished what we set out to do and found Zack's family, he said to himself. Now what? Zack and Little Wind will have choices to make: to stay or to go. But I? I don't belong here. I've come a long way with them—they are *my* family. But this is not my land, not my home. He looked up and into Isaac's eyes and there he saw wisdom and kindness and sadness, all comingled. What would the old man say and do once Zack told him the truth?

Zack was thinking similar thoughts. Yes, he would have a choice to make. He listened politely to the chatter at the dining table. Silverware clinked against china plates that the first Catherine had brought with her from Pennsylvania all those years ago. Clatter combined with chatter made a soft, subtle rhythm that reminded Zack of riding on the railroad. It was a constant background noise that lulled him somewhat, but couldn't derail his anxious desire to reveal himself.

Zack knew enough to wait for the proper moment to tell Isaac Grosh that he believed his own father was Issac's long lost son—and that he believed James Grosh to still be alive. But would Isaac believe him? He was debating whether to broach the subject when Catherine Grosh turned to him with a question he had hoped wouldn't arise:

"It's remarkable that four such young people could travel so far on their own. Where will you go from here?"

"Well, Ma'am, I was sort of wondering if maybe you and the Mister needed some help on the farm. We're very good workers."

"Oh, no…Isaac doesn't need…"

"Cath, hold on," Isaac said. "I'll be the judge of whether I need help or not." But rather than answering the question, Isaac fell silent. A dark mood crept over him, apparent to all.

This is not going well, thought Zack. Not how I wanted it to be. He looked at Tommy. Tommy was shaking his head. Maybe I should have told him right away, Zack thought. Gotten it over with.

"Mister Grosh," Zack began, "I would like to tell you a story. Little Wind and I were very young when our father left the village where we lived. He was a good man, a good father to us and a good provider for our mother. But he left because of the conflict between our people and the whites.

"You see, Father was a white man. He had been climbing the sacred mountain when he was attacked by a bear and nearly killed. My mother brought him to the village and nursed him. They joined together and I was born. Then Little Wind was born, and everything was as it should be. Our father adopted the ways of the Wintu and the people accepted him as one of their own.

"But the whites and the tribes living around the sacred mountain were always fighting. Little conflicts at first. The settlers had taken our lands, chopped down the trees we needed for acorns, killed many of our game animals, and ruined the waters so that the fish died. Now and then some of us would steal from them because we were hungry. Now and then a white man would be killed in a fight with one of us. When that happened the whites would attack a whole village in retaliation, killing many.

"Not all of the people wanted war, but some were so angered they decided to attack the white settlers. Our father had to choose. Would he go with the raiding party and fight the white people who were also his people? Maybe kill friends? Or would he stand with the whites against us who were also his friends and his family? He told our mother that in his former life with the whites he had lived by a religion and that religion told him not to kill, not to go to war.

242

"So Father left the village. It was said he climbed the sacred mountain for the second time to seek guidance from the spirits. We never saw him again but I am sure he is alive. Some time after that the soldiers came and took all the people from our village and from other villages and made us live in what they called a reservation. They said it would protect us. But still we starved. I resolved to leave and find my father.

"I climbed the sacred mountain looking for him, but I didn't find him. I met a man who lived as a hermit on the mountain. He was the same man that our father mentioned having met when he made his first climb. That man told me to come here, to find you."

"What are you telling me?"

"My Wintu name is White Cloud but the name my father gave me is Ay-Zack. His name was…is James Grosh."

The clatter of silverware had stopped. The silence was thick and impenetrable, like a wall of stone. No one breathed for a few moments. Isaac turned steel-gray eyes from Zack to Little Wind and back again. Could there be a resemblance? It was possible, but unlikely. Two half-breed Indian children claiming to be…no, it wasn't credible. They had heard about James and now they were trying to cash in on…on what? Yet, there was something that rang true. And there was that eerie feeling of familiarity Isaac had felt all along

"Let me tell you a story now," Isaac said. "A story told me by my other son, John, who was there."

He doesn't believe me, thought Zack. I've come all this way for nothing.

"James and John had a mining concern along the Whiskey Creek. It was doing well thanks in part to James' newfound organizational skills—you know, I never saw that in him when he was a child, but I guess he changed, matured and got serious. But something troubled him. John told me that James believed he was responsible for another man's death and it haunted him.

"One day James just up and left. He said—and I don't know how *you* ever learned this—he said he had to climb that mountain, that Mount Shasta. They never saw him again. John waited and waited for him to return. And then he received word that James had been killed by Indians.

"Now this is how it was figured. A vigilante group had chased a band of Indians into the hills. The Indians had raided one of the settlements and killed some men there. The Indians were all killed and when the vigilantes searched their camp they found a long wooden staff, the kind they put feathers on and carry into battle. One of the men took it for a souvenir. But when they examined it more closely…"

"It had markings on it," interrupted Zack. "The markings were in the white man's language and spoke the name of my father."

"How did…how did you know that?"

"My father had this staff by him when my mother found him bleeding and half dead from the bear attack. My people revered it because it had been to the top of the mountain; it had magic to it. I remember seeing it. There were marking that ran around and around…"

"In a spiral. The lettering read, 'JAMES GROSH, SEP 9, 1855, SHASTA.' But it must mean that he is dead. Why would the Indians have it? And how do you know about it?"

"I know," said Zack who was now on the verge of tears, "because when Swift Eagle and the other warriors left our village to fight the white settlers, my father gave him the staff to take into battle. It was magic, see? It was all my father could contribute to the war that was starting. It doesn't mean he is dead."

"It doesn't mean he's alive. Why do you believe he still lives? He never returned to John or to you and your sister."

"I have something that is magic as well. A talisman. It's this," said Zack as he produced the watch from his pocket. "As long as it runs it means my father is alive."

Isaac looked at the watch. An ordinary pewter-cased watch like many people used day in and day out. Nothing fancy, nothing unusual about it, except he saw that there was an inscription on the back of it. "May I see that?" he asked. Zack handed him the watch. Isaac turned it over and read the words and began to cry.

24

The Pewter Pocket Watch

"Where did you come by this watch," asked Isaac. Zack shook his head, his dark hair which was in need of cutting swung wildly dislodging road dust. "Please tell me. It could be important."

"It was given to me by the Old Man of the Mountain, the hermit who I found living on Bohĕm Puyuk, the sacred mountain. He told me he'd always possessed it but now it was to be mine…for good luck. That's how I know it is magic."

"And what did you think when you read the inscription?"

"Sorry, Sir," answered Zack, embarrassed to admit it, "but I never learned to read."

"And this old man…who did he say he was?"

"He didn't. He told me he had lived there so long he had forgotten his own name. He was…yeĉewiskoyit…dreaming but awake, like a man who walks when asleep…you know what I mean?"

"Addle-brained," said Mary Ann. David gave her a swift kick under the table.

"I'll tell you what it says," Isaac said, turning the watch over in his hand. "It reads, 'To My Son James on his 18th Birthday from his father, Isaac.' This was James' watch. He took it with him to California."

"But that means…"

"It means *maybe*…maybe the man who gave you the watch was my son, James. Or maybe the Indians who killed him, Indians from your own village, took his staff and his watch."

"No!" Zack protested. "It happened the way I said. Father was well liked by my people. Tell him, Little Wind. Tell him I speak the truth!"

But Little Wind was in tears. She could only nod in the affirmative. Tommy stirred, ready to vouch for Zack, but Zack placed his hand on Tommy's shoulder, shook his head. "He'll have to believe me," Zack told him. "He'll just have to!"

Morning brought a veil of pink fog that rose lazily skyward leaving the plowed fields damp and glistening under the soft yellow sun. The cows began their incessant complaining joined by snorting hogs and cackling hens. Off in the distant somewhere a lone coyote yipped in defiance of hunger pangs. A pot of coffee gurgled and sputtered to life on the cast iron stove in Catherine's kitchen.

Zack and Tommy had shared David's bedroom, curled up under old quilts on the cold pine floor. They had slept under far worse conditions; being in a house for a change was a luxury. Little Wind and Mei Lim had found it too cramped in the loft where the three young daughters of Catherine's first marriage slept. The parlor had served them well enough, Mei Lim on cushions and Little Wind squirreled into an upholstered chair. Catherine had insisted the visitors stay at least for the night. Isaac, still unsure of his feelings acquiesced, intending to sort things out in the morning.

After breakfast, David had been assigned to escort Zack and Little Wind down the road to the farm of the man who might just be their uncle, John B. Grosh. Isaac wanted John to hear their story, wanted to get his reaction. As they climbed the slight rise at the intersection of another road they could see a large, freshly whitewashed barn and a long split rail fence.

"That way goes to the school where Phillip teaches," David explained, pointing up the crossroad. "That's John's barn up ahead. Just built last year. Everyone had a hand in putting it up."

The farmhouse was a neat, two-story clapboard structure with roofed front and rear porches. Like the barn it was painted white. It was set back from the road against an ancient stand of pines. A checkerboard of small vegetable gardens next to the house stretched along the expanse of a fruit orchard. This butted up to a corral where a spirited colt bucked playfully.

"John has fields on both sides of the road," David told them. "Should be a really good year if the price of wheat holds strong."

Zack guessed that their guide was showing off, boasting about his older brother. David wasn't so very much older than he and Tommy, and certainly hadn't seen as much of the world as they had. But he liked the boy and unless he was completely wrong, David was his uncle! As they entered the driveway to the farm a man came from the barn with a bale of timothy over one shoulder. He hefted it over the corral fence, brushed particles of dry grass from his overalls and walked toward them.

"Hello, David," he said. "Who are your friends?"

They sat on the front porch while Zack told his story from beginning to end. John listened, asking a question now and then, nodding if he got an answer that he expected. He examined the watch. "Yes, that's James' watch," he said. He studied Zack and Little Wind as if he could distill the truth of the matter from their faces. He shook his head.

"It's extraordinary. It could be true—James living with Indians! Fathering two children! Yes, I could believe it...I want to believe it...but it's so fantastic!"

"My people wouldn't have killed him. If you knew of the Wintu, you would know they aren't hostile like the Modoc."

"I did know of the Wintu. And of the Modoc. You realize that there is only one way for me to really know the truth. If that was really James on that mountain..."

"We have to go back and find him."

"I can't do that. I have a baby on the way, a farm to run. If I were younger..."

"You do believe me then?"

"I don't know, son. I just don't know. All these years believing James to be dead! It's as if I abandoned him. I should have been the one to climb the mountain. I should have saved him. It's easier not to believe you, my boy. Much less painful."

As John sat, lost in thoughts of grief and guilt, a small girl bounded across the porch and jumped up on his lap. She threw her arms around his neck and kissed him repeatedly. "Hello, Daddy," she said.

"Hattie Emma!" cried an older girl who had followed the three year old across the lawn. "Don't jump on Daddy!"

"It's all right, Ida May," said John. "It's just what I needed." Ida May was eight and sometimes became overly zealous in acting the little mother to her sister. John just smiled; the girls brought so much joy to him and to Mary Jane. And now a third child was coming. So difficult to think of the darkness of the past when the present shown so brightly and the future could only be even more radiant.

"What's that, Daddy?" asked Hattie Emma, pointing to the watch. "It's pretty."

"It's a pocket watch that belonged to your Uncle James. And there's a surprise inside of it. A picture of my mother."

"A picture of Grandma?"

"No, of my mother who died long before you were born. The watch opens up. I'll show you." John pressed the hidden catch on the side of the watch and the back flipped open to reveal a small portrait of a woman. At the same time a slip of yellowed paper fell out of the watch. A gust of wind picked up the paper and tossed it across the lawn.

"I'll get it," said Ida May who chased after the tumbling paper, finally grabbing it before it could blow into the road. John had passed the watch to David who had asked to see the picture of the woman who was also his mother; the woman who had died the year following his own birth. Zack and Little Wind leaned over David's shoulder.

"She was beautiful," said Little Wind.

"You said she died?" asked Zack.

John nodded. "Before I even went to California, she was gone."

"Why did your mommy have to die, Daddy?" asked Hattie Emma. Then she added, "Is *my* mommy going to die?"

"No, little one. Your mommy isn't going to die. It's just that…sometimes people die because it's their time. But don't you ever worry about your mother dying."

"Daddy, Daddy!" Ida May called out. "I got the paper. Don't you want it?"

"What's that? What paper?"

"It fell out of the watch. The wind blew it and I got it for you." She handed her father the yellow page that had been folded over several times to fit inside of the watch. John unfolded it and smoothed it against his knee. It was a handwritten note. He read it carefully, then read it again. Then he read it out loud:

"To John Grosh, Whiskeytown. Dear John, I have returned to the mountain for reasons I may someday be able to explain to you. There is danger for me where I was. I want you to do something for me. Look after my wife and two children. They are in the Wintu Indian village along the Cotton Creek. My wife is called Little Deer and the children are White Cloud and Little Wind. Tell them I love them and I'll come back for them. For now, I seek help from the Great Spirit. James Grosh, Shasta Mountain, 1860."

John folded the paper and placed it back inside the watch. "I wonder why he never sent it," he said.

"He didn't even recognize me when I saw him on the mountain," added Zack.

"Mary Ann was right," said David. "Addlebrained."

"Actually," said a soft female voice from behind the group, "there is a condition called amnesia. It can be caused by great trauma. I've read about it." Mary Jane Grosh had been standing at the door long enough to have gotten the gist of the conversation. "Oh, John…your poor brother!"

"Mary Jane! Come out," John told her. "Meet your niece and nephew. And David, would you do me a favor and go tell Father all that has happened here? Tell him White Cloud and Little Wind will be staying with us, that is, if it is all right with Mary Jane."

"And what about the other two?" asked David.

"What other two?"

"We have two traveling companions," Zack explained. "Not related. But they helped us get here. I was sort of hoping…they could maybe work on the farm?"

Spring gave way to summer. The wheat had started to sprout and so had a variety of weeds which kept Zack and Tommy busy. The soil was good and black, perhaps slightly less rich than that of the nearby prairies but the pioneer farmers around Pine Creek had broken plows on the roots of prairie grasses that reached down a foot or more and believed, as their Pennsylvania ancestors had, that the best farm land was where the forests grew. By the time they had cleared the trees and dug out the stumps the steel plow had been invented at Grand Junction a few miles south along the Rock River. John Deere's plow cut through roots and broke up clods with ease. Now there were farms everywhere, or so it seemed.

Zack loved the feel of that soil, thrusting his hand into the furrows and letting the moist granules slip between his fingers. An earthworm, a grub, a beetle slithering or scurrying across his palm merely signified as to the health of the land. He could smell the sweet aroma of Mother Earth in that handful of dirt, savor her taste in the wind that blew across her pastures and her meadows, feel her rhythms in the incessant scraping of the tiny claws of ground squirrels and the poignant yipping of red foxes and the soft hooting of morning doves and the passionate songs of pond frogs. And he could hear the heartbeat of that land echoing in the footfalls of white-tailed deer that came out of the pine groves to drink at the streams.

Mary Jane gave birth on July 14th. They named the child James Alexander, after John's missing brother, but right away began to call him Alex. Little Wind, Mei Lim and Ida May saw to the household duties and helped with the baby and with little Hattie Emma. Mary Jane was weak after the birthing and the doctor had advised her to rest and stay off her feet. But of course she was back lending a hand with the cleaning and the cooking and the gardening. Most of her attention went to baby Alex and to visits from neighbors anxious to see the child.

One of the visitors to the Grosh farm was Deacon Blecher of the Pine Creek Brethren Church. Although the child would not be baptized until he was a young adult and able to understand the meaning of the triple immersions, the deacon wanted to register the birth properly. And Deacon Blecher had a secondary purpose: he wanted to meet—to scrutinize the new arrivals at the farm. By now the rumor had circulated about two Indian children who might have more than a just a working relationship to the Groshes. Not that there was anything wrong with that, but Deacon Blecher *was* in the business of baptism and he was fairly certain that here dwelt two souls needful of salvation—at least two, for he had also heard about Tommy Wepa and Mei Lim. A harvest of plenty for the Lord!

When the deacon finally got Zack alone he got right to work. "We don't see you or your sister at church," he said.

"Sorry, Father, but we didn't go to church in my village. We had the shaman for spiritual questions."

"I'm not a 'Father,' my son. That's a Papist term. We're all equal in the eyes of God and within our church."

"There were Franciscan Fathers who taught us at the reservation. I guess I just assumed you were called that. I know about your Jesus from them. He seemed like a good man."

"Do you believe Jesus died for your sins?"

"The white man's sins. Not the Wintus. And if that's true then he needs to die some more times! The white man makes war on us."

"Not all whites are like that. We Brethren don't believe in going to war."

"I know that. I hope...I hope the part of me that is white is good. I don't want to have to fight against myself."

"Do you feel conflicted, my child? Are you searching for your true identity? Perhaps you could look to Christ...find yourself in him."

"I'm living in two worlds now, Father. I don't need to live in a third as well."

Several days later Tommy and Zack were sitting in the shade of the apple orchard having a lunch break. They were discussing their feelings about living and working with the Groshes. Zack told Tommy that no matter how hard he tried to see himself as part of the family he still felt alien, out of place. It would just take time, Tommy assured him. Time healed wounds. And Little Wind, Zack said, was homesick, missed their mother. If only they could bring her here. Then there was the question of James, Zack's father, still on the mountain.

"Sometimes I feel so strongly that I should go to him. Go back to Bohěm Puyuk and find him again. I am being pulled in so many directions all at the same time."

"I have to tell you," Tommy said, "that I do like it here very much. It's peaceful, there is work to do, nice people to talk to..."

"But?"

"But I think it is time for me to go. I stayed with you throughout your quest...well, most of the time. But the quest is at its end. It is not my quest. I only came along because I am your friend. Now..."

"You want to go back?"

"No! I want to go forward. I have gotten a taste of the world and I want to see more of it."

"Where would you go?"

"There is a large city close by called Chicago."

"I would miss you, my brother."

"I would come to visit."

"Stay with me here for a while yet, Tommy. I still need you. At least until I feel more at home here."

"For a while. But soon I will go."

Byron Grush

★ ★ ★

The autumn harvest was fast approaching. Some of the farmers, those with fields of wheat or oats, met at the Brethren Church one evening to discuss plans for the year's harvest. The church was a long box-like building constructed of local stone. It had three doors: one for the men, one for the women, and a third which led to a spacious kitchen. The Brethren often banded together to share resources; in the early 1840s they had pooled their money to purchase a McCormick reaper. Now there was to be much discussion about this machine.

Cyrus McCormick had patented his father's design for a mechanical harvesting machine in 1837 although its origins dated back, so they said, as early as 1831. Before the introduction of mechanical reapers, wheat was cut by hand with sickles and cradles. This slow, backbreaking work required farmers to take on extra help. Three or four hours of work produced only about a bushel of grain whereas the reaper could do the same job in only ten minutes. But the machine was expensive and many farmers didn't trust the new technology.

The Brethren of Pine Creek Township held no such prejudice against progress. Here was a wonderful machine that could be pulled through the field by one or two horses, which cleaved through the wheat with sharp blades and pushed the stalks off into neat piles where they could be bound for thrashing. However, the ownership of a single reaper to service the entire community, a community that had grown substantially over the years, presented scheduling problems. There was only a short time span when the wheat could be cut: after the grain ripened but before the seeds fell to the ground—and this might be a matter of only a few days.

The original McCormick reaper that the Brethren had bought was old. It didn't have any of the features that had been added to the newer models such as a seat for the driver or re-designed blades. It tended to break down or become jammed; it needed to be replaced. The meeting at the church proceeded, as meetings concerning essential life issues often do, with guarded tensions escalating into outright bickering.

There were those who opposed spending so much as a penny to replace the reaper. It was time, they said, for each individual farmer

252

to acquire machinery of their own. There were others who pleaded a lack of funds and pointed to the Christian principles of fellowship and brotherhood, the need to work together for the common good. One man reported that a gentleman down in Dixon was advertising traveling reaper services. For a percentage of the crop he would bring his three new machines to your field and clear it in less than a day.

Nothing seemed to satisfy everyone. In the end they split into two groups: the wealthier farmers who wanted to go their own way and the rest who pledged to raise the price of a new reaper. George Holsinger was among the second group. "We can run both reapers side by side and finish each field in half the time," he said. Lewis Cornelius, one of the oldest of the farmers present snorted. "That is if the old one doesn't break down," added Cornelius. John and his father had also pledged to help pay for the new reaper. "Who will go to Chicago to buy the machine?" John asked. There were no immediate volunteers.

"I'll go," shouted Daniel Meyers from the back of the room. There was a chorus of laughter.

"Danny, you're only 11 years old!" said Samuel Meyers, Danny's father.

"I can run a buckboard, Papa," Danny replied.

"Anyone else?" asked John. "Well, I know you are all busy with your farms. Perhaps sending some of the younger boys…and an adult…would give them a good experience and it wouldn't take away from much of the farm labor we need right now."

"Experience? Of *Chicago*? I don't know if I want my boy in that dangerous place."

"Someone will go with them, Sam. Maybe one of the farm hands."

When the day came for the expedition to Chicago to pick up the McCormick reaper Danny Meyers was disappointed not to be allowed to accompany the other boys. He was just too young, his father had told him. Maybe next year. A farm hand who worked for old Lewis Cornelius named Avery Geiger was the official adult in charge. Geiger, twenty-six, would oversee the safety and conduct of his three young helpers, Charlie Hildebrand, Henry Adler and another young man who was as eager to go as Danny Meyers had been: Tommy Wepa. The boys were fifteen, sixteen and fourteen, respectively. Tommy had barely made the cut although his experience working on the railroad should have, in his mind, put him in charge of the rest. Tommy hadn't mentioned to anyone except Zack that he didn't plan to return once he arrived in Chicago.

"Why don't we just have them ship the reaper to us on the train?" Geiger had asked. The farmhand was satisfied with the explanation that the shipping costs by rail were prohibitive. They would only be gone for three or four days at best and besides, seeing the big city would be a thrill—if only he didn't have to baby-sit three children!

Avery Geiger brought the old hay wagon to Hildebrand's hog yard where the boys were waiting to load a barrel of pork they were bringing to sell at the market in Chicago in order to offset some of their expenses. The pork had been smoked to preserve it and hopefully would survive the trip without spoiling. As there hadn't been time for a decent hog butchering they would have to be satisfied with the single barrel.

"Saved some of the best parts for scrapple," said old man Hildebrand, Charlie's grandfather. "Snouts and tails and ears, kidneys and bladders and..." As he itemized the various offal that would be boiled down and mixed with cornmeal and fried to make the traditional dish, Geiger chuckled to himself: "Everything but the oink!"

The hay wagon rumbled along the dirt road toward the town of Dixon. Someone was standing along the road waving. As they got closer, Tommy saw who it was and he was not pleased.

"I wonder what's happened," said Geiger. "Better stop and see."

Mei Lim with a well-stuffed knapsack by her side was flagging down the wagon. "Wait!" she called. "I go with you."

25

On the Road Again

John Dixon had taken over operation of Ogee's ferry in 1830. It was the only river crossing south of Rockford. The new settlement and its post office (of which Dixon would become postmaster) soon took the name of Dixon's Ferry. In 1832 a small fort was built along the river, a strategic location and command post during what would come to be called the Black Hawk War. A young volunteer to the Sangamon County Militia named Abraham Lincoln was ordered with his company to Fort Dixon. His first duty was to reach the battle field thirty miles up river where the first encounter of the military and Black Hawk's followers had occurred. There they buried the dead of Major Stillman's force who had been obliterated by the Indians.

Dixon's Ferry became a major crossroads for commerce stemming from the mines at Galena. There were several trails to Galena proceeding from Fort Clark at Peoria which converged at Dixon. Kellogg's Trail passed up through Pine Creek between Mount Morris and Polo. A realignment of Kellogg's route called the Boles Trail also crossed the Rock River at Dixon. Later, the Galena-Peoria Trail would intersect the Galena-Chicago Trail at Dixon and the Illinois Central Railroad would pass through the town on its way to Galena.

Now the wagon driven by Avery Geiger entered the town. Avery had argued against bringing the Chinese girl with them. Tommy hadn't been too keen on that idea either. In the end, Mei Lim had won out, due perhaps to her refusal, once she had climbed onto the wagon, to budge an inch. No one had been willing to try to force her to get off; her fierce defiance was all bared teeth and clinched fists.

"I don't belong on the farm," she explained. "I'll find my own people in the big city."

"Maybe she can cook," Geiger proffered.

"I wouldn't count on it," Tommy retorted.

"You do not want me to come with you?" Mei Lim asked Tommy, somewhat confused concerning his apparent and uncharacteristic animus.

"I just don't want to have to be responsible for you once we get to Chicago."

"You will not be. And *I* will not be looking after *you*."

Dixon, once a handful of log cabins set upon the muddy riverbank, was now a grid of tree shaded avenues lined with houses and buildings of painted wood, brick or quarry stone. The first stores to appear had been Chapman & Hamilton's and the S. M. Bowman Dry Goods Company. Over the years the Government Land Office, the Courthouse, several churches, offices for lawyers, doctors, cabinet makers and its first newspaper, the Dixon Telegraph and Lee County Herald appeared. By 1855 over 135 buildings had been erected, many built of brick and one in particular, the Union Block, rose four stories—but being deemed unsafe, this upper floor was subsequently removed.

Now in 1869, Dixon no longer resembled a frontier town. It was a thriving community that had survived an Indian war, a cholera epidemic, and several fires—the city fathers were in the process of purchasing a new fire engine to insure the safety of Dixon's citizens. In earlier years, a constant stream of passers-through had spawned the inevitable taverns that the good people of Dixon disdained. The resultant lawlessness and the organized thievery of the so-called Banditti had been addressed by the Dixonites who formed their own Society of Vigilance. Law and order had prevailed.

Handcarts filed with local produce and drays heaped with boxes and barrels of every imaginable commodity passed through the dusty streets. Old men sat on benches on the wooden sidewalks in front of stores. They watched promenading women in fine dresses who perused the fashions on display behind the plate glass windows or who chased after children engaged in youthful rascality. The only incongruous element was what appeared to be a feral dog, bedraggled and muddied. It began chasing after Geiger's wagon.

Tommy, seeing the dog and understanding its hunger, opened the barrel of butchered pork and retrieved a chunk of meat which he tossed to the dog. The dog stopped to devour the morsel. Geiger was apparently unaware of the canine encounter. He stopped to ask directions to the Galena-Chicago Trail from two men standing idly on a corner.

One of the men, a big man with the ruffled look of a laborer, directed Geiger to take Second Street under the stone arch bridge and turn south on Galena Avenue, continuing past Bloody Gulch Road. The other man, his appearance no less rough, shook his head in ardent disagreement. He waved his arm in the opposite direction. Follow Chicago Avenue out of town toward Lee Center, he told Geiger. That's the route the Frink and Company Stage Line takes, he insisted.

Tommy and the other boys listened to the argument from the back of the wagon when suddenly, a mud-caked form that might have been white with brown spots under its calcified mantle of muck leaped onto the wagon.

It had a pushed-in face and beady eyes, no neck to speak of and a long tongue that extended down to its chest and dripped slobber. Its enthusiasm could be seen in the furious vibration of its stub of a tail. Avery Geiger turned to see the dog nuzzling up to Tommy. "Get that mutt offa there," Geiger cried. It took all three boys, Charlie Hildebrand, Henry Adler and Tommy Wepa to force the dog off of the bed of the wagon. "Can't have no dogs along on this trip."

"Boy, what an ugly dog!" Charlie Hildebrand said as the wagon pulled away leaving the dog sitting in the middle of the street chewing on its fleas.

"Not as ugly as some people," said Mei Lim who had been the only one on the wagon unhappy to see the dog go. "I thought he was cute."

They reached Lee Center around midafternoon. Geiger pulled up to a livery stable where he could get food and water for the horses. Like Dixon and other nearby villages, Lee Center had been plagued during the 1840s by the Banditti of the Prairies. The Banditti had been notorious for murder, robbery, counterfeiting, and the bribing of local politicians. Like Dixon, Lee Center had formed its own vigilance committee to eradicate the villains. An ominous artifact of those days was the hanging tree near the outskirts of town, now lightning stricken and barely alive. The townspeople declined to cut the tree down; it was thought that it might serve as a deterrent to anyone with Banditti-like aspirations.

Outhouse visits were made. Avery Geiger left to explore a nearby tavern while the crew broke out the sandwiches packed for them by the ladies of the church back in Pine Creek Township. Tommy and Mei Lim sat leaning against the back of the driver's seat while Charlie and Henry dangled their feet over the edge of the wagon bed.

The wagon had no sides as it was intended for carrying bales of hay or wheat. It was all the crew had been able to do to keep from tumbling off as the wagon had rumbled along the bumpy, rutted roads. The barrel of pork was secured with a stout length of rope to the driver's seat but the boys and Mei Lim had had to maintain their balance any way they could. It was a pleasure now to be stationary, to enjoy a repast and relief from the creaking and clattering of the hay wagon. While they ate, a familiar looking ball of dirty fur bounded up the road and leaped once again onto the wagon.

"Uh-oh! Look who's back," shouted Henry.

"We'd better get rid of him before Geiger comes back," said Charlie. "He'll have a fit."

"Oh, I wish we could keep him," said Mei Lim. "He looks so lonely. I'm sure he is a nice puppy."

"Yeah," said Charlie, "you probably want to take him home for dinner. I hear there's an old Chinese recipe for puppy stew."

Tommy was barely in time to block Mei Lim's open palm as it flailed out toward Charlie's face. "He's just kidding, Mei Lim," he told her.

"Ha! Very funny. You want to hear old Chinese saying?"

Oh, oh…here it comes, thought Tommy. He had heard many of Mei Lim's proverbs before, and they often had a stinging quality.

"I tell you," she continued. "It is said that when the people are hungry the house pets tremble. And when the house pets are all gone, the peasants tremble. You like story, *peasant?*"

Tommy had managed to coax the dog across the street with the left-over half of his sandwich. He had timed it just right as Geiger was now stumbling back from the tavern. Henry offered to take the reins so that Geiger could curl up in the back, a prospect that no doubt would have pleased the inebriate had he been more coherent. Tommy leaped onto the wagon bed just as Henry urged the horses back onto the trail. The road signs now identified the trail as Shaw Road.

A few miles out of town Henry was forced to pull off the road to avoid a collision with an approaching Frink and Company Concord Coach. As the four-horse team galloped past, Henry exclaimed, "Boy! That one's a beauty, ain't it?" It was, in fact, beautifully decorated with yellow trim against heavily varnished red panels and golden curlicues that accented its interior. A fairy princess might ask for no less a luxurious vehicle.

Tommy watched the hapless passengers through the coach window as it flew by. Squeezed together on the narrow benches were a woman holding an infant so tightly it seemed to be turning blue, a man in a stovepipe hat that repeatedly bounced against the roof of the coach, two small children who were laughing with glee and an enormous fat man with chin whiskers that must have doubled his weight. Seated across from this group were even more weary travelers with pallid faces that indicated extreme physical discomfort. In spite of the Concord Coach's unique suspension system of leather braces, the coach swayed and swung often inducing seasickness in those who had chosen this mode of travel.

The elegant Concord Coach would soon become obsolete, like the roads and routes it followed. The railroads could do everything the coaches did and faster, more comfortably and more efficiently. And the contracts for carrying the mail, a major income source for stage lines, were being awarded to the railroads. Certainly the old roads were the slow way to travel; Geiger's wagon was to make the 40 miles between Pine Creek Township and the town of Paw Paw Grove in just under 10 hours. They would be only one third of the way to Chicago.

With the morning a brief light shower brought fresh and fragrant breezes through the open windows of the Datemore House, one of the town's two hotels at the intersection of the Chicago Road and the Princeton Road. Seated at a round oak table, the travelers ate a hearty breakfast of coffee, fried pork fat, boiled potatoes and hot baking soda biscuits. They looked forward to getting back on the road but lingered for a while in the pleasant dining room.

The village of Paw Paw Grove was named for the abundance of shrub-like pawpaw trees found growing throughout the surrounding landscape. The trees produced a yellowish-green fruit looking like a fat banana with a soft, custardy flesh dotted with large black seeds.

The earliest residents of the area, the Pottawattamie Indians, considered the fruit a delicacy. Their leader, Chief Shabbona, selected part of the grove where there were more oaks and maples than pawpaws for a burial ground. Here the tribe placed their dead between two hollowed out logs and stood them upright in the crotches of the hardwood trees.

The wagon rolled out of Paw Paw Grove. As they gained some distance from the groves, the prairie through which the Chicago Road stretched flattened into a great pan, the horizon seemed to reach to infinity and the dome of the sky loomed endlessly blue and empty of all but tiny wisps of cloud. The road was straight and narrow and occasionally striped with ruts and spotted with potholes. The order of the day was monotony—they traveled through a simple, uniform, changeless, boilerplate of a world. Even the random appearance of a farm or a tavern was marvelous to observe.

Just before they reached Indian Creek, a small gray-brown dot appeared in the road behind them. It grew bigger as it drew closer and resolved all at once into the galloping form of an ugly but familiar dog. It barked. Furiously. Barked a kind of frantic, warning bark as if it desperately needed them to understand something impossible to communicate—a thing that dogs can know and humans can only wonder about—a thing that should concern humans as much as it did dogs.

Tommy jumped to the driver's seat beside Geiger and grabbed the reins. He pulled back on them and the horses bucked, then stopped trotting. Geiger shouted an oath. The dog jumped onto the wagon. All the humans turned to look back down the road. A cluster of gray forms was bounding toward them. They could see yellow eyes and sharp white teeth as the forms drew near. Geiger took back the reins and snapped them, shouting at the horses to "giddy-up and be quick now!"

The pack of wolves closed in on the wagon. The dog stood his ground, barking and nipping at a wolf that had tried to jump up on the bed. There was pandemonium among the wagoneers as they realized they would be unable to outrun this wolf pack. Then Tommy remembered the barrel of smoked pork. It must be what the wolves were after, he reasoned. Certainly a scrawny dog wouldn't satisfy their hunger—nor would four scrawny human children—but then there *was* Avery Geiger. Geiger's bulk could probably keep them well fed for a week!

Tommy opened the barrel and pulled out a good-sized piece of meat which he flung to the advancing wolves. The pack stopped in their tracks and began to fight over the pork. But one wolf, the largest of them, claimed it for his own and the rest of the pack continued the chase.

Now all three boys had procured a hunk of meat from the barrel. One by one they threw these at the wolves. Each time the ritual of who-gets-the-meat was repeated by the pack. Each time the remaining wolves, now four in number, resumed their pursuit. And the dog barked. And Geiger swore. And Tommy had a new idea.

He unlashed the rope holding the barrel in place, tipped it over and rolled it toward the back edge of the wagon bed. Waiting for the moment when all four wolves were within a few feet of the wagon, Tommy gave the barrel a shove. There were yelps and howls. One wolf lay bloodied in the road. The others had disappeared into the fields.

"Aren't you going to go back for the barrel?" Tommy asked Geiger who was still snapping the reins at the frightened horses.

'The hell with it," he answered. "There may go our profits, but at least we still have our own hides!"

The new road between Chicago and Dixon's Ferry had been surveyed in 1833 by George Snow and Captain Joseph Naper, for whom Naperville was named. They had begun at the southeast corner of Lake and West Water Streets in Chicago and had followed an old road, the Peoria-Galena Road that connected a series of busy taverns: Kellogg's, Chambers', Crane's, Winter's, Avery's and Snyder's. Passing the taverns they entered the bare landscape where they staked out a path across Straddle Creek, Leap Creek, Mud Creek, and Smallpox Creek. The only settlements they noted on their survey were Laughton's and Forbes' claims, the taverns along the Des Plaines River, and Joseph and John Naper's small fort which stood about 28 miles southwest from Chicago.

In 1851, because of the need for better roads to service the stagecoach and teamster routes out of Chicago, a plank road was built out through Riverside, Fullersburg, Naperville and Oswego as far as Little Rock. Sections of the plank road were owned by private companies who established toll booths at intervals as close together as one mile. Early tolls were 37 cents for a two- or 50 cents for a four-horse vehicle, 25 cents for a single team, 10 cents for a horse and rider, 4 cents per head of cattle and 3 cents for a sheep or a pig.

The eight businessmen of Naperville who had funded the plank road had done so in part because of their opposition to the passing through Naperville of the Galena and Chicago Union Railroad: an extraordinary act of short-sightedness as this particular railroad soon acquired the Cedar Rapids and Missouri River Railroad which had been the first railroad to reach Council Bluffs and hence connect with the Union Pacific and therefore the Transcontinental Railroad. The folks in Oswego, to the west of Naperville, were of like mind in rejecting the railroad in favor of the plank road and even raised funds for an extension to Indiana, which was never completed.

Constructing a plank road was something like building an upside down railroad track: wooden stringers were set down and covered with planks three inches thick and eight feet wide. The Southwestern Plank Road, part of the Chicago-Galena Trail, was one lane wide and well traveled, but not always well maintained. Boards warped and rotted and the resulting ride could be quite bone-rattling. When Geiger and company reached Little Rock in the late afternoon they encountered a section of the road that had deteriorated. The tollbooth had likewise been abandoned but at least (Geiger thanked God) the taverns were still open.

Past Little Rock the road signs identified the route as Galena Road. As they got closer to Oswego there was more and more traffic on the road; carriages and drays had difficulty passing one another on the single lane of planks. Now there was a toll about every 5 miles.

"Crap!" Geiger complained. "I wish we'd gone back for that barrel. How we gonna pay all these tolls?"

Ah, changed your tune now, thought Tommy. And Geiger was supposed to be the adult on this trip! Geiger wouldn't run out of money, Tommy was sure of that. But Geiger would not realize extra money from the sale of the pork, some of which he had planned to pocket.

Across the river in Oswego, the road followed an old trail, Wolf's Crossing. At the first tollbooth, traffic was backed up waiting for some kind of dispute to be resolved between the toll collector and the driver of a dray piled high with crates. The collector wanted a higher fee as he had spotted several hogs behind the crates. One by one the waiting drivers left their vehicles to form a half circle behind the driver of the dray—a half circle of very tough-looking and angry men. The collector wisely decided to raise the gate.

It was just past suppertime. Twilight was fading as the sun disappeared below the horizon. Geiger halted the wagon next to the Pre-emption House on the northeast corner of Water and Main Streets in Naperville. The large, rambling hotel, dining hall and saloon dominated the block. With its Greek Revival styling, siding of black walnut, white-trim and lettering that stretched the length of the main two-story building reading "P R E - E M P T I O N H O U S E" it was the largest hotel west of the Alleghenies.

Built in 1835 of locally grown oak and walnut trees it boasted 19 bedrooms, a kitchen, dining room, sitting rooms, maid's room, office and Jessie Oldham's "Sample Room," a long spacious chamber with an outside entrance for visitors to "sample" the local spirits. The rooms had tongue and groove white rock maple floors and trim of white pine. Abraham Lincoln had slept there in 1858, the night before one his debates with Stephen Douglas, and had stood on the building's porch roof to address a crowd gathered below.

"We'll stay here tonight and make Chicago tomorrow," Avery Geiger told his crew. "Only thing is, I don't know what you're going to do with that dog."

"Let him go," Henry Adler suggested. "He's got street smarts."

"I want to keep him," said Mei Lim. "I think I'll call him Lao. He warned us about the wolf pack, you know."

"He was more likely in cahoots with 'em," said Charlie Hildebrand. "Led them right to us."

"You can keep him," said Geiger. "But you're not getting back on the wagon with him. You can go or stay…I could care less."

Mei Lim looked at Tommy, hoping for a glimmer of support for her position. He merely shrugged. Anger flared up in her breast. "Come on, Lao," she said and stomped off into the darkness. She walked across the street and along the river, trying to gain some composure. Lao, the dog, followed her, somehow sensing who his new master might be. But dogs and angry girls make impractical adventurers when they haven't a plan. So soon Mei Lim returned to the Pre-emption House to rejoin the others. At the door she bent to stroke the dog's head. "Stay here, Lao," she said. "I'll see you in the morning."

When the morning sun struck the dark siding of the Pre-emption House, Mei Lim was out the front door looking for her dog. Lao was no where to be seen. "Oh no," she said out loud. The others were still in the dining room. They wouldn't be leaving immediately, so Mei Lim decided to search for Lao. Maybe she could convince Geiger to let her bring the dog back onto the wagon. If not, maybe Lao could run alongside—but did he have the strength to do that? She did so want to get to Chicago; surely there would be a Chinatown there. She shouldn't have to choose between a Chinatown and a dog, should she?

Avery Geiger brought the three boys from the hotel to help to hitch the horses to the wagon. All up and down the street there were teamsters securing produce on their drays and families loading supplies into prairie schooners. Shop keepers were unfurling awnings. The sounds of a small town waking to meet the day met the ears of the travelers. But Tommy, hoping to hear the barking of a small dog, was disappointed.

"Where could she be?" Tommy asked.

"If she ain't here by the time we're ready to go she gets left," said Geiger. "Probably she's out chasing after that damn dog."

"What have you got against dogs, Mr. Geiger?"

"I hates 'em, that's what."

"And Chinese girls? You hate them too?"

"It's all the same to me. She's here when we leave, she can come. She's not here...we leave anyway. You wanna go lookin' for her?"

26

Picnic in the Pines

"It's time you had a white person name," Zack told Little Wind. "Father named me Ay-Zack but the people called me White Cloud instead. When you were born he let the people name you without giving you a white person name."

"I never cared about that," said Little Wind. "I never felt self-conscious about being half white until I had to live among them. Now…"

"Now you have a new family. Your Wintu name, it refers to the sound the hummingbird makes with its wings: Lakas Ku-k'aluma, 'wings to make the little wind blow.' "

"That boy from San Francisco used to call me 'Windy.' I don't think it was to be nice to me."

"Windy…K'aha…well, we could call you Kathy. That's a white person name."

"They have a Kathy already. A couple of them, I think. Anyway, why do I have to have a white person name?"

"It will make Uncle happy. It will be easier for our new family to accept us."

"Oh…I don't know if you are right or not. Anyway, I don't want to be 'Windy' or Kathy. How about…"

"Well, I guess you can choose your own name if you wish."

"Thank you for realizing that," she said not disguising her sarcasm. "How about this: our mother's name is Kut'et nop which means 'a little deer' or what the white people call a 'fawn.' How about Fawn for my name? It will make me think of Mother whenever anyone says it."

"Fawn. Yes, I think that will do. I don't think they already have a Fawn."

John Grosh had a small grove of pines not far from his house. When he was developing the land for farming, cutting trees and pulling up stumps, he had left these alone. The grove was shaped like a crescent moon and bordered a large pond fed by a cold spring. The clear area by the pond was an idea place for a picnic.

John wanted to bring his siblings together to celebrate the news that their brother, James, might still be alive somewhere out west and for them to meet James' children. He sent word to Philip, Elizabeth, Emma and Mary Jane to bring their spouses, their children and of course, lots and lots of food. Isaac and Catherine, and David, who would bring Mary Ann Snyder, would complete the family reunion; William and his family and Katy and hers lived faraway in the wilds of Iowa and would not come.

Philip and Catherine were the first to arrive with their children, Isaac, Mary, Anna, Sarah and James...

Here the narrator is obliged to digress from the story for a few words of explanation designed to forestall any confusion the reader may experience concerning the names of the characters in our story. Isaac and his progeny seem trapped within a vortex of limited names, but this is not for their lack of imagination. They are following the naming tradition established by their German ancestors which dates back to the eighteenth century. In this tradition, the first born son was usually named after the father's father (hence Phillip is named after Isaac's father) and the second born son is named after the mother's father (Philip's twin was named Isaac—that child died very young.) The first born daughter is named after the mother's mother, the second after the father's mother, and so on. There were variations on these patterns, of course, but the result can generate many duplicate names that can give a genealogist—or a novelist—a migraine.

Isaac's first wife was Catherine Burns. Her parents were Catherine and Isaac Burns. Isaac's father, Phillip, was married to Catherine Zentmyer and their children were named Isaac, William, James and Elizabeth. So Isaac had sons named Philip and Isaac, another son named William and one named James, as well as a daughter named Elizabeth and another named Catherine (who we've been calling Katy). Confused yet?

Isaac's oldest daughter is named Mary Jane (one of my favorite characters from the previous novel about the Groshes, *Once Upon a*

Gold Rush). Isaac's son William has married Catherine Tennis and John has married her sister, Mary Jane Tennis. At the time of our story Isaac has 25 grandchildren and there will be many, many more. There are Marys, Johns, Williams, one or two named James, and so on. The narrator therefore offers the reader a list of Isaac's daughters' married names to refer to in times of confusion. They are: Mary Jane Ayers, Elizabeth Bomberger, Emma Arnold, and Catherine Palmaiter. John's wife, Mary Jane will be referred to as 'Mary Jane' and Isaac's wife, Catherine, will be 'Catherine' or 'Cath.' Philip's wife, Catherine, will be 'Philip's wife, Catherine.' And now, let's go to a picnic!

Philip and Catherine were the first to arrive with their children, Isaac, Mary, Anna, Sarah and James. Eight year-old James headed straight for the pond where a long rope had been hung from the branch of a tall cottonwood tree on the pond's opposite bank and where he promptly stripped down to his underwear. Philip's wife, Catherine, had brought beef kidneys which she had cleaned of the fat and fiber, seasoned with salt and pepper, floured and fried in fresh lard. Her own mother would have parboiled the kidneys then broiled them, but Catherine preferred the crispy outer coating, plus she could make a nice gravy by adding more flour and some water to the cast iron pan once the kidneys were cooked through.

John and Zack had set up tables to hold the food and Mary Jane had spread four large quilts on the ground. A picnic basket held plates and silverware. A jug of freshly squeezed lemonade and decorated ceramic cups were also at the ready. Mary Jane's dishes included Apple Brown Betty and a stuffed leg of pork which she had prepared by cutting deep incisions parallel to the bone and stuffing these with a mash of boiled potatoes, butter, cayenne pepper, chopped onion and a little rubbed sage. Pork was always a good choice even though someone was bound to bring soused pig's feet (boiled until the flesh is tender and almost falling off the bone, then cooled and soused with equal portions of the cooking liquid, sharp vinegar, whole allspice, clove and salt and pepper).

Ida May was watching Hattie Emma who had run to the pond when she saw James swinging on the rope out over the water and dropping with a splash. Hattie Emma was only allowed to venture as deeply into the pond as her waist but Ida May watched her carefully anyway. A boy had drowned in the river over at Dixon only last year. Baby Alex was sleeping soundly in a perambulator under the shade of the trees near the food tables. A carriage rolled up the drive back by the house; Mary Jane and Charles Ayers and family had arrived.

"Uncle John! Aunt Mary!" shouted Elsie, the Ayers' eldest. "Mom's brought her new camera. Wait 'til you see it."

Mary Jane Ayers had gone to California in 1852 for the gold rush with her brothers, John and James. There were not many jobs there for women, at least not ones a decent woman would consider, so Mary Jane took up photography. She learned the art of the daguerreotype, the use of the view camera, the darkroom techniques required to coax the latent image from the plate—and fell in love with the process. She also fell in love with Charles Ayers. The couple had four children now.

Photography had evolved; wet colloidal negatives and paper prints had allowed photographers to be much more mobile; cameras were smaller and the process much less complicated. For their fifteenth wedding anniversary, Charles Ayers had sent away to Paris for a present he knew his wife would love: an Appareil Dubroni Number 3 camera. When Charles had proposed to Mary Jane he had promised her that she need not abandon her involvement as a photographer. He supported (and loved) her independent spirit and creativity. The reality of marriage and motherhood, however, left her little time for photography. But the Dubroni Number 3 was to reawaken her former love and enable its pursuit.

It was beautiful: a square box of polished rosewood with brass fittings, a brass-bound lens, a red glass viewing window and an internal chamber of clear glass. The wet plate needed to be developed immediately after exposure or the image would be lost. This camera allowed the development process to take place *inside* the camera in a mere thirteen steps by introducing the needed chemicals through a pipette with a rubber bulb. It was truly revolutionary. Mary Jane intended to make a family portrait once everyone had arrived.

Elizabeth and Josiah Bomberger and their children, William, Mary Ellen, and Ida were the next to arrive. William was 10, only two years younger than Mary Jane Ayre's son Sammie, so the two boys took off into the pine grove to play at wild Indians (not realizing that Zack and Fawn were actual Indians). Elizabeth had brought beets stewed with a little salt and pepper, vinegar and a good slice of butter rolled in flour, and a chicken pie of two small chickens cut up and seasoned with salt and pepper and placed with some water in a pie pan lined with puff pastry and layered with pieces of another stick of butter rolled in flour, and then covered with thin strips of pastry and decorated with scalloped edges. She had also brought her specialty, an apple cornmeal pudding (thinly sliced pippin apples in a quart of fresh milk with a quart of well sifted cornmeal, a little salt, a spoonful of chopped suet and a teacup of good molasses, baked in a buttered dish for four hours).

Next Isaac and Catherine arrived with Catherine's children, Minnie May and Elsie, followed by Emma and John Arnold and their two children, Ben and Albert. David was the last of the family to come, late as usual. David had brought Mary Ann Snyder and her sister, Sarah Elizabeth. Sarah was only 12 but had an enormous crush on her sister's boyfriend, David. She had needled Mary Ann to let her come to the picnic until Mary Ann had relented. David was a little annoyed at this but he was focused on an announcement he wished to make later after the feast.

Now the tables were piled with food; each dish was a specialty of one of the women's and there were several traditional items, like the soused pig's feet, about which the women were dubious. There was a tub of lemon jelly made from the soaked rinds of fresh lemons, lemon juice, crushed sugar, egg whites and sherry wine. There was Fruit Charlotte, a baked desert made from apples, currants, raisins, grated stale bread, brown sugar, ground cinnamon, grated lemon peel and brandy. There was a mincemeat pie and a beefsteak pudding (trimmed and tenderized rump steak cut into small pieces and baked with onions, potatoes, veal broth, mushroom ketchup and a beaten egg yolk). There were piles of green corn boiled in the husks, plates of cornmeal bread cut into squares, wheat muffins baked in a ring, and smoked sausages still attached in a long string. There was a bowl of sauerkraut boiled with pickled pork and another of parsnips fried in lard. And of course, fried chicken.

Isaac had brought the scrapple he had made the day before. He had spent most of yesterday afternoon scraping and washing the various parts of the pig (everything but the oink) and boiled them down with a little salt until the flesh was soft and loose from the bones. He had used a whole pig's head and feet after cleaning them and had added kidneys, liver, heart and stomach cut into small pieces (but had saved the intestines to make sausage casings). After removing the bones from the pot and cutting the meat into even smaller pieces he prepared the cornmeal with rubbed sage, sweet marjoram and salt and pepper. The meat and the cornmeal were returned to the cooking liquid and boiled until they were the consistency of mush. Finally, Isaac had poured the mush into pans to cool, then sliced the scrapple into squares. Early this morning he had fried the pieces in some lard.

Mary Jane Ayers had set up her Dubroni Number 3 camera on its tripod. She put a piece of ground glass against the rear of the glass chamber where it was held in place by a spring. Everyone was summoned and arranged by family groups with children in front of the adults. Zack and Fawn were in the middle, just in front of Isaac and Catherine and Catherine's two girls. Everyone squeezed together as Mary Jane Ayers focused the lens and then locked the focus by tightening a screw on the brass cylinder.

"Everyone stay where you are…don't move now," she said. "You don't have to smile just yet." She removed the camera from the tripod and carried it to where she had set up her chemicals.

The camera had come with a kit of glass plates and various chemicals. She had washed a plate with alcohol and now she poured a bottle of iodized collodion over it. She then removed the ground glass from the camera and replaced it with the wet plate, put a lens cap over the lens and closed a wooden flap to make the camera lighttight. Silver nitrate was introduced into the camera with a pipette and rubber bulb and this sensitized the plate as it flowed over it. She drained the silver nitrate from the camera and reattached the wooden box to the tripod.

The children had been fidgeting and some of the adults were also getting restless. With the woman photographer back at her station, a semblance of order began to take effect (but anticipation of the waiting array of food—next on the program—added little in achieving the desired decorum). Smiles and keeping still were ordered as Mary Jane removed the lens cap to make the exposure, and then quickly replaced it.

"Okay, you're all released now. Go and enjoy the food!" she called. She removed the camera from the tripod and carried it back to where her chemical kit was set up. Fawn followed her.

"Can I watch what you do next?" Fawn asked.

"Of course you can. See, there's a red window here we can watch the development process as it takes place. It's fascinating!"

Mary Jane Ayers introduced pyrogallic acid into the camera and they watched as the image gradually appeared. The plate would be washed and fixed while still in the camera. It would be a negative, with lights and darks reversed, and could then be printed onto sensitized paper to create a positive. In fact, Mary Jane could make prints for each of the families at the picnic once she returned home where Charles had built a darkroom for her in a shed behind the house.

"Are you interested in photography, Fawn?" Mary Jane asked the girl.

"I was helper to a photographer...sort of. I went to Alaska with him. His name is Edward Muybridge."

"Excellent! I've seen some of the stereo slides he made of Yosemite. Wonderful work."

"Your camera is so much smaller, and you don't need the portable darkroom."

"You will have to tell me all about your adventures. Would you like to come over to my darkroom and help make prints of this plate? Yes? We'll do that. You know, your father and I...he was so special to me growing up. We were very close."

"And you got into all sorts of trouble together as I recall," said John, who had just come to tell Mary Jane and Fawn to go get a plate of food.

"I suppose we did. But Fawn doesn't want to hear about that."

"Yes I do."

"Well, we used to steal rhubarb from Mr. Finkbeiner's garden."

"Oh, that was just the least of it, Mary Jane," said John. "Tell her about the time with the pumpkins."

"The pumpkins. Ah, yes...you see, I was probably about your age, maybe a little younger. James and I often dawdled on the way home from school...this was back when we lived in Pennsylvania. It was near the end of October and we saw that people were already decorating their porches with pumpkins and cornstalks."

"Decorating with pumpkins? What for?"

"It was the Irish that had moved to Shirleysburg at the beginning of the century. They brought this custom with them. We of course didn't give credence to a belief in witches and goblins, nor Saints for that matter. That comes from the Papists. They have something called All Saints Day. The day before All Saints Day is celebrated as All Hallows' Eve. They let their children go from door to door on that night begging for something they call a soul cake. But no one ever had a soul cake, what ever that was, so they would give the children an apple, a pear, a plum, a cherry, maybe just some nuts…"

"Oh, that sounds like fun!"

"Yes, we thought so too. But we weren't allowed to go out on that night. That's why, when we saw all those pumpkins…"

"But why pumpkins? Why did they decorate with pumpkins? I would think they would just eat them."

"Did you ever hear of a Jack-o'-Lantern? No? There is an old story about a farmer named Jack. He disliked work above all things and wished for some way to avoid it. One day he met the Devil coming up the road. The Devil told Jack it was time for him to die but Jack wasn't ready for that. He tricked the Devil into climbing up a tree and promptly carved a cross into the tree's bark. This trapped the Devil who couldn't pass a Holy symbol like that.

"Now Jack went out and led a sinful life and when he was tired of all the crimes he had committed and all the evil deeds he had done he returned to the tree where he had trapped the devil. 'Promise me you won't take my soul to Hell and I'll let you down from the tree,' said Jack. The Devil made Jack the promise and Jack released him. When Jack finally died, however, the Lord would not let him enter Heaven because of the bad life he had led. The Devil, wishing to heap revenge on Jack but being unable to bring him down to Hell threw a burning ember at him, an ember that would cling to Jack and burn for eternity. Jack found a pumpkin and carved out a hollow inside it and placed the ember there where it shown brightly. He had to walk the earth carrying his pumpkin lantern endlessly looking for a place where he could rest, but he never found it."

"So what did you do with the pumpkins?"

"It was the night before All Hallows' Eve. We snuck out of the house and walked down the hill to the village. We had borrowed a handcart from behind old Mr. Vail's store and we loaded it up with pumpkins as we went down the street, taking them from porches until we had nearly every pumpkin in town. It took both of us to push that cart but we finally got it to the end of the street where there was a cistern that served to hold water for the entire town. We struggled to open the wooden door on top of the cistern. We were going to drop all the pumpkins into the water. We thought it was the funniest trick we had ever played!"

"But something stopped you?"

"Constable McGarvey. He was patrolling around Cooper's tavern. We were lucky that Mr. McGarvey was a good friend of my Grandfather Burns who operated the wheelwright shop next door to the tavern. Grandfather Burns had been working late that night so Constable McGarvey ushered us into the shop and turned the two of us pumpkin snatchers over to him. That was probably a worse punishment than if he had thrown us into jail!"

"My father and you remind me of my friend Tommy. A trickster, like our Coyote. Tommy's name, Wepa, means coyote. I can't wait for him to get back, I miss him."

Zack had just taken a big bite from a square of scrapple which he promptly spit out. "What is this stuff?" he cried.

"You don't want to know," said Philip who had come to sit next to the boy. "Actually, you should have some maple syrup to eat that with."

"It tasted a little like squirrel. Not my favorite food."

"Tell me something, Zack. How is it that you speak such good English but you can't read or write?"

"None of us ever learned. You see, the Fathers taught us English so they could preach to us. There was something about their Bible…it was only for the Fathers to read…in some other language, I guess. We Wintu don't put down our words with marks. So we didn't care to learn and the fathers didn't care to teach us."

"School starts pretty soon," said Philip. "I'd like to invite you and Fawn to come to my classroom where I teach. There are children of all different ages learning to write and read and do numbers. The school isn't faraway and I could give you special help."

"You don't teach that bible, do you?"

"No, not at school. If you are interested in that, we Brethren use one that is written in English. You can learn to read it."

As people were finishing their Apple Brown Betty and Fruit Charlotte, David Grosh stood and cleared his throat.

"Everyone! Everyone listen. I have an announcement to make. I've have asked Mary Ann to be my wife and she has said yes! We plan to marry this coming November."

Everyone—everyone, that is except Sarah Elizabeth—applauded. Sarah watched with envy as David and Mary Ann embraced. The picnic goers were about to disperse into smaller groups: swimmers (the younger children), ball players (the older children), nappers (the men), and cleaner-uppers (the women). But a wagon rattling up the lane caught their attention.

"Hallo!" came the cry. "I heard you were having a party so I brought some refreshments for you."

George Funk, the son of Sammy Funk, the man who had first met Isaac and his family on their arrival in Illinois, jumped from his wagon and started to unload a crate of dark green bottles. "Been over to Brady and Dee's brewery in Dixon. Sorry it took so long. Got some nice cool porter for you." George Funk was a young man of 24 and, like the many Funks who resided in the Rock River Valley, was a great friend to the Groshes.

"George, come and have some of this food before the womenfolk clear it all away!" Isaac told him. "We're celebrating a number of things, it appears. I have two new grandchildren—the son and daughter of my son, James—and I'm about to have another child of my own, as well as a new daughter in law!"

"Magnificent, Isaac. Magnificent!" George uncapped a bottle of the porter and raised it in a toast. The other men scrambled to pull the stubby, short-necked bottles from the crate.

It was a grand day for a picnic in the pines; it was a splendid day for the making of memories. Isaac knew the importance of memories, how the blissful ones neutralized the lamentable ones—usually. He and his were blessed with good fortune, abundant family and faithful friends. But the universe had been constructed around the principle of change. In the next few years three of those present and another of their number who was living faraway would pass from this realm of the living. It would be said of them that they were gone but not forgotten.

27

The Pre-Emption House

It wasn't just a tavern and a hotel, it was a meeting place that figured in local politics and state and national issues as well. Naperville had been chosen as the county seat of the newly formed DuPage County in 1839. County officers held their meetings in the hotel's sample room until an actual courthouse could be built. Every Saturday there was a horse market in the streets just outside the Pre-Emption House. The horse traders spent part of the day in the sample room celebrating their purchases or sales.

Early settlers laid claim to lands by squatting; this was called pre-emption since the government hadn't yet surveyed the land. The pre-emption act of 1841 legalized the process allowing settlers to buy up to 160 acres at $1.25 per acre. Pre-Emption House, the first and largest hotel west of Chicago, had been named after that practice which had been in effect many years before it became law. There was something about the pioneering spirit, the laying claim to property gained through one's hard work and sacrifice, that pervaded the town and the hotel, and inspired the citizenry and the hotel's clientele to muddle through difficult times. And sometimes to act on impulse.

In 1868 the neighboring town of Wheaton called for another election (this had been an on-going legal battle for years) to determine where the county seat of DuPage County should be located. By a slim margin the vote went in favor of Wheaton. Some Napervilleans maintained that the ballot box had been stuffed. Naperville officials refused to recognize the results and would not turn over the county records. Just before dawn, by the light of partially shielded lanterns, a group of villagers from Wheaton, about forty by the count of those who later told the tale, crept through a window and into the Recorder's Office of Naperville's courthouse. They began carting boxes of record books down the wide courthouse steps to load onto a waiting wagon.

Two young girls, Franny and Grace Cody, happened to look out their window and saw the men moving the boxes. The alerted their father, Judge Hiram Cody, who rushed to the Congregational Church tower and rang the bell there to wake the town. By the time any defenders could be mustered however, the raiders had escaped.

The following afternoon a group of angry Napervilleans gathered at the sample room of the Pre-Emption House. There they hatched a plan to stage a raid on Wheaton to retrieve the records which the group felt were rightfully the property of Naperville. Sheriff James Hunt got wind of the hot-head party (as it was called) and determined to intercede, fearing violence. This might result if the hot-head group encountered the men from Wheaton who no doubt expected some sort of retaliation. Pretending to join in the plan, the sheriff began buying drinks for everyone in the room. Soon they were all too drunk to do anything but go home and sleep it off. Conflict had been averted—for a time.

Mei Lim had found the dog she had named Lao roaming the back alleys, searching for discarded food. The saloons, which were as numerous as the churches, often had a jar of hard-boiled eggs next to a cellar of salt, offered freely in order to make their patrons more thirsty. Once rotten, the eggs were jettisoned out into the alley; Lao was busy devouring a pile of these, and fending off aggressive rodents with long, ugly, pale tails that twitched and switched as they gnashed their sharp incisors at him.

Mei LIm had found a length of rope behind one of the buildings and looped this around Lao's neck. It was clear that the dog was unwilling to leave his hard-fought feast. Tugging Lao along, she returned to the Pre-Emption House only to find that her traveling companions had departed, stranding her in the town. The Cantonese oath she recited would have shocked even the most ruthless of the Tongs that had once pursued her.

She needed her belongings, as sparse as they were and so, knotting Lao's lease around a hitching post, she marched to the front door of the hotel and entered. This opened onto a long hallway with a dining room on her right and the hotel's office on her left. Ahead of her were stairs which led to the bedrooms for the guests. She was certain her knapsack would still be in the room. As she began to ascend the steep, narrow staircase, a voice rang out:

"Hey there, where do you think you're going?"

A man stood in the doorway of the office. Tall and thin as a young sapling, he was jacketless, his untied cravat drooped against his green, unbuttoned vest and his sleeves were rolled back to expose his forearms, thin and knobby as sticks. He seemed to Mei Lim to be like a scarecrow which had lost its straw stuffing, as if he might collapse at any moment. But the scarecrow bellowed, repeating his question as if she were the accused at an inquisition.

"Sorry," she stammered. "I go get my belongings. I leave then."

"I have your things in my office. Your party said you'd be back for them. Come in here." It was a command, not a request. Mei Lim hadn't been ordered around since her days in San Francisco. She stood fast and glared at the man.

"I won't bite you," he said. "Please come in and get your belongings."

The office was a large chamber, larger than four of the hotel's bedrooms combined. There was a roll-top desk against one wall but most of the work of the office appeared to be laid out on a square table in the center of the room. Papers were stacked in towers of disarray; the green blotter pad was stained with splotches of ink, looking like an early navigator's map of an unexplored world. A lush Persian carpet covered most of the floor and an ungainly gas-lit chandelier hung from the ceiling, protruding into the space defiantly. There was a copper gas line running from the ceiling fixture to a green glass-shaded lamp balanced on top of the roll-top desk. Against another wall was a large, ornate metal box with sculpted legs that resembled those of some impossible jungle animal. A plaque on the front of the box read, "Wilder's Improved Patent Fire-Proof Salamander Safe."

The man motioned for Mei Lim to sit on a spindle-backed chair on one side of the central table. He sat opposite her and peered across a mountain range of papers.

"Oh, I know exactly where everything is. Can lay my hands on anything that is wanted. Just looks disorganized."

"And my knapsack?"

"Presently. But let me introduce myself. I am Ellsworth Dunning, proprietor of this establishment. And you are?"

"My name is Mei Lim."

"And how is it that you have come here to this place, Mei Lim?"

"Long story. Come from China...with family...to work at Gold Mountain. Have job on train which brings me to Illinois. I am going to big city of Chicago to be with countrymen."

"And your family?"

Mei Lim hesitated. One little lie, she knew, had the capacity to grow like a many-headed hydra. Dunning let it pass and continued:

"And how do you expect to get to Chicago?"

"I really don't know. Now that my so-called friends have abandoned me. I don't have any money."

"You say you worked on a train. What did you do?"

"Waited tables in dining car. Made up beds in sleeper."

"I tell you what, Mei Lim. My maid quit yesterday to get married. To a terrible fellow from Wheaton! Anyway, why don't you work for me? Making beds and cleaning. Free room and board. And I can use you in the sample room. You'll get tips and you can save enough to ride in style to Chicago."

"What about Lao?"

"Who's Lao?"

"My dog."

The hotel was constructed diagonally on its corner lot. The west-facing façade along Main Street, however, was built to be parallel to that avenue and so gave an acute angle to the walls of the two rooms at that end of the building. The room at the northeast corner was the smallest of all the rooms in the hotel and seemed smaller still since no furniture, bed nor desk, could be placed in the corner with the sharp angle without blocking a good portion of the floor space. But to Mei Lim, who now occupied that strangely shaped alcove, it was sumptuous, luxuriant, palatial. It was the first private room she had ever occupied.

Lao had been sequestered in Laird's Livery Stable behind the hotel. Mei Lim's new boss, Ellsworth Dunning, had inspected the animal, then instructed Mei Lim to take the mangy mutt to the fountain that stood at the intersection of Washington and Water Streets and to return with a spotless canine or to return alone. Lao was dunked, scrubbed and completely humiliated by the washing. Now the dog dozed on a bed of straw while his new companions, the horses of hotel guests, shuffled and snorted in the dusty and dim ambience of the stable.

Lao dreamed of roaming freely once more. The town, although crowded with humans and their noisy conveyances, wasn't such a bad place for sniffing about. He had reservations, however, about the shop across from the hotel, the one along the river side of the street with the sign (which, of course, he couldn't read, being a dog) that spelled out "Knoch Brothers Cigar Manufacturers" and from which issued the foulest of foul smells. Lao had no use for Knoch's Fine Havanas, the Guvner ten-center, or the Jay-Eye-See five-center.

In fact, most of the stores near the hotel yielded up scents of human things which he could not chase, eat or destroy. Hillegas and Reiche's Hardware and Agricultural Implements sprawled across three store fronts and offered stoves and tinware and wagon-maker's supplies. Down near the dreaded fountain where Lao had nearly been drowned by the Missy (that would be the translation from Dog of the name he called Mei Lim in his dog mind) was Philip Beckman's Harness Shop. Now that *did* contain food—but for horses, cattle and chickens. Totally inedible!

Up around the corner he had discovered Williard Scott Junior's General Merchandise store in a very large building with plate glass windows. It was so large that here was a public hall spanning the upper story which could seat 400 people. Among the dry goods and notions, the oil cloth, carpet, crockery and millinery goods were an offering of grocery items: usually fresh eggs and vegetables from local farms and fruit shipped in from Wisconsin or Missouri. If he timed things correctly he could arrive in the alley behind the store when spoiled food was thrown out.

Strolling past the furniture and upholstery store, the dentist's office, the carriage shop, the blacksmith's and the boot-maker's, he had arrived at Valentine Dieter's grocery; more vegetable smells and the hint of fresh baked bread. But the greatest discovery an educated dog nose could ferret from among all those disgusting human smells was just up Jefferson Street, just east of Main: Seth A. Wescott's City Market. A butcher shop! Freshly killed carcasses swung from hooks high up on the walls; sausages dangled in strings; a glass case contained choice cuts of meat—meat rippling with veins of fat, meat that glistened in the window light, meat red, raw and bloody! And the trimmings were tossed outside.

But Lao still languished in the accursed stable. The Missy soon would come to loop the rope around his neck, perhaps to drag him off to some new humiliation. And the Missy did come but instead of the rope she brought him a bowl of food, leavings from the dining room—cooked, but still retaining some amount of its original flavor. And she sat with him, stroked him while he ate. Perhaps this imprisonment wasn't so bad after all.

The sample room extended nearly the entire length of the west wing of the Pre-Emption House. Adjacent to it were a separate kitchen and a private dining room, mirroring the same facilities of the hotel proper. There were outside entrances to the sample room to accommodate nonresidents who might be hungry and thirsty. In the very center of the room was a cast-iron stove that radiated heat in the winter, warming the outsides of imbibers whose insides were being warmed by the local ale from Stenger's Brewery. This autumn's burst of warm weather, which was called "Indian Summer" by non-Indians, had forestalled the lighting of the stove.

Along one wall was a long bar complete with brass foot rail. There was a scattering of tables where men could play cards or checkers. Mei Lim moved through the sample room with a tray and a towel, wiping tables, gathering empty glasses and bottles and doing her best to avoid the odd patron who reached to pinch her backside or accost her with obscene proposals. There was a time, she remembered, when she would have been obliged to reciprocate. But those California men had been more polite than these Midwesterners—most of the time.

At a table that had been pushed into a dark corner sat four men, bent over beer mugs and talking in low voices. Unlike the jubilant celebration of days-work-end that characterized most inhabitants of the sample room, this grouping of raggedy idlers seemed a sinister tableau. As Mei Lim passed the table a hand caught her arm; fat fingers clutched her with stern determination.

"Hey, sweetie," the man insisted, "come sit with us."

"So solly," said Mei Lim, wrenching her arm from his grasp, " no speakee ick-lish!"

She bounded away and avoided their table after that. As afternoon gave way to suppertime the locals had vacated the sample room and residents had repaired to the hotel dining room. Mei Lim was at her station next to the bar waiting to clear the one remaining occupied table: that of the cloistered raconteurs, the level of their conversational chatter now raised by intoxication to fill the emptied room.

"Not so loud," one said, gesturing toward the girl, the lone witness to their insobriety.

"Aw, the cherry...she don't speakee the ick-lish. Besides, what would she care?" answered another.

"Nuttin' I 'spose. Anyways, you was sayin' you was there?"

"I ain't sayin' I was and I ain't sayin' I wasn't."

"One man was killed, I heard," offered a third man.

"He shoulda been somewhere's else, is what. Home with the wife and kids. Well, see, we was puttin' back a few wet ones and getting' pretty riled up. Them thievin' Wheaton bastards got the legislature all tied up now. Can't get a bill through it as they's all still fightin' about the courthouse. We try to get it back and they block it. And they block anything else our side wants.

"Oh, I guess we were drunk enough to start the war all over again. About a half-dozen good lads of us decided it was time to stop talkin' about it and do something. Drove over Wheaton way intendin' to haul them records back. We got an empty courthouse just sittin' there, don't we?"

"My God, Pete, didn't ya think they was expectin' something like that?"

"Look, it'd been nearly a year since they raided us. Been a fist fight or two, that's true. But we thought they'd a relaxed their vigils...the 'chafers. They'd set a cussed watchman on the grounds. Raised the alarm he did and a dad-blam'd bunch of scalawags erupted from all directions as fast as...well, fast!

"Hell fire and tarnation if they didn't put on a good brawl! Well, we was beat. There was just too many of them. When we left though, one of them wasn't movin' no more."

"Whadda ya say, Pete," said the other man. "What say we goes over there again and sneaks up on 'em?"

"I don't know, Jack. Maybe some other time. Say! I'm still thirsty. How about another beer?"

Pete rose unsteadily to his feet and staggered over to the bar where Mei Lim was seated on a bar stool. Seeing the young woman, Pete forgot his thirst and lunged at her, encircling her shoulders with his meaty arms. Mei Lim was startled and it took her a moment before she realized the man was crushing her with a bear-like hug from which there was little hope of escape.

"Come on, you huzzy...you know you want it!" Pete said,

beginning to pull her from the bar stool.

Mei Lim twisted and turned within his strong grasp but it was to no avail. The lower part of one arm was free, however, and she flailed this in desperation. It was then that her hand came into contact with a smooth, cylindrical object that sat on the bar: a jar in which pickled eggs floated in a vinegar solution, glaring through the glass like eyeballs—wide-eyed, pupiless and horrified.

She closed her fingers around the jar. She relaxed her struggling and let the man put all his own energy into pulling her off the stool. Using the momentum this gave her she swung the jar with all her strength, connecting with Pete's cranium. Glass shattered, eggs flew, Pete's mouth dropped open as he fell straight to the floor, still holding on to Mei Lim. She wiggled loose and ran from the sample room. The laughter of the other men followed after her.

That evening Mei Lim thought about the old proverb: "without incident there is no lesson." What had she learned? That white men were all the same—that her station in life could change only through her own actions—that without discord there was no concord. But then, there was another old proverb: "strong dragon does not push local snakes." She would talk to Mr. Dunning. Ask him to take her out of the sample room, maybe to work in the restaurant instead. But would he be angered that she had struck a customer? Would she be fired? He had said nothing about it…yet.

The next morning she collected dirty linen from all the rooms and piled it into a wicker basket. This she dragged down the stairs bumping against each step with a loud thump. Each concussion jolted her; it was as if her past was chasing her. She pulled the basket through the door on the Water Street side of the hotel. Two doors east of the hotel was a laundry—a Chinese laundry. This would be her first visit to Jimmy Wong's Chinese Laundry.

"Hand Laundry" was painted in large red letters on the door. The jingling of a glass windchime announced her entrance. Inside, the hot air was dripping with the smell of wet linen and starch. A man was bent over a long board navigating a wooden-handled iron across a sea of damp cloth as steam sizzled and rose in the iron's wake. Without looking up from his work the man said, "Leave beside shelf. Write name on paper. Good morning."

"Dòngwèn," said Mei Lim. "Excuse me. These are for Pre-

Emption House."

Jimmy Wong turned, surprised to hear his native language spoken and doubly surprised to see Mei Lim standing in his shop. "Where did you come from?" he stammered.

"I told you, from the Pre-Emption House."

"I'm sorry. I didn't know there were any of my countrymen in this town besides myself and Grandfather."

"I am equally surprised. One may have a long period of separation and yet be together for a long minute."

"I hope our minute will be very long."

"You speak English very well. Why are you called Jimmy? I was told to take laundry to Jimmy Wong's."

"My name is Wong Kin Hei. People hear 'Jimmy' instead of Kin Hei, so it is easier to go by the name they give me."

"I am called Mei Lim...Chen Mei Lim, but I don't use my family name these days."

"And why is that?"

"A long story," she answered. Mei Lim considered relating her history to this young man but considered the consequences. She also considered the danger of being caught up in a lie; she was not skilled at deception. This Jimmy Wong, as he was known by his white patrons, had a wonderful symmetry to his features. His manner was soft, polite, and his interest in her seemed genuine. She wanted him as a friend. "Fáng rén zhī xīn bùkě wú," she thought to herself, being careful with others is a must.

"Neih sīkmhsīk góng gwóngdùngwá a? Do you speak Cantonese?" asked Jimmy Wong.

"I speak Cantonese and some Mandarin as well, although the different dialects can be confusing. I've even learned some Wintu...that's an Indian language. I've been associated with so many different groups of people since I came to this country that I've had to learn to understand at least the common things that are said. But please, tell me your story first. Mine is dull and boring."

"I tell you what. I must work now. Much to clean and iron. But please...won't you come back tonight? Share a supper with me and my grandfather. We'll have plenty of time to talk and get to know one another. Will you come?"

"I come to eat with you and talk with you tonight...for our long, long minute!"

28

Jimmy Wong

In the center of the table was a flat-bottomed clay pot containing bāozâifàn, a steaming dish of rice topped with small pieces of beef and boiled egg. Surrounding this were small plates of lou mei: bits of stomach and entrails of beef, gizzards and other odd scraps of chicken, stir-fried and seasoned with soy sauce. There were boiled vegetables in oyster sauce, and small bowls of hoisin, plum, and black bean sauces, and, of course, rice.

"Grandfather is an excellent cook," Jimmy Wong said proudly, speaking in Cantonese. "He understands some English but he is reluctant to use it. Too much history with the British occupation of our homeland on the island of the fragrant harbor."

"Hong Kong," said Mei Lim. "That is the port from which I sailed to America. The journey down the Dong River from Humen and through the Shizi Strait is one I'll long remember…but the long ocean voyage I would soon forget."

The old man at the head of the table, Wong Wai Keung, Jimmy's grandfather, hadn't spoken since being introduced to Mei Lim. He was sinewy as rope beneath his loose-fitting traditional jacket and wizened like an old mummy. Wai Keung's face betrayed no emotions, no evidence of displeasure at, nor cordial acceptance of his son's guest. That he was venerated she had no doubt. That his opinion of her was sacrosanct was a given.

Wong Wai Keung looked at Mei Lim with ageless eyes and drummed his fingers on the tabletop; those boney appendages resembled, at least to Mei Lim's dithering mind, the dancing legs of a pale, anemic spider. Why, wondered Mei Lim, did this man make her feel so anxious? Perhaps the memories of men (men like him?) who had taken her away from her family were suddenly slipping out from that dark corner of her brain where she had hidden them for so long. But beneath the elder's austerity there must be the faintest glimmer of kindness—at least she hoped so. She smiled her most heartfelt smile but the old man's stern gaze remained fixed, rigid.

"There is one way only," Wong Wai Keung said, breaking his silence like the first thunderclap of an approaching storm, "that a female comes across the big water to this land."

"Yes," she answered, "I was taken. Brought to Yee Fow—Sacramento—for the vilest of purposes. But I escaped! I have found other ways of making a living…and good friends who have helped me in my travels. You need not think…"

"Grandfather," interrupted Jimmy Wong, "this is America where you now live. Women can find work just as men do…as I have. It is not in service to the vices of wealthy men, of either Chinese or whites, that they are now obligated. This is called freedom."

"Freedom if you keep your place. Freedom if you, a male who will soon be head of family, does the work of women—washing dirty linen of others."

"Grandfather…"

Mei Lim touched Jimmy's arm. "It's all right," she said, "I understand all this—all that tradition requires." Then turning to Wong Wai Keung she asked, "But tell me, which is worse: that I had no choice then, or that I *have* a choice now?"

The Wongs' living quarters were in the back one third of the creaky old laundry building. Kitchen and eating area were in one room, the sleeping chamber in another. A door opened onto the alley where an outhouse stood next to a small vegetable garden, now overgrown with autumn weeds. The front two thirds of the building were devoted to the laundry: tubs for soaking, tubs for boiling and scrubbing, racks for drying, boards for ironing, shelves for storing.

The days were long and the evenings passed quickly for Jimmy Wong. Water had to be pumped. Wood had to be hauled. Fires had to be stoked and the iron kept hot. Customers had to be greeted. Before Mei Lim, there had been no guests in the Wong household. And now Grandfather was becoming more and more choleric and ill-tempered. It would be a shame, thought Jimmy, if the old man ruined this evening.

"Opium and gold," said Jimmy. Seeing puzzlement creep across Mei Lim's face, Jimmy explained: "You asked how I…we got here. Opium and gold—those were the two factors that influenced everything back in the old days.

"Grandfather had a farm near the fort at Kowloon, on the peninsula across the bay from the island of Hong Kong. There was plenty of water for growing things: potatoes, soy beans and peas, yams…all sorts of vegetables. My mother and father lived there and worked on the farm. Father would pick palm leaves and make fans from them to sell. I was born there in 1839, the same year that the Emperor Daoguang, the Son of Heaven, sent his commissioner, Lin Zexu, to Guangzhou to stop the drug trade.

"The British East India Company had been trading with our country for many years, buying silk and porcelain and especially tea, for which the British had so great a desire. They needed some commodity to sell to us to offset their expenditures. They found that commodity in the opium which they easily brought from the poppy fields they owned in India. But you know all this.

"The emperor banned the drug trade but it never stopped. Smugglers continued to bring the drug in through Guangdong province. The British refused to stop the trade and in fact, they doubled their sales. The Chinese people suffered greatly. As you probably know, Lin Zexu seized a great quantity of British opium and burned it. This started a war with the British, a war we could not win.

"To bring the war to an end the emperor ceded the port of Hong Kong to the British. I was only about two years old at the time. Grandfather called them barbarians and foreign devils. They were evil, he said, and had invented many evil things, especially their weapons of war that spoke with thunder and lit up the sky.

"But to a small boy growing up in a rural setting, playing with other boys and having little contact with the foreign devils, I had, I would say, a contented early childhood. When I was eight years old the emperor strengthened the fort at Kowloon with a great wall to guard the people against the British, but the British were selling Hong Kong land to their own countrymen and they came in droves. Some came to Kowloon as well. We began to feel their presence, and their prejudice.

"Later the Walled City was also ceded to the British. But even before that our peninsula was invaded by scores of the foreign devils seeking a foothold, seeking to gain a monopoly in trade. I remember one day playing with the other boys down along the wharves and watching as a Chinese man approached a white woman on the street and spoke to her. Immediately a British soldier struck him down. He was lucky not to have been killed as some had been for such insolence. This was the treatment we received from the barbarian invaders, as Grandfather would call them. And it escalated.

"One day a strange thing happened. A man named Cheng Li Jin returned to Kowloon from a sea journey to the American continent which he had embarked upon a few years before. He had been penniless, a peasant like most with no land or possessions, no wives or children and had borrowed the money for the passage from a banker who had been a distant cousin. He returned a rich man!

"Cheng Li Jin proceeded to build for himself a fine palace on a large plot of land. Around this he built a high wall of blue clay bricks and erected several other buildings for those who might come to him to be his servants. He built a summer house surrounded by lush gardens with streams and fine bridges where he could stroll among flowering trees and listen to the songs of the exotic birds he had acquired.

"Now he was an aristocrat and should have had nothing to do with the rest of us who struggled for a living—yet he never forgot his origins. He gave lavish parties with wonderful food and brought famous actors and musicians to entertain his guests. And who were the guests? The villagers, the farmers, the people he had known all his life. And his wealth? It had come, he freely told, from the discovery of precious metal—gold!—from the place in America which was called California.

"The Chinese were first on the scene on the American River where gold was discovered in 1848. They found the richest veins and largest nuggets. This of course angered the Americans who tried to drive them off. But Cheng had made his fortune. There was plenty gold for everyone, he told us. And many wished to go to Gold Mountain and see for themselves. My father was one of those.

"It was 1852. I was thirteen going on fourteen and the oldest of my father's children. Grandfather went to the banker and put up his farm against a loan of one hundred dollars...just enough to get my father and myself steerage passage on a steamer from Hong Kong to San Francisco, and to have a little left to live on once we got there. So I know, Mei Lim, a little of what you must have suffered on your own sea voyage. The heat and the smells, the constant rolling and heaving of the boat, the spoiled food, the sea-sickness—we were practically dead when we finally arrived!

"There is an old saying, 'to stay in a distant foreign country is a tragedy long grieved.' And Confucius said, 'while father and mother are alive, a good son does not wander far afield.' But the promise of great wealth, such as Cheng Li Jin had so aptly demonstrated, spoke louder than the sages.

"By the time we arrived in America, however, there was great resentment among the white miners against foreigners. California had passed a tax law in 1850 that required all foreign-born people to obtain a license in order to mine for gold. This cost $20. That part of the law had been repealed but a new law had just been enacted aimed directly at we Chinese which taxed us $4 per month. A lot of miners back then only made about $6 each month, so you can see how devastating the law was.

"We heard stories of our countrymen who had paid for their licenses upon arriving in San Francisco and then traveled to the mines believing these pieces of paper would protect their rights, only to find themselves turned away by the white miners. And there were men who falsely passed themselves off as tax collectors in order to rob the workers who spoke little English and had no way of knowing they were being cheated. If you could not pay the tax your property could be confiscated and you might be whipped or beaten.

"I remember digging and hauling dirt to the sluices, standing in the freezing cold river and swirling water over gravel in a big pan and waiting for the elusive glimmer of gold to appear. I remember our gold dust being stolen and our tents being torn down by angry white miners. I remember my father's despair. I remember hunger. And I remember that when it seemed the blackest, when it seemed as if we could not go on…I pulled from the gravel beneath my feet in the muddy water of the Trinity River, a lump of dull yellow stone big as an apple!"

Mei Lim placed her chopsticks neatly alongside her dish and looked to see if the others were still eating. After asking permission from Jimmy's grandfather, she cleared away the dishes from the table. She noticed a Yixing clay teapot sitting on a shelf above the stove.

"Honored Sir," she said to the grandfather, "may I make tea?" Wong Wai Keung nodded, his face still betraying no emotion. To Jimmy, she said, "Please go on with your story." She ran water into a kettle.

"The story," Jimmy Wong said, "now becomes concerned with Grandfather. You may be too young to remember that the Long-hairs, the followers of Hong Xiuquan, raised havoc even in our own remote countryside. Hong believed he was the younger brother of Jesus, the God of the Christians, and he thought to rid China of the Manchu and other followers of Confucius. Thus we had to contend with a war with the British over opium and a civil war with Taiping rebels over religion! Civilians died in great numbers—it is said that a million died in your own province of Guangdong.

"Grandfather lost his farm to the banker, who subsequently lost it to the British army, who wished to use it as a base of operations. My mother went to work for Cheng Li Jin and to live at his estate, bringing Grandfather and my brother and sister with her. One day the rebels attacked and many were killed. My grandfather and my mother and her children fled south to Hong Kong where it was thought the Taiping rebels would never dare to venture.

"By then I had found the gold nugget and so my father and I had enough money to bring the rest of the family to America. At first, Grandfather refused to leave the country of his birth. My mother said she would not leave without him—it was a bold declaration for a woman to make. But Grandfather acquiesced. The four of them left Hong Kong on a freighter. It was 1853.

"When father met the ship at San Francisco he learned that influenza had traveled along with the voyagers. My grandfather survived the sickness but the rest of the family perished. They were buried at sea in order to stem the spread of the disease—a circumstance which infuriated Grandfather as he had wished to take their bones back to China for burial. So his arrival in America was tainted with anger, grief and remorse.

"We took Grandfather home to the small dwelling we occupied in the town of Weaverville which sits at the foot of the great mountains of that part of California. There were many Chinese living there and a Joss House had been built, the Won Lim Miu, a splendid temple with brightly painted spirit doors, approached by a winding pathway. Inside were statues of the twelve gods and goddesses made from clay and painted gold, with wonderful silk and horsehair garments, just as you would have seen back in China.

"As you probably know from your time in Sacramento, there are the Six Companies who had organized in San Francisco to help people coming from the different provinces. There are also other associations that sprang up with different business or social interests—Tongs—and some of these spread across the state to the mining towns where Chinese had not yet been expelled."

Mei Lim flinched at the word, "Tong," but Jimmy Wong pretended not to notice. He continued:

"Weaverville had the Sanyi, Nigyung and Siyi Associations who were closely aligned. My father had joined with the Nigyung because it would help him with his mining efforts. But there was another association which was its rival: the Yanghe Association. All the Tongs, you see, had some political or religious ideologies in addition to their interests in commerce. These clashed quite often.

"A few incidents had taken place. A sluice along Weaver Creek was disputed as to its ownership. Once or twice there were fistfights. Then one man was shot through the heart by another using an old dueling pistol. Where he had acquired that, I don't know and can't even guess, as we Chinese typically owned no guns.

"As the hostilities escalated, each faction began to arm itself. They would go to the local blacksmiths and have them fashion swords after the designs of the curved dao or the hudiedao double butterfly sword or the straight jian, although these were crude by comparison to our military weapons. Some acquired pikes or javelins, or made these themselves from discarded mining equipment.

"City officials tried to discourage the blacksmiths from supplying these weapons, but some of the white miners liked the idea of a Chinese gang war so much they decided to get involved. Guns appeared—old, discarded muskets from the Mexican War—and not one of us knew anything about the use of them. The whites then volunteered to train us. What we didn't know was that they were placing bets on which side would win. They were encouraging a conflict that might otherwise have dissipated of its own accord.

"On the day the two sides were to meet in an open field outside of town, the volunteer trainers had painted their skin yellow and had hung long strands of horsehair down their backs to mimic our queues. Scores of white miners had come from surrounding towns to witness the battle and place their bets. It was said that a thousand whites were present, cheering on one side or the other. In spite of this humiliation there was pent-up anger among our men. Over two hundred of us had assembled and the two sides stood glaring and shouting at one another, waving our crude weapons—my father and I included!

"For a long time, no one made an aggressive move toward the other group. It seemed as though it might end without bloodshed. But one of the white miners, impatient for the battle to begin, raised his pistol and fired into the crowd. That started it. We came together swinging swords and pieces of pipe and wooden timbers and yelling insults at the top of our lungs. Those that had muskets fired them, but I don't remember if any one was shot or wounded from this. The miner who had fired his pistol, I heard later, was killed by being shot in the back of his head by another white man who had a grudge against him.

"I was frightened, of course, but the blood-lust that flowed through the mob spilled over onto me. I was armed with a piece of wood I had found and swung this in every direction, rarely connecting with anyone. Someone pushed me down and I lay on the ground for some time just watching, slowly realizing the horror of it all! It was as if the battles between the Long-Hairs and the Emperor's troops had surfaced here in this land so many thousands of miles from China.

"Certainly the dispute over the sluice wasn't cause enough for the two camps to clash—it was just an excuse to bring differences of belief, of loyalty, of religion to the surface of an already inflamed community of people—a frustrated people who were disenfranchised in a foreign world; a suffering people who were hated or feared by the white populous who themselves were usurpers, barbarian invaders.

"I watched as men fell from heavy blows or ran holding their sides as blood rushed between their fingers in spurts. I saw many using the boxing arts that came from Wudang Mountain, fearing neither the blade nor the pike of their opponent, but waving these aside as if by magic and striking with such little effort that it seemed impossible they could kill or maim—but they did!

"It lasted for most of the day. Eight were killed. Dozens were wounded. My father had received a gash across his chest from one of the homemade daos. I brought him home and put him to bed. The wound became infected. Grandfather applied herbs and powders that he got from an herbalist. Father died two days later. Oh, by the way, I think your water is boiling."

Mei Lim hurried to check the water on the stove. She looked to see if the size of the bubbles were like large crab eyes or like smaller fish eyes. She listened to the churning water as it gave off a bit of steam. "Not ready for tea, but good for warming pot and cups," she observed.

She found a towel which she used to grasp the handle of the kettle and poured a small quantity of the hot water into the clay teapot, swirled it around for a few seconds, then poured the water out into the sink. She repeated this with three porcelain teacups. She placed the pot and the cups on a shallow tray in the center of the table.

"I'm sorry to hear about your father. It must have been a shock. When men fight there can be no good to come from it," Mei Lim said to Jimmy Wong.

"Grandfather and I were all alone in a hostile world," Jimmy said. "I could not earn enough at mining to feed us and Grandfather could not do the heavy work that was required. We had just enough money to come east. We thought to go to New York where there was a large community of Chinese. We didn't realize the great distance we would have to travel. We got as far as this town. We are alone here, but the people are tolerant of us. They appreciate the service we do for them."

Mei Lim brought the loose tea leaves to the table and held them in the palms of her hands so that the others could inspect and smell them. She then dropped the leaves into the Yixing teapot. Holding the kettle high above the teapot, she poured hot water over the leaves until the pot overflowed. She scooped small floating bits of tea leaf from the mouth of the teapot and covered it with its lid, waiting several seconds for the water to seep through the remaining whole tea leaves. She poured this tea into the cups, waited for a few more seconds, then emptied the cups into a bowl. "A row of clouds," she said. "Running water."

Having ceremoniously rinsed the tea leaves, she began the second brewing. She poured hot water into the teapot, this time holding the kettle close to the pot's opening, scraping the bubbles from the surface and covering the pot again. Now she warmed the outside of the Yixing by pouring the first brewing from the bowl over the pot and catching it in the drip tray. The tea brewed for several minutes before she poured it into the cups, starting with a cup she placed before Jimmy's grandfather, then into Jimmy's, then into her own.

Grandfather Wong sampled the tea's aroma, looked at its color, felt the sides of the cup with his left hand. Now he sipped. Now a slight curling of his lips betrayed the impending escape of a smile which he quickly repressed. After another sip he moved his right hand onto the table and curled three fingers in gentle arcs as if they were the head and arms of a servant bending to kowtow to the emperor. He tapped softly.

"Good tea," he said. "You may come to visit us often. You will be welcomed. However, you must make tea again when you come."

29

Sweet Home, Chicago

HOG Butcher for the World,
Tool Maker, Stacker of Wheat
Player with Railroads and the Nation's Freight
Handler;
Stormy, husky, brawling,
City of the Big Shoulders...
—Carl Sandburg, "Chicago"

Tommy Wepa had seen large houses and tall buildings before: hugging the hills of San Francisco or scattered along the riverfront in Sacramento—blocks and blocks of them, built of wood or stone or brick. So Chicago's ornate mansions and five- and six-storied office buildings weren't unique in their grandeur and abundance. But the Cyrus Hall McCormick and Sons' Reaper Works was altogether another matter.

It sprawled. A dozen towering chimneys spewed black smoke skyward. Drays and buckboards filled its yards while docile horses swished their tails at pesky flies. Railcars lined up along its loading docks, as patient as the horses. It swathed the Chicago River. It was like a lazy giant, outwardly appearing in repose, but bristling with activity.

Cyrus McCormick had purchased the land just east of Rush Street on the north bank of the Chicago River in 1847. He had constructed his first factory there on the site where the Haitian mulatto, Jean Baptiste Point de Sable, credited as the founder of Chicago (or Eschikago, as he called it), had built his log cabin in 1779. Once a swamp filled with wild garlic, the watershed was called Shikaakwa, meaning "smelly onion," by the Miami-Illinois Indians who frequented the area. Now it was a cluster of foundries and warehouses: a spearhead for the industrial revolution.

Avery Geiger and his young helpers, Charlie Hildebrand, Henry Adler, Danny Meyers and Tommy Wepa rode the buckboard through the gate and got into a line of horse-drawn vehicles waiting for their turn at a loading dock. "Keep our place in line," Geiger told the boys, "while I go check on our order."

The three white boys chattered and giggled, retelling tales of their recent schoolyard exploits and questionable approaches to the female members of their age group. Tommy listened, attempting to relate to this strange new world having such people in it—people who never had known great hunger, never had thrilled in the chase of a deer with bow and arrow, never had experienced the fear of death during a coming-of-age ritual, never had seen a parent die along the side of the road. Their laughter, though appealing by its basic nature, failed to infect Tommy. He grabbed his rucksack, slipped off the side of the wagon and walked toward the gate.

"Hey! Where ya goin'?" yelled Danny Meyers. Tommy paused, but did not turn. He waved his hand in the air in a simple gesture of farewell and continued on.

"Aw, let him go," said Charlie Hildebrand. "Them injuns is too lazy to do any real work, anyway."

Tommy set off across the Rush Street Bridge. The wooden structure spanned the Chicago River at a point close to where the river, crowded with steamers and sailing vessels and filled with sewage and industrial waste, emptied into Lake Michigan. The braced-ribbed arch design of the Rush Street Bridge was a copy of the original iron bridge which it had replaced. The original, mounted on a masonry pier in center stream, could swing on a pivot to allow the passage of tall ships. One day in 1863, while a herd of cattle was being driven across the bridge, the pilot of a boat approached too rapidly, failing to heed a warning signal. To avoid a collision with the oncoming vessel, the bridge engineer swung the bridge around but the weight of the cattle caused it to break and topple into the river, destroying it and drowning or crushing the helpless cattle beneath falling iron fragments.

Tommy stopped near the center of the bridge to watch the traffic on the river. Small tug boats and freight-carrying side-wheelers churned through the murky water past grain elevators and warehouses, factories like the Reaper Works and docks where tall ships were moored, awaiting goods to carry across the Great Lakes. Flags and pennants were flying, wind-whipped on the topmasts of the sailing ships. Billows of smoke from steamboats and factories intertwined and were blown away by lake gales, a constant blast of turbid windstorm which would one day come to be known as "the hawk."

He stepped from the south end of the bridge, passing the metal sign on its railing advertising Bennet Pieters and Company's famous Red Jacket Bitters. Old Fort Dearborn had once stood on this spot; it had been torn down when the river was widened and the original bridge constructed. He paused...which way now? Where, in fact, was he going? What was he looking for?

To his left, toward the lake, was the Illinois Central Railroad's Depot Grounds. From the station at the foot of Randolph Street, the track ran on piles built along the shore, 400 feet into the lake, until it reached the south pier of the inner harbor, leaving a stretch of beaches and parks between the railroad and the city. But Tommy had had his fill of trains, so he turned to his right and walked down Water Street along the river. Fishermen lined the low wharves, their poles like a thicket of young saplings, denuded of branch or leaf. What could possibly live in that river, Tommy wondered? He knew a lot about polluted rivers.

He came to an intersection with a broad thoroughfare: State Street. This looked promising. He could see horse-drawn trolley cars riding smooth rails through the center of the muddy street, wide wooden walkways covered, at intervals, by awnings that jutted from tall buildings—buildings that seemed to take up entire city blocks. Pedestrians and horsecarts hurried up and down: women in billowing skirts and men in topcoats and silk hats, carriages and drays, handcarts and laborers shouldering heavy packages. He counted the stories on the taller buildings—one, two, three, four, five. Some were topped with mansard roofs which made them appear even more massive. Many flew flags.

He strolled. At State and Lake he gapped at massive buildings to his right and left: Burch's Iron Block to the east and Tremont House to the west. He continued south on State Street. He wandered. At Randolph Street a large banner hanging between two buildings caught his eye. It pictured a very fat woman, her arms as thick as tree trunks, her body a nearly perfect globe upon which her bud of a head seemed like an afterthought. Tommy couldn't read the lettering which announced, "Largest woman in the world weighing near 900 pounds," but he got the idea as he neared the site of Colonel Wood's

Museum and Theatre.

Attached to the building was a two-story tall statue of a soldier, complete with feathered cap and sword. Flags were hung everywhere and they seemed to flutter with the same excitement that emanated from the crowd surrounding the barker at the museum's entrance.

"Ladies and Gents," began the slim man in the bright red vest and black satin coat with tails, "for only one quarter of a dollar you will gain admission to the world's largest collection of wonders. Step right up, now, don't be shy. Inside you will see exotic insects from all over the world...birds and reptiles all stuffed and elegantly displayed...yes, and a scale model of the Parthenon, that eighth wonder of the world...a rifle used by Daniel Bone at the Alamo...the mummy of the great Mormon prophet, Joseph Smith...and more!"

Tommy began to creep away from the museum and the barker. Twenty-five cents! That was way too much just to see an old mummy. The barker's words trailed after him as he turned down Clark Street:

"The Great Zeuglodon awaits your scrutiny. Yes, folks, it's a ninety-foot long skeleton...a prehistoric whale, the experts tell us. And there's more! You'll get to examine Waino and Plutanor up close. Yes, folks, the freakish duo that together weight less than 100 pounds! Waino is a midget pinhead and Plutanor..."

The words were drowned by the clatter of wagon wheels and horses' hooves. He turned to his left and rambled up Randolph toward State Street where an enormous edifice dominated the corner: Field and Leiter's Department Store. But as he passed another stately building, Crosby's Opera House, he stopped in front of its arched windows to gaze longingly at splendidly dressed diners lifting forks full of delectable fare from china plates set on linen tablecloths inside Wright's Opera Restaurant. His growling stomach reminded him that he was hungry.

"I wouldn't waste my hard-earned money on that place," said someone standing directly behind Tommy. He turned to encounter a young man, a boy, really, not so many years older than himself, but with a stature and poise that spoke of maturity, and a smile that beamed unconditional regard. He was neatly dressed but not fancy: obviously just released from some workaday job that required clean-cut attire.

"It's overpriced and, I'm afraid, too rich for the palette of the common man. If you're hungry...I'm on my way to a great eatery, and I'd be happy of the company," said the boy. "I'm Harry, by the way."

"Tommy."

"Glad to make your acquaintance, Tommy. Say, are you...?"

"I'm what you call an Indian. Yes. Of the Maidu people of...of Nome Cult Farm now, I suppose. That's in California."

"I'm from Wisconsin. A town called Ripon. Anyway, let's go eat!"

They walked together the few blocks to Wells Street. The larger buildings of the business district gave way to more modest structures of wood and shingle. The street and raised wooden sidewalk were narrow by comparison to State Street, which had been widened to accommodate a market-house in mid-street—a market now defunct due to the diligence and ambition of Potter Palmer. Palmer had developed the area as the new commercial center of Chicago, buying land and erecting many of the grandiose buildings with their marble edifices and ornamental masonry where offices, hotels, theaters and stores found new homes. But Wells Street, where the two boys snaked their way along the crowded sidewalk, was a slice of the old Chicago—the rough, and raw, the rowdy—the city of the big shoulders.

As they ventured up Wells, Harry pointed out to Tommy which of the many saloons had brothels upstairs or gambling rooms in the back. There was Gentle Annie Stafford's place—she was known as the fattest madam in all of Chicago and the love interest of Cap Hyman, a notorious gambler and the terror of the nearby Hairtrigger Block up along Randolph Street where Hyman ran a gambling hall. One day in 1866, Gentle Annie had entered Hyman's place carrying an ugly-looking rawhide whip. She had dragged Cap Hyman out of the place and chased him up Wells Street. They were married a few weeks later. Then there was Robert Plant's place, a brothel and bawdy house called Under the Willow because of a willow tree on the corner where Plant dumped his trash and liquor bottles. Besides Under the Willow's saloon and brothels—three of them, Harry related—it was rumored there were rooms where white slaves were held.

Lill's Restaurant and Hotel was at 17 and 19 North Wells, next door to a haberdashery that seemed to specialize in last year's fashion. Inside the double doors was a rambling, high-ceilinged room with two long rows of tables covered in red- and white-checkered tablecloths, over which dangled spindly gaslight chandeliers, dingy from years of dust. The bar ran along one wall, separated from the dining area by a series of slender pillars supporting a lowered ceiling with a painted mural of sky and clouds. Dark-stained wainscoting surrounded the room, setting off a display of framed pictures of country landscapes mounted above it on yellowed wallpaper.

It was not an unusually shabby environment, certainly not by Chicago's working-class neighborhood standards, and it had that comfortable, old-world feeling of home and hearth that the city's immigrant populous expected. There was no brothel upstairs and no faro tables, no keno or craps or twenty-one in a back room. The food was good, or so Harry said, and it was cheap. Seeing Tommy's embarrassment when handed the menu, Harry read it for him:

"The five-cent dishes are baked beans with bread and butter, fish balls or hashed meat, also with bread and butter, fried onions or fried potatoes. Ten-cents will get you beef steak, veal cutlets, pork chops or mutton chops, liver with bacon or onions, oyster stew…although I wouldn't recommend that—there aren't any oysters in Lake Michigan, so who knows where they come from!

"Now *I'm* having the veal cutlets and a glass of Lill's Crème Ale, and maybe some minced pie for dessert. Oh look…there's Michael O'Byrne. He's the proprietor."

"I would have thought that would be a Lilly," said Tommy.

"Oh no. This is part of Lill and Diversey's enterprises. That's *William* Lill and Michael Diversey. They own that big brewery up on Pine Street, by the new water tower. They make really good beer. Oh, hey…Mister O'Byrne!" Harry shouted, waving at a stout, ruddy-faced man who was making the rounds of the tables.

"Well, well…if it isn't his nibs, Master Sheffield," said O'Byrne.

"Hi, Mister O'Byrne. This is my friend: Tommy…"

"Wepa," Tommy added.

"Tommy is a full-blooded…what did you say you were?"

"Maidu. From California."

"Oh?" said O'Byrne. "Yer a redskin then?"

"I don't know. Are you a *whiteskin*?" Tommy answered. There followed several uncomfortable moments of silence as O'Byrne's face color deepened. Harry was clenching his teeth. This could be bad, he thought. That man's face is redder than mine ever was, Tommy thought. O'Byrne was thinking as well…considering, perhaps, the advisability of taking one boy under each arm and throwing them out the door.

Then he laughed.

"Boys," he said, "your first drink's on the house. It'd be the beefsteak that I'd be recommendin'. Get a side of fried onions with that…you won't go wrong!"

As soon as O'Byrne had left their table, Tommy asked, "Drinks? Aren't we too young for…"

"Don't be a boob. This is Chicago! If you can get your nose over the bar you can get a drink here."

A waiter arrived and Harry ordered for them: the veal for himself and a beefsteak, rare (with fried onions), for Tommy, and two pints of Lill's Crème Ale. The beer came first, in two frosted mugs. Tommy sipped cautiously. It was his first experience with demon alcohol and he had been warned of its dangers by admonitions from the Franciscan Fathers, as well as through horrible stories the women of his tribe related to their children about what happened when the men of the tribe drank. It dulled the senses, made you crazy, rotted your insides. It sent men to their deaths in drunken fury, attacking one another without rational thought. It was the white man's most evil gift to the Indian. And, it tasted good!

Stories were traded. How Tommy Wepa had worked on the railroad. How Harry Sheffield had left school at age 14 and run through a variety of odd jobs: at a bank, a hardware store, a dry-goods store, finally acquiring the position of stock boy at Field and Leiter's in Chicago.

"That big building at State and Washington with all the awnings. The one they call the Marble Palace," he explained. "It's a good job. I get to go all over the store bringing things from the storeroom. And sometimes I carry packages to people's carriages. The other day, Mister Field had me deliver some purchases to the home of a very prominent family, the Buckinghams. What a mansion! And the daughter…I think her name was Rosalie…met me at the servant's entrance to give me a tip. She was a real looker! Say, want another beer?"

"Not just now. It's sort of going to my head."

"Not much of a drinker, huh? Well that's okay. Where are you staying?"

Tommy fiddled with his napkin, lining it up against the checkerboard pattern on the tablecloth. "I don't know. I just got here today."

"You don't know? Do you have a job lined up? What were you thinking?"

"No, no job. No place to stay. Just a dumb Indian hoping the Great Spirit will provide for me."

Harry Sheffield rubbed his chin in an effort to appear thoughtful. The waiter returned, placing their food on the table. A generous basket of freshly baked bread and a tub of butter accompanied the entrées. The waiter asked, did they want anything else? More Lill's Crème Ale, perhaps? Harry indicated with one finger that indeed, he would like another Lill's Crème Ale.

"Say, that's tough. No prospects, huh?" Harry said once the waiter had left. "Tell you what. You can stay with me tonight and tomorrow we'll find you a place. Now the job…that's another thing. You worked on the railroad, you said. Well, there are plenty of railroads in Chicago. Maybe…"

"What about a job like the one you have? I could do that."

"Maybe you could at that. Okay, tomorrow we find you a place to stay and we'll go talk to my supervisor at Field and Leiter's. It would be fun having somebody like you working with me. You see, I have all these ideas…"

"Ideas about your job?"

"About the store. How to improve business. Only nobody of importance would ever stoop to listen to a lowly stock boy."

"I would listen."

"If you work alongside me, I'll be jabbering nonstop. Someday I'll have my own store, bigger and grander even that Field and Leiter's. I'm aware of what the customers want, you see. And the customer is always right."

Epilogue

Dry leaves blew across the stones of the station platform; the smell of autumn, the honking geese winging through the cloudless gray sky, the crisp, damp air hinting of winter, the excitement of the squirrels gathering fallen acorns on the other side of the tracks—change was coming to the Pine Creek Valley. Zack waited for his train. Fawn had come with John and Mary Jane to Dixon to see him off.

"You won't come with me?" Zack asked his sister.

"No. I'm staying here. If you do find him again…"

"I'll bring Father home to Mother. Maybe the three of us…"

"You could visit us."

"I could send word. You could come home."

"I have a new home."

A shrill whistle announced the train's approach. The clanging bell, the wheezing of steam, and the grinding of iron on iron as conductors applied the brakes on each of the cars, made talking impossible. Mary Jane hugged Zack tightly. John took his hand, slipping a few bills into it. Fawn turned away so that he would not see her tears but Zack drew her to him and embraced her, perhaps for the last time—who could tell.

This train would carry Zack to Council Bluffs where he would board the Pacific Railroad for a 1,907 mile journey. He would reach and climb Shasta Mountain once again, searching for the mysterious Old Man of the Mountain who might possibly—no, surely *was* his father. He would find the fissure that led to the short canyon and the man's cave. But the cave would be empty; the blankets, the cooking implements, the few books: gone. The emptiness, the absolute absence of life, would be augmented by the roar of the wind racing across the opening of the fissure. As he would stand there, alone, dejected, the insistent wind would decelerate to a fluttering breeze; the sound would become flute-like. The trickle of the water that ran down the canyon wall would sound like the laughter of the Little People as it fell into the shallow pool next to the cave. Zack's quest, he would realize, was just beginning anew.

Fawn would not hear from her brother for many years. She remained at the John Grosh farm, becoming an essential member of the family. She saw her aunt often, visiting the woman's darkroom while she worked. Fawn became familiar with the particular smells of the chemicals and could tell each solution apart from the others, even in the dark. She loved watching the latent image gradually appear on the photo paper as it sat in the developer pan. It was a sort of magic beyond anything she had ever experienced, which might have reaffirmed her belief in the spirit world of her ancestors, had not Aunt Mary Jane Ayres explained the science of it to her.

Fawn had expected Tommy to return from Chicago along with the wagon hauling the reaper. He had not told her of his plan to remain in the city, a plan, he would be the first to admit, that he had not thought through thoroughly. Fawn felt hurt, but she believed Tommy would eventually be back, and this strengthened her resolve to stay at the Pine Creek farm.

The threshing of the wheat had been accomplished in record time with the addition of the new reaper machine. Cyrus McCormick's reapers, through his acquisition of patents from other reaper inventors, had evolved from a mere cutting device to a raker and bundler with a seat mounted strategically for the man who tied the bundles. This invention was revolutionizing agriculture, just as the railroad was revolutionizing commerce.

Back east, fortunes were being made; robber barons established monopolies. Steel, coal, oil, railroads, commodity trading—Mark Twain duded it, "the Gilded Age." His description was partly tongue-in-cheek. But on September the 24th, 1869, a day which came to be called "Black Friday," a financial scandal threw the stock market into a panic; speculators had tried to corner the gold market. It wouldn't be the last economic crisis the century would see.

Late in October, Isaac and Catherine had been blessed with a baby girl. She was named Verna. Verna was now an aunt to Alexander, who was three months older than she. Fawn enjoyed the babies, particularly baby Alex, whom she bathed and fed and rocked during the times when the mother, Mary Jane Grosh, was incapacitated by a recurring illness. The doctor was unable to identify the malady. There was little acknowledgement of the role of bacteria in certain illnesses, and few antibacterial treatments existed. It wouldn't be until 1884 that the term bacteriology was first used to describe what was essentially a new science. Mary Jane worsened.

On a cold February day of the following year, 1870, Mary Jane

Grosh died. She was laid to rest in the Pine Creek Brethren Cemetery, near the plot Isaac had purchased when his daughter, Harriet, had died and where his first wife, Catherine, was also interred. The ground was frozen and the grave digging was difficult. The sad little cemetery was receiving so many of the early settlers of that township now; there were several new plots.

The chronicle of life is punctuated by birth, marriage, and death—and remarriage. Isaac's youngest son, David, married Mary Ann Snyder that November. There were two children. Then Mary Ann passed away, after only three years of marriage. David took Mary Ann's sister, Sara Elizabeth for his second wife the following year. They would eventually move to Nebraska and raise nine more children, a brood rivaling even Isaac's progeny.

Death, it is said, is incestuous. Catherine Tennis Grosh, Mary Jane's sister, was married to John's brother, William. They lived in Iowa on a farm William had recently bought. They had five children together. Catherine died at the end of 1871, one year after her sister. William also remarried—it seemed to be a common occurrence for widowers to seek the companionship of a second wife—and to continue the family line—this, perhaps, stemming from deep religious convictions. But what of John Grosh, recently bereaved of his bride and left with three children to raise?

Her name was Annie. She had been born Anna Lee in 1838 in Frankford, New York, just east of Utica. She was not the Annabel Lee of Poe's kingdom by the sea, but John Grosh would have echoed Poe's famous lines:

> *For the moon never beams, without bringing me dreams*
> *Of the beautiful Annabel Lee;*
> *And the stars never rise, but I feel the bright eyes*
> *Of the beautiful Annabel Lee;*

John had met Annie at a Love Feast at the Brethren Church a few years before Mary Jane's death. She was then the widow, Annie Burger, with a young son named Charles, and had come down to Pine Creek Township from a small town in Wisconsin. Her husband had enlisted in the 2nd. Wisconsin Cavalry in 1862 but while the regiment was being sent to Austin, Texas, he mysteriously disappeared. The army called him a deserter. Annie was convinced he was dead. In 1872, John Grosh and Annie Lee Burger became husband and wife. They had one child whom they named Otis. John's household now included his own four children, James' daughter, Fawn, Annie and her son, and several farmhands who lived on the premises.

Mei Lim continued to work at the Pre-Emption House in Naperville, having convinced her boss to change her from a barmaid in the sample room to a waitress in the restaurant. She saw Jimmy Wong frequently; after all, the laundry was only two doors away. Lao, the dog, would beg for table scraps at the Wong back door. He developed a taste for lou mei. One day, however, Lao's inherent wanderlust drew him away to the open prairie west of the town. He could chase prairie dogs and rabbits and avoid the throngs of humanity there—until he got hungry enough to have to forage through back alleys once again.

Grandfather Wong Wai Keung died of pneumonia the following winter. Mei Lim and Jimmy had become close friends and so she grieved with him and comforted him. Mei Lim soon came to understand that Jimmy's growing dependency on her nurturing was mutual; she needed his needfulness. Something akin to love came to them that next spring, flourishing like the blooms of forsythia and hydrangea that sprang forth in the gardens of the fancy houses up Jefferson Street. They often walked along that avenue in the early morning, hand in hand. That summer they married. Mei Lim planted a cherry tree in the backyard of the laundry.

Mei Lim and Jimmy Wong were the only Asians in that small, mostly German, Midwestern town. Even in Chicago, where a Chinatown was yet to be established, there were few of their race. Most of the Chinese workers who had labored to build the First Transcontinental Railroad had either returned to China or moved back to California to work on new railroad projects or to start small businesses. Some returned to China in boxes.

The Elko Independent reported in January of 1870 that "Six cars are strung along the road between here and Toano, and are being loaded with dead Celestials for transportation to the Flowery Kingdom. We understand the Chinese Companies pay the Railroad Company $10 for carrying to San Francisco each dead Chinaman. The remains of the females are left to rot in shallow graves while every defunct male is carefully preserved for shipment to the Occident." The Sacramento Reporter stated "The accumulated bones of perhaps 1,200 Chinamen came in by the eastern train yesterday from along the line of the Central Pacific Railroad." They may have exaggerated the number; other reports claimed only 137 bodies.

Those that returned alive to California found that the climate of sinophobia had intensified. Since the foreign miners' taxes of 1852, there had been numerous laws and ordinances aimed at the Chinese. In 1858 the California legislature passed a Chinese Exclusion Law which prevented immigration of Asians to that state. It was declared unconstitutional in 1862 but remained on the books until 1955. In 1862 the law was amended as "An Act to Protect Free White Labor against Competition with Chinese Coolie Labor and to Discourage the Immigration of Chinese into California." It levied a tax against any Chinese in nonagricultural endeavors. It was also declared unconstitutional. In 1870, California Statute 330 stated that "Mongolian women emigrating to California must provide proof that they are of good character." In 1891 the state simply prohibited "The coming of Chinese persons into the State, whether subjects of the Chinese Empire or otherwise." It was overturned, but not until 1894.

San Francisco was even more specific in its passage of several anti-Chinese ordinances. 1870: "No Chinese may be employed by the government. Transporting goods on yeo-ho poles slung across the shoulders is prohibited. Gongs may not be rung at theatrical performances. No plays may be performed between midnight and daylight." 1873: "Laundries with animal-drawn carts must pay a $2 fee, but laundries without carts must pay a $15 fee." 1876: "Chinese prisoners must have their hair cut immediately after arriving at the county jail." 1880s: "Lotteries are forbidden. Building materials may not be imported from China." In 1878 the Federal Court in San Francisco ruled that Chinese were ineligible for naturalization. In 1882 the United States Government, taking an outrageously backward step, created the Chinese Exclusion Act that expressly forbid any court to grant citizenship to any Chinese person.

Perhaps because Mei Lim and Jimmy Wong were not perceived as taking jobs away from white workers, or perhaps because they were the only Asian residents of Naperville, they were treated with mild courtesy or simply ignored. The citizens of Naperville weren't any more ethical or virtuous than the citizens of San Francisco—they just didn't see Jimmy Wong as part of what Kaiser Wilhelm the Second would one day call the "Yellow Peril." The Wong family, which grew to include a baby girl and boy, had found their particular place in the economy and the social structure of Naperville. They stayed in it, content in the knowledge of their own self-worth, not needing recognition from others. Jimmy often repeated the words of the sage:

Those who understand others are intelligent
Those who understand themselves are enlightened*

In the 1870s, Native Americans suffered terribly. Buffalo herds had been thinned nearly to extinction. Mescalero Apaches were massacred in the Guadalupe Mountains of New Mexico by soldiers. This was followed closely by the slaughter of 173 peaceful Blackfoot men, women and children in Montana along the Marias River by U. S. troops seeking revenge for the wounding of a white boy. In March of 1871 the Indian Appropriation Act was passed which specified that no tribe could be recognized as an independent nation and therefore the government would make no further treaties. Tribal members were to become wards of the state.

In April of 1871, outside of Camp Grant in Arizona, members of the Tuscon Committee of Public Safety, acting in retaliation for sporadic raids by Apaches in various remote parts of the territory, rode against an encampment of Apaches who had been given asylum there. One hundred and forty-four were clubbed and hacked to pieces. All but eight were women or children. By 1873 General George Armstrong Custer and the Seventh Cavalry were on the job guarding surveyors for the Northern Pacific Railroad. Conflicts with Sitting Bull and Crazy Horse would follow. Custer would die at the Battle of the Little Big Horn in 1876 after waging war against the Sioux and the Cheyenne.

In California, the Modoc wars were beginning. Between 400 to 600 cavalry and infantry soldiers armed with two howitzers assailed 53 Modoc warriors at their stronghold in the lava beds near Tule Lake. The photographer, Muybridge, was there to record the battle. 13 warriors and civilians were killed; over 200 soldiers and volunteers died. The Modoc leader, Captain Jack, was finally captured and hanged.

Chicago, October 8, 1871: there has been only about an inch of rain in the last one hundred days; dry leaves cover lawns whose grass has turned brown; everywhere the wooden planks of the sidewalks are cracked from a lack of moisture. And now the city is preparing for winter. Hay is piled high in barns and cords of wood are stacked along the sides of houses. In the poorer districts like Conley's Patch, tenement buildings are built so close to one another that their wood shingle roofs nearly touch.

All across the Midwest the drought and unusually high temperatures have created fire hazards; in fact, small fires have erupted in dried-out cedar swaps and peat bogs in Wisconsin, Michigan and Illinois. The dead branches of trees and the dust from sawmill wastes have been dumped thoughtlessly into creek beds now devoid of water. Farmers have continued the dangerous practice of clearing forest lands by setting fires, some of which get out of hand.

There have been isolated fires everyday in the City of Big Shoulders. The fire department is a full-time regiment of 185 professional firefighters who do their jobs well, but who are becoming over-taxed. They have asked for new hydrants and water mains for some time, and have pointed out the need for building inspections and fire boats for the river, but the city has refused these requests for lack of funds. The five story buildings in the central business district are built with thin walls of brick and are trimmed with wood—and are firetraps waiting to ignite.

Yesterday, a fire had broken out that ravaged an area four blocks square: from Van Buren to Adams and from Clinton to the south branch of the river. The valiant fire department had battled the blaze for over 17 hours. It was contained and extinguished because they had arrived on the scene early. The fire companies of Chicago pride themselves on their ability to locate fires quickly. Their expertise is lauded. This tragedy of October 7 is considered to be a major fire in the annuals of Chicago firefighting—it is only a prelude.

It is Sunday. Tommy Wepa has been working in the stock room at Field and Leiter alongside his friend, Harry Sheffield, for nearly a year now. Sundays are his day off. He has spent the day strolling through the Lake Park, gazing at the brown-stone buildings of Park Row which face the lake. Yesterday's fire was just across the river from his neighborhood, the tenement district called Mother Conley's Patch. The smell of smoke still permeates his clothing. He is not anxious to return home but the sun is due to set shortly and night is not a good time to be walking through Conley's Patch.

The Patch along Monroe Street had once been the realm of the wealthy who had built mansions there resembling southern plantation homes complete with Greek columns and large gardens. But Conley's Patch was in decline. The Chicago Gaslight and Coke Company had built their plant on the corner of Monroe and Market. Lumberyards lined the river. North's National Amphitheater, which occupied Monroe Street between Wells and Clark, had brought an influx of circus and carnival people into the neighborhood. Property values pummeled. Criminals had found a fertile ground in the emerging squalor of the shanty town.

But it is cheap, a requisite for survival for the young Native American boy. He arrives at his boarding house after a quick meal at Lill's and climbs the stairs to his room. It is about 7:30 PM. He sits on the bed and opens his McGuffey's Reader, a first grade textbook he is studying in order to learn to read. His body is tired. His eyes are tired. He nods off. As he sleeps the earth is hurtling through space. It orbits the sun at a speed of approximately 69,360 miles per hour.

Also orbiting the sun, but at a greater distance, is a comet which astronomers have named, Biela. Biela, perhaps twenty or thirty years ago, split into two parts, trailing long debris fields in its wakes. The earth, on this 8th day of October, 1871, is intersecting those debris fields. Fragments are entering the earth's atmosphere and burning up. Eleven years from now, a man named Ignatius Donnelly, will publish a book entitled, *Ragnarok: The Age of Fire and Gravel,* in which he will present the theory that this comet, Biela, is responsible for the catastrophes which are about to take place tonight.

It is 9:30 PM. The McLaughlins are throwing a party in the house they rent in front of Patrick O'Leary's cottage. Daniel "Peg Leg" Sullivan has just left the party and is stumbling toward his own house just across De Koven Street from the McLaughlins. He looks back and sees flames licking up from the roof of the O'Leary's barn.

Near the small town of Sugar Bush, Wisconsin, at nearly the identical moment, a fire has broken out in a dried-out swamp and is about to touch off several tons of hay which have been stored in a nearby barn. Both of these fires will be whipped into whirling dervishes of firestorm by a fierce wind from the south-west. Flaming embers will sail in all directions as the fiery cyclone eats its way through Peshtigo and Door County in Wisconsin, Holland and Manistee in Michigan, and Chicago in Illinois. Simultaneously, acres upon acres of forests and city buildings will be destroyed; many thousands will die or will be injured.

Tommy Wepa has fallen asleep; his McGuffey's Reader has slipped from his hand. He doesn't hear the bells clanging as seven different fire companies hurry toward De Koven Street, a little over a mile to the south and west of him. This time the engines are not Johnny-on-the-spot: a watchman has seen the flames from his post on the courthouse tower but he mistakes the location. He tries to change his report but the telegraph operator decides not to confuse the issue and won't send out the change of address. Someone close to the O'Leary barn fire pulls the level on an alarm box but the signal fails to transmit.

It will be said that the firefighters were either fatigued or drunk or both, but in fact, the fire is out of control before their arrival. The wind has churned the hellish blast and sent it bounding across the rooftops and slithering dragon-like up the wooden sidewalks. The south-west side is just a pile of dry kindling waiting for the dragon's hot kiss. It is now 10:00 PM and Bateham's Mill at Clinton and Harrison is aflame. The dragon is moving west, toward the south branch of the river; it eats the Polk Street Bridge as it crosses. Waste and oil floating in the water ignites and soon the very river is burning. Lumberyards and warehouses filled with dry goods are feeding the hungry monster as winds push it back toward the city center.

It should be halted by the burned-out area from yesterday's fire. There is nothing left there that can burn. But it leaps and spits out tongues of flame that flail and fling out burning embers that land on the east side of the river. Shacks along Adams and Jackson are incinerated. It is 11:30 PM. Tommy is awakened by cries from the street below. Something is wrong. The sky is too bright for this time of night. The stables at Franklin and Jackson are burning. The screams of horses trapped and confused by the smoke can now be heard for blocks.

The Gas Works explodes. This dooms the Courthouse and all of Conley's Patch. Tommy is now out of the building. Its roof is burning. Smoke and dust fills the air. People are running in all directions, unsure of the route to safety. The bell in the courthouse has been sounding the alarm but the tower collapses and it comes crashing down making one glorious, final reverberation. Prisoners housed in the basement of the courthouse have been turned loose. The fire is sweeping toward the business district.

People are now rushing to cross the main branch of the river to the north side of the city. The bridges are crowded by carriages and drays. People are dragging bundles and hampers filled with what valuables they have had time to grab. A railing breaks and some of those on foot are pushed off into the water. Cinders are falling like blackened snow and firebrands are flung about in the superheated air. Flames shoot up from the roof of the Chicago and Northwestern Railroad Station like a golden crown.

Tommy is in the throng crossing the State Street Bridge. Many have faces reddened by the heat. To the east of them horses and wagons have been driven into the lake and women and children have waded out to climb upon the wagons; some are standing in the shallow water. North of the river would seem more likely to be where salvation lies, but it is not to be so. By 3:00 PM the roof of the Water Works is smoldering. By 3:30 PM, it collapses destroying the pumping machinery inside. Fighting the flames is now hopeless.

He reaches a stretch of the lakeshore just beyond the North Branch of the Chicago River called the Sands. Here and in nearby Lincoln Park, they have gathered: the now-homeless, the devastated, the despairing. Tommy witnesses heartbreaking scenes of families huddled around broken pieces of furniture, worn blankets, odd boxes and suitcases, their faces blackened by soot, their children sobbing. Rich and poor are clustered together here, perhaps encountering each other for the first time.

It is the morning of October 10th. A light rain is falling. The last of the flames are winking out. The city is still too hot to be reoccupied, but people are moving back to the burned-out areas to salvage what they can. There is nothing to salvage. The toll is monstrous: 18,000 buildings, 28 miles of streets and 120 miles of sidewalks, 300 innocent lives—gone. 100,000 homeless. An area four miles long and three-quarters of a mile wide is blackened and smoldering.

The Chamber of Commerce Building is gone. The Courthouse is gone, and with it, deeds and records of the other properties that have disappeared in flame and smoke. McCormack's Reaper factory is gone. Conley's Patch is a blackened prairie. The Tremont house, Crosby's Opera House, Field and Leiter's Department Store, the Palmer House, Colonel Wood's Museum, the Arcade buildings, all of Bookseller's Row, the Chicago Tribune and the Chicago Sun Times buildings, the City Water Works, churches, banks, stores, restaurants, houses: gone. Ironically, Patrick O'Leary's house still stands.

In Wisconsin, an area the size of Rhode Island has been destroyed; twelve communities have disappeared from the face of the earth. In Peshtigo, 350 of its citizens are buried in a mass grave; the death toll will be estimated as being between 1,200 and 2,500. Thousands are maimed. The burned carcasses of cattle and horses lie among ashes and still glowing embers. Everywhere there is devastation.

Fawn set up the camera in front of one of the garden plots at John Grosh's farm. Aunt Mary Jane was teaching her how to use it. She was attempting to photograph a row of pumpkins and gourds that had caught her eye. There was one gourd that looked like an old man with a crooked nose—and an agglomeration of warts. As she looked through the ground glass at the upside-down image of the world, she began to sing a Wintu dream song:

> *It is above that you and I shall go*
> *Along the Star Trail you and I shall go*
> *Along the flower trail you and I shall go*
> *Picking flowers on our way, you and I shall go*

There was a shadow falling across the pumpkin patch. She moved the camera slightly to avoid it. Then, inexplicitly, the song she was singing continued by itself!

Where will you and I sleep?
At the down-turned jagged rim of the sky
You and I will sleep

She turned. He stood smiling at her. His clothes, his face, were darkened with soot and road dirt. He had walked most of the way.

"We heard of the great fire," she said. "We thought you were dead."

"I thought so too, for a while." Tommy said. "Now I'm home."

Tao Te Ching: Annotated & Explained, Translation by Derek Lin. published by SkyLight Paths in 2006, web: www.Taoism.net

An Afterthought or Two

If some of it seems fantastic—well, those are the parts that are true. Of course, what we believe to be true, those events and people that have shaped our present through the past, have come to us through *history*. And history adheres to the equation: HISTORY = FICTION = HISTORY—a vicious circle which depends upon *whose-story* it is. There is a wealth of research material available about the Transcontinental Railroad and its building, about the Chinese and the Native American cultures that were affected by the incredible changes in the nineteenth century—and some of it is contradictory.

I picked, for example, the version of *whose-story* which told that the Chinese hung down the side of Cape Horn in baskets to set off explosives. This has been refuted by many. I did not, however, favor the *whose-story* that tells that Mrs. O'Leary's cow kicked over a lantern, starting the Great Chicago Fire. I like the comet theory better, although that has also been refuted by some experts. Statistics on how many Native Americans were massacred, how many Chinese worked on the railroads, and so forth, vary, but the representation I have given here of unfairness, prejudice, and out-and-out genocide is, unfortunately, accurate.

If I have mixed Mandarin and Cantonese, Pinyin and Wade-Giles indiscriminately, I apologize. The Wintu and Maidu words and phrases I used to make my characters more realistic will no doubt elicit some criticism, or perhaps a few guffaws, from tribal members, and again, I apologize. I wanted to come as close as I could to understanding what it might have been like for Zack and Tommy and Fawn, and for Mei Lim, to try to make their way in a white-dominated world. And I wanted, at least in my own *whose-story*, to include at least a few white persons who were not totally evil. That was difficult.

I enjoy writing historical fiction and I make every effort to blend the fictional narrative with the dates, people and places as they are documented (by history). I did adjust some time-lines and rename some characters to make the narrative work better. The Reverend Anthony Kulver, who travels on the ship to Alaska with Edward Muybridge, is based on the Honorable Vincent Colyer, a real minister and Native American advocate who was appointed United States

Special Indian Commissioner, and who did investigate the Alaskan territory—but did so a year later than in our story. Some of the events I depicted in Alaska are scrambled, but reasonably truthful, based on reports by various principle players who were there.

When Tommy Wepa arrives in Chicago he meets Harry Sheffield, a boy who works in the stockroom at Field and Leiter's Department Store. Harry is based loosely on Harry Gordon Selfridge, who founded Selfridge's in London, a high-end department store that became the model for similar retail businesses. Harry Selfridge did work for Marshal Field's in Chicago (originally Field and Leiter), but he came there around 1876, well after the era of the fire. He invented the marketing campaign, "Only _____ shopping days until Christmas," and he did marry Rose Buckingham.

There was a Chinese laundry in Naperville as early as 1886, and perhaps earlier. It was run by Tom Ley. I can remember such a laundry from my own childhood days growing up in Naperville in the 1940s and 50s. It was in a different location than Ley's, which was on Water Street near the Pre-Emption House. Genevieve Towsley, writing in an article about Naperville history (see bibliography), mentioned this laundry as being called "Sam Lung," possibly an anglicized variation of a Chinese phrase meaning "good luck." People called the owner "Sammy" although that was not his name.

My use of the word, "Tong," to refer to Chinese secret societies or Triads, some of which, but in no way all of which had criminal or violent tendencies, is liberal, if not prosaic. The term, meaning "hall" or "gathering place," probably didn't come into popular use until the 1880s. The Weaverville conflict of 1854 was called a "Tong War" in later *whose-stories* as was the 1869 confrontation between rival association members working for the Central Pacific Railroad. The characterization of "Tong Hatchet Men" became a cliché perpetrated in Hollywood movies, in a similar way to which Native Americans were portrayed as "savages." Just another *whose-story*.

Mark Twain apparently did have a friend named Tom Sawyer, but he claimed his fictional character was patterned after his own childhood experiences growing up in Hannibal, Missouri, and not after the real Tom Sawyer.

Born Edward James Muggeridge, the photographer changed his name several times, becoming Edward Muybridge and then settling, by 1882, on Eadweard Muybridge. In 1872, Leland Stanford hired

Muybridge to take a series of photographs in order to settle a wager on whether or not a running horse always had one foot on the ground. In approaching the problem, Muybridge used a bank of cameras equipped with high-speed shutters to capture the motion as a sequence of images. At a later date he placed transparencies of these images on a rotating disk and projected the motion study, effectively inventing the motion picture.

James and Hanna Maria Strobridge are interesting and complex historical characters. Hanna Maria was extremely sympathetic to the Chinese workers. She and her family lived in a converted railcar for much of the construction. Also drawn from real life are the characters of Sarah Winnemucca, Fong Dun Shung, Wong Fook, Lee Shao, Ging Cui, Ah Toy, Reverend Morgan Dix, Charles Crocker, Thomas Durant, General Grenville Dodge, and "General" Jack Casement. The reader is invited to separate the "real" historical actions of these characters from my fictional manipulations by exploring the bibliographical citations which follow. I have knowingly disparaged no one. The Mysterious Mr. M is quite fictional, as are most of the "villains" of the narrative.

It is unknown whether or not Annie Lee Burger's first husband was the same Charles Burger that deserted from the Wisconsin 2nd Regiment. The dates and places seem to fit. The real Baby Alex grew to manhood in Pine Creek Township, married my grandmother, herself the descendant of a veteran of the American Revolutionary War, and moved to the small town of Naperville, Illinois, where he became a partner in a butcher shop. In 1931, at the time of that town's centennial celebration, he was its mayor. He facilitated projects to bring relief from the on-going Great Depression of that time, including running a soup kitchen, rebuilding bridges, and constructing a recreational swimming beach and park which is still a major attraction of that town.

The story of the Grosh family is fictionalized in my two preceding novels *All The Way By Water*, and *Once Upon a Gold Rush*. A more detailed account of the Peshtigo fire of 1871 can found in my short story "The Fire Next Time," published in an anthology of short stories entitled *Romeo's Revenge and Other Wisconsin Stories*.

Byron Grush

Selected Bibliography

"Alaska ... Report of the Hon. Vincent Colyer, United States special Indian commissioner ... 1869," Washington, D.C. (document digitized by University of California Libraries)

"Annual report of the Commissioner of Indian Affairs, Made to the Secretary of the Interior for the year 1869."

Bailey, William Francis. *The Story of the First Continental Railroad, Its Projectors, Construction and History*. Pittsburgh: Pittsburgh Printing Company, 1906

Bales, Richard F. *The Great Chicago Fire and the Myth of Mrs. O'Leary's Cow*. Jefferson, NC.: McFarland & Company, 2002

Bauer, William J., Jr. *We were all like migrant workers here: work, community, and memory on California's Round Valley Reservation, 1850-1941*. Chapel Hill, NC: University of North Carolina Press, 2009

Baumgardner, Frank H. *Killing for Land in Early California: Indian Blood at Round Valley: Founding the Nome Cult Indian Farm* (Google eBook). Algora Publishing, Jan 1, 2005

Campbell, Robert. *In Darkest Alaska: Travel and Empire Along the Inside Passage*. Philadelphia: University of Pennsylvania Press, Jan 1, 2011

Chang, Iris. *The Chinese in America*. New York: Viking Press, a member of Penguin Group (USA) Inc., 2003

Chinn, Thomas W., Editor. *A History of the Chinese in California, A Syllabus*. San Francisco: Chinese Historical Society of America, 1969

Chung, Sue Fawn. *In Pursuit of Gold: Chinese American Miners and Merchants in the American West*. Urbana, Illinois: University of Illinois Press, 2011

Clemens, Samuel (Mark Twain). *The Letters Of Mark Twain, Volume 2, 1867-1875*. The Project Gutenberg, August 21, 2006 [EBook #3194]

Curtis, Edward S. 1907-1930. *The North American Indian*. 20 vols. (Wintu creation myth collected from Tommy Neal, vol. 14, p. 173.) Norwood, Massachusetts: Plimpton Press, 1924

Dixon, Roland B. *Maidu Texts, Volume IV*. Publications of the American Ethnological Society, ed. Franz Boaz, 1912. web: The Long Now Foundation, http://www.archive.org/details/rosettaproject_nmu_vertxt-1

Galloway, John Debro. *The First Transcontinental Railroad*. New York: Dorset Press, 1989

Graysmith, Robert. "The Adventures of the Real Tom Sawyer," Smithsonian Magaine, October, 2012

Haas, Robert Bartlett. *Muybridge, Man in Motion*. Berkley: University of California Press, 1976

Hirata, Lucie Cheng. "Free, Indentured, Enslaved: Chinese Prostitutes in Nineteenth Century America," Chicago Journal, 5/1/1979, pp 3-29

Hopkins, Sarah Winnemucca. *Life Among the Piutes: Their Wrongs and Claims*. Boston: Cupples, Upham & Co., 1883

"Indians of the Concow Valley, Yankee Hill and Cherokee, Part Two," Yankee Hill Dispatch, Vol. 4, No. 2, Oct 2011

Judson, Katharine Berry. *Myths and Legends of California and the Old Southwest*. Chicago: A.C. McClurg & Co, 1912

Kirkland, Joseph. *The Story of the Great Chicago Fire*. A. J. Cornell Publications, 2012; (The Story of Chicago. 1892) Amazon Digital

Knudtson, Peter M. *The Wintun Indians of California and their neighbors*. Happy Camp, California: Naturegraph Publishers, 1976.

Kroeber, A. L. "Handbook of the Indians of California," Smithsonian Institution Bureau of American Ethnology, Bulletin 78. Washington: Government Printing Office, 1925

Leland, Charles G. *Fusang, or The Discovery of America by Buddhist Priests in the Fifth Century.* New York: J. W. Bouton, 1875

Meade, Richard. *Hydrographic Notice #13-1869 [Command Book of Richard Meade, Jr. 1868-69]* Google ebooks

Naperville Centennial 1831-1931. Booklet, Fort Payne Chapter-D.A.R., 1931

Norton, Henry K. "The Chinese" In: *The Story of California From the Earliest Days to the Present.* Chapter XXIV, pp 283-296. Chicago, A.C. McClurg & Co., 1924.

Quaife, Milo, M. *Chicago's highways, old and new, from Indian trail to motor road.* Chicago: D. F. Keller & Company, 1923

"Report of General Halleck, Military Division of the Pacific," in *Annual Report of the Secretary of War, Volume 1.* United States. War Dept, U.S. Government Printing Office, 1868

"Reports from General Davis, Headquarters Department of Alaska, Sitka, Alaska, May 27, 1868," in *Proceedings of the Alaskan Boundary Tribunal: pt. 1., Alaskan Boundary Tribunal.* U.S. Government Printing Office, Alaska, 1903

Sabin, Edwin L. *Building the Pacific Railway: The Construction Story of America's First Iron Thoroughfare Between the Missouri River and California...* Philadelphia: J.B. Lippincott Company, 1919

Seagraves, Anne. *Soiled Doves. Prostitution in the Early West.* Hayden, Idaho: Wesanne Publications, 1994

See, Lisa. *On Gold Mountain: The 100-Year Odyssey of a Chinese-American Family.* New York: St. Martin's Press, 1995

Sheahan, James W. (text) and Kurz, Louis (illustrations). *Chicago Illustrated.* Chicago: Otto Jevne and Peter M. Almini, 1866 - 1867. web: http://chicagology.com/pre-fire-chicago/engravings/

Siebert, Wilbur H. *The Underground Railroad from Slavery to Freedom*. London : Macmillan & Co., Ltd. 1898

Solnit, Rebecca. *River of Shadows, Eadweard Muybridge and the Technological Wild West*. New York: Penguin Putnam, 2003

Spude, Robert L. and Delyea, Todd. "Promontory Summit, May 10, 1869..." [pamphlet] Cultural Resources Management, Intermountain Region, National Park Service, 2005

Steiner, Stan. *Fusang: The Chinese Who Built America*. New York: Harper and Row, Publishers, 1979

Strobridge, Edson T. and Sweet, Charles N. "The Sins of Stephen E. Ambrose, A review of Ambrose's new book, *Nothing Like it in The World*, and the summary of errors, misstatements and made-up quotes it contains." web: http://utahrails.net/articles/ambrose.php

Strobridge, Edson T. "The Central Pacific Railroad and the Legend of Cape Horn." San Luis Obispo, California: Published by Edson T. Strobridge, 2001 [June, 2003], web: http://cprr.org/Museum/Cape_Horn.html

Taylor, Leonard W. and Taylor, Robert W. "The Great California Flood of 1862," paper for The Forthnightly Club of Redlands, California, 2007, web: http://www.redlandsfortnightly.org/papers/Taylor06.htm

Towsley, Genevieve. *A View of Historic Naperville from the Sky-lines*. Naperville, Illinois: The Naperville Sun, Inc., 1975

Tsai, Shih-shan Henry. *The Chinese Experience in America*. Bloomington: Indiana University Press, 1986

Wei, William. "The Chinese-American Experience: An Introduction." web: http://immigrants.harpweek.com/chineseamericans/1Introduction/BillWeiIntro.htm

White, Richard. *Railroaded: The Transcontinentals and the Making of Modern America* (Google eBook) W. W. Norton & Company, May 31, 2011

Other fiction by Byron Grush

All The Way By Water
In which Isaac Grosh brings his wife and eight children to Illinois, traveling by flatboat on the Ohio and Mississippi Rivers.

Once Upon a Gold Rush
In which John and James Grosh journey by wagon train to California during the gold rush of '49. Introduces the characters of White Cloud and Little Wind.

Romeo's Revenge and Other Wisconsin Stories
An anthology of twelve short stories about towns and people of Wisconsin.

About the author

Byron Grush was born in Naperville, Illinois. He has been an independent, experimental film artist and an educator, teaching at The School of The Art Institute of Chicago and Northern Illinois University. He lives in Delavan, Wisconsin, paints, writes fiction, and studies Tai Chi.

Byron Grush

www.ingramcontent.com/pod-product-compliance
Lightning Source LLC
Chambersburg PA
CBHW062023170626
46813CB00001B/273